SURRY OF EAGLE'S-NEST

JOHN ESTEN COOKE

SURRY OF EAGLE'S-NEST

OR

THE MEMOIRS OF A STAFF-OFFICER

SERVING IN VIRGINIA

EDITED, FROM THE MSS. OF COLONEL SURRY

By JOHN ESTEN COOKE

AUTHOR OF "FAIRFAX," "HILT TO HILT," "MOHUN," "OUT OF THE FOAM,"
"HAMMER AND RAPIER," ETC., ETC

THE GREGG PRESS / RIDGEWOOD, N. J.

First published in 1866 by M.A. Donohue & Co.
Republished in 1968 by
The Gregg Press Incorporated
171 East Ridgewood Avenue
Ridgewood, New Jersey U.S.A.

Copyright© 1968 by
The Gregg Press, Inc.

Library of Congress Catalog Card Number: 68-23718

Printed in United States of America

AMERICANS IN FICTION

In the domain of literature the play may once have been the chief abstract and chronicle of the times, but during the nineteenth and twentieth centuries the novel has usurped the chief place in holding the mirror up to the homely face of society. On this account, if for no other, the Gregg Press series of reprints of American fiction merits the attention of all students of Americana and of librarians interested in building up adequate collections dealing with the social and literary history of the United States. Most of the three score and ten novels or volumes of short stories included in the series enjoyed considerable fame in their day but have been so long out of print as to be virtually unobtainable in the original editions.

Included in the list are works by writers not presently fashionable in critical circles—but nevertheless well known to literary historians— among them Joel Chandler Harris, Harriet Beecher Stowe, Thomas Bailey Aldrich, and William Gilmore Simms. A substantial element in the list consists of authors who are known especially for their graphic portrayal of a particular American setting, such as Gertrude Atherton (California), Arlo Bates (Boston), Alice Brown (New England), Edward Eggleston (Indiana), Mary Wilkins Freeman (New England), Henry B. Fuller (Chicago), Richard M. Johnston (Georgia), James Lane Allen (Kentucky), Mary N. Murfree (Tennessee), and Thomas Nelson Page (Virginia). There is even a novel by Frederic Remington, one of the most popular painters of the Western cowboy and Indian—and another, and impressive minor classic on the early mining region of Colorado, from the pen of Mary Hallock Foote. The professional student of American literature will rejoice in the opportunity afforded by the collection to extend his reading of fiction belonging to what is called the "local-color movement"—a major current in the development of the national belles-lettres.

Among the titles in the series are also a number of famous historical novels. Silas Weir Mitchell's *Hugh Wynne* is one of the very best fictional treatments of the American Revolution. John Esten Cooke is the foremost Southern writer of his day who dealt with the Civil War. The two books by Thomas Dixon are among the most famous novels on the Reconstruction Era, with sensational disclosures of the original Ku Klux Klan in action. They supplied the grist for the first great movie "spectacular"—*The Birth of a Nation* (1915).

Paul Leicester Ford's *The Honorable Peter Stirling* is justly ranked among the top American novels which portray American politics in action—a subject illuminated by other novelists in the Gregg list—A. H. Lewis, Frances H. Burnett, and Alice Brown, for example. Economic problems are forcefully put before the reader in works by Aldrich, Mrs. Freeman, and John Hay, whose novels illustrate the ominous concern over the early battles between labor and capital. From the sweatshops of Eastern cities in which newly arrived immigrants toiled for pittances, to the Western mining camps where the laborers packed revolvers, the working class of the times enters into various other stories in the Gregg list. The capitalist class, also, comes in for attention, with an account of a struggle for the ownership of a railroad in Samuel Merwin's *The Short-Line War* and with the devastating documentation of the foibles of the newly rich and their wives in the narratives of David Graham Phillips. It was Phillips whose annoying talent for the exposure of abuses led Theodore Roosevelt to put the term "muck-raker" into currency.

While it is apparent that local-color stories, the historical novel, and the economic novel have all been borne in mind in choosing the titles for this important series of reprints, it is evident that careful consideration has also been given to treatments of various minority elements in the American population. The Negro, especially, but also the Indian, the half-breed, Creoles, Cajuns—and even the West Coast Japanese—appear as characters in various of these novels or volumes of short stories and sketches. Joel Chandler Harris's *Free Joe* will open the eyes of readers who know that author solely as the creator of humorous old Uncle Remus. And there is a revelatory volume of dialect tales, written by a Negro author, *The Conjure Woman* by Charles W. Chesnutt.

In literary conventions and the dominating attitudes toward life, the works in the Gregg series range from the adventurous romance illustrated so well by Mayne Reid or the polite urbanity of Owen Wister to the mordant irony of Kate Chopin and the grimmer realism of Joseph Kirkland's own experiences on bloody Civil War battle-fields or the depressing display of New York farm life by Harold Frederic. In short, the series admirably illustrates the general qualities of the fiction produced in the United States during the era covered, just as it generously mirrors the geographical regions, the people, and the problems of the times.

PROFESSOR CLARENCE GOHDES
Duke University
Durham, North Carolina

December, 1967

JOHN ESTEN COOKE

John Esten Cooke was one of the few first-rate imaginative writers which the Civil War era produced. He was born in 1830 near Winchester, Virginia, the son of one of Virginia's First Families, educated at Charlestown Academy, and later studied law, but wanted to be a professional writer, and successfully submitted several of his early stories to *Harper's Magazine*. During the war, Cooke rose from the rank of private, served on J. E. B. Stuart's staff as captain, and with General Lee after Stuart's death at Richmond. He was in charge of a cannon at Bull Run, knew all of the generals of the Army at Northern Virginia, and saw most of the great battles in which Lee's army participated. After the war Cooke married Mary Francis Page, and settled at "The Briers," Clarke County, Virginia, where he remained until his death in 1886. Cooke, like Thomas Nelson Page, wrote in the tradition of James Fenimore Cooper, combining a vivid historical sense of the American past with love of an adventure story *per se*. He had the additional advantage of war experiences and first-hand knowledge of the people and geography which he described.

The critic and poet Richard Henry Stoddard said of Cooke: "His books have the charm of elegant comedy, the pathos of pastoral tragedy, sparkles of wit, flashes of humor, and everywhere the amenities of high breeding."

And Cooke said of his work: "My aim has been to paint the Virginia phase of American society, to do for the Old Dominion what Cooper has done for the Indians, Simms for the Revolutionary drama in South Carolina, Irving for the Dutch Knickerbockers, and Hawthorne for the weird Puritan life of New England." In spite of his sympathy with the Southern cause, he never harbored bitterness toward the North.

Surry of Eagle's-Nest appeared in 1866, and soon found a place in practically every Southern library, as an example of all that this conquered and occupied people held most dear in what remained of their devastated civilization. Like *Mohun,* it is a war novel, told through the person of a fictitious aide to Stonewall Jackson — a *persona* of Cooke, of course. *Surry,* in its mixture of melodrama, historical anecdote (footnoted), and idealized descriptions of the ante-bellum South, seems naïve to the modern reader; baroque and a little quaint. But to the student of Americana, who can skip over the short passages consisting only of rhetoric, or the conventional sketches of crinoline-clad belles, there emerges a valuable picture of Southern culture, and all that separated it from the industrial North. Particularly interesting is Cooke's outrage at the unprecedented scorched-earth policy which Sherman used to terrify and subdue the Confederacy. Like so many of his compatriots, Cooke saw the Civil War as an unequal struggle between gallant, high-born gentlemen defending their homeland, and brutal, prosaic Yankees aided by revenge-seeking Negroes. Occasionally a Northern officer redeemed himself by conducting the war according to the proper knightly code of conduct, and this Cooke praised highly. The rest was simply a rape.

There is, for example, a colorful portrait of Cooke's distant relation, J. E. B. Stuart, who appears as resplendent as the God of War himself, a warrior-saint out of Sir Walter Scott, who forbids swearing and drinking, but who cannot resist dancing a jig to the sound of a minstrel's banjo, and who can outride and outfight any ten Yankees. Today this sort of figure is apt to elicit an irreverent guffaw from anyone but a confirmed Rebel, but before laughing too loudly, we had better hear what the implacable Sherman had to say in his report of September 17, 1863:

". . . The young bloods of the South: sons of players and sportsmen, men who never did work and never will. War suits them, and the rascals are brave, fine riders, bold to rashness, and dangerous subjects in every sense. They care not a sou for niggers, land or anything. They hate Yankees, *per se,* and don't bother their brains about the past, present, or future. As long as they have good horses, plenty of forage, and an open country, they are happy. This is a larger class than most men suppose, and they are the most dangerous set of men that this war has turned loose upon the world. They are splendid riders, first-rate shots, and utterly reckless. Stuart, John Morgan, Forrest, and Jackson, are the types and leaders of this class. These men must all be killed or employed by us before we can hope for peace."

Surry of Eagle's-Nest is a delightful story written by a man who was in his personal life as kind, gallant, and unworldly as the Arthurian figures in his books, and who represented all that was most admired in the ante-bellum South, but who, in the end, confessed that "in modern warfare, where men are organized in masses and converted into insensate machines, there is nothing heroic or romantic or in any way calculated to appeal to the imagination."

F. C. S.

SURRY OF EAGLE'S-NEST.

I.

THE SURRYS.

HAVING returned to "Eagle's-Nest," and hung up a dingy gray uniform and battered old sabre for the inspection of my descendants, I propose to employ some leisure hours in recording my recollections, and describing, while they are fresh in my memory, a few incidents of the late Revolution.

This will not be a task, my dear, unknown reader—rather an amusement; for nothing delights more your old soldier returned from the wars than to fight his battles o'er again, boast of his exploits, and tell the children and grandchildren, clustering in fancy around his knees, what wonders he has seen, and how many heroic deeds he has performed.

I think those dear, coming grandchildren will take an interest in my adventures. They will belong to the fresh, new generation, and all the jealousies, hatreds, and corroding passions of the present epoch will have disappeared by that time. Simple curiosity will replace the old hatred; the bitter antagonism of the partisan will yield to the philosophic interest of the student, and the events and personages of this agitated period will be calmly discussed by the winter fireside. How Lee looked, and Stuart spoke—how Jackson lived that wondrous life of his,.and Ashby charged upon his milk-white steed—of this the coming generations will talk, and I think they will take more interest in such things than in the most brilliant arguments about secession

Therefore, good reader, whom I will never see in the flesh, · am going to make some pictures, if I can, of what I have seen.

1*

Come! perhaps as you follow me you will live in the stormy days of a convulsed epoch, breathe its fiery atmosphere, and see its mighty forms as they defile before you, in a long and noble line. To revive those days, surround you with that atmosphere, and reproduce those figures which have descended into the tomb, is the aim which I propose to myself in writing these memoirs.

I foresee that the number of "I's" I shall employ will be enormous, and beyond a peradventure you will call me egotistical; but how can the use of that stiff, erect character be done away with in an autobiography? Be magnanimous, therefore, O kindly reader, and regard me as a friend who is telling you his adventures, not as an author composing a feigned history. It is only a poor "prisoner on parole" who is talking: leave him that one resource to while away the time—that single consolation. We sit on the old porch at Eagle's Nest; yonder Lows the Rappahannock; the oaks sigh; the sunshine laughs—so I begin.

I always heard that the first of the Surrys in Virginia was Philip, the son of Philip, and that he took refuge here when the head of Charles I. went to the block. This Cavalier was a gay gallant, the family legend says, and did much hard riding and fighting under Prince Rupert; but the royal banner drooped, the Roundhead pikes carried the day; and, collecting such money and jewels as he could lay his hands on, Colonel Philip Surry repaired to the head-quarters of Cavalierdom, Virginia. Here everything suited him. Cavalier faces were seen everywhere, land was cheap, and foxes abounded; so he built this house of "Eagle's-Nest" below Port Royal, on a hill above the Rappahannock, gave it the name of the family estate in England, and, collecting a number of thorough-breds, and a pack of hounds, married and settled down. All I have heard of him thereafter may be stated in a few words: he went with Richard Lee to see Charles II., then in exile at Breda, where he offered to proclaim the youth King of England and Virginia at Williamsburg. When his offer was not accepted, he returned to Eagle's-Nest, where he dedicated his energies to fox-hunting and raising blood horses for the remainder of his life. His portrait hangs on the wall here—a proud, handsome face, with blue eyes, pointed beard, black mustache, and broad shoulders covered with Venice lace falling over a hauberk of steel; in the hand is a hat with a black, trailing feather. There is Colonel Philip Surry, dead this many a day.

He left in his will the curious injunction that the eldest son of the family in every generation should sign his name, "Surry of Eagle's-Nest;" so my father always called himself, and I have followed the family habit. My father was the fifth or sixth in descent from Philip I., and bore his name. He was the soul of benevolence and kindness. Intellectually, he was the greatest man I ever knew. At the bar of the Court of Appeals of Virginia he ranked with the old race of lawyers, Marshall, Wirt, Wickham, and Leigh—all his intimate friends; but as his hair had grown gray he had retired from the profession, and spent his days at home in the country. He has died since the beginning of the war, but his portrait is yonder, a tall and stately figure, with a noble countenance, clear loyal eyes, and a smile of exquisite sweetness. He is gone now, like all the Surrys of the past, but his memory still lives. His intellect was so powerful, his temper so sweet and kind, that the first men of his age saluted him with respect, and I never knew a lady or a child not to love him. He belonged to that old generation of Virginians who have disappeared, and the sun to-day, I think, shines nowhere on his like.

I shall only add to this family sketch the statement that my dear mother, who died in my boyhood, was Mary Annesley, of Princess Anne, and that she had but two children besides myself. One of these was my sister Annie, about sixteen years of age when the war began; and the other, my younger brother, was only nineteen at that time, but a graduate of West Point, and a lieutenant in the United States army.

Such was the origin of the writer of the present memoirs, and from this point of view he looked upon the struggle which was approaching.

II.

IN WHICH THE WRITER OMITS A NUMBER OF THINGS.

I HAVE not the least intention of inflicting upon the reader an account of my childhood, boyhood, or early manhood, spent at "Eagle's-Nest." It would not interest deeply—that life of a child who ran laughing and singing through the grounds of an old house, or conned his lessons at his dear mother's knee—who listened to the murmur of the Rappahannock flowing past the lofty hill, and dreamed his idle dreams of far-off lands—who rode all the colts he could catch, and was thrown by them, spun his top, tore his clothes, and drew down the denunciations of his gray-haired "mammy." Nor would the life of the youth and man prove more interesting.

All these details would be charming, my dear reader, if Colonel Surry was anybody—a great warrior, statesman, or general—and was dead. But he is none of these, and fortunately still lives; so all these particulars of his youth are omitted. The flowers bloomed brighter then, and the song of the birds was sweeter; but that was in *my* childhood, not in yours, reader. Mine for myself—yours for you, friend. Let us dream of the dead days sometimes, as the comedy of life plays before us and the voices laugh—we will never see those days any more, except in dreams!

I spent one session at the Virginia Military Institute; studied law at the University; commenced the practice in Essex and the surrounding counties—and in 1861, at the age of twenty-five, saw the country about to be plunged into war.

*   *   *   *   *   *   *   *

Fill that hiatus with the hundred octavo volumes which will be written on the causes of what our friends across the border call the "Great Rebellion." In the present memoirs I intend to weary neither myself nor the reader with that discussion. Let others trace back the torrent to its source—laboriously demonstrating how 1861 was the logical result of 1820—and show how tne antagonism of race and opinion became the antagonism of the bayonet. This is not the place for that logomachy. I who write am as firm to-day in my conviction of the right of secession as yesterday, or five years ago. But the question has been tried—the issue is dead, for the present, and let it rest. Besides, you know all that story now, reader mine—how the whole North roared at the wicked South, and John Brown with the pike carried out what Helper wrote with the pen. In 1860 the beginning of the end came. The "Republicans" triumphed: the Gulf States declared that the Union was dissolved—and, asserting their right to shape their own destiny, prepared to support their action with the sword.

Where was Virginia? it may be asked. I reply that she was trying to command the peace, vainly supposing that this storm could be hushed. I blamed her then, when my blood was hot— now I think that she acted with her ancient courage and dignity. The Virgin of her shield would not lightly touch the sword, because, when once she drew it, she meant to throw away the scabbard.

Whether she kept that resolution, let the blood and tears and desolation of four terrible years, in which she never shrank before her foe, declare.

III.

HOT BLOOD.

RICHMOND, which I visited at this stormy period, was the fiery heart from which flowed the blood of Revolution.

What a change had passed over the quiet old place! In past years the city was the picture of repose. The white walls of the Capitol rose from the deep-green foliage, silent, except when some aspiring young legislator thundered in his maiden speech: the falls of James River sent upon the air their soft and lulling murmur: the birds sang in the trees of the Capitol Square: children played there: the clouds floated: Richmond was all good-nature and repose.

Now this was a tradition—a lost page in her history. Fierce agitation had replaced the old tranquillity; and in the streets, the hotels, the drawing-rooms, nothing was heard but hot discussion. Men's pulses were feverish. Neighbors of opposite views scowled fiercely at each other. Young ladies wore the Southern colors, and would turn their pretty backs upon an admirer who was not for secession. The cockade of South Carolina—a red rosette with a palmetto tree upon it—was everywhere worn; and upon the wearers the advocates of the old order of things looked with ill-concealed hostility.

Meanwhile, the Convention, of which my father was a member, thundered on from day to day: the press poured forth its lava: the stump resounded with denunciations: and society was evidently approaching one of those epochs when, having exhausted the powers of the tongue, the human animal has recourse to the sword.

Altogether, the period was jovial and inspiring; and I declare to you, reader, that I would like to live it over, and hear the bands play "Dixie" again, under the "bonnie blue flag!"

The hot current dragged me, and I speedily had a rencontre which was not without importance in its bearing on my future.

I was sitting in the public room of my hotel, on an afternoon of April, when a party of young men came in, and among them I recognized a former acquaintance at the University, named Baskerville. I had never liked him, and he was generally unpopular, in consequence of his arrogance—the result, it was said, of very great wealth. As I glanced at him now, his appearance did not falsify the report. His costume was dazzling; his shirt bosom sparkled with diamond studs; his hands were encased in yellow kid gloves; and he carried a small ratan with a golden head. Baskerville was about twenty-six, tall, straight, and exceedingly handsome—but as arrogant in his bearing as a patrician among the common people. It was overpowering!

Such was the figure which came into the room where I was sitting, and began talking politics.

His denunciations of secession and secessionists were bitter and violent; and his laughing companions seemed to be urging him on. From secession, the abstract, he passed to the cockades, the concrete; and denounced their wearers as "shallow-brained traitors, who would suffer for their folly." As I was wearing a cockade, though it was invisible to the speaker, I did not much relish this, but I controlled my temper—when all at once Baskerville uttered some words which I could not possibly pass over.

"I heard a speech in the Convention to-day which deserves the halter," he said arrogantly.

"Who delivered it?" asked another of the party.

"That old traitor Surry!"

When he said that, I got up and went to the place where he was standing.

"That is my father, sir," I said.

His reply was a haughty stare and the words, "I am not acquainted with you, sir!"

"You lie," I said, "you recognize me perfectly;—but that is not what I wanted to say. You call me a 'shallow-brained traitor' for wearing a cockade—which proves to me that you are a fool. You insult the gray hairs of my father—that convinces me that you are a coward."

* * * * * * *

The above asterisks are gracefully substituted for what almost immediately followed. The by-standers speedily "separated the combatants," as the newspapers say; and, informing my adversary that I could be found at No. 45 in the hotel, I went to my chamber, to avoid the crowd which began to collect.

I fully expected a message from Baskerville; but none came that evening, or the next morning. Tired of waiting, I was about to go out, when a card was handed to me; and enter a few moments afterward, one of the party of the previous evening—a young gentleman elegantly clad.

At the grave and ceremonious air of my reception he began to laugh.

"Excuse me, Mr. Surry," he said, "but you are evidently laboring under a slight misapprehension. I have not come as

Mr. Baskerville's representative to bring you a challenge—but simply to make a friendly visit, at the risk, however, of appearing intrusive."

"Not at all, sir," I said, "but I naturally supposed——

"That Baskerville would fight? Well, you thought wrong," was the gay reply of my visitor, who balanced himself, with an air of the most graceful *insouciance*, upon his chair. "Our dear friend is a man of peace, not war—he insults people, but he does not fight. I have seen him this morning, and he declares that he remembers nothing whatever of the little affair of yesterday—says he was inebriated, which is a truly shocking thing —-and professes that he had no quarrel whatever with you, or anybody else."

With which words my visitor began to laugh, in a manner so careless and good-humored that it was impossible not to do likewise. When he left me an hour afterward, the whole affair appeared like a joke, and I forgot it.

But Baskerville was to have far more to do with my life than I dreamed at that moment. Many an inward groan was to salute the very mention of his name.

————

IV.

A PAIR OF EYES.

THREE days after this scene, I had reason to be exceedingly sorry that I had quarrelled with Baskerville.

It was at that time the habit of the young ladies of the city to promenade with their gallants upon the Capitol Square in the evening, and enjoy the music of a fine brass band which played from a rostrum opposite the City Hall.

The scene at such moments was really charming. The white walls of the Capitol rose dreamily in the moonlight; the great bronze Washington towered above; bright forms moved to and fro beneath the moon; eyes sparkled; smiles shone! O summer

night, with that wondrous moon! whither have you flown with
the curls that lay in masses on those snowy shoulders?

One evening I went to listen to the music, and, lost in the
crowd in front of the rostrum occupied by the musicians, was
enjoying that sad and beautiful air, the "Mocking Bird"—when,
all at once, I saw in front of me a face so lovely that something
like a thrill passed through my frame.

It was the face of a girl—let me try and draw her outline.
Fancy a maiden of about nineteen, with a figure rounded, slender, and as flexible as the stem of the river-flag—waving hair of
a deep chestnut, twisted up into a shining braid on the snowy
neck; and eyes—ah, those eyes!—they were languishing, brilliant, and of an intense and dazzling violet—that tint which the
summer sky wears when the purple of the sunset dashes against
the blue. That face and those eyes possessed a haunting beauty
such as I had never before seen in woman. As she stood there
in the moonlight, keeping time with her slipper to the strains of
the "Mocking Bird," I thought she was some fairy—not a girl
of flesh and blood!

Such was the exquisite face—and now do you ask, how I saw
her eyes? I was gazing at the clear and elegant profile half
turned from me, when some sound behind the girl attracted her
attention, and she turned her head. For an instant those wondrous eyes met mine—then they were withdrawn, and I heard
her utter some cold words to the gentleman upon whose arm she
leaned.

I looked at him—I had not wasted a glance upon him before.
It was Baskerville.

Nothing could be more unfortunate. I had made up my mind
to discover who his companion was—for I had seen her at none
of the parties which I had attended—and now there was an in-
separable barrier in my relations with her escort. I nevertheless
determined to ascertain her name, and chance seemed about to
assist me. The band soon ceased playing; the crowd began to
disperse; and the young lady and Baskerville approached the
western gate, through which the multitude were passing. I was
close behind them, and, just as they reached the gate, observed

that she had dropped her handkerchief. Here was the opportunity. She evidently did not observe the accident, and I hastily
picked up the handkerchief—resolving to read the name upon it,
and then return it.

Straining my eyes in the moonlight, I discovered in one corner
of the little perfumed affair of lace and cambric the young lady's
initials! "M. B." was all; and, disappointed, I looked round
for the owner.

She had disappeared—lost like a flower amid the crowd. I
tried in vain to discover her; and at last gave up the search.

In vain did I go to every concert, every party, every church
thenceforward—looking for her. She did not reappear. She
had vanished like a dream of the moonlight night.

I ought to have sent the handkerchief to Baskerville, you may
say, for transmission to its owner. So I ought to have done—
but I did not.

V.

WHAT I SAW ON THE BROOK ROAD.

The incident just related made a strong impression upon me;
and the face I had thus caught a glimpse of in the moonlight
continued to haunt me. But an affair with which I found myself mixed up, a few days afterward, for the moment quite
diverted my attention from the owner of the handkerchief.

Having brought an excellent riding horse from Essex, I was in
the habit of riding out in the evening for exercise, after the con-
finement of the Convention. The Brook road, extending in a
northwestern direction from the city, was a favorite ride; and
one evening I went in that direction, soon emerging from the
dusty streets into the broad highway, which unrolled itself like
a long brown ribbon upon a robe of emerald.

Three or four miles from the city, near the point where the
slender spire of the Brook Church rises from the trees, a horseman at full gallop passed me, and descended the hill in front.

As he shot by, I could see that he was tall and vigorous; his face was pale; and as he fled onward he looked over his shoulder with the air of one who is pursued.

Such proved to be the fact. As he disappeared beneath the crest of the hill, a second horseman appeared approaching at full speed; and he too darted by and disappeared like a vision of the night.

What could all this mean? Here were evidently flight and pursuit; and in the Middle Ages, nothing would have been more natural. Then, gentlemen rode down their adversaries; but, in this prosaic age, men generally go in pursuit of their loves or vengeances by the railway.

The apparition of the two cavaliers puzzled me so greatly that I galloped on to see, if possible, what would ensue.

In this I was fortunate. He who had first appeared had descended the hill leading to the brook, and, thundering over the little rustic bridge, would no doubt have distanced his pursuer, had not an accident arrested him. His horse placed his foot upon a rolling stone, stumbled, and, falling, threw his rider, who rose just as his pursuer came up. As the latter approached, however, the former drew from his breast a paper which he tore into a hundred pieces; after which he folded his arms and confronted his opponent with an air of defiance which was discernible even at the distance from which I regarded the scene.

A brief parley followed, and, from the violence of the gestures on both sides, a personal collision appeared about to take place. None ensued, however, and to my surprise both horsemen remounted, and returned toward the city.

As they passed me, I could see in the countenance of the one who had been pursued an expression of sullen and bitter hatred —in the face of the other a gloomy satisfaction, something like a ferocious joy.

Such was the curious incident I encountered in my ride. As the reader will soon perceive, I was destined to be present at the sequel of the affair, and witness, if not understand, the denouement.

V I.

THE VENDETTA.

IN the fine April mornings, often before the sun had risen, I was accustomed to take long walks, which more than once extended far into the country.

At daylight, on the morning succeeding the scene just described, I know not what chance directed my steps toward Hollywood Cemetery, on the banks of the James, above the city.

Entering the grounds, which at that early hour were quite deserted, I strolled on to the hill upon which Monroe lies buried, and, throwing myself beneath a tall elm which grows there, gazed with admiration upon the fair landscape. Below murmured the falls, foaming around the islands with their drooping foliage; straight across shot the long white line of the Petersburg bridge, and to the left appeared the crowding roofs of the city, above which rose the snow-white pillars of the Capitol, brilliant in the first rays of the sun.

I was gazing in silence at this beautiful spectacle, and listening dreamily to the song of an oriole in the elm above, when the sound of wheels on the gravel road by which I had ascended the hill attracted my attention. Looking in the direction of the sound, I saw two hacks, from which four gentlemen descended, saluting each other as they did so. Then, without loss of time, they ascended the hill, and the whole party paused in an open space not ten yards from my elm. They could not see me, as I was stretched upon the grass, and a row of cedar bushes around a group of graves intervened. But I could see perfectly, as I looked through an opening, and in two of the party recognized the horsemen of the previous evening.

These affairs are rarely private, and I had no hesitation in remaining. To this I was impelled by a strong sentiment of curiosity.

My attention was immediately riveted to the face of the pur-

ner on the preceding evening. He was tall, powerful, and with
a face resembling bronze. His eyes, as black as night, sparkled
under raven eyebrows, and his heavy mustache and beard were
of the same color. But his expression was more striking than
all else. Never have I seen a fiercer satisfaction in the human
face. A species of instinct told me that nothing but the gratification of some long-brooding passion—some cherished vengeance
—could bring that gladiator-like smile to the lips of a human
being.

His opponent's face expressed rather bitter hatred than satisfaction at the approaching encounter. It was plain from his
sullen and lowering brow that he thirsted for his adversary's
blood, but not so evident that he welcomed the prospect of a
fair and open contest. With his small keen eyes, his thin lips,
and overhanging brows, I should have set him down for one who
would prefer doing away with an enemy by treachery—and
afterward I came to know that this estimate of the man was
entirely correct.

It was evidently the snake opposed to the tiger—not so bold,
but equally dangerous.

The preliminaries were soon arranged. The seconds were
evidently old practitioners, and their proceedings were matter-of-
fact and business-like.

"This spot, I think, is suitable," said one of them, "except
for that ugly object there." And he pointed to a newly-dug
grave.

"It is a matter of indifference to us, sir," returned the other
second, "as the fire will naturally be across the line of the
sun."

"That is just, sir, and if entirely agreeable to you, we will
now proceed."

His associate bowed, and they proceeded to measure off the
ground. The sound of pistols striking against their case was
then heard, and the click of the triggers as they were tried.
A short pause then followed—they were loading the weapons.
When this was accomplished, they were handed to the principals.

One of the seconds then said :

"Gentlemen, I shall give the word, which will be, 'Are you ready? Fire! One, two, three'—the fire to be delivered after the word 'one' and before the word 'three.'"

The principals listened in silence, standing half-faced to the right and left, the weapons pointed toward the ground.

"Before, however, this affair proceeds further," continued the speaker, "I consider it my duty to make a statement in the hearing of all. I was called on last night by Mr. Fenwick, with whom I have only a slight acquaintance," and the speaker turned toward the individual pursued and overtaken on the Brook road —"who requested that I would act for him in an affair to take place this morning. I consented with pleasure, but to my surprise was informed by Mr. Fenwick that he could not state the cause of the meeting—he could only assure me that it was unavoidable. I need not say, gentlemen, that such a state of things is awkward. The affair is wholly informal. No correspondence can hereafter be published, and both principals and seconds may be placed in a most disagreeable position. I yielded to Mr. Fenwick's representations that he was an entire stranger and knew scarcely any one besides myself; but I again ask that the grounds of the present meeting may be stated, in order that the affair may be honorably arranged, or, in case it unfortunately is obliged to proceed, that none of the parties may be placed in a false position."

The speaker ceased, and a brief pause followed. It was broken by the deep voice of Fenwick's adversary.

"I reply, sir, that the affair cannot be arranged," he said.

"You will pardon me for asking why?"

"For reasons which cannot be now explained."

The second looked doubtful.

"I am not convinced, sir—" he began, when the man of the bronzed face, with a fierce glow in his eyes, interrupted him.

"Well, sir," he said, in a voice so cold and menacing that it sent a thrill through me, "I will endeavor to convince you that valid grounds exist for the encounter about to take place —as take place it will, with or without witnesses. Suppose, sir, that one human being has sworn against another that oath

of vengeance which, in Corsica, is called the *vendetta!* No
matter what may be the reason—it may be a family feud,
descending from generation to generation, or it may be for an
offence, personal to the individual—the origin of it is nothing to
the point! Well, suppose, sir, that you are the person who has
registered that oath! Say it is *your* soul that cries out for the
blood of this adversary, and that, after long years spent in
searching for and awaiting him, you find him! Say that you
discover him at the moment when he is skulking in the dark!—
when he is plotting against your country as the secret agent of
her enemies!"—

"Impossible, sir!" exclaimed the second, almost recoiling as
he spoke.

"A moment, sir—I have not yet finished," said the deep
voice. "Suppose that you pursue this man and he flies, tearing
up the paper which is the proof of his guilt! Suppose that,
mastered by a weak and silly deference to the so-called code of
honor, you offer this man a fair combat instead of putting him
to death!—suppose, lastly, sir, that the adversaries are placed
face to face—the pistols loaded, the hopes of long years of waiting about to be realized—suppose that, sir!—place yourself in
that situation—and then tell me if you imagine that the man
who has lived for this alone—that I—I, sir!—will forego my
private vengeance!"

There was something so cold and threatening in the deep tones
of the speaker—his eyes burned with a fire so dark and lurid—
that the person whom he had addressed seemed overcome and
unable to find a word of reply.

At last he raised his head, and I could see upon his countenance an expression of utter bewilderment.

"A stranger affair I never took part in!" he muttered; "and
if my principal is the man he is represented to be—"

The quick ear of the swarthy personage caught the muttered
words.

"Oh! understand me, sir!" he said; "I do not charge your
principal with any thing infamous. I am a gentleman by birth,
and am ready to meet him. You may, therefore, act for him."

"One moment, sir," was the reply· "I wish to see Mr. Fen-wick."

And, making a sign to his principal, he walked some paces apart. Fenwick had listened to the words of his adversary with sullen and lowering brow—with eyes cast down, but lips closely set. Unable or unwilling to reply, he had evidently resolved to let the affair take its own course. He was absent for about ten minutes, conversing with his second. when they returned, and the latter said:

"I shall continue to act for Mr. Fenwick and now withdraw all my objections."

His associate bowed, and in a moment everything was ready.

The word was given: two pistol shots followed, like a single report; and the man of the bronze face remained unmoved. Then I looked at Fenwick. For a moment he stood erect, then, uttering an imprecation, he fell forward on his face.

The seconds hastened to him, and one of them muttered:

"Shot through the lungs—he will be dead in five minutes!"

A hasty consultation was then evidently being held, and, from the words "gate-keeper's house," I had no doubt of their intention to leave the dying man there.

My glance then fell on the man whose bullet had produced this tragedy. He was standing motionless, with folded arms—the smoking pistol in his hand—and in his dark, cold features I thought I read that his vengeance was not even yet satisfied.

I was gazing at him still, when a signal was made to one of the hack-drivers, and the vehicle ascended the hill. The dying man was placed in it; his second followed—and then the other principal and second slowly descended the hill on foot, and entered their carriage, which rapidly disappeared.

The whole scene had vanished; and I gloomily took my way back to the city.

On the next morning I read among the "local items" in one of the journals the following paragraph:—

"MYSTERIOUS AFFAIR.—Yesterday morning a fatal rencontre took place at Hollywood Cemetery, the particulars of which are set shrouded in mystery. About sunrise, the gate-keeper, who occupies a small house at the entrance of the cemetery, heard the discharge of pistols, and, hastening in the direction of the sound, met two hacks returning, one of which contained a gentleman mortally wounded. He was conveyed to the gate-keeper's, and subsequently to his hotel, where he now lies at the point of death. The name of the gentleman is Fenwick—that of his opponent we have not been able to discover."

On the next day an additional paragraph appeared, headed, "The Affair at Hollywood."

"This mysterious affair," wrote the sensation journalist, "continues painfully to excite the curiosity of the public. But as yet no new developments have been made. The seconds and princepals—all but Mr. Fenwick—have disappeared, and the causes which led to the meeting are entirely unknown. Mr. Fenwick was yesterday somewhat easier, and may possibly recover, his physicians say. If the bullet of his adversary had passed the one-thousandth part of inch nearer to the femoral artery, the wound would have instantly proved fatal. We expect to be able, in a day or two, to throw additional light upon this singular affair."

Three days afterward the public were inundated with this additional light.

"We are now able to explain the affair at Hollywood," wrote the journalist. "The meeting resulted from a violent scene which took place between Mr. Fenwick and a noted abolitionist and tool of the Yankees, who has lately been lurking in this city. Mr. Fenwick arrested him, and discovered the proofs of his guilt, but, misled by a false sense of honor, accepted his challenge. The unhappy result is known; but we are still unable to give the name of the other party in the duel. Mr. Fenwick, we are happy to say, is steadily improving, and his physicians declare that he will soon be able to leave his bed."

Such was the flood of dazzling light poured on this "mysterious affair."

This paragraph, as I learned long afterward, never met the eye of the person against whom it was directed, or his second, as they had left the city on the morning succeeding the encounter.

2

I dropped the paper, and asked myself, for the hundredth time, the meaning of the whole affair. Who was that man with the shin, cunning lips, and the eye of the snake?—who that dark personage with the black eyes and the face of bronze, who had sworn the *vendetta* against his adversary?

The curtain fell upon the mystery, and all was dark.

VII.

MY COMMISSION.

ON the floor of the Convention the advocates and opponents of secession meanwhile thundered on from day to day, and in the committees the leaders grappled furiously, as though in a breast-to-breast struggle for life or death.

The shifting phases of that great contest will some day be delineated by the historian. They will not be followed here. These memoirs hurry on to other scenes, and cannot dwell upon those fierce battles of the tongue preluding the conflict of bayonets. I will here record, however, my conviction that I, for one, did injustice to many who opposed the adoption of the Ordinance of Secession. I then thought they were untrue to the honor of the Commonwealth. I now think that they only differed with their opponents upon the expediency of secession at the moment. They thought that Virginia would be able to mediate between the extremes of both sections—that she could " command the peace "—and that her voice would be heard across the storm. Vain hope! All at once these mists of delusion were divided by the lightning flash. President Lincoln called for seventy-five thousand men to coerce the Gulf States, and Virginia was directed to furnish her quota.

From that moment all opposition to immediate secession ended. Its advocates triumphed—its opponents were paralyzed, or, rather, acknowledged that no other course was left. The choice was now between fighting with and fighting against the Southern States, and the Convention no longer hesitated.

It was on the 18th day of April, I think, that, hastening toward the Capitol, whither I had been attracted by a sudden rumor, I saw the Confederate flag rise in the place of the stars and stripes.

The Convention had just adjourned for the day, and I met my father in the throng. His countenance glowed, and in his earnest look I read deep feeling. Many of the members' faces exhibited traces of tears.

At my ardent expressions of joy, my father smiled—rather sadly, I thought.

"We have done our duty, my son," he said; "and you know I have advocated this step from the beginning, when I think the war might have been prevented. Now it is a fixed fact. What do you propose to do?"

"To return at once to King William, and set about raising a company. If they choose me to command them—good. If not, I will serve in the ranks."

My father walked on in silence, evidently reflecting.

"Wait two or three days," he said; "there will be time enough."

And we continued our way.

Three days afterward he came into my chamber, and said, with a smile:

"Good morning, Captain."

I laughed, and replied:

"You give me my title in advance."

"No; I have addressed you properly."

And he handed me a large envelope, upon one corner of which were stamped the Virginia arms. I tore it open, and found that it contained my appointment as captain in the Provisional Army of Virginia, with orders to report to Colonel Jackson, commanding at Harper's Ferry!

Never did lover greet more rapturously the handwriting of his mistress. I rose to my full height, waved the paper round my head, and uttered a "hurrah!" which shook the windows.

Turning with flushed face and sparkling eyes toward my

father, I saw him looking at me with inexpressible tenderness and sweetness.

I addressed myself to the task of procuring my equipments with an ardor which I now look back to with a satirical smile. Ah, those good days of the good year 1861! How anxious we all were to get to horse and march away under the bonnie blue flag! How fearful we were that a battle would be fought before we arrived; that we would not have an opportunity of reaping the glory of having our heads carried off by a cannon ball! That romance soon passed, and the war became a "heavy affair"—but then it was all illusion and romance.

At the end of a week I had procured my uniform and equipments. The first consisted of a suit of gray, the sleeves of the coat profusely decorated by my fanciful tailor with the gold braid of a captain: the latter of a light sabre, pistol, saddle, and single blanket, strapped behind. My slender wardrobe was carried in the valise upon the horse of my servant, an active young negro, who had figured as my body servant, and was delighted at "going to the wars."

I bade my friends good-by, and then went to have a last interview with my father. I still see his noble face, and hear his grave, sweet accents. There were tears in his eyes as he pressed my hand, and I think my own were not dry.

I got into the saddle, waved my hand, and, followed by my servant, set out upon the untried future.

VIII.

THE LONELY HOUSE.

It was the end of April when I commenced my journey toward the Potomac. The weather was charming, the birds sang in the trees, and the face of nature lay before me, all smiles and sunshine, her form clothed in that tender green with which she salutes the spring.

Such was the fine and pleasant season when the writer of the present memoir, clad in Southern gray, with his horseman's boots, and gayly-clattering sabre, set out for the wars, his mind full of rosy dreams, his pulse thrilling with anticipations of adventure.

To-day he seems quite a stranger to the old battered soldier, whose pulse rarely thrills, and who is tired of romance and adventure—or almost.

I made about thirty miles the first day, and stopped that night in the neighborhood of Beaver Dam, at the house of the hospitable Colonel 1——, who gave me a cordial reception. On the next morning I again set out, turning my horse's head toward Raccoon Ford, on the Rapidan.

The country through which I now passed was thinly inhabited, and toward the afternoon I began to feel convinced that I had missed my road. This, I soon ascertained from a wayfarer, was the fact; I had inclined too far toward the right, and my shortest route now to Culpepper Court-House was by way of Germanna Ford. Long before reaching that point it began to grow dark, and I found myself in the region near Chancellorsville known as the "Wilderness."

All around me extended a dense and unbroken expanse of thicket, which the eye vainly tried to pierce. The narrow and winding road through the gloomy undergrowth resembled rather a dusky serpent than a highway, and, as I penetrated deeper and deeper into this mysterious wilderness, the lugubrious sights and sounds which greeted me were ill calculated to raise my spirits. The silence was unbroken, save by the melancholy cry of the whippoorwill, buried in the swampy thicket, and no living object was seen, except when some huge owl, startled by the tramp of the horses, flapped his heavy pinions across the road, as he sought refuge in the shadowy depths of the wood. The moon had risen, and was struggling amid a bank of clouds; but the solemn light served only to bring out in clearer relief the sombre details of the wild and deserted landscape. The long branches depending above the narrow road resembled the shaggy arms of goblins, reaching down to grasp and carry the traveller away;

and I know not what melancholy influence, born of the place and time, weighed down my spirits, filling me with almost superstitious depression. Here night and a solemn gloom seemed to reign undisputed, and the notes of the whippoorwill resembled, to my fancy, the cries of unhappy beings imprisoned in these mournful solitudes.

That strange Wilderness, now associated with so many scenes of blood and death, had enticed me into its depths. I was the captive of its funereal shadows, its ominous sights and sounds, and, as will soon be seen, I was to explore some of its mysteries.

The depressing influence of the scene evidently affected my servant also. He drew nearer to me, and suggested that the horses were too much fatigued to go further.

To this view I assented, and, telling him we would stop at the first house, continued my way, still pursuing the narrow road through the unending thickets. I went on thus for another hour, and, despairing of reaching any house, was about to bivouac in the woods, when all at once a light was seen glimmering through the boughs on my right. Never was any sight more welcome, and pushing on, I came to a brush fence at the foot of a hill, skirted with pines, upon which the moonlight enabled me to discern a small house.

Leaping the low fence, I ascended the hill, found myself before a sort of cottage, with flowers growing round the porch, and a light in the window ; and, dismounting, knocked at the door.

What was my astonishment, to hear, in a sweet and eager voice, in response to my knock, the words:

"Come! come! you are expected."

Overwhelmed with surprise, I opened the door and entered.

IX.

THE WOMAN IN WHITE.

THE apartment in which I found myself was small, with a rag carpet on the floor, split-bottomed chairs, a walnut table, and a broad fireplace, above which ticked an eight-day clock.

This I took in at a glance, but my eyes were speedily riveted upon the person who had uttered those singular words, "Come! come! you are expected."

It was a lady of about thirty-five apparently, who still exhibited traces of extraordinary beauty, though she was thin to emaciation. Her hair had once been auburn—it was now sprinkled with gray; and the magnificent eyes were deeply sunken in their sockets. They still possessed, however, a wonderful brilliancy, and it was impossible not to be struck with their mingled gloom and tenderness. The dress of this singular personage still further excited my astonishment. I+ was of white muslin, low-necked, and with short sleeves. The shoulders and arms thus revealed were thin to a painful degree, and their pallor was frightful. To complete the singularity of her costume, there fell from her carefully braided hair a long bridal veil of snowy lace, and around her neck she wore a superb necklace.

As I entered, the lady rose with sudden animation and a beaming expression upon her countenance, but immediately sank back, murmuring:

"It is not my darling! He will not come—he will never come!"

This strange scene had so completely taken me aback that I remained standing in the middle of the apartment without uttering a word. There I might have continued to stand, deprived of all power of utterance; but all at once a door opened, and a woman of about fifty, hard-featured and morose in manner, and plainly dressed, hastily entered.

"What will you have, sir?" she said in tones as cold as an icicle. I explained that my horses were worn out, and that I wished to secure a night's lodging—a statement which was greeted with the freezing reply:

"This is not a house of entertainment, sir, and we cannot lodge you."

I would have retired upon receiving this ungracious answer, but the pale lady came to my succor.

"No, no," she said in her sweet and mournful voice, "he must not go away. I thought it was my darling—and he is tired. I also am tired, oh very, very tired."

And she sighed drearily, relapsing into silence. Her hands were clasped upon her lap, but from time to time she played with a little golden cross suspended from her necklace. Suddenly the clock struck, and the sound produced a singular effect upon her. She rose to her feet, turned toward the door, and, throwing back her long lace veil with a movement of inexpressible grace, exclaimed with sparkling eyes:

"That is the hour; and he will soon be here. He is coming now!"

In fact, the hoofs of a horse were heard upon the ground without, and with flushed cheeks the lady hastened to the door, to which my servant had just ridden up. The mysterious lady evidently mistook the noise for that made by the person whom she expected, and, throwing open the door, stood with clasped hands in an attitude of passionate expectation.

The scene, however, came to a sudden end. The harsh-looking woman hastened to the lady's side, and, with a singular mixture of deference and roughness, exclaimed:

"What are you doing, madam? Do you suppose he will be glad to see you, if you make yourself sick by going into the night air? Besides, your hair is all coming down, and it makes you ugly. Come, and let me fix it up again."

"Oh, yes!" was the mournful reply, "he always loved to have my hair neatly arranged. He will not like to see me thus! But will he come? I fear he will never come! No, no!—he will never, never come!"

And, hiding her face with her hands, she wept bitterly, and permitted herself to be led away. She passed through an inner door, and I was left alone.

To describe my astonishment at this extraordinary scene would be impossible. I stood motionless in the midst of the apartment, gazing at the door through which the lady had disappeared, and it was not until I heard a voice at my very elbow that I realized my whereabouts.

It was the voice of the harsh-looking woman, who now re-

turned to inform me, with greater emphasis than before, that I
must go further on to secure a night's lodging. Her mistress, I
must see, was insane, she said; and any company made her
worse.

She had scarcely finished, when a musical voice behind me
said:

"It is not necessary for this gentleman to go, Mrs. Parkins.
We will soon have you some supper, sir. Pray sit down. You
are very welcome."

X.

THE MYSTERIES OF THE WILDERNESS.

I PASSED from one enchantment to another. I had seen a mysterious bride. I now found myself vis-a-vis to a young beauty
of seventeen, whose appearance was sufficiently attractive to
monopolize my whole attention.

Let the reader figure to himself an oval face exceedingly sweet
and winning; large blue eyes full of unclouded serenity; and a
delicate mouth, which expressed at once extreme modesty and
very great earnestness. Around this countenance, at once feminine and full of character, fell a profusion of auburn ringlets—
not curls—reaching scarcely to the neck. The figure, clad in a
light spring dress, was slender and graceful—the hand small and
white as snow. In the depths of the tranquil blue eyes, I thought
I could discern unknown treasures of goodness, and great was
my surprise at finding this aristocratic girl buried in an obscure
abode of the wilderness.

She welcomed me with an air of simplicity and ease which no
princess could have surpassed; and under the influence of this
manner, so firm yet unassuming, even the morose woman, who
now reappeared upon the scene, seemed to grow less harsh.
She placed some supper on the table—muttered a promise to see
to my servant and horses—and then withdrew.

The young lady, who had calmly introduced herself as "Miss
2 *

Grafton," took her seat at the tea-tray, and conversed during the meal with the same unaffected tranquillity. She spoke of the lady in white without being urged; but simply said that ner mind was disordered—especially upon "a certain anniversary in April," which had chanced to be the night of my arrival. Then she glided to other topics, and finally suggested that I must be weary. My bed was ready—would I retire?

So I retired to a small, neat chamber above—to lie awake for hours thinking of her.

At last I fell asleep, but I had a singular dream. I thought I heard in my chamber low, cautious footsteps, as though a woman were walking with bare feet upon the floor. Tip!—tip!—tip!— I could have sworn the sound was real. As I listened, too, with a quick beating of the heart, I thought I saw a dusky figure flit before me—something rustled—then the whole disappeared, and silence reigned in the chamber.

Was it all a dream? I asked myself as I opened my eyes at dawn. For the life of me I could not decide, and I finally dismissed the subject from my mind.

At that moment I heard the hoof-strokes of a horse beneath my window, and a long acquaintance with the indolent character of my servant convinced me that the horse was not my own.

Going quietly to the window, I raised a corner of the white curtain, and, looking out, saw a horse standing, ready saddled for a journey, before the door.

On the steps the woman Parkins was conversing with a man wrapped closely in a dark cloak, and wearing a drooping hat. In spite of this disguise, however, I recognized one of the participants in the duel at Hollywood—the person called Fenwick.

He was thinner and paler, no doubt from his recent wound; but I saw before me the same dark and sinister face; the same bold yet lurking glance; the same lips, thin, compressed, and full of cunning.

I heard only the last words which passed between these worthies.

"This officer must not see me," muttered Fenwick, "and I am going. Curse that girl! how I love her and hate her!"

The woman uttered a harsh and grating laugh, which sounded strangely from those morose lips.

"That's her feeling for you, except the love," she said; "she don't seem to like you, sir."

"And why!" exclaimed Fenwick in a sort of rage, "because I have told her I love her!—because I cannot live away from her!—because I would give up all for her!—therefore she hates me!"

And I could hear the speaker grind his teeth.

"Well, it is not my fault, is it?" came in harsh tones from the woman. "I do what I am paid for——"

"And you would sell your soul for gold!" interrupted Fenwick, with a bitter sneer

"Suppose I would!" was the reply; "but I can't make the young lady care for you. You had better give her up, and pursue her no longer."

"Give up the pursuit!—do you think I will do that? to be foiled and beaten by a simple girl!—No! I swear by all the devils in hell she shall not escape me!"

He spoke so loudly and violently that the woman growled in a low voice:

"You will be overheard. After hiding all last night, you will be seen by the officer—I hear him stirring in his room."

Fenwick hesitated a moment; ground his teeth; glanced at my window; and then, shaking his clenched hand, leaped upon his horse.

"What is delayed is not lost!" he exclaimed bitterly.

And putting spur to the animal, he disappeared at full gallop in the thicket.

Such was my third meeting with this personage, who went and came on secret errands, fought duels with nameless adversaries, and had loves or hatreds to gratify wherever he went. While musing upon the singular chance which had again thrown him in my way, I was summoned to breakfast, at which Miss Grafton presided. The lady in white did not reappear.

"My cousin is sick. and I hope you will excuse her, sir," was

the calm explanation of the young girl; and with this I was
obliged to remain content.

When the meal was ended I ordered my horses, and at my
request Miss Grafton walked out with me upon the knoll before
the house, where I repeated to her the conversation I had overheard between Fenwick and Mrs. Parkins.

It seemed to excite no surprise in her whatever, and I observed
no exhibition of emotion in her countenance.

"I owe you many thanks for your friendly warning, sir," she
said tranquilly; "but this is not the first intimation I have had of
these designs."

"But I am sincerely uneasy, Miss Grafton," I replied; "this
man is dangerous and perfectly unscrupulous."

"I do not fear him, sir," she said. "God will defend me."

Her voice was so brave and firm that I could not restrain a
glance of admiration.

"You have witnessed some singular things in this house, sir,"
the young lady added, "and I am sorry that they attracted your
attention. In regard to Mr. Fenwick, I shall say nothing; but I
trust that you will not speak of the condition of my unfortunate
relative, whose derangement is very painful to me."

"Most assuredly I shall not, if you wish it."

"She is quite ill this morning, in consequence of the excitement last night, and I should feel no surprise if she died at any
moment. Her life is a sad one; and it will gratify those who
love her—I am almost the only one—if her condition is not made
the subject of speculation or remark. She has long been buried
here, and if she is to die, it is better that no notice should be
taken of the event. She is not happy!"

And deep silence veiled the eyes of the fair girl as she slowly
returned to the house.

A few minutes afterward I bade her farewell, and got into
the saddle. A bow, a motion of the hand, which she responded
to by an inclination of her head—and we parted.

XI.

THE PACKAGE.

CROSSING the Rapidan at Germanna Ford, I pushed on through Culpepper Court-House, toward the mountains, intending to pass the Blue Ridge at Ashby's Gap.

The strange scenes which had greeted my eyes and ears in the Wilderness still absorbed my whole attention; and I taxed my memory to recall every circumstance, however minute, connected with my sojourn in the abode of the White Lady. I was thus engaged, and rode on musing deeply, when, chancing to put my hand in my coat pocket, it struck against something.

I drew this something out, and found that it was a package of papers in a large envelope, securely sealed in several places, with a crest stamped on the sealing wax—but the astonishing circumstance was that the envelope bore no direction whatever.

All at once I saw something in one corner, in the delicate handwriting of a woman, and deciphered the words:

"Read these when I am dead—and remember
Your own FRANCES."

That was all! But that little was a whole world of wonder. Who could this "Frances" be, and whence came this package? All at once came the recollection of that vision of the preceding night. I remembered the faint footfalls on the floor of my chamber, as though delicate feet without slippers were tipping along, and something told me that *the White Lady had entered my chamber and placed that package in my pocket.* The more I reflected, the stronger was my conviction of the fact. She had, no doubt, experienced a confused impression of my identity or acquaintance with the person whom she had expected on that "certain anniversary in April" mentioned by Miss Grafton—had entered my apartment—deposited the package in my coat pocket for delivery to the unknown, and, before I could detect her, had glided away, with the cunning of insanity, and disappeared.

Such was my explanation of this singular circumstance; but another question now presented itself : What was I to do with the package ? I could not lose a whole day's journey and return —that was impossible ; and yet I did not wish to retain the papers of the poor, deranged lady. What should I do? The best decision to which I could come was, to take care of them until I had an opportunity of returning or sending them back by a safe hand ; and, having thus decided upon my course, I re-placed the package in my pocket, pondering deeply upon that strange indorsement :

"Read this when I am dead—and remember *your own Frances.*"

Then her name was Frances. What was the rest ?

XII.

HOW I ENCOUNTERED A TRAVELLER, AND OF WHAT WE CONVERSED.

I FOLLOWED a winding road through the woods, and was now approaching the Rappahannock.

I had found the country on fire with the war fever, and at every cross-road crowds of idlers had congregated, who discussed and rediscussed the events of the day. These would gladly have stopped me to ascertain every circumstance which I had ever known, heard, or imagined. But I had no desire to delay my journey for the idle amusement of gossips and busybodies. So I turned a deaf ear to all their allurements, and steadily pressed on toward the Rappahannock.

I had reached a point within a few miles of the river, when I saw in front of me a traveller on a superb white horse. Of the animal's action I soon had a convincing proof.

A bridge on the road, over a stream with precipitous banks, had been swept away, and I heard the roar of the waters. The traveller, I supposed, would seek a crossing above or below, but in this I was mistaken. All at once I saw him put his horse at

the opening—the animal rose in the air—and, with a gigantic
leap, cleared the chasm.

As I approached, the traveller halted, and I saw him look over
his shoulder. I glanced at him—then at the stream. It was
fully fifteen feet, and I assure you, my dear reader, I had not the
least idea of attempting it.

Ignominiously riding along the beach, I discovered a crossing,
and in a few moments had joined and saluted the man on the
white horse, who was courteously waiting for me.

He was low of stature, apparently about thirty, and his
costume was the careless dress of a gentleman. The face was
a striking one—very dark, heavily bearded, and rather brigand-
ish. But no bandit ever could boast a pair of eyes like the
stranger's. They were brown, and sparkled with unmistakable
good humor; the whole countenance, indeed, was full of gayety
and courtesy. Altogether, there was something in the cavalier
on the white horse which irresistibly attracted you.

"What a splendid animal, sir!" I said, when we had exchanged the greeting of wayfarers; "I really envied you when
I saw you take that leap!"

"I have cleared wider places," was his smiling reply, as we
rode on; "and I don't think the Yankees could catch me very
easily."

"Do you belong to the army?"

"To a cavalry company of this county, sir. I fear that we
shall soon be cutting right and left."

"You *fear* that?" was my rather discourteous question; but
the stranger did not seem to observe the word.

"Yes," he said in his mild voice, "I am sorry to fight the
North. War is terrible, and, do you know, I have a lingering
affection for the stars and stripes still?"

"I felt as you do once, but we must choose a new flag.'

"Yes."

"What will it be?" I said, "the Southern cross? the Palmetto? We have a number of emblems to choose from."

"Yes, but I have chosen mine," said the stranger simply.

"What is it?"

He took off his hat and drew from it a small square of silk, upon which was painted the Virgin of Virginia trampling upon the neck of the tyrant, with the motto traced beneath, "*Sic sem- per tyrannis.*"

"This is the flag I intend to fight under,"* he said in the same mild voice.

"It is the best of all!"

"Yes," he said; "I had it painted the day before I left Rich mond, and, sink or swim, live or die, I intend to fight under it tt the last!"

There was something so noble and chivalric in the dark face of the stranger as he spoke, that I gazed at him with uncon- cealed admiration. Again I observed, too, his perfect mastery of his powerful white horse, his sinewy frame, his flashing eyè —and I thought, "You would be dangerous in a charge!"

But the traveller did not seem to observe the effect which his words had produced. The glow disappeared from his counte- nance, and he rode on—the picture of a kindly, unassuming gen- tleman.

Of that kindness of temperament I soon had an illustration. On the road we came up with a little girl in a tattered frock, without shoes or stockings, who limped along painfully over the rocky way. My companion observed her weariness, and, check- ing his horse, asked where she was going. The mild voice seemed to disarm any fears the child had, and, looking out with large eyes from her tangled hair, she replied that she had been some miles to carry a message, and was returning home.

"How far is *home?*" asked the stranger, smiling.

"About two miles, sir," replied the child.

"Two miles!" exclaimed the stranger; "you can never walk that far, little one, with your sore feet. Come, get up, I will give you a ride!"

And reaching down, he lifted the child and placed her before him on the saddle. He did not seem to notice that the dirty and tattered dress rubbed against his spotless shirt bosom, as,

---
* His words.

resting in ms arms, the child looked at him out of her great
eyes.

The stranger quietly rode on, still conversing. until we reached
a point opposite a poor house seen across the fields: he [,] the
child slid down, and disappeared.

We then continued our ride, conversing as before, and I found
my companion a very delightful talker. He was perfectly modest and unassuming, but a man of excellent sense. I should
have classed him with those persons who are described by the
phrase "they would not hurt a fly"—but at times his brown eyes
flashed, and a chivalric glow lit up his dark face, as we spoke
of the coming contest.

When we reached a cross-road, not far from the river, and,
checking his white horse, the stranger informed me that he must
leave me, to pay a visit to a friend, I really regretted the parting.

"I hope, however, to see you again, captain," he said, addressing me by the title which my uniform indicated. "My house is
on your road, and I shall be at home to-morrow. I live at Markham's, near Manassas Gap, and trust you will make use of my
house to-night. My name is Turner Ashby, and my brother
Richard is at home. I shall expect to see you when I reach
home to-morrow morning." I accepted this obliging offer with
many thanks, as my day's journey would terminate in the vicinity of Markham's; and, with a friendly pressure of the hand, my
travelling companion disappeared at full speed on his white
horse.

I fully intended to make my way to his house, but, as the reader
will soon see, was prevented from doing so by "circumstances
over which I had no control."

XIII.

THE OWNER OF THE HANDKERCHIEF.

FORDING the Rappahannock near the little hamlet of Orleans, I stopped to dine and feed my horses at the hospitable mansion of Mr. M——; and then continued my way, drawing nearer and nearer to the long blue wave of the Ridge.

I lost no time, as heavy banks of clouds piled up on the horizon indicated an approaching storm; and the thunder already began to mutter in the distance. The declining sun, threatening and bloody, poured its crimson light upon field and forest as I hastened on; and from time to time vivid flashes of lightning lit up the dark masses slowly gathering overhead. Then all at once, without warning, and ere I dreamed of its approach, rushed down from the mountains a veritable hurricane.

Never before had I encountered anything like this sudden tornado. It blinded me, and took my breath away. Roaring as it came, like a thousand wild beasts unloosed, it tore across the fields, whirled amid the boughs of the forest, and carried everything before it.

I had entered a belt of woods, through which the road ran, ere I realized the extent of the hurricane; and now went on at full speed, to escape the dangerous vicinity of crashing boughs and tree trunks. The air was filled with limbs torn from the trees, and more than once, as I passed beneath, I narrowly escaped being struck by them.

All at once, as I went on at full gallop, I saw a horse shoot out from a side road, a hundred yards in front of me, and a second glance told me that the rider was a young lady. Her hair was flowing in heavy curls upon her shoulders, from beneath the coquettish little hat and feather; her habit streamed like a meteor; and, with head thrown back, and slender form erect in the saddle, she seemed to be enjoying the hurly-burly of the storm.

Behind her came a servant, urging his horse violently with

hand and heel—as perfect a specimen of terror as his young mistress was of "game."

I was charmed with the enticing figure which sped on before me, and pushed my horse to his utmost speed, not only to escape the storm, but also to keep up with the young lady. As I did so, the hurricane increased in intensity. The air was full of flying boughs: twice I was obliged to leap trees which had crashed down between myself and the young lady: finally my enjoyment of her splendid horsemanship came suddenly to an end. The storm came on with a roar which surpassed all its former fury; a huge limb above me snapped—the next moment I was struck violently upon the head, and hurled from my horse to the ground.

I must have been completely stunned for some moments. When I opened my eyes and came to my senses, I saw the young lady kneeling beside me, and felt her arm under my head. At ten paces the frightened servant held her horse. The storm raged as furiously as before, but the young lady seemed perfectly indifferent to it.

Suddenly I recognized in the face close to my own something familiar; then a thrill ran through my frame. It was the owner of the handkerchief which I had picked up, on that moonlight night, in the grounds of the Capitol at Richmond!

There was no sort of doubt about the identity of the young lady. There were the same beautiful lips, as red as carnations; the same waving chestnut hair; the same eyes, half haughty and half languishing—great violet eyes, which had haunted me ever since that evening!

I must have looked at her fixedly, for a slight rose-color came to the cheeks. Then it faded, and she said, with the most perfect calmness:

"Are you much hurt, sir? Your arm seems to be broken."

"I do not know," I murmured. "I am ashamed to trouble you!"

"You do not trouble me at all, sir," was the reply of the young lady. "I will assist you to rise."

Was anything ever less romantic? Instead of rescuing the

young girl, of whom I had dreamed so long, here she was coming to my own succor and rescuing *me!*

Rising faintly to my feet, with a sort of vertigo in my brain, I managed to mount my horse, which was led up at the moment, and the young lady, too, got into the saddle.

" You must not ride rapidly : I fear you are seriously hurt," she said. " I am in no haste, and will accompany you until you feel stronger, sir."

And she calmly rode on by my side.

She was in no haste!—and yet the forest was a whirlpool of falling limbs and crashing trees, as the storm roared on with unabated fury! My fair companion exhibited not a single evidence of fear—her face was as calm and cold as before. You would have said that she was riding pensively along on a tranquil May morning.

We soon issued from the forest.

" Will you come to my father's house, sir, until the storm is over ?" my companion now said. " I think you need some rest before riding further."

" Thanks!" I murmured, in a sort of dream, as I listened to that voice.

And she led the way into a by-road which ran in the direction of a house which I saw rising from the woods upon a distant hill.

Still stunned, bewildered, and scarcely realizing my situation, I rode on by the side of the young lady, who seemed not to observe the rain which now drenched her chestnut curls and her riding habit. She did not again open her lips; and I was too faint and weak to address her.

In a quarter of an hour we reached a large white gate, ascended a grassy hill, and stopped before the portico of an old mansion of very considerable size, overshadowed by magnificent oaks. I remember some dogs were lying upon the portico, and a peacock was cowering with wet plumage beneath one of the trees. Memory is a curious faculty and deals in trifles.

I had dismounted, with the vague feeling that I ought to assist the young lady from the saddle, when a gentleman, with long gray hair falling upon his shoulders, came out and approached us.

After that, I don't remember much more. My arm seemed on fire; a mist passed before my eyes, and, only dimly realizing that the arm of the gray-haired gentleman was around me, I lost consciousness.

Again, my dear reader, can you possibly imagine any incident less "heroic" than this first meeting with the lady of the handkerchief?

XIV.

A FOLLOWER OF CALHOUN.

I HAVE no intention now of drawing a vivid and affecting picture of an amiable family turned topsy-turvy and running to and fro.

Here is what I saw when I opened my eyes: an old lady in a white cap, busily bandaging my broken arm; an old gentleman with long gray hair, who was superintending the operation; and a young lady with chestnut curls, who reclined in a chair opposite, and did not seem greatly interested in the scene.

Five minutes after regaining consciousness, I had the satisfaction of knowing that I was not among strangers at all, but was the guest of Colonel Beverley of "The Oaks," one of my father's oldest and most intimate friends.

"M. B.," on the handkerchief I had picked up, stood for Miss May Beverley, his daughter.

On the evening of the same day, my arm felt perfectly easy; and I was talking politics with my host.

He was really a character. Imagine, my dear reader, a tall, thin gentleman, nearly seventy years of age, with long gray hair falling in elf-locks on his shoulders; eyes as keen and piercing as those of an eagle; but a smile so soft and sweet that no woman's ever exceeded it in suavity. In every movement of my host was the elegance and distinction of the old race of cavaliers;

and in the gray-haired gentleman with the sweet and winning
smile, I was utterly unable to recognize the stern old *doctrinaire*
whom my father had often described to me—the politician of
passions so fiery, invective so withering, and a combativeness so
fierce and implacable. I knew that in the great war for State-
rights, when South Carolina opposed Jackson in 1832, no man
had been more violent and resolute than Colonel Beverley, who
had passionately espoused the views of Mr. Calhoun, and proved
himself a fire-brand of agitation and revolution.

I need not record the conversation which took place between
myself and my host. Great was his satisfaction when he heard
that I was a son of " old Phil. Surry, one of his very best
friends. I must stay as long as possible. What was the news
from Richmond? These cursed Yankees were going to invade the
South—the bludgeon against the rapier—the crop-eared Puritan
against the Cavalier! Curse the Pilgrim Fathers, and the whole
canting breed of 'em! The South had been fighting them for
fifty years in Congress, and was ready now to meet them on the
battle-field! John Brown nor John Devil should put the heel
on *him!* Old Patrick Henry and Randolph of Roanoke saw
clearly how the thing was going to work—saw the 'poison
under the wings' of this Federal contrivance, which had proved
a dead failure from the start! The South had paid two-thirds
of the revenues of Government; had furnished all the Presidents; had built up the shipping and manufactures of New
England; and now these people had grown presumptuous and
greedy—they must put to death the bird that laid the golden egg,
and get all at once! But the South was ready to meet them—
she would resist with the bayonet! She might be overwhelmed
by numbers, but she would fight to the last. With the denial of
the doctrine of State-rights every thing went; old John C. Calhoun saw the working of the venom of Federalism and warned
the North of the consequences; but they scoffed at him. War
was now at hand, and the only hope for the country was in the
triumph of the South. If she failed, all was over; mobocracy
would rule, and all go to ruin. Against this the South was the
only breakwater. She must spread the old State-rights banner

to the winds—meet the enemy breast to breast—and if she fell, let her fall with the old State-rights flag around her—glorious even in her death !"

As the old *doctrinaire* thus spoke, his face flushed, his eyes burned, his form quivered. It was the fiery outburst of a veritable volcano—you could smell the hot odor of the hissing lava!

XV

PYGMALION.

I HAVE no doubt my fair readers—if, indeed, I am honored with such—have carefully omitted perusing that tirade upon politics—hastening on to some imaginary "love scenes."

Alas! mesdames, there were none at all to record. It would charm me, not only upon your account, but my own too, to describe some romantic interviews with this young lady; but I should be compelled to draw upon my imagination. That would not become the narrator of real events—and thus, all these expectations must be disappointed.

The young lady did not melt—indeed, she seemed to freeze more and more. I can scarcely describe the phenomenon which I then witnessed. Liking is apt to conciliate liking in return—to a certain extent, at least; but the more she knew of me, the less Miss May Beverley seemed to care for me. It is impossible to describe the chill and stately air with which the young lady received my attentions. It was the bearing of a duchess who repels one of the commonalty; and it commenced the very day after my arrival.

She came into the parlor where I was lying on a sofa, and slightly bending her head, upon which the bright chestnut hair was now disposed in rich braids, inquired calmly how I felt.

"Thank you—a great deal better!" was my reply, as I gazed with unconcealed admiration upon the beautiful girl. "My hurt is very trifling, and I am only too glad I received it--for it has given me the happiness of knowing you."

I must have spoken with ardor, and betrayed what I felt, fcr, as her eyes met my own, full of eager feeling, her cheek colored slightly, and she turned away.

"I have spoken too warmly for a stranger, perhaps, Miss Beverley—a mere acquaintance of yesterday," I added, "but you will pardon me, I hope—these are not times of ceremony. Feeling ripens rapidly now, and the acquaintance of to-day becomes the friend—perhaps more than the friend—of to-morrow!"

She turned toward me—as I caught her expression, my heart sank. It was a statue of ice which I saw before me—or marble, if you like the comparison better.

"Pardon my words, Miss Beverley," I murmured, "but you are not a mere acquaintance. You exposed yourself to danger to assist me in the wood yonder"—

"Not at all, sir!" she interrupted, in a freezing tone; "it was nothing; and I would have done as much for any one."

I sank back, silent, and cruelly mortified.

"Does your arm pain you much, sir? I hope it is better this morning. The sun is coming out, I think, and the weather promises to be fair again."

With which words, Miss May Beverley moved calmly to the window; looked out; raised her snow-white hand to arrange the braids of her hair; and then slowly glided out of the apartment —cold and stately to the last.

There is the first interview, my dear feminine reader. Do you think that it promises any thing "thrilling," or "romantic"?

It was a specimen of all. Miss Beverley did not thaw—she grew colder and colder as I grew warmer.

For I no longer tried to deceive myself upon the subject of my sentiments toward her. In a day—an hour, as it were—her love had become the only thing worth living for. Her eyes were the stars of the evening sky—her chestnut hair the golden waves of sunset—in her smile was the splendor of the pensive moon that shines in the summer night!

In other words, it was a world all "moonlight, love, and flowers" which I inhabited, my dear reader. See the song for the rest.

When my mind was not reduced to an imbecile condition about May Beverley, I used to lie on my sofa, and flush with anger at a thought which incessantly recurred. Had Baskerville, with whom she had been walking that evening, basely uttered in her presence something to my discredit? Had he misrepresented that encounter at the hotel, and thus poisoned the young lady's mind against me? When that thought came to me, I clinched my hands, and fell into silent rages. More than once I determined to ask, plainly, the truth ; but the cold face of the young lady always repelled me. That pride and disdain, too, which is the vice of the Surry family, withheld me. If she would take that man's word, and condemn me without a hearing, she cared nothing for me! Why should I make myself ridiculous?

In other words, I was in love with Miss May Beverley, and my choice seemed to be unlucky. It is an old story. I don't mean to prose on with it.

I will only say, that "day after day," as sighs the hero of "Love's Chidings," the same phenomenon was presented—a man burning, and a woman freezing. The longed-for thaw never took place in May Beverley; and even in her selection of songs—for she played and sang exquisitely—she seemed to repel her unfortunate wooer.

See! she strolls to the piano, yonder, with that "regal, indolent air," of a born duchess, half haughty, half careless, all graceful. The April sun lights up her waving hair, and crowns the bright head like a glory.

Listen! she touches the piano, and then commences singing in a voice which echoes through the old hall. Do you know what she is telling, whoever listens, in that song? Here is the cheerful and jovial view of life and human nature which I listen to for my mental improvement, as I lie on my sofa, or bend over her, my face close to the perfumed hair and the snow-white neck, encircled by the thin golden chain.

(Favorite air of young ladies in the land of "Dixie," as sung
by Miss May Beverley, *con espress. :*)—

> "In the birth of spring to meet!
> In the morning air so sweet!
> And woman's love is sweeter than roses in May:
> But the birth of spring will fleet,
> Like the roses at her feet!
> And love, like the seasons, must soon pass away.
>
> "The summer sun is bright,
> And the swallow's wing is light—
> And woman's love is warm as a fair summer day;
> But the sun will set at night,
> And the swallow wing his flight—
> And love, like the summer, must soon pass away?
>
> "The leaf on autumn's bough
> In the moonlight glimmers now—
> And woman's love is as pure as its soft silver ray;
> But the leaf goes on the gale,
> And the silver moon will fail—
> And love, like the autumn, must soon pass away!
>
> "Gay winter sweeps us by,
> Joy beams in every eye—
> And woman's love is gayer and brighter than all
> But chill 's the winter's breath,
> And the eye must close in death—
> And love, death, and winter must all pass away!"

The young lady ceases—her voice dies away, and I observe:
"That is a lively and inspiring air you have selected, Miss
Beverley. It is my favorite song—after the 'Miserere' in
Trovatore."

I laugh as I make this brilliant jest, but no smile touches the
beautiful face of the young lady.

"Do you like Verdi?" she says, indifferently. And touching
the piano, she commences singing—

> "Ah! fors' è lui."

As she sings, her voice soars, triumphs, and the silver trills
ring through the old hall and the adjoining grounds. This time
I do not joke—I hang upon her lips. With eyes glowing, bosom

heaving, and cheeks full of passionate feeling, the young lady gives to the music of Verdi an effect which I never dreamed it possessed.

The ice had melted, roses had tinted the marble face—it was a passionate girl, not a cold and stately woman, which I saw before me.

Then the air died away; the color in the cheeks faded: she was marble again.

"You spoke of the 'Miserere,'" she said, in a tone of careless indifference, as she ran her hands over the instrument before her.

"Yes, it is the soul of sadness."

"Then you do not wish to hear it?"

"On the contrary, I should be delighted if you would sing it."

"I will try, then; if I weary you, tell me, and I will stop."

If she wearied me! The idea seemed curious to the hapless individual who could have stood there, beside her, and listened to her forever.

So, in slow, measured strains, came that singular air which Owen Meredith heard Mario sing, "Aux Italiens," and which brought back his early love from the grave. That is a tenor song, my dear reader, as you doubtless know; and before I heard May Beverley, I thought no woman could sing it. She made the music magical, and I still hear that strain, echoing forever in my memory. Was it her own heart speaking in the mournful music? Had she ever bidden farewell to any love in those wild accents? I knew not—I only knew that her voice produced an indescribable effect upon me, and that, on that day, I did not ask her to sing again.

I pass on from that period of enchantment. It was only for a moment, now and then, that the violet eyes glowed, the cheeks filled with color. The young lady remained as obstinately chill as before; and yet a little incident at the time seemed to indicate that she possessed deep and earnest feelings.

There was a young Charley Beverley, her brother, who had been off on a visit somewhere, but returned now to "The Oaks" to get his equipments and join the forces on the Potomac.

Charley was a gay youngster, of about seventeen, with only one
passion in the world—to ride unbroken colts: only one ambi-
tion—to shoulder a musket and go and fight "the Yankees."
He was a favorite with all, but his sister May seemed his special
adorer. She hung around the youth with the deepest fondness
and devotion ; sewed night and day at his articles of clothing;
could not bear, apparently, to have him out of her sight, and
when he was leaving her, covered his face with passionate
kisses, and burst into an agony of tears. As the youth disappeared, she passed by a certain gentleman with an air of utter
unconsciousness of the fact of his existence, and, going to her
chamber, did not reappear again until the next morning.

She then made her appearance, as cold and haughty as before.
All traces of emotion had vanished from her face ; her tones
were calm and indifferent ; her walk as measured, stately, and
queenlike as before.

Altogether, I came to the conclusion that Miss May Beverley
was a singular character, and I only regretted that I had been
so unfortunate as to become the victim of her beautiful eyes.
Things are in a desperate condition with a wooer, my dear
reader, when he is sorry that he ever met "her." If you are
young and susceptible, I strongly advise you to avoid the *filles
du marbre.* Sunshine and roses are much better than the gray
skies of winter, when the shining flowers seem destined never to
bloom again!

XVI.

THE GUEST WHO DID NOT COME.

Two or three more scenes will terminate those days at "The
Oaks." I shall now ask the reader to be present at a grand
dinner which the hospitable Colonel Beverley gave in honor of
his chance guest.

Here is the company seated at the broad table, in the large
dining-room, through which go and come, with shining faces,
the ebon subjects of the well-known "irrepressible conflict."

After the dessert is finished, the ladies disappear—Mrs. Beverley bland and smiling, her daughter silent and *distraite*.

The old Colonel then begins to talk politics. He has surrounded himself with a Spartan phalanx of "original secessionists," every one of whom is a passionate admirer of the great Calhoun, and the unanimity of the company, upon politics, is almost painfully perfect. It is hard to find points of difference sufficient to afford discussion; but the Colonel manages to pick out an old gentleman who injudiciously "doubts if the views of Mr. Calhoun were entirely practicable"—and then the storm begins. Let us close our ears to it, reader, and remain quiet; it will soon expend its wrath. Listen! it is already over, and Colonel Beverley is addressing your humble servant.

"Captain Surry," he says, bowing and drinking a glass of Madeira to my good health, "you are here in the midst of the leading traitors and chief gentlemen—the two being the same—of the County of Fauquier. There is not a single neighbor of mine absent to-day—yes, one is not here, but no invitation ever tempts him."

"Who is your hermit, Colonel?"

"You may well give him that name. I sent him a pressing invitation to meet you to-day, but he very politely refused."

I began to laugh.

"I am more anxious than ever to hear who he is—as not even the charms of my society can move him."

"His name is Mordaunt."

"I do not know him."

"But surely you must have heard of him?"

"Not in the least. We are too good Virginians down there on the Rappahannock, to hear of, or care for, anybody out of our own county."

The old Colonel laughed and replied:

"Well, that accounts for it; but I must tell you about Mordaunt. He is one of our celebrities, though few people have ever seen him. In one word you have described him—he is an absolute hermit."

"And where does he live?"

"On a spur of the Blue Ridge, a few miles from this place. His life of seclusion is only a part of the singularity about him."

"You excite my curiosity more and more, Colonel."

"Well, I'll try and gratify it, though I really know little, of my own knowledge, in regard to him. There is something mysterious about the man and his history—a somewhat doubtful recommendation you will say—but our Mordaunt is unquestionably a gentleman. He is still a young man, between thirty-five and forty at least; but is known to have served against the French in Algiers, where he fought for many years, taking the side of the Arabs. It is even said that he became a leading chief among these wild bands, and was as active against their enemies as if he had been a good Mussulman."

"That is a curious story, Colonel."

"Is it not? But the man and his surroundings are even more singular. I have met him two or three times—purely by accident—and can describe him to you. He is tall and dark—in fact, burnt nearly black by the sun of the tropics; but his manner is very distinguished, and it is impossible not to see that he is a gentleman born and bred. Now, as to his mode of living. It is said that his house, which is situated in a secluded part of the country, near the mountain, is full of tiger skins, strange weapons, and a hundred outlandish mementos of travel in distant lands. An ample estate enables him to gratify every whim, but he is said to live very simply, spending most of his time in his study. When not thus engaged, he is hunting, or taking long and solitary rides among the mountains. All the old hunters know him, and look upon him as a demi-god. He prefers their society, apparently, to that of all other persons—though he scarcely ever opens his lips, it is said, except to speak in Arabic to a Moorish attendant he has brought with him from Algiers. Is not all that rather curious?"

"A real chapter from the pages of romance, Colonel; but what is the mystery of his life?"

"I really do not know—nor does anybody. He came to live in this country a few years ago, but he goes nowhere, discourages visitors, and it was only by accident that I made his acquaintance.

I have invited him to come and see me, two or three times, but he always sends a cool, though perfectly courteous, refusal. I thought I could tempt him to break his rule to-day—but you see I have failed."

"I am sorry, for I really should like to meet your singular hermit."

And the conversation glided to other topics. Soon afterward the company rose, and, hearing the piano, I went into the drawing-room and found Miss May Beverley singing the "Tempesta del mio cor." Was there really a storm raging in the heart of that statue? I had never seen her look colder, or less repellant in her manner, though the music of Verdi had brought a faint rose-tint to the beautiful cheeks.

She ceased singing as I entered, and strolled carelessly to the window.

"It is a very fine day," she said, beating a tattoo on the pane.

"Superb," I replied, " and I am sorry that the company to-day prevented the ride you promised to take."

"Yes—I think I should have enjoyed it."

"Will you ride to-morrow, then?"

"If you wish, sir."

"What were you playing?"

"Nothing."

And she strolled away languidly, preferring her own thoughts, apparently, to my society. Pygmalion sighed—his statue seemed never destined to glow with human feeling.

XVII.

THE "LAST RIDE TOGETHER."

THERE is a piece in Browning called "The Last Ride Together." Did you ever meet with it, my dear reader? It is worth your notice. Read that wonderful extravaganza, that supreme cry of passion from a heart that fails in the struggle, and you will have some idea of the feelings of a friend of yours when he took his last ride with May Beverley.

The month of flowers had come now—May had bloomed in all its glory—and the girl who bore the name of this month of months seemed blooming too. The balmy breezes blew against her cheeks just tinted with the rose, made the ribbons of her bodice flutter gayly, and just stirred the bright waves of her chestnut hair, in which nestled a single flower of spring. The lips, pensive and half parted, had the ripe red of the carnation— the great dreamy eyes were as blue as the sky above us.

Then I knew what the poet meant when he made his unfortunate hero utter that prayer, that he might "ride forever, forever ride" by the side of the woman he adored.

The young lady had promised to conduct me to a lofty hill, from which there was a superb view, and we were soon flying along through fields and forests toward the Blue Ridge. In half an hour we reached the hill, and I saw far beneath me the green slopes of Fauquier, crowned with white mansions, embowered in the young spring foliage. To the right, and in rear of us, rose the shaggy, pine-clad sides of the Blue Ridge.

She checked her horse, and, leaning her cheek upon her hand, murmured, as she gazed at the beautiful landscape:

"What a contrast to the tedium and sameness of society!"

Then looking at me with her large, pensive eyes:

"I believe I will turn hermit," she added.

"Like the Solitary of the Blue Ridge? He must have inoculated you with his enthusiasm for retirement."

"I have never seen him," was her reply.

"And you do not know where he lives?"

"No, I have never heard."

And she relapsed into silence.

I see her now as I saw her then—leaning her fair cheek languidly upon the delicate gauntlet, and gazing pensively toward the blue horizon. She wore a brown habit which revealed every outline of the exquisite figure—slender, and swaying like the reed, or the lily; the plume in her riding-hat just shaded her white forehead, and against the snowy neck shone the glossy braids of her hair. There, sitting upon her docile bay, in the bright spring afternoon, May Beverley was "a sight to make an old man young."

You fancy, perhaps, that the spring sunshine had at last thrilled her pulses, and that the marble statue had become a happy girl. Listen!

"Life is a dull affair," she murmurs; "nature the only solace, and even that is not very gay. Come, sir, you must be tired of waiting. Let us ride on."

So we descended the hill, and rode in the direction of another. Pausing to enjoy every new view, the young lady did not seem to observe the lapse of time. The light slowly faded, darkness approached, and we found ourselves many miles from "The Oaks," in a wild and unknown region.

"We had better return," I said. "But do you know the country?"

She looked round carelessly, and replied:

"Not in the least, sir?"

"Then I really think we had better lose no time in retracing our steps before the light entirely disappears."

She bent her head indifferently, and turned her horse into a road which led through a belt of woods.

"This is the direction to 'The Oaks,'" she said. "I know by the mountain."

And she tranquilly rode on; but I was by no means satisfied. We were in a wild and rugged country—I knew how easily a road is lost—and night was now upon us. We had entered what resembled an interminable forest, and soon the winding character of the road we pursued rendered it almost certain that we were not proceeding in the direction of "The Oaks."

"I am very sorry to inform you, Miss Beverley," I said at last, "that we have lost our way. This a slight affair to myself, but the air is growing cold, and you are very thinly clad."

"It is nothing," she replied coolly; "I never take cold, and we can inquire at the first house we find."

But none appeared—still stretched on and on the interminable forest.

3*

It was then that I thought of the "Last Ride" of Browning. If we never reached "The Oaks" any more forever, but continued thus to ride, side by side! would that destiny be hard? I would have accepted it.

But suddenly a light glimmered through the foliage to the left, and we soon reached a tall gate, which evidently led into the grounds of a dwelling-house. We passed through it, rode on through an avenue of magnificent trees, and, ascending a gentle slope, found ourselves in front of a low, brick mansion, with extensive wings, over which drooped the arms of some enormous black oaks.

I dismounted, and at the first sound of the knocker—I remember it was a scowling face, in bronze, like the mask of the old tragedians—the door opened, and a singular figure presented itself. It was that of a young Moor, about eighteen apparently, with a slender frame, swarthy face, and sparkling black eyes. He wore an ornamented caftan, a braided jacket, and around his waist was tied a shawl by way of girdle.

I briefly explained the object of my visit, but the young Moor shook his head, evidently to indicate that he did not understand my words. I was about to repeat my attempt to make him comprehend me, when all at once my eyes encountered an object which drove everything else from my mind.

The door leading into an apartment on the right of the entrance was open; a chandelier hanging from the centre of the ceiling lit up a strange scene of furs, weapons, and pictures; but what at once riveted my gaze was a portrait hanging on the wall of the apartment, full in the light of the chandelier.

That portrait was the most exact likeness of the young lady I had encountered at the house in the Wilderness—Violet Grafton.

I gazed at it with very great astonishment. Why was that picture hanging here? Could the Solitary of the Mountains—for this was plainly the house of Mordaunt—know the girl buried yonder in that obscure mansion? Here plainly was her portrait; what relation did she bear to him?

I was still gazing, lost in astonishment, at the beautiful face, with its mild eyes peering out from the golden ringlets, when the hoof-strokes of a horse resounded on the avenue, and the young Moor, who had remained standing by me motionless, at once hastened to the door.

A man riding a powerful black horse had halted there, and across the pommel of his saddle I saw the dead body of a bear, still bleeding from a deep gash in the throat. The light then fell upon the features of the horseman. I recognized the unknown adversary of Fenwick in the duel at Hollywood Cemetery.

Mordaunt—for the reader no doubt understands that this was the solitary—saluted Miss Beverly with profound but ice-like courtesy. Then he bestowed a bow of the same description upon me.

I hastened to break the awkward pause by an explanation of the object of our visit. Mordaunt replied in a tone of formal politeness that he would send a servant to guide us back—meanwhile, as Miss Beverley must be fatigued, would she honor him by dismounting? When this proposal was declined, the formal personage uttered three words in Arabic, to the young Moor, and in a few minutes a mounted servant was ready to accompany us. Mr. Mordaunt was evidently accustomed to talk little and to be served promptly. He did not utter another word, and his formal air—mingled with deep gloom—had not changed for an instant.

"You have a magnificent bear there," I said as I mounted; "was he killed in the mountain, sir?"

"Yes, sir," was the brief reply; "he gave me a hard fight, but I mastered him."

A slight color came to the swarthy cheek. The recollection of his combat seemed to please the stranger. But he seemed to have little desire to describe it or to prolong the interview. His manner was perfectly polite, but no ice could be colder; and, thanking him for the guide, I set out with the young lady for "The Oaks."

A ceremonious bow from the tall, gloomy figure—a slight movement of Miss Beverley's head in return—so we parted.

"Well, what do you think of the hermit?" I said, laughing, as we rode on.

"He is very cold in his manners," was her indifferent repiy.
"Something in his past life must have made him melancholy."
In an hour we had reached "The Oaks."

XVIII.

THE ALGERINE.

On the next morning I mounted my horse, and, following the
road by which we had returned on the preceding night, soon
found myself again in sight of Mordaunt's house.

The object of my visit is easily explained. I had never ceased
to remember the cold and yet passionate tones of that deep
voice which had resounded before the duel in Hollywood Cemetery; and I know not what it was that told me, that some great
tragedy had darkened this man's life—some mortal poison imbittered a character grand, noble, and magnanimous. I could
read that great nature in the clear bold eyes, the proud curl of
the lips, and the dignity of his most passionate utterances. Now,
this man, in whom I took an irresistible interest, was about to
be the victim of a plot devised by his bitter adversary. The
young lady whose portrait was hanging on his wall—his friend
or his kinswoman—was the object of the dark designs of Fenwick, as I had ascertained that morning in the Wilderness. It
was certain that these designs were unknown to Mordaunt.
Was it not absolutely incumbent upon me, as a man of honor, to
put him on his guard by revealing them?

It did not take me very long to decide that question; and the
result was my visit. I entered the tall gate, passed between the
long rows of trees, through the extensive grounds, and, dismounting, grasped the scowling knocker, and let it fall. This time a
negro answered my summons, and, showing me into the room on
the right, containing the portrait, went to announce my visit to
his master.

The apartment in which I found myself was curious. It was
evidently the private sitting-room of the owner of the mansion:

and, as I afterward discovered, I had been shown into it by mistake. Nothing more *outré* than the appearance of this room, can possibly be imagined. The furniture was antique, with grotesque ornaments carved upon the wood; ánd, in place of a carpet, the floor was covered with the most magnificent skins, preserving the outlines of the animals from which they had been torn. Here were the shaggy spoils of the lion of Morocco; the mottled and tawny skins of the Bengal tiger; and the brilliant fur of the East India leopard, as soft as and more pliable than the finest velvet. With these were mingled other rich furs; and the peculiarity which struck me was the extreme care taken to preserve the appearance of the animals. The eyes were replaced by dazzling globes of agate; the teeth grinned threateningly beneath the curled lips; and the sharp claws seemed ready to tear any one who approached.

On two sides of the apartment the walls were covered with books in every language. The opposite wall was filled with pictures, representing combats on foot or horseback; encounters between French Zouaves and Arabs in white burnous; hunting scenes, and every species of conflict with man or animal. Between the pictures hung, crossed as trophies, weapons of every description, including beautiful specimens of the Moorish yataghan, the Turkish scimetar, the deadly crease of the Malays, and, by way of grim jest apparently, one of the long rude pikes used by John Brown and his followers when they invaded Virginia. On the table lay pipes of every form, chibouques, hookahs, narghilès, meerschaums carved into grotesque or beautiful figures, and the plain but excellent Powhatan pipe of Virginia. In porcelain jars beside them were a dozen varieties of tobacco— the pale Latakia; the dark Shiraz; the Peerrique from New Orleans, black, fibrous, and powerful; and the milder brown, that which is raised on the south side of James River.

Across an open volume of Hugo's "*Les Misérables,*" which had then just appeared, lay a black meerschaum, which its owner seemed to have been lately smoking.

Such was this curious apartment; and it was impossible not to speculate upon the character of the individual whose tastes it seemed to reflect. Here were the spoils of war and the chase; the best books of all languages; and pictures which seemed to start from the walls as you gazed upon them. Was my host, then, a mixture of the soldier, the hunter, the student, and the amateur of art? One thing was very plain—that he had little taste for female beauty: not a picture of the entire collection contained a single female figure. The portrait of Miss Grafton was the sole recognition of the existence of her sex.

I was gazing intently at this portrait, whose resemblance to my beautiful young hostess of the Wilderness struck me still more forcibly than before, when the door opened, I heard a step behind me, and the owner of the mansion entered.

His manner, as he greeted me, was characterized by the same cold yet perfect politeness which I had observed on the preceding evening. But in this there was no affectation whatever. It seemed never to have occurred to him that he ought to ask, "To what am I indebted, sir, for the honor of this visit?" That is a phrase, my dear reader, which is used only in novels, or by charlatans. Mr. Mordaunt's bearing was gloomy, but that of a Virginia gentleman welcoming a guest. He was evidently a man of the world, however, and, like the Black Douglas, "his hand was his own." He was perfectly polite—seemed to regard my visit as a courtesy bestowed upon him—but there everything ended. Behind the host was the man—and with that person Mr. Mordaunt evidently thought that I had nothing to do.

His voice, as he conversed upon the events of the day, deep, measured, and sonorous: his manner, although gloomy, high-bred, and what we call, for want of a better word, "distinguished." In half an hour I saw plainly that this hermit of my imagination was not only a deep and powerful thinker, but a trained and self-collected man of the world.

From the fugitive topics of the moment, the conversation passed to art, and I said, as I pointed to the picture of Miss Grafton:

"I was admiring that fine head when you entered. Mr. Mordaunt. It is a portrait, is it not?"

"Yes sir." was his reply, in a voice of perfect coolness.

"I think I know the original."

"The original!" he said, with a sudden glow upon his swarthy face; "you *know* the original? That is impossible, sir—she is dead."

"Dead!" I exclaimed, in my turn, "why, that is impossible! I saw her only a few days ago."

My host greeted this statement with a look of unmistakable astonishment. He did not speak for a moment; and then said, coolly, in his deep, measured voice:

"You have doubtless met some lady who resembles this portrait, sir. I repeat, that the original is long since dead."

"Are you certain, Mr. Mordaunt?"

"Perfectly certain, sir."

And I saw something like a shadow pass over his broad forehead.

"Your statement fills me with the utmost astonishment," I said. "Then you do not know a young lady named Violet Grafton?"

"I have never heard of her, sir."

I looked at my host. It was impossible to believe that this man, with the proud and loyal look, the deep, earnest voice, and the bearing so cold and grave, could be deceiving me. And yet it was utterly impossible that this portrait was not intended for Miss Grafton. The likeness was positively startling.

Curiosity had now mastered me and absorbed every other sentiment. I determined to penetrate, if possible, that armor of reserve in which my singular host had encased himself.

"You have never heard of Miss Grafton, Mr. Mordaunt?" I said. "Well, at least, you know a Mr. Fenwick, do you not?"

The question struck home. The head, which had drooped as though bowed down by some gloomy recollection, suddenly rose erect, and Mordaunt gazed at me with a glance so piercing that the dark eyes seemed straining to penetrate my inmost soul. Then the head sank again, and he replied, in tones more cold and formal than I had yet heard from his lips:

"Yes, I know a person named Fenwick, sir."

"This person, at least, is alive, is he not?"

"I believe so," he said; and a flash of unmistakable hatred lit up his black eye.

"Well, I know it, Mr. Mordaunt."

"You are, then, acquainted with him?" was his cold interrogatory.

"I have never exchanged a word with him, but I have seen him twice, and under somewhat peculiar cirsumstances. On the first occasion he was engaged in a duel—on the second, he was plotting against the peace of a young lady."

Mordaunt looked at me fixedly, and said:

"Where did that duel take place, sir?"

"In the grounds of Hollywood Cemetery, at Richmond."

He did not reply for a moment, and his dark eye still remained fixed upon my own. Then he said, with perfect coolness:

"I really do not see how your presence, upon that occasion, could have escaped me, sir. I thought that the principals and seconds in the affair were the only persons who witnessed the meeting you refer to."

In ten words, I recounted everything. Mordaunt listened without interrupting me, and, when I had finished, said, with cool indifference:

"Well, that was really curious; and your explanation shows that, in this world, many things pass us by without attracting our notice. I thought the parties in that affair were the only persons present."

"You thought, also, that your adversary was dead, Mr. Mordaunt—but he is not. He is not only alive, but at this very moment is engaged in a conspiracy against a young lady who, if not the original, is the exact image of the portrait hanging yonder on your wall."

And I briefly informed my host of that encounter with Fenwick, at the house in the Wilderness; repeating the words which I had heard him utter on the steps. Mordaunt listened with close attention, and seemed especially struck with my description of Miss Grafton.

"The image of my portrait!" he muttered; "that is very strange—these singular resemblances!"

His eye wandered to the picture as he thus muttered to himself, and he seemed to pass in gloomy thought to other scenes. His brows contracted, his lips became rigid; then something like a bitter smile came to them.

Suddenly he seemed to realize my presence, and his glance was lowered. His face resumed all at once its former expression of impenetrable coldness.

"You will pardon my absence of mind, sir," he said, in his formal tone. "I am almost a recluse here, and the habit grows upon me. Thanks for your visit, and this information in regard to that person and his plots. You know more of my relations with him than I thought you could; but I am sorry to say that circumstances of a private nature will not permit me to explain an enmity which must appear somewhat singular to you. You heard the words I addressed to my adversary's second, when he attempted to stop that affair. Thus you know in what light I regard this person. I have sworn the *vendetta* against him, Captain Surry," continued my host with a flash of the dark eyes which resembled lurid lightning, "and I will keep that oath! There is something more sure and fatal than the instinct of the bloodhound: it is the eye and hand of the man who has sworn to have his vengeance!"

"I tell you this, sir," he said, more coldly, after pausing for a moment, "because you are a gentleman of mind and discretion, who will feel no temptation to repeat my words. So much for the relations which exist between myself and that wretch. Of this Miss Grafton, I declare to you again, that I know nothing. If she resembles this portrait, as you seem to think, the resemblance is purely accidental. As to the plot of that person, and the danger she is exposed to, I shall only say that I hope soon to remove all possibility of annoyance from that quarter."

There was no mistaking the meaning of these words, so cold and full of menace; but the speaker seemed to suppress, by a powerful effort of his will, any further exhibitions of enmity, and plainly wished to change the topic.

"My servant has shown you into my private study, sir," he now said with his former air of courteous reserve, "and these decorations, no doubt, appear to you eccentric. They are the rubbish of travel, and were intended for no eye but my own."

"They interest me much," was my reply. "You have visited Europe?"

"Yes, I spent some years there."

"In Algiers."

"Ah! you discover that from my pictures and weapons."

"No, I heard it before I ever saw you."

"Well, gossip is right for once, sir."

"You served against the French."

"Yes, I took part with the Arabs."

"And have brought back one of the faithful."

"You mean my Moor, Achmed?"

"Is that his name?"

"Yes. The youth took a fancy to me when he was a mere child, and, since the death of his father, who fell in battle, has remained with me. I am very much attached to him, and I believe that he would lay down his life for me."

"Were you often engaged with the French?"

"Frequently—they are the best troops in the world. I did not rank myself on the side of the Arabs from any dislike of their enemies, but because their soil was invaded."

"The same principle will, doubtless, lead you to offer your sword to the South."

"Assuredly."

"You, then, think of entering the army?"

"I never thought upon the subject. I am a Virginian—I fight, therefore, as a matter of course."

"You are right, Mr. Mordaunt. And what branch of the service, may I ask, do you intend to enter?"

"The cavalry—it is that with which I am most familiar. I have already raised a company, and it is nearly ready for the field. The men are all mountaineers of this region, excellently mounted, and have done me the honor to choose me for their captain, from having heard, I suppose, that I am not entirely a novice in military matters. But I am indulging in egotism. Will you smoke? Here are several sorts of pipes and varieties of tobacco, sent me from Europe. I prefer a plain meerschaum, and the Lynchburg in that jar near your hand: you will find it excellent."

I declined, and, pointing to the volume upon which his own pipe rested, said:

"I see you are reading ' *Les Miserables.*' It absorbed me, in Richmond, where I found a copy. Do you like it?"

"It is a mournful book," replied Mordaunt, "and at times affects even as rough a husk as my own. It is rather too long, perhaps; but then the subject is an inexhaustible one, the history of ' the wretched.' "

"It is the story of humanity."

"You are right," said my host, " a tragedy, that is to say."

" Are all lives tragic?"

" When they are not dull. Life is a poor affair, to my thinking Captain Surry, and the shadow predominates. But we are growing didactic. Are you fond of arms? I have a tolerable collection."

And taking down weapon after weapon, Mordaunt pointed out, with evident interest in the subject, their various merits.

"Man is a blood-thirsty animal," he said, "and cudgels his brains to invent improved instruments of death. But after all, this mediæval bludgeon, studded with points of steel, is as effective as the last invention. My own favorite is the light French sabre, pliable and pointed. Held at tierce-point, with the horse at a gallop, it easily pierces through from breast to back."

And he passed to other weapons. When they were exhausted, he called my attention to the pictures.

When, an hour afterward, I parted with my host, I felt that I had been conversing with a remarkable man. Beneath the cold exterior I could easily see the traces of a powerful organization; in the flash of the dark eye there was a latent force and passion which would make this man equal to the most desperate undertakings. Such should have been the commander of the French cuirassiers who charged the living volcanoes of English infantry at Waterloo: such the officer at the head of the "Six Hundred " who rode through the Russian fire at Balaklava. Something told me that, in work like this, the stern and passionate spirit under that mask of ice would rejoice—and I lived to see the hour and the man both come.

XIX.

THE STATUE SPEAKS.

THE moment now approached when I must leave this domain of enchantment, and forget all the dreams in which I had indulged. My arm was well, and duty called me.

I went without reluctance, for it was plain now that my suit was hopeless. It is not an agreeable confession, but I am compelled to state that Miss May Beverley seemed to care no more for me on the last than on the first day of my visit. I go further, and say that I think she cared less for me.

I had kept her handkerchief, picked up on that evening, intending to return it when the moment came, with "a few remarks," such as we read in novels. How absurd did this "silly romance" now appear! That pretty little drama quite hung fire, and I thought I saw her laughing instead of blushing! Now, when a young lady laughs upon such occasions, you might as well pocket your romance, get into the saddle, and wave her "adieu for evermore!"

That is all excellent advice, and I bestow it upon the reader in the gayest manner to-day. You see the wound has healed: at that time it was bleeding. I jest now, but then I was the prey of anger, disappointment, outraged pride, wounded vanity, and wretchedness generally. Those poisonous distillations of the human heart are not wholesome, and did not contribute very greatly to my happiness at the time.

When one day I announced my intention to set out for the Potomac on the next morning, I found the Colonel and Mrs. Beverley much more deeply impressed by that important statement than the young lady; and indeed it seemed to be a matter of perfect indifference to her whether I stayed or went away. I found myself alone with her that evening on the steps of the portico, and it is impossible to imagine any thing more coolly indifferent than her demeanor.

Disappointment, anger, mortified pride!—see an allusion above to the feelings of one of the parties to that interview.

The moon was shining, and the dreamy splendor lit up the beautiful head with the waving hair and the great violet eyes. I had never known May Beverley look so beautiful, but there was an expression upon her face which I had never seen there before. Pride, weariness, and a sort of scornful despair—all were written in those eyes, and upon those lips, in characters that could not be mistaken. I could scarcely extract a word from her: she seemed brooding over something, and from time to time looked furtively toward me, instantly withdrawing her eyes when they met mine.

"What does all this mean!" I said to myself, with a sort of gloomy surprise. "Mademoiselle seems *distraite* to-night, and with something on her mind. Well, I'll try and see if I can't arouse her."

And, suppressing a bitter laugh which rose to my lips, I said:

"This is a charming night! It reminds me of one in Richmond not long since—on the Capitol Square, where the music was playing."

She did not seem to hear me, but I saw her face flush and then grow pale.

"I saw you there that night," I went on; "did I never tell you I saw you? That day in the storm was not our first meeting."

She turned and looked at me.

"You saw me!" she said, in a low tone.

"Certainly! I had that great pleasure; and you don't think it possible that I should forget it?"

She must have observed my bitterness, for a strange expression came to her face.

"You were walking with Mr. Baskerville: is that gentleman a friend of yours?"

A lurid light came to her eyes, and her roses all faded.

Looking me straight in the eyes, she remained silent for several minutes, and I could see her face in the moonlight flush crimson. Then this was succeeded by a pallor so deadly that I thought she was about to faint; she placed her hand on her heart, and, still looking straight at me, murmured hoarsely:

"I am engaged to Mr. Baskerville!"

The blow I had received from that falling limb in the forest was nothing to those words. I gazed at the speaker with an air, I am convinced, of imbecile wonder, and in vain attempted to utter some reply. She must have seen, or fancied she saw, an expression of scorn upon my pale face, for suddenly her brow flushed again, and she haughtily exclaimed:

"You seem exceedingly surprised, sir! Do you find any thing very extraordinary in this announcement? Yes, sir—I repeat that I am engaged to be married to Mr. Baskerville!"

What could I reply? There are moments when all language fails, and the very blood seems to stagnate. I remained thus dumb and bewildered, looking at the person who had uttered these words; and then slowly came the full conviction of my misery—slowly, as the gloomy moon rises, blood-red and menacing, over some battle-field covered with the dead. This, then, was the end of all my romantic dreams!—this was the mortal blow which had struck me to the very heart—May Beverley was to marry *Baskerville!*

As I muttered that name audibly, in a tone of inexpressible scorn, the young lady uttered a hoarse moan, and exclaimed, with cruel sarcasm:

"One would really suppose, sir, that you did not approve of the match, and were going to refuse your consent to it!"

Those words revived me, like a bitter tonic. They aroused all my pride, and made me a man again. Suppressing every exhibition of emotion, I said, in a tone as cold and measured as I could assume at the moment:

"I beg that Miss Beverley will pardon any thing in my manner which is offensive or disagreeable to her. She must be aware that my approval or disapproval of any course she may pursue amounts to nothing whatever; and I am quite sure that my opinions even are a matter of complete indifference to her. I did fancy, at one time, that there was something like friendship between us; but that, too, is scattered to the winds at this moment. I will not intrude further upon your presence, Miss Beverley."

And, with bitterness at my heart, I rose and was about to leave her. She retained me with a single movement of her hand—the other was twitching convulsively at the gold chain around her neck. She had turned her head away—she now looked at me, and her eyes were full of tears.

"Pardon me," she said, in a low voice, "I did not mean to offend you. I have known you but a short time, but I would not willingly forfeit your regard. I am very wretched, sir! No one seems to care for me. You think me cold, my temper disdainful—do not deny it, sir, I have read it in your eyes. I am very proud, sir—I do not value the good opinion of everybody—but I would do much to retain yours."

She paused: her voice trembled; but I saw in her eyes the light of a determined resolution. She had evidently made up her mind to pursue some course from which her feelings recoiled.

"I have informed you of my engagement, sir—do you know why? I am about to utter words which no woman should speak lightly, without a good reason."

She stopped again—then her cheeks were covered with blushes, and she said, hurriedly:

"You are attached to me—I could not avoid seeing it! You are an honorable gentleman, and I should have despised myself forever if I had suffered you to be deceived—to remain in ignorance of what I have told you! I have resolved many times to tell you—I had not the courage. Every day I formed that resolution—every day it has been broken! I have tried to discourage you—I have made myself very disagreeable. I have been cold, satirical, even bitter—when I would have given worlds to have appeared in my natural character, and won your friendship! You know all now—I am very unhappy, sir—but I am a proud person, and I acted honorably, did I not? This avowal is almost killing me, sir!—but I must go on until I have finished! It has made me sick at heart to reflect that you regarded me as a young lady whose hand was disengaged, when I was the victim of a formal contract. Yes, victim! I say victim!" she exclaimed, in a voice of inexpressible anguish; "the victim of a hateful, an intolerable engagement! You shall know all, sir—you *must* know it! My father was the friend of Mr. Baskerville's father —he is dead now—and an agreement was made between them that when Mr. Frederick Baskerville and myself grew up, we should be married. He came to see me when he was a child, and continued to do so as he grew older. I was educated in the idea that I was some day to marry him—I admired him as a boy, for his grace and ease of manner—and, when I was but fifteen, engaged myself to him. His father, who was very fond of me, died soon afterward, rejoicing that the marriage would now surely take place; and my own father, who is the slave of his word, declares that I am doubly bound, first by his promise to his friend who is dead, and again by my word to Mr. Baskerville!"

Again she paused; her voice had a cold and desolate intonation now, which jarred upon the ear. I pitied her, but at the name of Baskerville all my rage and misery overflowed.

"You do not speak!" she murmured in a piteous tone, "perhaps I weary you."

"Your words tear my heart!" I said. "Why do you utter them? Why not simply say 'Go! I care nothing for you!' Your confidence honors me—but I scarcely understand its object!"

"You shall soon understand?" she exclaimed bitterly. "I mean that I am engaged to be married to Mr. Baskerville, and that I cannot bear him!—that for years past, since I have discovered his real character, I have shuddered at that contract!—that my life is imbittered by the very thought of marrying him!—and yet nothing I can do or say will change my father's purpose, or prevent him from insisting upon this marriage with a man I actually loathe!"

It was a wail of despair I listened to—the cry of a broken heart. I forgot my own anguish as I listened to that voice, and would have given all I hoped to possess of fame or wealth or happiness to have drawn the poor girl to me and sheltered her in my arms.

Setting my teeth together, I could only mutter:

"When is this marriage to take place?"

"When I am twenty-one," she murmured.

"And you will marry that man?"

"I must."

The words sounded like a knell. What was there to reply? I looked at her as she held down her head, crying silently.

"Do you remember that moonlight night in Richmond?"

"Yes."

"Here is your handkerchief, which I picked up—I return it to you."

And I placed it in her hand.

"I saw you for the first time that night—and now that my dream is over—now that you deny me all hope, and have resolved upon this marriage with a man you abhor—I can now tell you calmly, and *will* tell you that I loved you from that moment!—that I love you now—as a man loves with his blood and his heart! I did not know your name when I saw you that night—I never expected to meet you again—and yet that day in the storm I opened my eyes to see you bending over me! I thought that Good Fortune smiled upon me then—but you steadily grew colder from that hour. To-day, I know why, and I honor you! You are a noble girl! The misery of miseries is, that you are going to marry this man, whom you despise. You are right—he is a poor creature!—pardon me! there is something here at my heart that fills me with bitterness—it is the thought that *you* are to be the wife of that person! That resolution disarms me—I have no strength to contend against it! What can I do? Kill him? Would you marry me then? I am conquered—unless you do what you have a right to do before God and man!—refuse to fulfil that contract! *Will* you refuse?"

"I cannot!" came in a low moan from the girl.

"Then farewell."

Both rose at the same moment. Her face was as white as a

4

sheet, and the hand she gave me as cold as ice. She placed the
other over her eyes and retired, without uttering a sound, to her
chamber.

On the next morning she did not appear, and I left "The
Oaks" without again seeing her.

XX.

THE RUINED CHURCH AND THE STRANGER

I ENTERED the great Valley of Virginia through Ashby's Gap,
on a May morning which rendered the scene inexpressibly lovely.
The Shenandoah glided away beneath the mottled arms of the
huge sycamores upon its banks, with a murmur as soft and
sweet as the distant tinkling of silver bells; green fields extended
on every side; and in the west rose the blue ramparts of the
Massinutton and Great North Mountains, as beautiful and tranquil as some happy dream. It was hard to realize that war
would ever stamp his red hoof upon this Arcady, all loveliness
and repose; or that the day would come when the threat of a
Federal commander would nearly be carried out, that "a crow
flying over the region should be obliged to carry his own rations."

And now as I enter upon new scenes of my memoirs, I beg
leave to notify the kindly reader that I shall endeavor hereafter
to entertain him with something more interesting than my private feelings. Why should I inflict upon that amiable personage
a long and lachrymose paragraph all about the heavy heart
which a friend of his bore away from "The Oaks"—or describe
the tragic emotions of that unfortunate individual at the prospect of seeing his sweetheart marry his rival? Alas! human
life is so full of these unlucky affairs, that I think the less we
hear of them the better!

I am therefore obdurately "resolved to be gay," and am resolutely determined that, if possible, not a single wail of anguish
shall be heard from the hero of these memoirs. Is not life a

comedy, and the music lively? Reader mine! I who write have
seen both good and bad fortune in my time; and it has always
seemed best to me to bear the first with a modest, the latter with
a courageous heart.

So we pass away now from those days at "The Oaks." From
the mast the long streamers wave farewell to the little bark that
glided across our course, and has disappeared. *Bon voyage!* fair
May Beverley! May the sea be smooth before you! You and I
go different ways!

Turning to the right at Berry's Ferry, I passed a mansion pic-
turesquely perched upon a hill with a background of woods,
around the portico of which, I remember, some young ladies
were trailing a sweetbrier rose in full blossom. All this was
the very opposite of war—and yet I lived to witness a hot
fight upon that very lawn, and to see the spring grass dyed with
blood.

My horses were fresh, and I expected to reach the neighborhood of Harper's Ferry before evening, but, when in the vicinity
of Charlestown, I found the sky, which had long been threatening,
suddenly indicate the approach of a storm. A huge bank of
black cloud, against which, from time to time, vivid flashes of
lightning shone, like a fiery crack in the dark mass, admonished
me of the wetting which awaited me unless I found shelter; and
very soon those heavy drops, which are the skirmishers thrown
out by an advancing tempest, began to patter on the leaves.

I looked round for some shelter, but saw no house anywhere.
In a clump of trees, however, a few hundred yards from the road,
rose the ruins of an old church; and to this I hastened, dismounting and taking refuge within, just as the storm burst. The ruin
was almost roofless; but a projection over the altar-place furnished some protection from the rain; and to this spot I hurried.

All at once I stopped. A man was kneeling there, with his
forehead buried in his hands; and at the same moment I heard
the neigh of his horse, which was tethered to a bough behind the
ruin, and had escaped my notice.

The falling rain and the rumble of the thunder must have
drowned the noise of my approach; for the kneeling man re-

mained in the same posture, and perfectly motionless, for at least a quarter of an hour.   At the end of that time, the clatter of my sabre, as it accidentally struck against a fallen stone, attracted his attention, and, slowly rising, the stranger turned toward me.

He was a man apparently about forty years of age, tall, gaunt, and awkward-looking.   His beard and mustache, worn tolerably full, were of a reddish brown, inclining to black; and his eyes were dark, piercing, and with a peculiar glitter in them.   The stranger wore a plain gray uniform, entirely without decorations, and his forehead was covered by the rim of a small cadet-cap, pulled low down, with the top trailing forward.

The expression of the stranger's countenance was mild, benevolent, and modest—his smile, as he greeted me with an air of simple courtesy, very winning.

"I am afraid I interrupted your devotions, sir," I now said, "and I pray you will pardon me."

"I had finished, or very nearly," was his reply, in a voice of peculiar abruptness, but unmistakable courtesy.   "This storm is very violent, sir."

"And our place of refuge very dilapidated."

"Yes," he said, smiling; "but there seems great fitness in taking refuge in this holy place."

"I understand.   You mean that the church is the best shelter from the storms of life.   I am not a Christian myself, but you will not find me differ with you upon that point, sir."

"I am truly glad to hear it," was his simple reply, in the same brief voice.   "God has prescribed but one refuge, and the chief duty he inculcates is prayer."

There was something simple and noble in the man's bearing as he spoke; and his words seemed the most rational and natural in the world—so little of the professional air of the preacher, so to speak, did I discern in them.

"You belong to the army, sir?" I now said, glancing at his uniform.

"Yes, sir," was his reply.

"May I ask if you have ever served before?"

"Yes, in Mexico."

THE RUINED CHURCH.

"Ah? in the last war! Then you must have seen some hard fighting?"

"I was at Churubusco, Chepultepec, and other battles."

"You are fortunate in having returned safely," I said.

"God spared me," was his reply, in the same simple tone.

His eye wandered as he spoke, and he seemed to be thinking, as the thunder roared above the ruin, of those battles, which had resembled it.

"I was many times much exposed," he added, "but no man ever dies until his time comes. It was the good pleasure of the Almighty, sir, that I should be spared for another conflict."

"And you doubtless carry similar convictions into the present contest? I mean the doctrine of predestination."

"That word is much abused, sir," replied the stranger gravely, "yet it expresses the only rational view of human life. Who can tell when he will die? The bullet which is to strike me down may now be moulded, and I may fall in the first skirmish —or I may pass through a hundred bloody battles untouched. If I am to fall now, I am to fall—if years hence, not until then— if never, never! If Providence has decreed that I shall die in my bed, surely the enemy cannot harm me."

"You are right, sir," I said, not a little moved by the earnest tones of the speaker. "All rational men believe in the doctrine you assert. But do you entirely discard free will?"

"No, sir, by no means—I believe in that, just as strongly. But we touch upon the profoundest of all questions. It is better to obey than to question. It is easy to understand the precept, "Love one another," if the doctrines of free will and predestination *are* difficult!"

"Love one another!" I said; "that is a curious principle for a soldier to adopt, is it not, sir?"

"I do not think so."

"And yet we are at the beginning of a long and bloody war."

"War is not opposed to the will of God, sir."

"But it is terribly bloody."

"So is the surgeon's knife. It is disagreeable, but necessary."

"You, then, regard this war as just and inevitable!"

"I do, sir. I would cheerfully have laid down my life to have prevented it; but I believe that it could not be avoided."

"I agree with you. Will it be long? When will it end?"

"I know not—nor do I expect to see its end."

"You expect to fall?"

"Yes, sir."

"And yet you enter upon it cheerfully?"

"I try to do my duty—God will take care of the rest."

As the stranger spoke in his simple and earnest voice, he raised his right hand aloft, looked upward, and, closing his eyes, muttered some inaudible words which seemed to be a prayer. So singular was this proceeding that I set my companion down for a confirmed eccentric; and, not wishing to disturb him, went to the dilapidated opening, once serving as a window, and looked out. The clouds were clearing away—the blue began to appear here and there—the storm was over.

As I turned round, I saw the stranger at my side, with a smile of exquisite sweetness upon his features. At the same moment, a dove, which had made its nest in a crevice of the ruin, winged its way out, uttering a plaintive coo as it disappeared.*

"We have spoken of the probability of a long and bloody war," said the stranger mildly, "but perhaps we err in our views upon that subject. This dove may be the blessed emblem of peace and sunshine, as when one brought the olive-branch to Noah after the deluge."

"I hope so," was my reply, with a smile; "but I am afraid that fierce bird the 'Spread-Eagle' is going to tear our poor little Southern dove, and make us return to the 'great and glorious Union,' sir."

"There will be much blood shed first," was the response of the stranger. "But I see the rain is over, sir. May I ask what route you take?"

"I am going to Harper's Ferry."

"Then we will travel together, as I am riding in the same direction."

* Colonel Surry stated to me in conversation that this little incident had never escaped his recollection, and always came back to his mind with a peculiar charm.—*Ed.*

" Most willingly."

And we went toward our horses. The stranger walked, I observed, with a peculiarly awkward stride, and his seat in the saddle, as he joined me, was very ungraceful. But he was evidently
a practised rider, if not a very graceful one.

Conversing as we rode, we passed through the town of Charlestown, and, as night fell, approached Harper's Ferry. My companion had informed me that he was returning from Winchester
when the storm arrested him, and he now rode on with the assured air of one who was returning to his own quarters.

The hills around were covered with white tents, which shone
like groups of waterfowl in the last rays of day; and, reaching
one of these groups, very plain and unassuming in appearance,
the stranger drew rein, and seemed to have reached his journey's
end.

"Will you stay with me to-night, sir?" he said, very courteously. "I can offer you a good bed of straw, and soldier's fare."

"Thanks for your kind offer, but I am looking for the head-
quarters of Colonel Jackson," I replied.

My companion smiled and said:

"Do you want to see him?"

"Yes; I am assigned to duty with him as aide-de-camp, sir."

"Ah! then you are —— ?"

"Captain Surry, of the Virginia forces."

"And my name is Jackson," was the stranger's smiling reply.
"I am glad to make your acquaintance, Captain, and to welcome
you to my quarters. I think we shall be very good friends."

And Colonel Jackson gave me his hand. Such was our first
interview.

XXI.

ON REVIEW.

In these memoirs, my dear reader, I intend to carefully avoid
writing a history of the war. See the histories for that. I aim
only at giving you a few pictures and relating some incidents.

Therefore, go to the grave and strictly reliable "official documents" for an account of the situation in May, 1861. I need
only say, that at that moment the Federal Government threatened Virginia with three great columns—from Wheeling, Williamsport, and Alexandria; and that the second, commanded by
Major-General Patterson, was about four or five times as great as
the little "Army of Observation" at Harper's Ferry.

But that army was composed of excellent material. All classes
were mingled fraternally in its ranks, by the hand of that great
leveller called War. Here was the high-spirited boy, raised in
his elegant home on the banks of the Shenandoah, and the hardy
and athletic mountaineer from beyond the Alleghanies. The
pale and slender student lay down side by side with the ruddy
son of the poor farmer, who had dropped the handles of the
plough to take up the musket. All were alike in one thing—
their eager desire to meet the enemy.

On the day after my arrival, Colonel Jackson reviewed the
troops. As he rode along the line, above which rose the glittering hedge of bayonets, I heard many a smothered laugh at his
singular appearance. In fact, the Colonel's odd costume and
manners were enough to excite laughter. Fancy a sort of Don
Quixote, reader—gaunt, bony, and angular—riding an old, stiff
Rosinante, which he pushed into a trot with great difficulty. This
figure was clad in a gray coat already growing rusty; a faded
cap resting nearly upon the wearer's nose; top-boots, huge
gauntlets, and a leather stock which propped up his chin and
sawed his ears.

He rode leaning forward, with his knees drawn up, owing to
the shortness of his stirrups; raised his chin in the air in order
to look from beneath his cap-rim; and from time to time moved
his head from side to side, above his stiff leather collar, with an
air of profound abstraction. Add to this a curious fashion of
slapping his right hand against his thigh, and the curt, abrupt
"Good!—very good!" which was jerked from his lips when any
report was made to him: and there is Colonel T. J. Jackson, of
the Virginia forces.

The young volunteers evidently expected to see a gallant and imposing figure, richly clad, and superbly mounted. When this scarecrow appeared, they with difficulty restrained their laughter. When the review was over, and the young men were marched back to their quarters, I learned, afterward, that they made themselves exceedingly merry on the subject of their commander's appearance—not a few, who had been to the Lexington Institute, repeating his former nickname of "Fool Tom Jackson."

What was the opinion, it may be asked, of his aide-de-camp, who saw him every hour, and had ample opportunity of observing the man? He did not impress me greatly: and I am obliged to disclaim the deep penetration of that mighty multitude who—long afterward—"always knew what was in Jackson from the first." I thought him matter-of-fact in character, rather dull in conversation, and possessed of only average abilities. He seemed a plodding, eccentric, commonplace martinet. That was the light in which I regarded this immortal.

If I did not admire his intellect, I, however, very greatly respected his moral character. His life was perfectly blameless, and he had not a single bad habit. Spirit never passed his lips, and I should as soon have expected the Potomac to flow backward as to have heard him utter an oath. He regularly said grace at his simple meals, spread on the lid of a camp-chest, and spent hours daily in religious reading and prayer. He was habitually charitable in his estimates of men, and seldom yielded to any sort of irritability. "Eccentric" he was, in the highest degree—but it was the eccentricity of a man whose thoughts were half the time in heaven.

Three days after my arrival, he called me into his tent, and began to talk to me about the war. He listened with an air of great modesty and attention to my crude views, and, when I expressed an opinion that Harper's Ferry would not be attacked, replied briefly:

"I think so too; it will be flanked."

He remained thoughtful for some moments, and then said:

"I wish you to carry a message for me to Colonel Stuart, Captain; you will find him near Martinsburg. Desire him to picket heavily the whole front toward Williamsport, and to es-

tablish relays of couriers to give me intelligence. I should like
to hear what his scouts report. Before Patterson crosses I must
be out of this place, ready to fight him on the "—

Suddenly the speaker paused, and looked keenly at me.

"Captain," he said, abruptly, "never remember any thing
but the message I send. My intentions must be known to no
one but myself. If my coat knew my plans, I would take it off
and burn it."*

I saluted, ordered my horse, and in half an hour was on the
road to Martinsburg.

XXII.

I VISIT COLONEL "JEB. STUART."

PASSING rapidly through the beautiful country skirting the
banks of the Potomac, I approached the Opequon.

When in sight of that picturesque stream, with it grassy banks,
studded with huge white-armed sycamores, I met a cavalryman,
who informed me that Colonel Stuart, with a squadron from his
regiment, was at that moment passing through the woods beyond.
I hastened to come up with him, and, fording the stream, galloped on beneath the boughs of the gay spring forest, which was
ringing with the songs of birds.

Ere long I heard the tramp of hoofs, and a sonorous voice
singing one of my favorite songs, "The dew is on the blossom."
Five minutes afterward there appeared at a turn of the road,
clearly relieved against the green background of the leafy covert,
the head of a column of horsemen, in front of whom rode the
singer.

Let me draw his outline. He was a man of twenty-five or
thirty, of low stature, athletic figure, and with the air of a born
cavalryman. There was no mistaking his arm of the service.
He was the cavalier all over. His boot-tops covered the knee;
his brass spurs were models of neatness; his sabre was light,

---

* His words.

flexible, and "handy;" his gauntlets reached to the elbows. The young cavalier was evidently at home in the saddle, and asked nothing better than "a fight or a frolic." He wore the blue undress uniform coat of the United States Army, gathered at the waist by his sword-belt; an old brown pair of velveteen pantaloons, rusty from long use, and his bold face was surmounted by a Zouave cap, from which depended a white "havelock," giving him the appearance of a mediæval knight with a chain-helmet. Upon that proud head, indeed, a helmet, with its flowing plume, seemed the fittest covering.

But I have not finished. I am drawing the portrait of one of the immortals, reader, and you can afford to listen to every detail. His saddle was a plain "McClellan tree" strapped over a red blanket for saddle-cloth; behind the cantel was his oil-cloth, containing a single blanket, and on the pommel was a light india-rubber overcoat for stormy days. The chest of his sorrel was decorated with a brilliant yellow breast-cap, a blazing heart in the centre, and the spirited animal champed a strong curb bit, to which was attached a single rein.*

I did not notice these details when I first saw Stuart that day. I was looking at his face. It was the picture of martial gayety and enjoyment. A lofty and massive forehead, blue eyes as brilliant and piercing as the eagle's, a prominent nose, a huge brown beard, and heavy mustache, whose long ends curled upward—there was Stuart's countenance. In that face and form, immense health and physical strength shone. This man, it was plain, could remain whole days and nights in the saddle, never growing weary; could march all night, fight all day, and then ride a dozen miles and dance until sunrise.

Such was the splendid war-machine which I saw before me; such the man who now paused in his song, looked at me keenly out of his clear blue eyes, and gave me the frank military salute with his gauntleted hand.

---

* Colonel Surry laughed, and said, when I read this passage: "Don't you think that long description will bore the reader fifty years hence?" My reply was: "The result will be just the contrary. Stuart will then rank with Harry of Navarre and Prince Rupert." Do you doubt that, reader?

84 SURRY OF EAGLE'S-NEST.

I introduced myself, delivered my message, and rode on with Stuart, who had cordially shaken hands and said:

"Glad to make your acquaintance, Captain. Come, and ride back to camp with me."

So we rode on, side by side, Stuart talking carelessly, with the ease and unreserve of the *bon compagnon*, instead of the stiffness of the West-Pointer.

"Jackson is right," he said, musing, with an absent air; and as he spoke he took off his cap, made a salute, apparently to some imaginary personage, and then replaced his cap. This curious habit I frequently observed in him afterward.

"The enemy will cross near Williamsport," he added; "I am convinced of that. The pickets are already doubled, Captain, and the relays established. I intend to inspect my pickets along the whole front to-morrow. Will you ride with me? You can then make an exact report of every thing."

I accepted this invitation, and Stuart then seemed to banish all "official" affairs from his mind. He turned his head, called out "Sweeny!" and there rode forward from his escort a tall, mild-looking man, of deferential bearing, who carried under his arm an old-fashioned Virginia banjo.

"Come! strike up, Sweeny," Stuart exclaimed, in a jovial voice. "Here is Captain Surry—give him a specimen of your music."

Sweeny saluted me with sad and deferential courtesy, and I expected him to play something like a dead march upon his instrument. Never was any one more mistaken. He struck up that popular song—"O Lord, ladies! don't you mind Stephen!" and if ever the spirit of wild and uproarious mirth spoke from any instrument, it was heard in the notes of Sweeny's banjo. After finishing this gay air, with its burden, "Come back, Stephen!—Stephen, come back!" he played a medley, with wonderful skill—a comic *vis* that was irresistible; and then Stuart, lying back on his horse for laughter, cried:

"Now give us the 'Old Gray Hoss,' Sweeny!"

And Sweeny commenced that most celebrated of recitations, which I heard and laughed at a hundred times afterward, but

never without thinking of that gay spring scene—the long line
of cavalry winding through the May forest, with Stuart at their
head, shouting with laughter as he rode, and joining in the
chorus, like an uproarious boy.

Sweeny played then, in succession, "O Johnny Booker, help
this nigger!" "Sweet Evelina," and "Faded Flowers"—for
this great musician could pass from gay to sad, and charm you
more with his sentimental songs than he amused you with his
comic *repertoire*. In the choruses Stuart joined—singing in a
sonorous voice, with a perfectly correct ear—and thus the caval-
cade passed over mile after mile, until, at sunset, we reached
Stuart's quarters, near Martinsburg. That individual appeared
to me more like some gay knight-errant of the elder-time than
a commonplace cavalry officer of the year 1861; and I never
afterward, through all his arduous career, could rid myself of
this idea. I saw him everywhere during his long, hard work, as
commander of the cavalry of General Lee's army, and as that
great chief's "right hand"—but I could never think of him except as an ideal personage. He was not so much a soldier of the
nineteenth century as a chevalier "from out the old romances."

Are you weary, my dear reader, of this long description? I
should be sorry to think so; and I have still some words to add.
In these pages Stuart will speak often, and perform many things.
Here I wish, "once for all," to give you his outline. Then
you will know what manner of man it was that spoke the
words and struck the great blows. So I linger still in those old
days, spent in the Shenandoah Valley, recalling every incident
of my brief visit to the afterward celebrated "Jeb. Stuart."

XXIII.

A MOONLIGHT RIDE WITH STUART.

STUART's head-quarters consisted of a single canvas "fly"—that
is, the outer covering of a tent—stretched over a horizontal pole.
One end of this pole was placed in the crotch of a large oak;

the other was supported by uprights, joined at top and tied
together—there was the tent. A desk, a chair, a mess-chest,
and bed of blankets on some straw—there was the rest. Overhead drooped the boughs of the oak; in front stretched a grassy
meadow, reaching to the "Big Spring;" the horses were picketed near, and a small flag rippled in the May breeze. In a
wood, near by, was the camp of the regiment.

Stuart called to his body-servant, a young mulatto, to know
if supper was ready, and then directed a company to be detailed,
with orders to report to him at once, for picket duty.

It soon appeared, and not only the officer in command, but
every squad, received the most explicit instructions from him.
If before I regarded Colonel Stuart as a somewhat boyish individual, I had now good reason to consider him an excellent
cavalry officer. His directions were so plain and concise that a
child could understand them—and the manner of the speaker
was no longer gay and thoughtless. It was grave, almost imperious. I can best describe it by saying that it was the manner
of a man who intends that his orders shall be obeyed to the
very letter, and who will not be trifled with.

But even with "business" that genius of mirth which seemed
to accompany Stuart everywhere was mixed up. He was instructing, one after another, the sergeants and corporals commanding squads, when there came up, in his turn, a huge,
black-bearded giant, with a voice like the rumble of distant
thunder, and the assured air of an old acquaintance of the
young Colonel.

"This is Corporal Hagan, one of my very best soldiers, Captain," said Stuart.

I saluted the tall corporal; and, exclaiming deferentially
"Captain!" Hagan made me a rigidly military salute in return
—two fingers to the cap, body erect, eyes front.

"Hagan," said Stuart, "you must make your squad pay particular attention to what I have explained."

"Yes, Colonel," came in tones of low thunder from the heavy
beard.

"I will hold you responsible."

"I intend to be, Colonel."

"You are an old soldier, Hagan, and know what is expected of a good picket."

"I think I do, Colonel—to keep one eye skinned for snakes and the other for bees!"

And the giant looked as grave as if he had never smiled in his life.

Stuart uttered a laugh, and said;

"What do you mean by that, Hagan?"

The tall corporal assumed an air of the deepest solemnity, and, advancing a step, inclined his head to one side, and put two fingers of his right hand in the palm of his left, with the manner of a man about to explain some great problem. Then, with unmoved solemnity, but a twinkle of the eye and a slight movement of the mustache which indicated lurking fun, Hagan thundered, in low tones:

"Well, you see, Colonel, you never know which way the inimy will come. Maybe out of the ground," and Hagan pointed to his feet, "maybe down through the air," and the giant pointed, like a great orator, toward the sky. "Now, there's only one way to sarcumvent 'em, Colonel. You must keep one eye skinned for snakes—that is, down on the ground; and the other skinned for bees—that is, up in the air. You are then bound to know when the inimy is coming, and you can give the alarm!"

This grave explanation highly tickled Stuart, who slapped the big corporal on the back in a manner which evidently delighted that worthy. Hagan ordered his squad to fall in, in a voice of thunder, made his former salute with even deeper solemnity, and then commanding "Forward!" disappeared like a moving mountain.*

At the same moment the neatly dressed mulatto announced supper, which was served on the lid of the camp-chest, under the great oak; it was altogether a gay affair. The sunset lit up the

---

* "I think that is Hagan to the very life, and I have remembered all his expressions!" laughed Colonel Surry, as he read me this.

form of Stuart splendidly, and he exchanged with his excellent
adjutant, Captain Tiernan Brien, a hundred jests.

"This is the best beverage in the world, Captain," he said,
holding up his silver mug; "only give me coffee and candles,
and I am satisfied."

"You drink nothing else?"

"Only water: when I was a child I made a pledge to my
mother that I would never touch liquor, and I never drank a
drop in my life."

"That is certainly uncommon."

"Well, an officer ought to do his duty up to the hilt; and he
can't do it if he drinks."*

In fifteen minutes Stuart rose and said.

"I am going on a little excursion this evening, Captain. Will
you ride with me?"

"At your orders, Colonel—dispose of me."

"Then, to horse!"

And calling for Sweeny and his banjo, Stuart proceeded to
make a rapid toilet. His heavy boots were exchanged for a
lighter pair, ornamented with golden thread; around his waist
he tied a new and elegant sash over his sabre belt; and then
issuing forth—a splendid cavalier, ready for a raid, a charge, or
a frolic—with a single bound he was in the saddle. Sweeny followed us with his banjo. I put spurs to my horse, and we set off
at a rapid gallop through the moonlight, I knew not whither.

Stuart rode as if the wild huntsman were on his track, and
sang as he went. We soon left the high road, and, striking into
the forest, fled onward beneath the moonlight foliage, my companion paying no attention to obstacles, and more than once
leaping some fallen tree which obstructed the narrow road.

"Give me a gallop by moonlight!" he said, with his gay
laughter. "Come, captain, boot to boot! Your horse is a good
one, and I am riding 'Skylark,' who never gets tired."

The gallop became a run; the wood was passed; we followed
a road skirting the Opequon; descended an abrupt hill; forded

---

* These expressions are all Stuart's, as I can testify.

the stream near a little mill; and, passing through a gate which
led into some beautiful grounds studded with old century oaks,
the finest I had ever seen, ascended a hill, and stopped before a
large mansion, on the portico of which a group of ladies and
gentlemen were sitting in the moonlight.

"It is Colonel Stuart!" was the exclamation of the ladies;
and in an instant the young officer was shaking hands with,
everybody; after which he introduced me as "one of his friends,
young, gallant, and not, like himself, married."

The laughter of Stuart was contagious; I was received like an
old friend; and "Oh! there's Sweeny!" having indicated the
general joy at the advent of the banjo, a dance was immediately
proposed, and rapturously assented to by the young ladies—a
portion of whom had come that afternoon, on a visit, from a
neighboring village.

I have never spent a gayer evening, or enjoyed myself more
with new acquaintances.   The piano and the banjo made excellent
music, and such ardor was thrown into the cotillons, reels, and
other dances, that the very portraits on the walls, of old-time
people in stiff cravats and piled-up curls, seemed to look on
with a smile.

Then commenced Sweeny's performances — his songs, his
recitations, and the wonderful solos on his magical instrument.
Quiet, sad-looking, with a retiring and respectful demeanor which
would have done no discredit to the finest gentleman, he assented to every request, without idle excuses; and soon the
whole company, but more especially the small boys, were convulsed with a sort of ecstasy of enjoyment.   The appreciation
by those small boys of "The Old Gray Hoss," "Stephen," and
the song commencing—

> "If you get there before I do,
> Oh! tell 'em I'm a-coming too,"

was immense, unspeakable.   They hung around the great musician, watched his every gesture, and evidently regarded him as
the most remarkable personage of the epoch.

Having wound up with a tumultuous, deafening, wonderful

solo, which made the windows shake, Sweeny bowed and put
his banjo under his arm. It was past midnight, and, urging his
long ride on the morrow, Stuart rose and bade our kind entertainers good-by.

An hour afterward, I was sleeping by Colonel Stuart's side
under his canvas, and dreaming that the Southern army had
advanced to attack the enemy, led by Sweeny, playing his
banjo!

I assure the reader that fancy has nothing to do with these
scenes. The picture to the minutest particulars is a transcript
from life, and the words uttered the Colonel's own.

XXIV.

JOHN BROWN AND HIS BULL-DOG.

WE were up with the dawn, and before sunrise had break-
fasted and were on the way to visit the pickets.

Passing through Martinsburg, we pushed on toward the Potomac, and, ascending the river's bank, inspected the pickets along
the entire front, returning only after nightfall.

This ride through a beautiful country was delightful ; and Stuart's gay and varied conversation made the hours glide away
almost unnoticed. One of his anecdotes—an account of the part
he had taken in the capture of John Brown—will be here recorded.

"I was in Virginia at that time on furlough," he said, "and,
singularly enough, had run over to Washington, when the news
of the riot at Harper's Ferry came. I immediately went to the
War Department to offer my services, but could not find the
Secretary. Some of the employés of the Department were talking, and one of them said, 'I'm going straight to Virginia, to look
after my wife and children,' as a negro insurrection was expected;
but I thought to myself, 'The best way to defend my wife and
children is to go to Harper's Ferry,' and I hurried to the White
House, where I found General Lee, then Colonel, Secretary Floyd

and President Buchanan. I saw the General for a moment, and told him how anxious I was to go, but he said he did not know that I could. The President then called him and said, ' You wil. take command of the marines, Colonel, and proceed at once to Harper's Ferry—but act prudently, Colonel.' Lee bowed, and was turning away, when Floyd came after him to the door, and said, ' Give 'em hell, Colonel !' This was the time to prefer my request, so I begged the Secretary to let me go, and, after looking at me for a moment, he said, ' Well, go.' I hurried off, met Colonel Lee at the cars, and we were soon flying along toward Harper's Ferry.

"When we arrived, Brown was in the engine-house, with his band and the prisoners he had taken. It was a small house inside the grounds of the arsenal, exactly like an ordinary fire-engine house in cities—with large folding doors. The Virginia troops had been deliberating upon the best means of assault, but upon Colonel Lee's arrival he assumed command, and the first step which he took was to send me forward to demand a surrender. I accordingly walked into the enclosure, and approached the engine-house, waving a white handkerchief, and, when I got to the door, called out that I wished to speak with ' Captain Smith.' I forgot to say that, up to this time, Brown had passed as Captain Smith, and I thus addressed him. At my call, he came and opened one fold of the door a little way. Behind it was a heavy rope stretched across—better security than a bar, as it would yield if a battering ram of any sort were used, but not give way.

"Well, the old fellow appeared at the opening of the door, with a carbine in his hand, and below appeared the head of a big bull dog, who kept snarling at my knee and growling angrily during the whole conversation. As soon as I saw the man, I knew that I had met with him before, and in a moment I remembered him.

" 'You are Ossawatomie Brown, of Kansas, are you not?' I said.

" ' He looked at me keenly for a minute from under his grizzly eyebrows, and then said coolly, addressing me by my title :

" ' Well, they do call me that, sometimes, Lieutenant.'

" ' I thought I remembered meeting you in Kansas,' was my reply. ' This is a bad business you are in, Captain. The United

States troops have arrived, and I am sent to demand your surrender.'

" 'Upon what terms ?' he asked coolly ; in fact, he displayed no sort of excitement during the entire interview.

" 'The terms are that you shall surrender to the officer commanding the troops, and he will protect you from the crowd, and guarantee you a fair trial.'

" Brown shook his head.

" 'I can't surrender on such terms,' he said. 'You must allow me to leave this engine-house with my comrades and the prisoners, and march across the river to the Maryland side: there I will release the prisoners, and, as soon as this is done, your troops may fire on and pursue us.'

" I replied that I had no authority to agree to any such arrangement, and was ordered to demand his surrender on the terms first proposed.

" 'Well, Lieutenant,' said the old fellow, 'I see we can't agree. You have the numbers on me, but you know we soldiers are not afraid of death. I would as lief die by a bullet as on the gallows.'

" 'Is that your final answer, Captain?' I asked.

" ' Yes.'

" I then stepped aside, and he closed the door. When I re ported the result to Colonel Lee, he ordered the marines to attack the engine-house, and this was done with a ladder which was used as a battering ram. As they approached, Brown and his men opened fire from the air-holes in the wall, and killed one or two of the men ; but the door soon yielded, and after a short struggle the whole party were captured."

Such was the narrative related to me by Colonel Stuart, and finished just as we reached head-quarters.*

* This is given nearly in General . tuart's words.

XXV.

THE RAID OF THE BEE-GUM.

I WAS about to set out on my return, on the following morning, when an amusing scene, interrupted by a rather comic incident, delayed my journey.

The men of the regiment had discovered a bee-gum, in the vicinity of the Big Spring—that is to say, a hollow tree in which a swarm of bees had taken up their abode, and stored away the rich proceeds of their raids among the flowers. The hollow tree thus contained a huge mass of honeycomb, and it was not long before it crashed down before the quick blows of the men's axes, and was split open.

The scene which followed was ludicrous. The jovial troopers crowded round the bee-gum, and, scooping out the rich contents with their hands, eagerly devoured them, smearing their faces with the honey, and laughing like a party of schoolboys let loose on a holiday.

The noise and confusion were at their height, the "general joy" unbounded, and the shaggy beards and mustaches of the cavalry men, to say nothing of their hands, were clogged with the liquid honey, when suddenly a horseman appeared on the brow of the neighboring hill, approaching at a furious gallop.

All heads were raised—all tongues hushed. On came the horseman, making violent gestures, and, as he came within hearing, the honey devourers distinguished above the clatter of his horse's hoofs the exciting words, "Look out! The Yankees are coming!"

In a moment all was confusion worse confounded. The men abandoned their bee-gum, dropped their honeycomb, and ran to their horses; but, as no attack was expected, all were unsaddled, and they were compelled to seize the equipments with their honey-covered hands, and saddle up in hot haste, without removing the yellow liquid from their faces. The quick notes of the bugle sounded "to horse!" and in a moment the regiment

was drawn up in line, with Stuart in front of them. A more
ludicrous spectacle I never witnessed. Every man's face resem
bled a yellow mask, every mustache dripped, every beard disap
peared in masses of honeycomb.

Stuart burst into uncontrollable laughter, and when the officer,
whom he had hastily ordered to gallop forward and ascertain the
truth of the reported advance, returned and announced that it
was a false alarm, the young cavalier leaned back in his saddle,
and there issued from beneath his heavy mustache a "guffaw"
which made the air ring.

The men were ordered to unsaddle their horses, and were soon
securing the remainder of the honey, but all the life and spirit
were gone. The laugh was turned on them, and they soon disappeared in the direction of their quarters.

I never heard an explanation of the alarm. Whether it was
brought by some excited picket who took "trees moving" for
Yankees, or was a practical joke gotten up by some wag of the
command, I never learned. It is certain that Stuart enjoyed it
too much to make very rigid inquiry, and I never before saw
such intense relish for a practical joke displayed by any human
being. He often mentioned this incident to me afterward, styl-
ing it "The Raid of the Bee-gum," and never without laughter.*

I soon afterward took leave of my gay host, and set out on my
return, promising to visit him again whenever I could do so. I
made my report to Colonel Jackson, and when he asked me how
I liked Stuart, I declared myself delighted with him.

Jackson smiled at my enthusiasm.

"Yes," he said, "Stuart is an excellent companion. He is
more : he is a remarkable man "

* An actual occurrence.

XXVI.

MY FIRST SIGHT OF THE BLUE-COATS.

IN the latter part of May additional troops reached Harper's Ferry, and General Joseph E. Johnston arrived, and assumed command.

This soldier, since so eminent, was a man of about sixty, with gray hair, piercing eyes, and the stiff carriage of the West-Pointer. His manner was phlegmatic, his voice grave and formal, and he wore his uniform with the air of a man born in it.

Johnston vigorously continued the organization which Jackson had commenced. The latter had been assigned to the command of a brigade raised in the Valley. They were entirely Virginia troops; but the Georgians and South Carolinians, under the brave General Bee, were now mingled with them in the little army. All was life, bustle, and activity: the news came from Bethel about this time, and cheer after cheer indicated the enthusiasm of the troops.

Then the words passed from lip to lip in the small army, "Patterson is advancing!" This intelligence was soon confirmed, and Johnston promptly broke up his camp to go and meet him. The surplus stores were burned, the arsenal destroyed, and, setting fire to the fine railroad bridge over the Potomac, the Confederate commander fell back toward Charlestown.

The spectacle, as I gazed upon it from a hill, was superb. The flames were roaring and crackling, the long bridge a sheet of fire, and the walls of the arsenal fell in one after another. On the right and in front, Loudoun and Maryland Heights, with their huge rocks and shaggy evergreens, were illuminated by the glare of the waving flames. The Shenandoah glowed in the light of the great conflagration; the Potomac was completely hidden by the lurid smoke, and through this murky cloud one of the hottest suns I ever experienced plunged its burning rays. It was the first time I had realized the full meaning of the word War.

The column fell back through Charlestown, where crowds of

beautiful girls filled the streets, waving their white handkerchiefs.
Bivouacking in the woods just beyond the town, on the next day
we moved by the right flank through country roads, and emerged
upon the Winchester and Martinsburg turnpike.

Here the army faced Patterson, advancing toward Williamsport, and soon it was announced that his column had reached
the river.

Jackson had been sent with his brigade to support Stuart, in
advance of Martinsburg, and one morning, at daylight, we
received intelligence that Patterson was over, with a large army.

When this dispatch reached Jackson his face actually glowed.
Hitherto I had looked upon him as almost a non-combatant, but
from that moment I knew that he loved fighting for its own sake.
The *gaudium certaminis* flamed in his regard. The grave and
serious Presbyterian was almost gay.

A reply was sent to Stuart's dispatch, but, remembering soon
afterward an important point which he had omitted, Jackson
sent me to find Stuart and give him the message.

I set out at once, and passed Falling Waters before I could
hear any thing of him. I soon encountered, however, a detachment of cavalry falling back before the enemy, whose dark
masses—infantry, cavalry, and artillery—were plainly seen in
front, and from the officer in command learned that Stuart was
moving with his main body on the right flank of the Federal
column.

Taking a bridle path which led in the direction indicated, I
soon found him with a squadron, dogging the enemy's movements, and gave him my message.

"Thank you, Captain," he said, his eyes glowing with ardor; "I
will do as Colonel Jackson wishes. Remain with me a short
while; I wish to send a message by you. Look at that column!
Their force must be at least two divisions."

And, leaving his command, Stuart galloped straight toward the
Federal column. We approached so close that their words were
distinctly audible, and I was endeavoring, as far as possible, to
ascertain their force, when Stuart suddenly pointed to a field in
our immediate front. I followed the direction of his finger, and

saw a company of infantry flankers, who had advanced ahead of the column, and were lying down resting until it came up.

"I am going to capture that party, and I wish you to help me. Do you see that clump of trees yonder? Bring my squadron round through them—bring it like lightning,* Surry!"

I instantly obeyed the order, and moved the squadron at a rapid trot by the route indicated. Then instructing the commanding officer where to bring it, I pushed ahead, and rejoined Stuart just as he galloped up to the fence behind which the infantry flankers were lying.

There was a pair of bars in the fence, and Stuart rode straight up to them, commanding one of the Federal soldiers to "take down those bars!"

His blue undress coat doubtless deceived the man, though this was certainly no part of his design. The infantry-man touched his hat respectfully, hastened to remove the obstacle, and then, again making the military salute, stood erect, awaiting further orders.

Stuart passed through the gap with one bound of his horse, and thundered:

"Throw down your arms, or you are dead!"

At the same moment his squadron was seen approaching at a gallop, and the whole company—forty-four, if I remember rightly, in number—not only threw down their arms, but fell prone upon their faces.†

In ten minutes Stuart had hastened away with his prisoners, and I speedily rejoined Colonel Jackson.

The engagement at Falling Waters followed.

This brief but spirited affair need not be here described, though its issue had an undoubted effect upon the *morale* of the troops —discouraging the enemy, and inspiring the Confederates with confidence.

Jackson met the advancing column with the Fifth Virginia Infantry, and one gun of Captain Pendleton's battery, and,

---

* This was Stuart's favorite expression in any emergency.
† General Stuart mentioned this incident to me more than once, and seemed greatly amused by it.

E

deploying his three hundred and eighty men—the exact number—
held his ground for some time with great stubbornness.

His thin line was, however, forced to fall back to avoid a flank
attack; and, as a column of Federal cavalry advanced to charge
it, the artillery was used for the first time in the action.

Captain Pendleton, who had been an Episcopal preacher, gave
the characteristic order, "Aim low, men, and may the Lord have
mercy on their souls!"*—the piece was discharged—and the shot
struck the head of the cavalry column, which recoiled and
retreated behind the infantry again.

The Federal artillery immediately opened in reply, and for the
first time i witnessed in Jackson that perfect coolness for which
he was afterward so celebrated. While he was seated beneath
a tree, writing a dispatch to General Johnston, a round shot
tore the trunk above him to atoms, and covered him with splin-
ters. He did not move a muscle, but finished his note with
entire coolness—it was hard, indeed, to realize that he had
observed the incident.

He continued steadily falling back, and, rejoining his main
body, retreated through Martinsburg, which the enemy pressed
on and occupied.

That night, the brigade bivouacked at "Big Spring," about
two miles from the town, on the road to Winchester; and an
odd incident marked the occasion.

About midnight, the weary troops were disturbed in their
slumbers by a dusky figure which moved among them, stumbling
over the sleepers. Many an imprecation greeted this unceremonious personage; but, when the men afterward ascertained who
the intruder was, their anger gave way to laughter and admiration.

The figure was Jackson's, and his errand was simple. General
Patterson had captured some of his tents, made by the young
ladies of Jefferson; and when he stumbled over the sleepers,
Jackson was looking for Colonel Allen, of the Second Virginia,
to order out his regiment, attack Patterson, and recapture the
tents.

* His words.

What induced him to abandon this scheme I do not know ; but
it was a characteristic idea—to attack two divisions with a single
regiment !*

Falling back still farther to the little village of Darkesville,
Jackson drew up his brigade, and determined to retreat no farther.

" Here I am ready for Patterson, whenever he comes," he said.
" I want my brigade to feel that they can whip his whole army;
and I believe they can do it !"*

Johnston had moved forward from Winchester to Bunker's Hill.
about midway between that place and Martinsburg; but General
Patterson did not advance.

Events were, however, hastening on—the great struggle about
to begin.

XXVII.

THE ENCHANTMENTS OF BOGY!

ONE morning I went to see Stuart, who held the front with
his cavalry toward Martinsburg, and found him lying, as usual,
on his red blanket, under a tree, waiting for the enemy.

He was listening to a report from our friend Corporal Hagan,
who, with a beard longer, mustache shaggier, and a voice more
closely resembling thunder than before, gave the particulars of
the capture of two or three prisoners he had just brought in.

" We charged 'em, Colonel," continued Hagan, after bestowing
upon me a punctilious salute, " and they run like the very old
devil was after 'em.   I come up with this young man here,"
pointing to one of the blue-coats, " and I jest grabbed hold of
him by the nape of his neck, and says I, ' Young man, the Judg-
ment-Day is come, and you are unprepar'd.'   He give right up,
without making any row ; and I really do believe, Colonel, he
thought I was the old devil himself—ha ! ha !"

* Historica'

When Hagan laughed, the ground seemed to shake. His merriment was Olympian, and partook of the earthquake.

"I got his weep-on, Colonel," continued the giant, exhibiting
a fine carbine, "and I thought, as I had the dead wood on him, I
would go through him, and take his boots. But then I remembered that that was ag'inst your orders. Ain't that the truth?
Speak to the Colonel!" thundered Hagan, and he scowled in a
truly terrific manner at the prisoner.

The unfortunate individual confirmed every particular ; and then
commanding "About face!" Hagan marched off his prisoners,
grave and solemn to the last.

"Hurrah for Hagan! He is a character," I said, laughing.

"True," said Stuart ; "and, if you will ride with me to-day, I
will make you acquainted with another."

"Who is that?"

"My dear Surry, a good soldier never asks any questions—
come! I'll show you a real curiosity, and give you an excellent
dinner. Do you accept?"

"Do I accept!—when I have been living on hard bread for a
whole week!"

"Agreed, then. But who is that yonder?"

"General Johnston and Colonel Jackson."

Stuart rose and went to meet them, receiving and returning
the salute of the two officers.

"So we have nearly caught the indefatigable Stuart* napping!"

Such was General Johnston's greeting, as he shook hands with
the commander of his cavalry.

"Not quite, General ; but I was not expecting an advance on
my rear."

"Well, Colonel, we are going to the front. Will you ride
with us?"

Stuart replied by getting into the saddle, and the whole party
set forward for the front. A complete reconnoissance was made,
the ground thoroughly examined, and then, as the sun began to

* See Johnston's report of operations in the Valley

decline, the heads of the horses were turned again toward Darkesville.

I began now to think of that famous dinner which had been promised me, greatly fearing that the visit of the two command-ers would interfere with it. Stuart solved this interesting prob-lem, however, in the most agreeable manner. He invited them to accompany him, highly extolling the cuisine and the hospitality of his friend—and they accepted. Generals are just like the rest of us, my dear reader: they get hungry. So we set out for the head-quarters of the "real curiosity."

His name, I soon heard, was Captain Bogy; and we found the worthy intrenched beside a limpid spring, in a glade of the woods. Horses were picketed near, for Captain Bogy was a cav-alry-man. The canvas cover of a wagon was visible through the bushes; not far off, a sable individual was seen busily cooking; and in the foreground, beneath a mighty tree, some planks, stretched across saplings, which rested in turn on forks driven into the ground, formed a rustic table.

Such were the preparations for the entertainment; but how shall I describe the host? Imagine Falstaff in an old cavalry uni-form, his mighty paunch encircled by a sword-belt half buried from sight; his legs cased in enormous horseman's boots, with spurs of fabulous proportions, which jingled as he moved. The Captain appeared only about forty-five, but his hair was grizzled and his mustache gray. A lurking smile seemed ever upon his features; and it was plain that the worthy loved the good things and the good jokes of life better than all the glories of arms.

Bogy greeted his guests with the ease of an old soldier, declar-ing himself much honored by their visit; and then, as though in matters so serious as eating and drinking there was no time to spend in idle talk or ceremony, he applied himself assiduously to the great work before him.

His whole soul was evidently in the matter of dinner, and he had secured an able staff-officer in the person of the old negro, who presided at the fire with an air as grave and serious as his master's. From that fire came the soothing music of frying meat and a savory odor invaded the nostrils of the guests.

Soon the golden moment came when all was done to a turn; and then, directed by Bogy, who was solemn and preoccupied, the dilapidated African staff-officer made his appearance with a pile of plates. My attention was attracted by them. They were china, snow-white, and richly gilt!

Had Bogy, then, discarded the military tin-platter, and did he revel habitually in this gorgeous service? The idea was incredible—but there they were!

The white plates were succeeded by shining knives with ivory handles, and then every eye stared—Bogy had silver forks!

Gilt plates and silver forks!!!

Bogy was modest, unassuming; he would not observe the general wonder and admiration. He made some innocent jests; he coughed slightly, and disappeared in the direction of the wagon.

What does Bogy return with? Is it not a brace of bottles? It is a brace of bottles, with rich labels and green seals. Bogy sets them on the table—all eyes admire!

His aid brings him mint and ice from the spring—a glass dish of white sugar from the wonderful wagon; and then behold! a long row of rich cut-glass goblets! The guests cease to wonder farther; they gaze in silence at the great magician.

He responds to that look by another, serene and smiling. He seems to say, "Have confidence in your host, my friends; he is equal to the present great occasion!"

Bogy draws a cork—a rich bouquet of Otard brandy, old and mellow, is inhaled. Some young officers who have joined the company look faint. That odor overcomes their sensitive nerves. Old Otard on the outpost!

With the hand of the master, Bogy mixes his liquids, and behold, a long row of cut-glass goblets full of julep, from whose Alpine heights of ice springs the fragrant mint! As the contents of those bright goblets disappear down the throats of the guests, their eyes close, and Bogy towers before them, the greatest of mortals.

This is the preface only, however. Bogy now opens the volume. Dinner is ready, and is placed upon the board. At the head is a Virginia ham, which Lucullus might envy; at the foot a saddle of mutton; at the sides, chickens, cutlets, and steaks, interspersed with all the esculents of the season!

By the side of each plate the sable aid places three wine-glasses, and these are filled with Rhine wine, Champagne, and Madeira!!!

The guests take their seats—they proceed from enchantment to enchantment. The *entrées* are followed by ice-cream in a silver holder! Almonds, raisins, English walnuts, olives, and Havana cigars!! Coffee with condensed cream, served in small gilt cups, with spoons of solid silver!!!

No allusions are made; we are too well bred. Bogy enjoys his triumph without interruption. He is the model of a host. He gently urges his guests to renewed attacks on the viands. Under his urging they perform wonders.

Nor does the great master allow the conversation to flag. He keeps the ball in motion, and his anecdotes are so pithy and so richly humorous that every face relaxes into a smile.

Stuart stimulates and seconds him, laughing loudly as the entertainment proceeds. At last it draws to a conclusion, and Stuart raises his coffee-cup.

"I wish to offer a toast!" says the gay cavalier.

Captain Bogy looks gratified, modest—he smiles sweetly. It is Falstaff just after dinner.

"To the health of your friend, who has sent you 'a small box,' Bogy! The present company honors him, and long may he wave!"

Bogy bows his head with the air of a girl who is overcome and blushing at a declaration.

"I will write to him and tell him of your good wishes, Colonel. He will then immediately send me another."

"In which case everybody will be happy to dine again with you," said Stuart. "But you have omitted one thing."

"What is that, Colonel?" exclaimed Bogy, with a sudden look of anxiety.

"To tell us the name of your friend."

"His name, Colonel?"

"Yes."

"Hum! I really have forgotten it"–

"Then perhaps I can assist you."

"You! Colonel?"

"Shall I try?"

Bogy smiled. That smile was evidently a challenge.

"Well, here goes for a guess, Bogy," said Stuart, laughing.
"Your friend's name is Patterson—is it not? Don't deny it!"

And he pointed, with a loud laugh, to the wagon in the bushes.
Upon the side of the vehicle all now saw a large "U. S."

Bogy's head slowly drooped; he swallowed a glass of wine.
Then rising to his feet, he spoke as follows:

"It is impossible, Colonel, to hide any thing from your knowledge, and from this moment Bogy don't mean ever to attempt
it. That individual now throws himself upon the mercy of the
court, and confesses that he really has received all these good
things from the individual whose honored name has just been
pronounced by my friend upon the right. That wagon was captured in a little raid last night, and its contents were soon found
to be varied and extensive. What could Bogy do, gentlemen?
What better use could he put those contents to than to feast his
commander and his friends? That is his plea in bar of sentence—
and he appeals to the quality of his brandy in justification!
What head-quarters has he rifled and made desolate by this capture? who can tell?—perhaps the mess of General Patterson
himself! We have appreciated, however, his selection of wines,
and his coffee and cigars have been favorably criticised. I would
have wished that his Madeira had been a little older; that his
cayenne pepper had been stronger; the pair of boots that I
found in the wagon, about four sizes larger. But the great mistake in life is being too fastidious. It is the place of a soldier to
put up with inconveniences, to make the best of his lot, and to
suppress all discontent. With these few remarks, Colonel, unac-
customed as I am to public speaking, I beg leave to conclude by
offering this honorable company:

"The good health of our friend over the way, who is dining
out to-day! and may he soon send another little present to his
comrades!"

" He was cursing you awfully when I left him, Captain."

All started as these words resounded behind us; and every eye was turned in the direction of the sound.

There stood a gay youngster of about eighteen or nineteen, tall, handsome, and elegantly dressed. The features of the youth were lit up by a smile, and he sustained the looks levelled at him with a species of joyous pride and *insouciance*.

"Why, where did you come from, my young friend?" exclaimed Bogy; "you appear to have started from the earth!"

"I came through the lines, Captain," was the reply of the gay young man, as he saluted with a movement full of graceful freedom. "I am from Maryland, and yesterday I was at the head-quarters of a Major Somebody in the Yankee army. He was cursing and swearing at the loss of his wagon, and I rather think, Captain, that you have fallen heir to it!"

There was so much gay courtesy in the air of the young man, and his face was illuminated by a smile so bright and glad, that I could not help admiring him.

In reply to our questions, he briefly explained that he had come over to join the Southern army. His name was Harry Saltoun; he had many Maryland friends in Stuart's Cavalry. Among others, Captain Brien, who could vouch for his loyalty.

"Will you have me, Colonel?" he asked, turning to Stuart; "I would rather fight under you as a private than have a commission!"

I saw from Stuart's smile that the words had won his heart.

"All right!" was his gay reply, as he made room for the young man by him. "That's the way I like a soldier to talk!"

The guests soon rose, and Bogy made a last address. I shall not attempt to record it: what great orator was ever correctly reported? Imagine Falstaff, my dear reader, doing the honors of his own table, and you will have formed some idea of the remarks of the great Bogy!

When we left him, I think it was the opinion of everybody that his equal, as a host. was not to be found in the whole universe.

So we returned to Big Spring, and thence I rode back with
Jackson.

The young Marylander had remained with Stuart.

XXVIII.

THE COUNCIL OF WAR.

ON the next day, a council of war assembled at General
Johnston's head-quarters, near Bunker's Hill.

An advance of the enemy was expected at any moment. Every
thing made such a movement probable. The enemy already had
armies in the field when the Confederacy had only detachments;
and news had just arrived of two affairs in which they had struck
a heavy blow at the dawning hopes of the South. General Pe-
gram had been compelled to surrender at Rich Mountain, and
General Garnett was defeated and killed at Carrick's Ford, in
Western Virginia—the enemy rode upon the summit of the
wave of success.

They would undoubtedly, now, push forward with their two
armies at Washington and in the Valley. Stuart had harassed
their foraging parties and pickets incessantly with his three
hundred cavalry, and Johnston had faced them in line of battle
every day; but it was very plain that, when once their great
forces were in motion, every resource of generalship would be
needed to oppose their predominance in numbers. Above all, a
thorough co-operation must be secured between the column
under Johnston and that under Beauregard at Manassas.

I rode with Colonel Jackson to head-quarters, and waited,
conversing with the staff as usual, while the council of war took
place. While thus engaged, I was summoned to attend General
Johnston.

I found him seated at a table, surrounded by his chief officers
in full uniform, and wearing their sabres. Jackson was quietly
examining a map; Stuart was drumming upon the table, and
reflecting.

I saluted, and waited to be addressed.

"Captain," said General Johnston, in his measured voice, "you are suggested as a competent person to carry an important communication to General Beauregard at Manassas, and explain to him the situation of affairs here. Have you a good horse?"

"Yes, sir."

"When can you set out?"

"In half an hour."

"At daylight will do, but lose no time on the road. Here is the dispatch—it embraces the main points. I depend upon your good sense and judgment to reply accurately to General Beauregard's questions."

I bowed and took the dispatch.

"Any further instructions, General?"

"That is all."

I saluted and withdrew.

Half an hour afterward Jackson came out and mounted his horse, holding in his hand a large envelope, which evidently covered an "official document." It seemed to embarrass him, and he said:

"Captain, will you carry this?"

I took it, but said: "I may forget and take it to Manassas with me, Colonel, when, in case it is important"—

"It is not important. You may read it."

I opened the paper, and glanced at it. It was Jackson's appointment as Brigadier-General.

He was riding on absently, in deep thought.

XXIX.

THE CAVALRY PICKET.

AT daylight I was in the saddle and on the road to Manassas. My horse was fresh, the weather fine; and, passing to the left of Millwood, I forded the Shenandoah, and rode rapidly through Ashby's Gap.

At Paris, a little village perched on the eastern slope of the mountain, I looked toward the south. Two or three hours, at the farthest, would take me to "The Oaks!" and, as the thought occurred to me, something like a thrill passed through me. Then, as the novelists say, any one who had been present "might have seen" a bitter smile distort my lip. Why should I go there to covet my neighbor's wife, and groan for the amusement of the future *Mrs. Baskerville.*

I pushed on. Soon the bitterness disappeared from my heart. "Poor thing!" I muttered—that was all.

Passing successively through Upperville, Middleburg, and Aldie, I turned, late in the afternoon, into a road leading by way of Sudley Ford to Manassas.

Darkness gradually descended, and I had seen no human being for more than an hour, when, as I approached Bull Run, I suddenly heard the quick "Halt!" of a picket.

"Friend!" was my reply; and "Advance friend, and give the countersign!" came back.

"I have no countersign," I responded, fording the stream as I spoke. "I am carrying a dispatch to General Beauregard, and am your prisoner. Where is your officer?"

The carbine of the cavalry-man was lowered at these words, and, calling a comrade, he announced who I was. I was then conducted forward, and soon descried, through the boughs, the glimmer of a light, which issued from a camp-fire in front of a small tent.

At ten paces from the tent, as I approached, I saw a dark figure about to mount a powerful horse in the shadow of the trees.

"Here is a prisoner, Captain," said my escort, saluting.

"Bring him up," was the reply, in a deep voice which I recognized.

And, turning round, the person about to mount approached the fire.

The light fell on his features, and I saw before me the dark face and powerful form of Mordaunt.

XXX.

THE STONE HOUSE AT MANASSAS.

He met me with a cordiality which really surprised me. His face was gloomy still, and his voice as deep and measured; but the weary air of the recluse had yielded to the martial ardor of the soldier.

At the door of the tent stood the young Moor, Achmed, who evidently filled something like the position of a confidential body-servant near my host. At sight of me, the young Moor saluted courteously; and then, at a sign from Mordaunt, busily set about preparing some supper for me. This was set out upon a camp-chest, by a negro, under the Moor's orders—and soon I tasted once more that bitter black coffee, which revived my weary frame like some *elixir vitæ.*

As I supped, Mordaunt conversed; and I had soon put him in possession of the situation in the Valley. In return he explained the state of affairs at Manassas, and informed me, in brief words, that he had been with General Beauregard since May.

As he spoke I could see more than ever the change in him. He evidently enjoyed the life of the bivouac far more than that of the library. His gloomy air of languor and cynical disdain had disappeared; and, although his melancholy seemed too deeply rooted to be eradicated, he was altogether a different individual. As I listened to his sonorous voice, and looked at his large and muscular frame, I was confirmed in my former conviction, that action and not meditation was the forte of this powerful organization.

When I had finished my supper, and my horse had ground between his teeth the last handful of a plentiful supply of corn, I rose and informed Mordaunt that I must go on to General Beauregard.

"I will ride with you a portion of the way," was his reply. "I was just going on my rounds to inspect the pickets, but I will show you your road, and take my ride when I return."

I accepted this friendly offer, and, mounting our horses, we soon reached Sudley Ford, where Mordaunt passed me through his interior picket. We then rode on through the darkness, which had become intense.

"I never saw a blacker night in all my life," I said.

"It is dark enough," replied my companion, "but I know the road."

"Is this country familiar to you?"

"Naturally, as I have been picketing it."

"But you never were here before the breaking out of the war ?"

My companion did not reply for a moment. He then said : " Yes."

There was a sudden gloom in his tone as he uttered this monosyllable, which I could not avoid observing.

"Then we can't lose our way," I replied, as we rode on. I am fortunate in having you to show me the road, as I really cannot see my hand before me. What a country! I don't see any signs of an inhabitant. Are there any houses near us?"

"There is one not far off," was Mordaunt's gloomy reply, "but it is not occupied."

"A deserted house—ah!" I said, with a laugh. "Well, that is exactly in keeping with the funereal landscape. One would really say that this country was intended for some bloody battle-field—to become the scene of suffering and death! It is as lugubrious as the grave, and your deserted house must resemble a spectre. Come, relate some ghostly story connected with the place, and the influence of the landscape will be complete."

Mordaunt did not seem to participate, in any degree, in my merriment. For some moments he preserved silence, and when he spoke his voice was as gloomy as death itself.

"I have no story to tell," was his brief response ; but this only piqued my curiosity.

"Come, acknowledge," I said, laughing, "that there is some mysterious and tragic affair in your memory! Confess that this spectral mansion you refer to was the scene of it—and that no

human being can be induced again to set foot inside of its accursed walls!"

"You are right, sir," said Mordaunt, suddenly, in tones as cold
as ice, "the place is accursed!—trebly accursed!"

So abrupt was his reply, and his accents were so filled with
gloomy menace, that I started in spite of myself. Before I could
make any reply, he seemed to have realized his indiscretion, and,
uttering a harsh laugh, added coolly:

"You see, I partake of your superstitious feelings. I agree with
you, that these 'haunted houses,' as they are called by children,
produce a singular effect upon the imagination—you see that this
one has had that effect upon me."

He spoke with perfect coolness, but his nonchalance did not
deceive me. His exclamation had been far too gloomy to be at-
tributable to any mere sentiment such as he described. His reply
was an evasion—I was sure of that—his former speech the outburst of some hidden tragedy.

We rode on, however, without further reference to the topic,
and soon I saw before me a dark object, which was doubtless the
house in question. It was a gloomy-looking building, of dark
stone, near the intersection of the Warrenton and Sudley-Brents-
ville roads, and in the very heart of the subsequent battle. Thou-
sands of my readers will, no doubt, remember it as the "Old
Stone House at Manassas."

"That is your spectral mansion, I suppose," was my comment.
"Well, you did not exaggerate in describing it as looking accursed.
The very owls seem to have deserted it!"

"Yes," came briefly from my companion. Then he suddenly
checked his horse, and said, in a low tone:

"That is strange!"

"What?" I said.

"I see a light yonder!"

I looked, and, in fact, a light was seen glimmering through
what seemed to be a window or doorway in the house.

"That is singular," I said, "as you say the place is not occupied; but doubtless some straggling soldiers have made their den
there."

"It is probable."

But the low tones appeared to say, "It is *not* probable."

As Mordaunt spoke, the light moved, disappeared for an instant, and then reappeared, moving along the ground in rear of
the house. Some one seemed to be carrying a lantern.

My companion remained motionless for some moments, gazing
at this weird will-o'-the-wisp: then he touched his horse with
the spur, and rode straight toward the house.

"We have stumbled upon something very much like an adventure," he said, with a harsh laugh. "Come! it is very little
out of our way—let us ride by, and see what is going on!"

I followed without a word, and we rode on through a field in
the direction of the house. It looked inexpressibly dreary, as
the gloomy gable loomed out indistinctly against the dark back-
ground of the sky. It was ink upon ink: the gloomy thing
seemed to rise up before the eyes like some monstrous animal; to
approach and weigh upon the chest.

Fifty yards from the sombre mansion, a thick hedge of Osage
orange arrested us. Through this, however, the light was still
seen to glimmer—stationary now upon the ground—and I could
make out, around it, a desolate and weed-encumbered garden,
containing only a few stunted fruit-trees.

Under one of these trees stood a man and a woman. In the
shadow of the tree, a third figure, apparently that of a female,
was dimly visible. On the ground was a coffin beside a newly-
dug grave.

Mordaunt did not utter a word, but I heard his low breathing
at my ear.

"Look!" I muttered in a whisper. "I told you this spot had
something ghostly about it. They are burying a dead body!"

My companion did not reply, but a ray from the light fell upon
his face, and its expression was startling. I never saw a deeper
pallor on the human countenance; and his singular expression
of stupefied surprise astonished me. What connection could
Mordaunt have with this scene, and why did it move him so? I
thought my eyes must have deceived me; but the next moment
served to explain a part of the mystery.

The man at the grave turned round, and the light fell upon his face. I recognized Fenwick—and at the same instant made out the face of his companion. It was the woman Parkins: The third figure I could not see, as the shadow of the tree-trunk concealed it.

Mordaunt laid his hand on my arm, and said, in a low, set tone, as cold as ice:

"You recognize that man, do you not?"

"Certainly. It is Fenwick."

"And that woman"—

"I know her too."

"It is well," said Mordaunt, through his clinched teeth. "What devil's errand they have come upon, I do not know, or why they should be here burying any one—but I know that the hour I have long looked for has come."

There was a concentrated hate in the low tones of his voice, which made further words unnecessary.

"Let us wait," he added, coolly, "and see the comedy out."

And, leaning forward on his horse's neck, he seemed to devour with his eyes the movements of the figures in the garden.

Fenwick had, meanwhile, hung the lantern on a bough of the stunted tree under which the grave had been dug; and now, with the assistance of the woman Parkins, inserted ropes beneath the coffin. Without further delay, or any burial service, it was lowered into the grave, and Fenwick seized a spade lying near. A harsh and grating sound was then heard—it was the dirt falling on the coffin. Fenwick worked with great energy and rapidity, and the grave was soon filled. Throwing the last spadeful on the hillock, he wiped his forehead, exchanged some hurried words, apparently with the woman Parkins, and, taking down the lantern, proceeded with rapid steps, followed by his two companions, toward the house.

I was leaning close beside Mordaunt, and could see his face. It was paler even than before, and there was a deadly meaning in his eyes.

"Well," I said, gloomy in spite of myself at this nocturnal

adventure, "we have seen the play through. What is the after-piece?"

"Follow me, and you will see," said my companion. As he spoke, I heard the click of his pistol as he tried the barrel. His voice was so cold and steady that the hand must be equally so. "This time, Fenwick is a dead man," I thought.

XXXI.

WHAT TOOK PLACE AT THE STONE HOUSE.

LAYING his hand upon my arm, Mordaunt drew me away from the hedge, and, moving carefully over the turf, which muffled the sound of the horses' hoofs, made a detour, reaching thus the front of the house. Before it stood a light one-horse wagon, which had, doubtless, served to convey the dead body beyond this, a riding horse was standing beneath a tree.

"Listen," said Mordaunt, in a whisper. "I know this house and the grounds perfectly. There is no means of exit from that garden, except a small gate close against the gable end of the house. Do me the favor to take your place there, and allow no one to pass."

"You are going into the house?"

"Certainly."

"To find Fenwick?"

"Ah! you have guessed that?"

"It don't require much penetration. But take care."

"Of what?"

"He is a treacherous animal—there may be many persons in that den."

"It is nothing."

"If so, call me promptly."

"Thanks—but it is not ten men, or one hundred, that can keep me from driving my sword's point through that man's heart."

This rapid dialogue had taken place in a low tone, and Mordaunt had quickly dismounted, throwing his bridle over the fence. I imitated him, and ran to the gate, just as the interior of the house was illuminated, and the sound of footsteps upon the creaking floor indicated that the party had entered by the door in the rear.

A rapid inspection told me that the side gate was securely fastened, and, finding it unnecessary to guard it, I hastened to follow Mordaunt, who had rushed into the house.

The scene which greeted me was long engraved upon my memory. The apartment was bare, desolate-looking, and repulsive. The window-panes were broken, the fireplace full of soot and ashes, and the walls were festooned with cob- webs. These details I made out by the light of the lantern, which had been placed upon a dilapidated pine table, sole fur- niture of the mansion. By the fireplace stood the woman Parkins, grim and lowering, with contracted brows, and still holding the spade which she had brought into the house. Opposite Mordaunt I saw Fenwick, pale and desperate; and, as I entered the doorway, his hand clutched and drew a revolver from his belt.

What followed did not occupy thirty seconds.

Mordaunt rushed upon his adversary, Fenwick's pistol was raised and discharged, the ball whistling past my head—when suddenly, before he could fire a second time, the form of a woman interposed itself between the combatants.

It was Violet Grafton, with the same golden ringlets, the same delicate, earnest face, and the same wonderful likeness to the portrait in Mordaunt's study.

The effect which her appearance produced upon him was ter- rible. He recoiled, as though he had seen a ghost, his sword's point fell with a clattering sound to the floor, and, with his eyes glaring upon the young lady, he turned so ghastly pale that I thought he was going to faint.

From this stupor, however, he was aroused in a manner equally sudden and disagreeable.

Disappointed in his first aim, Fenwick had deliberately raised his pistol, aimed at Mordaunt's heart, and fired. The result would have been fatal but for Miss Grafton. She struck up the weapon as it was discharged; the bullet buried itself in the wall; and in an instant Mordaunt would have driven his sword through his adversary's breast, when all at once the whole scene was plunged in darkness.

Fenwick, by a quick movement, had extinguished the light: his figure was seen for an instant as it passed through the open window; and a moment afterward the hoof-strokes of a horse departing at full gallop were heard upon the ground without.

With one powerful bound Mordaunt passed through the doorway, threw himself upon his horse, and followed the retreating horseman with the fury of a tiger despoiled of his prey.

I was close upon the heels of his flying animal—for an irresistible desire mastered me to be present at the execution of his vengeance.

"Do you hear him?" I said.

"I think so," was the hoarse reply.

And the speaker continued his headlong pursuit.

We went on at a furious speed for more than half an hour—then all sounds in front had ceased. Fenwick seemed to have vanished. Taking some by-road known only to himself, he had escaped.

A mile further, Mordaunt uttered something like the growl of a wounded lion, and drew rein. For some moments he listened—then he said through his clinched teeth:

"He has got off! The devil takes care of his own!"

And I heard his teeth grinding together as he spoke.

Without further words, he turned the head of his horse, and we rode slowly back. On the way, Mordaunt did not utter a single word, and I did not intrude upon his thoughts.

Soon the gloomy Stone House again appeared before us, and we rode toward it. No light was visible now, and the wagon, we found, had also disappeared. Miss Grafton and her companion had vanished like Fenwick. The Stone House resembled a gigantic tomb—and was as dreary, mournful, and deserted.

XXXII.

BEAUREGARD.

I HAD scarcely come to realize that Miss Grafton had disappeared, when my attention was attracted by the noise of horses' hoofs coming from the direction of Stonebridge.

"Halt! who goes there?" was Mordaunt's quick summons.

"Friends," said a firm and sonorous voice. "What picket is this?"

"It is General Beauregard," Mordaunt said to me, and he added:

"Advance, General—I am Captain Mordaunt."

"Ah! an amateur picket?" said General Beauregard, riding up, followed by a staff officer and an orderly. "I have been the rounds, and am glad to find you on the *qui vive*, Captain—but that you always are. I wish the infantry were as vigilant. The picket at Stonebridge has actually allowed a wagon with two women to pass to-night toward Alexandria, contrary to all my orders."

Then Miss Grafton and her companion had gone in that direction.

After a few words more, Mordaunt presented me to General Beauregard, and, declaring that he must return to inspect his pickets, took leave of us. In a moment he had disappeared, and I turned to General Beauregard, who had greeted me with grave courtesy.

"I have a dispatch, General."

And I handed it to him.

"Thank you, Captain; I will read it at once."

And, making a sign to his orderly, he soon had a light. As the wind was near putting it out, he dismounted and entered the deserted house, where, leaning against the old table, he read General Johnston's note.

As he did so, I looked with much interest at the "Man of Sumter." His appearance was decidedly French, and realized my conception of Napoleon's marshals. He was apparently about forty-five or fifty years of age; of medium height; gaunt, square built, and wearing the blue dress-coat of the United States Army, buttoned to the chin, on each side of which rose the points of a stiff white collar. The forehead, half covered by a Zouave cap, was broad, with thin, dark hair at the temples; the complexion sallow and brunette; the eyes large, black, and thoughtful; the thin lips nearly concealed by a heavy black mustache. The powerful jaw indicated hard "fight" in its possessor, and in the slumberous eye I read something of the dormant fire of the bloodhound.

The face was wholly un-Virginian—rather a creole, tropical countenance; but there was a noble simplicity in its expression, and a vigor in the poise of the head which made a strong impression upon me. A single glance told me that this man possessed military genius.

"I have read the dispatch you were good enough to bring, Captain," said the General, issuing forth and mounting his horse, " and I will be glad if you will be my guest for a day or two. I wish both to ask you a great many questions, and to ride over and show you the ground here. It is desirable that General Johnston should have an officer near him who has examined it— as you doubtless understand."

I bowed; assured the General that I was entirely at his or-ders; and rode back with him to Manassas, where he had his head-quarters in a small farm-house.

An hour afterward I was shown to an apartment containing a comfortable pallet; but the singular events which I had witnessed at the Stone House kept me awake until long past midnight. Finally I sank to sleep.

XXXIII.

THE LINES.

ON the next morning I had just risen from my straw pallet when General Beauregard entered and saluted me with grave courtesy.

"I will be glad if you will ride with me this morning, Captain," he said, "and I will explain the position of affairs here."

I bowed, and informed the General that I was at his orders. After a plain breakfast, we mounted and set out for a ride along the entire lines.

General Beauregard had taken up a strong position along Bul. Run, a small watercourse, with thickly wooded banks, running around Manassas, and emptying into the Occoquan. Three miles in front was Centreville; three miles in rear, Manassas. From Union Mills, the extreme right of the line, to Stonebridge, the extreme left, was about seven or eight miles. Mitchell's Ford, on the main road from Manassas to Centreville, was the Confederate centre.

"The enemy will attack here first," said General Beauregard; "but I have the advantage of position. If they strike with their main body at either flank, it will lay them open to an attack in return."

We passed on, following the earthworks along the high banks of the stream. The position appeared impregnable—the troops defending it, in excellent spirits. In front of Stonebridge a heavy abatis of felled trees, commanded by artillery, defended the approach by the Warrenton road.

Passing near the afterward celebrated Henry House, General Beauregard said that, if the enemy succeeded in crossing on the left, the battle would be there.

"The battle of Bull Run," he said in a low tone, as if to himself.

"That is rather an unclassic name, General."

"It is as good as 'The Cowpens,' Captain." *

* His words.

And the white teeth shone under the black mustache.

After a long ride, in which General Beauregard pointed out every detail of the ground, we rode back to head-quarters, where a good supper awaited us. On the next morning the ride was repeated, and this time we visited Fairfax Court-House, where General Bonham was in command of the advance force.

"The enemy are about to move," said General Beauregard on the way back. "Now is the time for General Johnston to put himself in motion."

"At your orders, General."

"Do not go until the morning. I wish to send the last news from the front."

I was aroused at three in the morning by an orderly, who said: "Captain, General Beauregard would like to see you."

In a moment I had buckled on my sword and was in the presence of the General.

XXXIV.

THE HEROINE OF MANASSAS.

THE first person I saw was Mordaunt. That iron calmness which habitually characterized his dark features was unchanged, but I could see black marks under his eyes, and his pallor was frightful.

As I afterward ascertained, he had brought General Beauregard a detailed statement of the numbers and composition of the Federal forces, which one of his scouts had arrived with, an hour before. The same scout had brought the additional intelligence that the enemy had begun their advance.

General Beauregard had not slept, having been up all night receiving reports and sending orders. His face was sallower than ever, but his black eyes were undimmed.

He handed me a paper in an envelope, and said:

"I will be glad, Captain, if you will immediately return to General Johnston with this dispatch, and inform him that the enemy's column is 'n motion to attack me."

I bowed, and waited to hear any thing further.

"That is all, Captain—except that you can tell General Johnston that, if he wishes to help me, now is the time."*

I was leaving the apartment when the voice of the General arrested me.

"Upon reflection, you had better remain until daylight. I expect to hear from the front soon, and you can carry the last intelligence.

As he spoke, an orderly entered, and said:

"Here is a prisoner, General—a woman."

"From whom?

"General Ewell, sir."

"I will see her at once."

The door opened, and suddenly I saw Mordaunt's eye flash. I turned quickly, and looked toward the door. On the threshold stood the prisoner. It was Violet Grafton.

She wore a long dark riding-skirt, and in her right hand carried a small whip. Her manner was perfectly composed— two red spots burning in the centre of her cheeks, otherwise pale from fatigue and want of sleep, were the only evidences of emotion which she exhibited.

The General rose, and gravely saluted her.

"Are you the prisoner mentioned, madam?"

"I suppose so, sir," was her reply, in the calm sweet voice I knew so well.

"General Ewell sent you?"

"Yes, sir."

Suddenly, as she looked around the apartment, the young lady's eyes encountered my own. She made a step forward, and, holding out her hand with that inexpressible grace and frankness which characterized her, said:

"Captain Surry, I am very glad you are here! They insist upon regarding me as a spy and a prisoner, when I have ridden until my strength is broken down to bring important news. If this is General Beauregard, tell him that you know me, and that I am worthy of credit. It is hard, after all my trouble and ex-

* His words.

posure—a girl riding by herself at night through an army—it is *very* hard to be considered a spy."

A few words from myself at once placed the young lady in her proper light, and she made her statement. It was important. She had passed through the Confederate lines a day or two before, she said, on her way to Alexandria, when, on reaching Annandale, she and her travelling companion received the intelligence that the enemy were advancing. Before they could leave the place, the Federal column had entered it, and the house at which Miss Grafton had stopped was taken as the headquarters of one of the Generals, whose division encamped in the adjoining fields. The Federal General seated himself, without ceremony, at breakfast with the family, and indulged in many jests at the expense of General Beauregard and the Confederates. " They knew all about his lines on Bull Run," said the Federal officer ; " they had no intention of attacking the centre, opposite Manassas—nor the right. The attack would be against the left of the rebel line above Stonebridge, and they would be run out of their holes before they knew it." Miss Grafton had listened attentively to all this, not, however, without some expression of disdain upon her countenance. The Federal officer now added that he was supplied with a number of Confederate flags, which he intended to make use of to deceive the rebels ; and Miss Grafton asked, if he was not afraid to speak so freely before every one. " Pshaw !" was his laughing reply, " you can't get through our lines. Before you could arrive, even if you did, we'll have the rebels in full retreat on Richmond." Ten minutes afterward, an order came for the division to march ; it moved on—and Miss Grafton hastened to present herself before General McDowell in person. She informed him that the advance had caught her at Annandale, and asked for a pass to return to her friends in the country near. This was granted—she rode alone through the crowding Federal camps—between long lines of red Zouaves—pushed her horse to a gallop, and, travelling all night, came into General Ewell's lines toward morning.*

* A real incident

"That is all, General," said Miss Grafton; "it may not be very important, but I am sure from the manner in which the Federal officer spoke that he was in earnest."

"Your communication is very important indeed, madam," said the General, with a thoughtful salute, "and you have done the South good service. Now you must be fatigued. I beg that you will repose yourself."

And, summoning an old dame, the owner of the mansion, the General intrusted Miss Grafton into her hands, holding open the door, and again saluting with profound courtesy, as she retired.

"I believe that is their plan," I heard him mutter; "yes, the left! Captain Mordaunt, let us examine the papers brought by your scout, once more."

In the midst of the consultation I left the room, and sent to request a few minutes' private conversation with Miss Grafton.

XXXV.

I RETURN THE PACKAGE.

My object was to return the package which had been so mysteriously deposited in my pocket at the house in the Wilderness.

For more than two months, now, I had constantly carried it about with me, trusting to find some opportunity to return it, but none had presented itself. I had heard of no one travelling toward the Wilderness, and I knew of no post-office. The package threatened to wear out in my pocket, when all at once chance threw me once more with Miss Grafton, and I could rid myself of the unpleasant responsibility.

To my request for a brief private interview she gave a prompt assent, and in a few moments I found myself alone with the young lady, in a plain sitting-room, lit by a single tallow candle.

"I am afraid I am keeping you from your rest, Miss Grafton," I said, "but I trust you will excuse me. I expect to set out for the Valley in half an hour, and am anxious, before I go, to ask your assistance in an affair which has not a little annoyed me."

I then explained the origin of the package, which I drew from my pocket, and stated my belief that it belonged to the white lady. It had no directiou. I could not venture to open it; would Miss Grafton return it, or, *if the owner was dead*, dispose of it in such manner as seemed best to her?

At those words, "if the owner is dead," the young lady, who had listened with drooping head, suddenly looked up.

"I see you know all," she said, in a low tone. "Yes, the person we buried the other night, at that desolate spot, was my poor cousin—your acquaintance, sir, in the Wilderness."

"Poor thing!"

"Yes, she was truly to be pitied. Something pressed upon her heart, and it killed her. After your visit she did not leave her bed, and, a few days since, she died."

Such was the dry, bare statement of the young girl. It was plain that she did not design more confidential communication. I was to remain in ignorance still of the meaning of the strange scene at the Stone House. Between the impassive coolness of Mordaunt and the gentle reserve of my companion, my curiosity threatened to be crushed.

"And you really believe that my poor cousin placed this in your pocket, sir," said the young lady, pensively.

"I am sure of it, Miss Grafton."

She sighed unconsciously, and glanced at the worn and discolored envelope.

"'Read these when I am dead, and think of *your own Frances!*'" she murmured. "Yes, her name was Frances."

And, as she gazed at the delicate handwriting of the dead woman, her eyes filled with tears.

"Captain Surry," she said, passing her handkerchief over her eyes, and speaking with calm sadness, "you became connected with some very sorrowful persons by stopping, that night, in the Wilderness. It is annoying—even painful—to me, to appear to you ever surrounded with mystery—for mystery is generally discreditable—but I cannot help it. Some day you may know all. Now I must go on and do my duty as I can not speaking of affairs which do not concern me."

"You will pardon me, Miss Grafton, for asking if you design returning to the Wilderness."

"Never, sir."

"Have you a protector?"

"None."

"You pain and shock me," was my earnest reply. "Who will watch over and guard you in these troubled times?"

"God, sir," was the calm reply.

I looked with pity and admiration at the beautiful girl who spoke so calmly. There was something inexpressibly revolting in the idea that she had no protector from Fenwick—actually no roof over her head. Here was a delicate girl of seventeen, without friends, relatives, or home—and yet so calm and confident, that you felt that such confidence could not be misplaced!

I begged the young lady to accept a home at my father's house, but she declined.

"Where was she going?"

"She did not know."

As she spoke, a knock was heard at the door, and Mordaunt made his appearance, pale and gloomy.

He bowed low, and said with freezing coldness:

"I shall have the honor to conduct Miss Grafton, as soon as she has rested, to a place of safety. This house may be exposed to the enemy's fire in the battle about to be fought, and General Beauregard wishes Miss Grafton to proceed to the rear."

What could have induced Mordaunt, the cynical woman-hater, to accept such a commission? I vainly puzzled my mind to solve the question.

Miss Grafton rose. Her perfect calmness had not altered in the least.

"I do not feel at all sleepy, sir," she said, "and am ready to set out whenever you wish."

"I will, then, order Miss Grafton's horse," was Mordaunt's reply in the same cold tone; and with another inclination he left the apartment.

I took advantage of his absence to utter a few parting words.

"Your fate is a singular one," I said, "to be thus tossed to and fro in these dangerous times. Where are you going?"

"I do not know," was her calm reply.

"And yet you are not disquieted?"

"Why should I be, sir?"

"You do not know Captain Mordaunt—you do not know whither he is about to conduct you—and yet you are perfectly composed!" I said, with a sort of admiration. "Allow me to say, Miss Grafton, that your equanimity is something wonderful."

She looked at me with her large, thoughtful eyes for an instant, and replied with unmoved calmness:

"God will watch over me, and I shall find friends."

I could say no more. In presence of this supreme resignation and reliance upon a higher power than man's, I stood abashed.

Mordaunt entered.

"Miss Grafton's horse is at the door."

"I am ready, sir."

"I trust Miss Grafton will not be alarmed by the darkness," he said with grim courtesy.

"By the darkness, sir?" she said.

"It is heavier than before, madam."

"I rode by myself all night," she replied simply.

"Miss Grafton may rely upon my exertions to make her ride as agreeable as possible," came from Mordaunt in the same cold tone.

"I am sure of it, sir," was her calm reply, as she gave him her hand with an air of confiding simplicity which struck me.

Something like a slight color came to the swarthy cheeks of Mordaunt as he took it and assisted her to mount at the door. He then got into the saddle and took his place at her side.

I exchanged a grasp of the hand with him, and turning to Miss Grafton:

"You will not forget me, I hope, or cease to remember me as your friend," I said.

"I shall gladly think of you as such," was her reply, with a

courteous little inclination of her head. And leaning down, she
said in a low tone, as her horse moved :

" I think I have discovered for whom the package of papers
was intended."

A glance of the large blue eyes, which I long remembered—
a pressure of the small ungloved hand—and Violet Grafton
disappeared with her escort in the darkness.

XXXVI.

A RIDE IN THE DOG-DAYS.

I HASTENED back to General Beauregard. His horse was at the
door, and he was preparing to mount. In his measured voice
he gave me my last instructions. They were, to return as
rapidly as possible to General Johnston; inform him that the
Federal army was advancing; and urge the necessity of a
prompt junction of the Army of the Shenandoah with that of
the Potomac.

" The enemy's force is now ascertained to be about fifty-five
thousand men," he added ; " mine is somewhat less than twenty
thousand effective. I do not doubt my ability to hold this
position, but more troops are necessary for ulterior operations."

I clearly understood this allusion. It pointed to the projected movement of Johnston's force, by way of the Little River
turnpike, against the Federal right flank.

" That is all, I believe, Captain—the dispatch you bear will
convey the rest. Are you well mounted ?"

" Yes, General."

" If your horse fails, impress the first you find. Your message must arrive to-day."

" It shall, sir."

General Beauregard gave me his hand, mounted, and set off
at a rapid gallop for the front, followed by his staff.

In ten minutes I left Manassas, at full speed, following the road to Thoroughfare Gap.

The first light of dawn glimmered in the east as I looked in the direction of the Stone House. I almost fancied I could see it—weird and desolate in the dim light. What was the mystery, I asked myself, hidden beneath the sombre curtain, a corner of which I had just lifted? What tragedy was this in which Mordaunt, Miss Grafton, Fenwick, and the woman Parkins were all mixed up—and what had that lugubrious stone mansion to do with the history of all these lives?

All speculation was vain—I pushed on.

My roan was in excellent order, and moved under me like a bundle of steel springs. The distance I had to go was only about fifty miles; I expected to accomplish it in six hours. But I had not calculated upon the oppressive heat of the weather.

Passing through Thoroughfare Gap, I reached White Plains soon after sunrise, and then, leaving the main road to Salem, struck across toward Rectortown and Paris.

The sun became burning hot, and my roan was as wet as if he had just swum a river. His speed was undiminished, however; and, finally, the Blue Ridge drew near.

At Paris there was a group of loungers upon the tavern porch.

"What news?" they shouted, as I passed at full gallop.

"Nothing," I replied.

As I left the town, I heard a Dutch-looking farmer say:

"That officer is riding his horse to death."

It was true. Going up the mountain, my roan began to toss his head and wheeze: I allowed him for the first time to walk, and thus reached the "Big Poplar," but there I resumed the gallop.

Two miles further I forded the Shenandoah, looking with covetous eyes upon the cool green turf of the banks, shaded by the giant sycamores reaching their mottled arms over the current.

The cool bath and long draught of the fresh water gave my horse new life; but the scorching sun poured down all the hotter as we entered again upon the interminable, blazing turnpike. The heat seemed to descend—to rise from the earth in quivering steam—and the very puffs of air which came at times resembled the breath of a furnace. The dust filled the air, motionless as fog; the minute particles burned the face and choked the throat.

Beyond Millwood my horse began to stagger. His jaws were reeking with foam, his eyes glaring and bloodshot.

Pressing him steadily with the spur, I reached and passed the Opequon, came in sight of Winchester, and saw across the fields General Johnston's head-quarters tent.

A hundred yards from it my roan reeled and fell. I saw General Johnston in his tent, and hastened to him.

"Ah! Captain," he said, "what news? Are you from Manassas to-day? It is not possible!"

"To-day, General: the news is important. The enemy are advancing. By this time they are not far from Bull Run."

"And General Beauregard?"—

"Says, if you wish to help him, now is the time."

And I handed him the dispatch.

Johnston read it, asked me a few questions, and then summoned his adjutant-general.

"Any thing further, General?"

"Nothing, Captain. Thanks for your promptness."

I saluted and went to look after my horse.

He was dead.*

XXXVII.

THE FLANK MOVEMENT.

I HAD arrived at the crisis. Patterson was extending his left to cut Johnston off from Ashby's Gap, and in twelve hours the Confederate General would have found it impossible to evacuate the Valley without a battle, if at all.

Those twelve hours I had gained by killing my horse.

Rapid arrangements were made to move through Ashby's Gap, and in a very few hours the whole army was in motion.

* A true incident.

6*

Stuart picketed the rear so admirably from toward Bunker
Hill, by Smithfield, to Rippon and the Shenandoah, that a mouse
could not get through ; and, safely moving within this magic cordon, which kept off all intruders, Johnston's column left Winchester, passed through Millwood, forded the Shenandoah at Berry's Ferry, and defiled through the Gap.

The men were crazy with delight, singing and dancing as they
went along.   The prospect of a battle seemed to intoxicate them.

Stuart brought up the rear, passing last through the Gap ; and
then pushed on to the front.

The movement by the Little River turnpike was found impracticable, and at Piedmont Station, on the Manassas Gap Railroad,
the bulk of the infantry took the cars ; the rest were to follow.
Jackson's brigade went by the first train ; we disembarked in the
evening at Manassas, and the column was marched to a wood of
pines in rear of Mitchell's Ford.

The roar of artillery which greeted us as we approached indicated that the adversaries were face to face, and the decisive
struggle about to begin.

XXXVIII.

TWO BROTHERS.

SHALL I tell you, my dear reader, what I saw of the battle of
Manassas ?   It possesses a perennial interest; but then it is so
familiar!   Still I can't well omit some notice of it in these memoirs of my times.   Those who know it all by heart can turn the
leaf.

It was about three in the morning, on the famous 21st, that I
was waked by General Jackson as I lay under a tree, and sent
with a message to General Johnston.

Your toilet is not a heavy affair on the eve of a battle: I had
only to take my riding-cape, buckle on my belt, and rub my eyes.
Then I mounted, and set out for the farm-house where Johnston
and Beauregard had established their joint head-quarters.

The place was in a great bustle. To the fences and the boughs of the trees were affixed the horses of the staff and couriers, ready saddled; and mounted men constantly went and came. A sullen gun, at intervals, from the front, mingled with the clatter of sabres and the sound of horses' hoofs.

The two Generals, were closeted in an inner room. My name was sent in, and in ten minutes I was informed that I could enter.

Generals Johnston and Beauregard were seated at a table, upon which was spread a topographical map of the region, and the former rested his finger upon Stonebridge.

"This is the key of the position," he said. "I think the attack will be here, General."

I saluted, and was about to deliver my message, when a dispatch was brought in. Beauregard read it with attention.

"The enemy are moving in heavy force to the left," he said, in a low tone. "Captain Mordaunt's scouts report the main body massing between Centreville and Stonebridge."

As he spoke his face glowed.

"Now is the time, General," he said. "Ewell and Bonham can strike their flank and rear before sunrise."

Johnston inclined his head.

"Then, no time is to be lost, General."

This was the authorization for which Beauregard evidently waited. In an instant he had ordered couriers, and was ardently dictating orders to his adjutant. I could not help hearing them. The orders directed the officers commanding the right and centre to hold themselves ready to advance at a moment's notice, and attack the Federal rear at Centreville.

Meanwhile, I had delivered my message, which referred to the disposition of the artillery, and, receiving the orders of General Johnston, hastened to return. I had scarcely reached camp, and communicated the result of my mission, when the roar of artillery was heard from the direction of Stonebridge; and Jackson ordered his brigade to be gotten under arms.

Orders soon came for him to move and re-enforce Longstreet, at Blackburn's Ford, below. Before the troops had reached that

point, new orders arrived, directing him to go to the assistance
of General Cocke, near Stonebridge. As the column approached
this point the sun rose, and from the extensive plateau in front
came the sharp crack of musketry. The roar of artillery from
beyond the stream had continued steadily.

"This must be only a demonstration," muttered Jackson,
and, turning round, he directed me to ride toward Sudley Ford,
and ascertain if any movement was taking place in that direction.

I hastened to obey, and, striking across into the Sudley-Brents-
ville road, was soon at the ford, where I found Mordaunt sullenly
falling back, and disputing the ground inch by inch, with an overwhelming column advancing rapidly from the woods beyond. As
I joined him, a storm of bullets came hissing from a dark line
rapidly advancing, and a portion of the cavalry came back at a
gallop. Mordaunt's face flushed hot, and, drawing his sabre, he
thundered:

"I will kill the first man who attempts to pass me! Form line.
I am falling back—I am not running!"

His voice had its effect; line was formed facing the enemy,
and the men slowly fell back fighting.

"Well, Surry," said Mordaunt, with entire coolness, "things
are going on badly in this part of the field, and, unless General
Beauregard hurries troops here, he will be flanked and driven out
of his defences on Manassas. There is nothing to check the
enemy. I will die here, if necessary; but it is perfectly useless.
What can I do with one company? That column advancing
numbers at least thirty thousand. I have sent courier after
courier, but yet no reply."

"I will see that General Johnston knows the extent of the
danger." And I went back rapidly to report it.

Reaching Colonel Evans first, near Stonebridge, I informed
him of the state of affairs, and he instantly put his command—
about one regiment—in motion, and advanced to check the
enemy.

Then I found General Jackson, and gave him the intelligence.
He at once sent a staff officer, on a fresh horse, to Johnston:

and at that moment a long roar of musketry beyond the hill announced that Evans had engaged the enemy.

It steadily increased in intensity, but did not recede or approach. Evans was evidently holding his ground. In an hour, however, it drew nearer, and the meaning of this was unmistakable. Then all at once the glitter of bayonets was seen behind us, and Bee and Bartow appeared, rapidly moving to the threatened point.

The troops pressed on with cheers—they were seen to form line of battle on the Henry House hill—then they disappeared beneath the crest, and the redoubled roar of musketry told that Bee had engaged the enemy.

The firing from that moment became incessant, and indicated a desperate conflict. It continued for more than an hour. Then it rapidly approached, and the cheers of the Federal troops echoed among the hills. Bee was evidently falling back.

Jackson listened with an unmoved countenance, but a glitter of the eye, which indicated much in him. All at once the roar of triumph drew nearer—Bee's men began to appear, straggling over the hill.

"Attention!" came in Jackson's curt tones, and the men, who had been lying down, rose to their feet and formed line of battle.

"Ride to General Bee, Captain, and inform him I am coming to re-enforce him," said Jackson.

And I hastened, at a gallop, toward the firing. A regiment was forming line of battle along the Warrenton road, just to the right of the Stone House.

"What command is this?" I asked of one of the men.

"The Hampton Legion."

"What number?"

"Six hundred muskets."

I rode on rapidly, passing hundreds of stragglers. The roar of guns was now near at hand—incessant, obstinate; and Bee was falling back in utter confusion. His broken lines were torn by shell, canister, and musketry—the struggle was over—the triumphant enemy were pressing forward with wild cheers.

Suddenly, I heard the sharp crack of Hampton's skirmishers on the right, and Bee rode up, breathing heavily, covered with dust and sweat, and holding in his hand his drawn sword, with which he had been rallying his men. I knew him very well, and at once delivered my message.

"Thank God!" he replied, hoarsely. "They have broken my line to pieces—by pure weight of numbers. Men never fought better. What troops are those, Captain, in the road, yonder?"

"The Hampton Legion."

"Oblige me by telling Colonel Hampton he must hold his position until entirely flanked—to the very last."

I obeyed, and reached Hampton just as a heavy column pressed down from the direction of Red House Ford and opened fire upon him.

"Present my respects to General Bee," said Colonel Hampton, a tall and fine-looking man, with an air of entire coolness, "and tell him that I hope to give a good account of the force in my front. This position will soon be flanked, however, and I shall be compelled to fall back."

A volley from the enemy came as he spoke, and he ordered his men to rise and fire.

The effect was decisive. The six hundred muskets were discharged almost like a single piece, and the Federal line in front broke, and retreated under cover of the high ground in their rear.

I hastened back, and found Bee making desperate efforts to rally his men. Sword in hand, he rode among them, beseeching them by all they held dear to re-form their line. His voice was scarcely heard in the roar of battle, and the enemy pressed on, driving the Southern lines back in utter disorder.

Finally, they reached the ground near the Stone House I had visited with Mordaunt, and planted their artillery in the road, forcing Hampton to fall back. Then there was nothing further to resist their advance, and Bee, with a look of despair, galloped in the direction of Jackson. I was with him, and heard the brave Carolinian groan out, as they came face to face:

"General, they are beating us back!"

Jackson looked for an instant toward the enemy, his lips moved, and he said, coolly:

"Sir, we will give them the bayonet."

Bee seemed to gather new resolution from these words, and, galloping toward his straggling lines, shouted:

"Look! Yonder stands Jackson, like a stone wall. Let us determine to die here, and we will conquer!"

Jackson had, meanwhile, turned to me, and said, with his habitual coolness:

"Captain, go to the colonels of all my regiments, and tell them that my instructions are, as soon as the enemy gets close enough, say within fifty yards, to charge with the bayonet."*

This order I conveyed to the different colonels, as they formed their lines along the eastern crest of the Henry House hill. The men were ordered to lie down, two pieces of artillery were thrown forward and opened fire, and under their protection Bee formed his shattered line in a ravine on Jackson's right.

In face of this new line of battle the enemy did not immediately advance. They were checked, and the day was saved.

I was looking across the hills to the left, where Mordaunt's cavalry was seen falling back to take position on the flank, when Jackson called me and said:

"General Johnston must know exactly the condition of things here. Present my compliments to him, and tell him that the enemy are checked, but I must have re-enforcements. If this hill is lost, all is lost. I am going to seize and hold it; but I must be supported. Bee is overwhelmed. Hampton is driven back. If the enemy fortify yonder, all is over. Explain this, and lose no time."

In half an hour I was at Johnston's head-quarters, still at the farm-house opposite Mitchell's Ford. He and Beauregard were in the saddle, anxiously listening to the continuous fire from the left.

"Well, Captain," came from Beauregard, the more ardent of the two.

* His orders.

I saluted, and explained the state of things near Stonebridge. It evidently produced a deep impression upon both
officers.

"All now depends upon the movement of the right and
centre," muttered Beauregard, looking in the direction of Centreville. " Why don't the firing commence ?"

"I fear it is too late," was Johnston's cool reply.

At the same moment, a staff-officer came up, his horse foaming.

" Well, Major.?" exclaimed Beauregard.

"General Ewell never received your order, sir, and General
Bonham only just now."

Beauregard made a gesture in which it was impossible to say
whether anger or disappointment predominated.

" We must fight it out on the left," said Johnston. " Counter-
mand the orders to Ewell and Bonham, General, and let us ride
to where the fight is going on."

In five minutes, the two generals were proceeding at full gallop toward the scene of action.

They arrived at the moment when the enemy had gained possession of the Henry House hill, and were pressing forward to attack Jackson, whose two pieces of artillery were steadily firing in
front of his line.

The attention of the two generals was immediately turned to
the disordered ranks of Bee. Johnston seized the colors of a
Southern regiment, and, leading the men forward, re-formed their
line in face of a heavy fire. Beauregard meanwhile galloped up
and down the lines, his swarthy face glowing, his eyes flashing,
his sonorous voice calling upon the men to stand their ground.
He presented at this moment a splendid picture. The fire of the
born soldier flamed in his regard, and his martial spirit rode, as
it were, upon the wave of battle, rejoicing in the storm.

Under the passionate appeals of the two commanders, the men
speedily rallied, and line of battle was at once formed. Other
regiments and additional artillery had hurried forward, and,
thanks to the bold stand made by Jackson, time had been given
for something like an adequate force to arrive. It amounted, as

I afterward discovered, to only about six or seven thousand men; but this was enough to show fight until re-enforcements came.

The enemy had now formed a long and heavy line of battle, upon the Henry House hill, and their artillery crowned every knoll. They continued to pour a heavy fire of all arms upon the Southern line, and the only response was from two or three batteries, under Colonel Pendleton, in Jackson's immediate front. These were just under the crest, and engaged the Federal batteries at close range.

Jackson was riding up and down behind them, watching the fire.

"I expect these boys will all be killed," he muttered; "but the occasion demands the sacrifice."

As he spoke, a fragment of shell struck him in the hand, and I saw the blood flow.

"You are hurt, General," I exclaimed.

"It is nothing," he said, wrapping his handkerchief around it; and, seeing that the attention of the men had been called to it, he rode up and down the line, repeating quietly, "Steady, boys, steady! all's well!"

The fire now became very heavy, and the enemy were steadily advancing. All at once an officer galloped up, and said, in great agitation :

"General, the day is going against us."

Such things peculiarly displeased Jackson. He gave the officer a quick glance from beneath his old faded cap—such a glance as I for one should not have liked to encounter—and said, in his curtest and gruffest tones :

"If you think so, sir, you had better say nothing about it!"

The officer turned away, with a sudden flush upon his countenance. At the same moment, a loud cheer on the left attracted our attention, and we saw Colonel Cumming, commanding one of the regiments of the brigade, charge and capture a Federal battery.

Jackson's face glowed, and he uttered an exclamation which proved that all the soldier was aroused in him. But the triumph was short-lived. Cumming could not hold the battery in face of the withering fire directed upon him, and we saw him slowly fall back, as the enemy's whole line swept forward.

It was at this moment that I discerned for the first time in Jackson the supreme attributes of the man of military genius. He seemed to rise under pressure, and to grow cooler and more invincible as peril drew near. The air was full of balls, the whole scene was one glare of musketry and cannon, and on all sides were heard groans, cheers, and shouts of triumph or despair; but it was impossible to discern upon his face any traces whatever of emotion. It was like a mask of bronze; and his movements were as calm and measured as if upon parade. In three minutes now the shock must come, I saw plainly; but Jackson appeared as indifferent as though perfectly certain of the result.

The long, dark line pressed on, blazing from end to end, and the artillery was withdrawn at a gallop. It passed around the right of the line, and then I knew that the moment had come for the decisive struggle.

Rushing forward with triumphant cheers, the Federal line was within about seventy-five yards, when I heard Jackson command, "Charge with the bayonet!"

The men responded with the wildest ardor, delivered a staggering volley as they rose to their feet, and then rushed up the slope.

This movement was executed with such suddenness and determination, that the Federal line recoiled and gave way as the Southerners dashed upon them. The fire which greeted them was frightful, but the charge was not checked; and in five minutes Jackson had pierced the Federal centre, and his troops were fighting on the ground near the Henry House.

The men never fought better; and, as one after another fell, the ranks closed up, and the troops kept to their work like veterans instead of recruits. The boys were even more ardent than the men; and, as I was carrying an order to the right, I heard the voice of young Charley Beverley, with whom I had become well acquainted, though I have not before mentioned the fact, call out to me in great glee:

"Look, Captain, look! We are driving 'em!"

The young fellow fired his musket as he spoke; but the next moment I heard him utter a groan, and saw him stagger.

"What's the matter, Charley?"

"Only a scratch," he replied, turning pale, and trying to smile. I had just time to throw myself from my horse and catch him in my arms before he fell. He had been shot through the arm.

Two men whom I called carried him to the rear. I had no time to attend to him further. Remounting my horse, I hastened to find Colonel Hampton, near the Henry House. As I went on, some men were bearing off General Bee. I had no time to speak to the mortally wounded officer; but I heard him, as I passed, murmur, "Tell my men not to give up the field!"

Colonel Hampton was rushing forward at the head of his men, when, just as I reached him, he was struck and fell. The great Carolinian attempted to rise, but strength failed him, and, waving his sword for his line to press on, he was borne from the field.

At the same moment I felt my horse stagger—then he fell. A ball had pierced his chest, and I found myself on foot. The close roar of musketry drowned every other sound, and officers and men were falling all around me.

All at once I saw, not far from me, one of the companies of the brigade which was entirely unofficered, and began to waver. I ran in the direction of it, and found the men only wanted some one to lead them. At a word they closed up, and advanced unbroken, on the Federal line, then rapidly pushing forward.

So close were the opposing lines at this critical moment, that, in spite of the dense smoke, I could see almost the "whites of their eyes." Suddenly a chill, like that of death, passed through my frame, and my blood ran cold: in the officer leading a company of Federal infantry directly in front of me, I recognized my younger brother Will.

He was on foot in front of the line, waving his sword and cheering wildly. All at once, as the smoke drifted, his eyes encountered my own; and I saw, in an instant, that he had recognized me.

He turned pale, and his sword sank. The cry died away on

his lips. At that instant, I felt a sharp pain in my breast, and a sort of cloud passed before my eyes. When I opened them, I saw that the Federal line had swept past me, driving back the company I had commanded; and bending over me I saw the pale face of my brother. He supported my head upon his shoulder, and with his right hand was holding a white handkerchief to my breast, which was bleeding profusely.

"Brother!" exclaimed the boy, for he was hardly more, "God forgive me!—you are shot—mortally wounded—and by my own men!"

I tried to smile.

"I'm afraid they've done for me, Will," was all I could say, for the faint feeling came back, and my voice died away.

"How could I know!—to think that we should meet thus!—to kill you, brother," he used my old name, "when I love you more than the whole world!—when I would die for you!"

And I heard a choking sob, mingled with a groan, as, straining me close to his bosom, he pressed to my cheek his face wet with tears.

Strange meeting of two brothers after years of separation! But the interview quickly terminated. The battle had roared on, and the storm of balls swept over us, as, thus lost in the bloody gulf of conflict, we had spoken with the old love and tenderness to each other. Now we were to be torn asunder again. The Federal line, which had advanced triumphantly a moment before, was now driven back. The long crash of musketry from Jackson's line filled the air; and suddenly my brother's company was seen retreating in disorder.

He wrung his hands, and uttered a sob of agony.

"What can I do, brother!" he exclaimed. "If I stay here, I am a prisoner—worse still, disgraced! But I would rather die than leave you dying here!"

I rose upon one arm and pointed to his men.

"Go, Will," I said; "a Surry can't desert his colors. It's not your fault that I am shot. Go!—in a moment you will be a prisoner!"

A sort of convulsion passed over the youthful face, and his

bosom shook. He enclosed me in his arms, and kissed me as he had done when we were children.

"You are right, brother," he said, gloomily. "Farewell! I am going yonder to die!"

With these words he left me, and his figure disappeared amid the smoke.

All that I remember after this was a frightful commingling of cheers, yells, groans, and dying cries, over which rose the heavy roar of artillery and the long, deafening roll of musketry. For nearly an hour, the opposing lines seemed staggering to and fro on the extensive plateau, in a breast-to-breast struggle for its possession. All that I could make out distinctly was, that the Southern lines still held their ground.

Then a quicker and heavier fire came from the flanks; it advanced; wild cheers rose from the men of Jackson near, and I knew that our re-enforcements had arrived, and that the enemy were giving way. The roar around me redoubled, and all the furies seemed to be let loose. It was no longer a battle, but a sort of Pandemonium. But the wild turmoil of battle steadily receded westward; the Southern lines were seen sweeping forward like a huge wave; and then I knew that the Federal line of battle was broken from end to end of the great field.

I half rose, and, clutching the bloody handkerchief which Will had dropped, tried to wave it above me and cheer.

As I did so, the blood gushed over my bosom—a cloud passed before my eyes, and, falling heavily back, I lost consciousness.

That is all I remember, my dear reader, of this famous battle.

XXXIX.

ELM COTTAGE AND ITS INMATES.

I HAD afterward a faint recollection of being lifted in the arms of some one, and then of travelling somewhere in a carriage, and being carried into a house through a porch covered with flowers. I thought it was all a dream when I saw bending cver me, with flushed cheeks, a figure which resembled that of May Beverley.

It was that young lady in person. Not to weary you with long explanations, my dear reader, I was at Elm Cottage, near White Plains, a small vine-embowered mansion belonging to Mrs. Fitzhugh, an excellent old lady, and a sister of Mrs. Beverley, of The Oaks. The entire family from The Oaks had come down to be near Charley, in case he was wounded in the battle about to be fought; the Colonel had speedily discovered him, and the youth had been promptly moved. As the carriage was leaving the field, Charley saw me lying beneath the tree to which I had been carried, cried out that I had been his friend, and no urging was necessary to induce the old Colonel to take charge of me. So I was to be nursed by the gentle hands of women, and not by "detailed men" in a hospital.

I am not going to bore the reader with my experiences of the effect of a gunshot wound. Everybody, including the surgeon who attended me, thought I would certainly die, but I did not. I had a burning fever, and, I have no doubt, got at one time to the very brink of the grave—but there the clutch of the Death Angel relaxed. My wound began to heal.

There were some incidents connected with this fever, however, which were far from unpleasant. I could not for the life of me determine, at the moment, whether I dreamed them or they actually occurred.

The figure of May Beverley haunted me, and I thought that she was almost constantly sitting by my bed, holding my thin hand, and looking at me with tears in her eyes. When she disappeared, her place was taken by Violet Grafton; and her silken ringlets in turn faded away to be replaced by the tender face of my young sister Annie and the mild eyes of my father.

When I grew stronger, and the fever left me, I knew that all these figures were real. Violet Grafton had been conducted to Mrs. Fitzhugh's by Mordaunt, on the night when they left Beauregard's head-quarters, and my father had hastened with Annie from Eagle's-Nest.

It was surrounded by all these kind faces that I slowly began to recover. Charley was nearly well already, went about with his arm in a very handsome sling, and distributed his jokes, anecdotes, and warlike reminiscences on every side, especially in the direction of Miss Annie Surry, between whom and the youth seemed to exist the very best understanding.

It really did appear at one time that relations equally pleasing were going to be established between two other persons. May Beverley was much changed, and I longed, but was afraid, to ask whether she had broken her repulsive contract. You have seen her, my dear reader, during those days at The Oaks. She was now a very different person. Surely something had occurred to make her future less threatening! In her eyes, her smile, every movement of her person, there was an exquisite gayety which I had never seen before. Her glance at times was full of such sweetness, that it very nearly intoxicated the poor invalid who met it. He watched every motion of the slender and graceful figure—her voice was like music to him: his state of mind was imbecile in the very highest degree! If her smile disappeared, it was to give way to tears at some pathetic story or some incident of heroism. Then her bosom heaved, her cheeks filled with blushes, and a pensive languor seemed to weigh down the beautiful head. When, drying her eyes, she turned and looked at me with a smile, those great violet orbs made my pulses leap. I was a thousand times more enthralled than before.

It is the " old story of a man and a woman " which I am relating, you see, reader. Has the fable never been narrated of *you?* My little drama was played, however, under somewhat peculiar circumstances.

Did you ever lie upon a sofa, my dear reader, while recovering from a gunshot wound, and pass the hours listening to a musical voice reading to you—the voice of the woman you loved, but who, unfortunately, was engaged to another individual? The sensation is peculiar. You feel in a delightful state of uncertainty as to your *status* in the eyes of the fair damsel. That voice is exquisitely musical, but it is probably going soon to say "I will," where that reply is called for in the Form for the Solemnization of Matrimony, and *you* are not going to be the individual to make the other responses. Those eyes are charming, and look at you at times in a manner which makes your heart beat; but they may have a richer light still to bestow upon that hateful personage known in pathetic love-songs as "Another." Those lips, so red and soft, which thrill you, at certain moments, with their sweet and tender smile, you think, with a groan of rage and jealousy, to what uses they may be put, and mutter, if you are poetically inclined:

> " Dear as remembered kisses after death,
> And sweet as *those by hopeless fancy feigned,*
> *On lips that are for others.*"

That obstinate "Another" thus thrusts himself in, you see, on all occasions. You are called upon to decide upon your course with the promptness of a general in face of the enemy. Will you brace yourself against a "hopeless attachment," and "tear her image from your heart " (see numerous romances), or will you accept the goods provided by the kind immortals, close your eyes to the past and future, and, seeing nothing but the face beside you, let your bark drift on wherever the waves may bear it?

—I drifted.

So, amid the songs of birds and the perfume of a thousand flowers, with May Beverley reading "old romances " to me, I passed the happy hours of my convalescence. But the cloud was coming—the storm approached. Suddenly one day, all the sunny light disappeared from May Beverley's face; her girlish happiness and abandon vanished: the beautiful brow of the young lady was overclouded, and the fair Hebe "stiffened into stone."

There had come to the vine-embowered cottage of Mrs. Fitzhugh a superbly clad officer, in a new uniform all shining with gold braid—and this officer was Captain Frederick Baskerville, Volunteer Aide-de-Camp to some general of Beauregard's army. In regard to Captain Baskerville, Volunteer A. D. C., the reader knows that I am not a fair witness. But others said that he never would go into action. The taunts, even before him, of the young ladies of the country, whose brothers were in the army, had induced him to seek his easy position, it was said; but he was always sick or on furlough. Jealousy! envy! illiberality! I hear my readers exclaim. Doubtless—for who ever could see any merit in a rival? It was curious, however, that nobody that knew this man could bear him.

The person who liked him least of all, apparently, was May Beverley. She treated him with unmistakable coldness—but I wish to guard the reader from supposing that she was much more cordial in her demeanor toward another person. From that unlucky moment when Captain Baskerville made his appearance, all the young lady's sunny smiles disappeared; the thaw stopped; she froze again.

No sickness lasts forever, and you finally recover, even from a bullet through the lungs. Soon after the appearance of Bas-kerville at Elm Cottage, the Beverleys returned to The Oaks, and very soon thereafter I set out with my father and sister in the rickety old family carriage for Eagle's-Nest.

I have said nothing of Violet Grafton, and yet she had been like a ministering angel to me in my illness. She had become a decided favorite with Mrs. Fitzhugh, a woman of great warmth of heart and strength of character, who liked or disliked you vigorously, and "spoke her mind" on all occasions; and this excellent lady now declared that Violet should not leave her. "She is a perfect darling," said the old lady, busily knitting, "and never shall want a home as long as I have one." So the beautiful girl seemed moored in a serene port at last, secure from storms. There was but one other member of the household, Miss Henrietta Fitzhugh, niece of the old lady, and a perfect witch of gayety and abandon. Scarcely sixteen, she already began to "make eyes" at the male sex, and had the contagious playfulness of a kitten. I cannot speak further of Miss Henrietta at this time; she will probably reappear on the scene. I bid all these kind friends farewell, enter the old carriage, and, traversing Fauquier and Stafford, we cross the Rappahannock and are safely landed at Eagle's-Nest.

XL.

A CHAPTER ENTIRELY WITHOUT INCIDENT.

It was already autumn when we reached Eagle's-Nest, and the
September days had begun to tint the woods with the rich colors of the fall.   The old house, perched upon its lofty hill above
the Rappahannock, seemed to hold out arms of welcome; and I
greeted all the old familiar scenes and sights with the ardor of an
exile coming home, once more, after years of absence.

The sight of the ancient mansion, buried in its trees, was

> " Welcome as the hand
> Of brother in a foreign land,"

as says the sweetest and most musical—to my ear, at least—of all
the Northern poets; and I know not what emotion of boyish
yearning came to me as I entered the old hall, and murmured,
" After all, there is nothing like home!"

The old pointer on the porch came forward frisking to receive my salutation; the portraits seemed to smile upon me; and
as I passed the picture of Philip Surry the cavalier, I thought the
eyes followed and spoke to me.

My wound was slow in healing, and I was driven to my books
for amusement.   What a world of thought and emotion lies open
at the feet of the student!   Books are the depositories of the
thoughts of the great—and these thoughts, more than all else,
stimulate the intellect.   I have known some men, whose minds
were a very thin soil indeed, but who had read so much that a
very good crop was the result!   When the soil is naturally
strong, the culture of the student makes the intellectual giant.

Unfortunately, the present writer read only for amusement,
and had an "ill-regulated mind."   It was the honey that I sought,
not the fruit; and in the sunny mornings, in my chair upon the
portico, it was a volume of romance or poetry, not history or
philosophy, which enabled me to pass the hours so pleasantly.

Sometimes the open book lay for hours almost on my knee,
and I mused upon a hundred things—upon my visit to the Wil-

derness, Violet Grafton, Mordaunt, May Beverley, the meeting
with Will, and then came the gay laugh of Stuart breaking on
the silence, and heard almost with the material ear.   The trees
rustled in the fresh September airs; Annie ran to place in my
button-hole a bunch of autumn flowers; the great river flowed
below the hills—a ribbon of silver on a tissue of emerald; and
Eagle's-Nest, and all thereunto appertaining, was a lazy, tranquil
picture of an old Virginia home.

With the advent of October I grew stronger, and finally ven-
tured out with my gun after the partridges.   Then, enamored
of the glorious days, I fitted up my boat, and went duck-shooting
on the Rappahannock.   One day, when I had gotten thoroughly
wet at this sport, I returned with a hot feeling about the head.
On the next morning I could scarcely get out of bed, and that
evening had a burning fever.

It lasted me almost until spring, and brought me to death's
door.

During my illness I heard little of politics or war.   I only knew
that the North had determined to carry on hostilities with greater
energy than ever, and that immense armaments were marshal-
ling by land and sea to force the South back into the Union.
Johnston and Beauregard remained at Centreville, facing the Federal army, now commanded by General McClellan; and Jackson
had been appointed Major-General, and, proceeding to Winchester, had made an expedition against the enemy on the Upper Potomac, which had resulted in their retreat from that region.   I
had received a letter from him, enclosing an official document,
and this had proved to be my appointment as Major, which, I had
no doubt, his friendship had secured for me.

Among the figures which peopled my musings, you will no
doubt understand, my dear reader, that a certain young lady had
a prominent place.   I have not insisted upon raving about her,
but she was seldom out of my mind.   I always got back, however, after my extensive trains of reflection, to the point from
which I started—that my best plan was, to stay away from her.
"It is for every young lady to decide her own destiny," I muttered with gloomy pride; "and she has decided to marry that

man. I would like to go and cut his throat, but that would not
mend matters!" And, turning over in my bed, I would try to
think of something else.

In February I left my bed, and by the first of March had nearly
regained my strength. My purpose was to return at the earliest
possible moment to my duties, and, thanks to my father, I was
supplied with a good horse to replace those which I had lost.

My servant had followed me from Manassas to Elm Cottage,
and from Elm Cottage to Eagle's-Nest. He responded with
grins to my announcement that I was ready to return to camp,
the lazy life of which the sable individual dearly loved; and in
the first week of March I set out to rejoin General Jackson.

This time I had not the sign of an incident upon the way, and
I did not stop at The Oaks. Crossing the Blue Ridge at Ashby's
Gap, and passing through the little village of Millwood without
drawing rein, I was directed to, and on a raw March evening
reached, General Jackson's head-quarters near Winchester.

XLI.

THE DISPATCH FROM RICHMOND.

WHEN I entered his tent, Jackson was reading his Bible, which
rested on his knees. At sight of me, he closed the volume, and,
rising, cordially pressed my hand, offering, after his habitual
fashion, to take my hat.

"I am pleased to see you again, Captain, or Major, as I must
now call you," he said, smiling; "your escape has been truly
providential."

"Thanks, General, for your good wishes, and my appointment,
which I suspect I owe to your friendship. Are you well of your
own wound?"

"Entirely; it was a trifle. I have reason to be thankful, when
so many brave men fell. Did you receive a message by flag of
truce from your brother? I mean Lieutenant Surry, of the
United States Army."

"Thank you, General—yes; and replied to it."
A fact of which I have neglected to speak. Will announced that he was unhurt; and I had written from Eagle's-Nest.

Jackson shook his head, and said:

"This is a most unhappy conflict; and the enemy seem bent upon our complete destruction. But the South must do her duty and trust in Providence. I shall try to hold this region; but my force is wholly inadequate."

"I do not ask your plans, General, but would like to know the state of affairs."

"It is simple : the army is reorganizing—a bad arrangement; and my plan is to put on as bold a front as possible, until the troops are in a condition to take the field. What I desire is, to hold my ground until we can advance then; with God's blessing, let us make thorough work of it!"*

"What force has the enemy, General?"

"Nearly fifty thousand men. General Banks is at Charlestown with about thirty-five thousand. General Kelly, succeeding Lander at Paw-paw, with about eleven thousand; and others are distributed along the Potomac."

"Why, that is sufficient to swallow us!"

"I do not feel discouraged; and we may now look for war in earnest.* I have long ago made up my mind on the point, Major. If this Valley is lost, all is lost!* And, in defending it, I gratify my own feelings. It contains the homes of my brave soldiers;* and, with God's blessing, I intend to hold every foot of it, whatever may be the force that is brought against me!"

I listened in silence, and more than ever admired this determined leader.

"It is incredible to me, General," I said, "that the Government does not send you more troops. They must understand as well as you do that, if the enemy gain the upper Valley, Richmond will be seriously threatened."

The General shook his head.

* His words.

"I don't think they have a great deal of confidence in me, Major," he said; "and I must do what I can with the force I have."

"Nearly fifty thousand to four thousand! It is monstrous, General!"

"Our place is to fight, not to count numbers. I intend to oppose the advance of the enemy by every means in my power: the rest I leave in the hands of Providence."

Soon afterward, I rose to take my leave.

"To-morrow, if you have nothing for me to do, I will ride over and see my friends in the First Brigade, General," I said.

Jackson smiled.

"You must not call it the First Brigade, Major."

"Why not, General?"

"Do you remember General Bee's exclamation at Manassas, as he was rallying his men?"

"Perfectly, sir: he pointed to you, and compared you to a stone wall."

"I see you remember the very word. Well, the men insist upon giving me the nickname of Stonewall; and they call the old brigade the 'Stonewall Brigade.'"

"They deserve the name."

"True; they are a noble body of men. The name belongs to them, not to me; and, after this war, the survivors will be proud to say, 'I was a member of the Stonewall Brigade,' to their children."*

So it was the "Stonewall," not the "First," Brigade, I visited next day, to greet my many old friends there. The aspect of the camps at this time was inexpressibly dreary. They were situated in the great fields north of the town, where the March winds had full sweep; and, on the morning of my visit, a gust came which prostrated the small "A" tents of a whole regiment. Every thing was bare, bleak, chill, and gloomy. When I reflected that Jackson's only dependence was the small and ragged force shivering in these dilapidated tents, whose torn canvas fluttered drearily in the wind, my heart sank.

* His words.

The troops, however, were in perfectly good spirits. I never saw men more ragged or merrier. The smoky canvas dens resounded with songs—and I well remember the gay group around the smouldering sticks in front of our tent, listening to a song whose burden was:

"Oh! he was the boy with the auburn hair,
And his name it was MacElroy."

It was sung by a brave youth of the Second Virginia, who afterward passed gallantly through nearly every battle fought in Virginia; became orderly sergeant of his company; and, when it was swept away nearly to the last man, continued to call the roll regularly every morning, going conscientiously over the names of the dead and absent. The "Here!" which he uttered, when calling his own name, was often the sole response to this singular roll-call.

After passing some hours with my friends, I left them, and rode forward to look at the ground north of Winchester, where the enemy would probably make their attack.

I was riding along the chill, dreary, and wind-swept turnpike, whose pulverized particles rose with every gust and blinded the eyes, when a courier appeared, coming at full speed from the direction of Martinsburg, and soon reached me.

"What news?" I said.

"The enemy are advancing, Major."

"From Martinsburg?"

"And Charlestown, both."

"Who are you from?" I called after him as he receded.

"Colonel Ashby."

The next moment he disappeared in a dust-cloud.

I at once turned my horse's head, and rode back to General Jackson. When I arrived I found him calmly engaged in issuing orders for the disposition of his forces. The staff were soon riding in every direction, and I assisted in the transmission of the orders—disposing the regiments as directed, and returning toward nightfall.

So rapid had been the enemy's advance that their infantry

were now engaged with our cavalry only a few miles from the town. The firing was rapid and continuous, and it was soon evident that the cavalry required support. A force of infantry was accordingly sent forward to their assistance, and Jackson then drew up his entire command in line of battle, evidently determined to give battle, whatever force was brought against him.

I was riding with him about nightfall, when the firing in front had ceased, and he said, with that quick glitter of the eye which always showed that he was aroused:

"I do not intend to leave Winchester without a fight. With the blessing of Providence, I believe I can check, if not drive back, the enemy's force. At all events, Major, I am going to try."

He soon afterward rode back to head-quarters, drank a glass of milk, and said to me:

"I am going into Winchester, Major. If you would like to accompany me, I will make you acquainted with a most estimable family, and we can talk upon the way."

"I will be very glad to go, General," was my reply, and we set forward.

Jackson stopped before a neat house, on one of the side streets, and, fixing his bridle to the fence, entered the house, where he was received and greeted with great cordiality by a clerical-looking gentleman and his family.

Our host was in fact the Rev. Mr. G——, of the Presbyterian Church, and those who knew the preference which Jackson always exhibited for the society of clergymen will not be surprised at hearing that Mr. G—— was his chosen friend.

An hour then passed in friendly conversation, and Jackson then said:

"With your permission, Mr. G——, I will now read a chapter in the Bible, and offer a prayer."

"I will be glad if you would, General."

The books were brought; Jackson read a chapter with great solemnity, and then all knelt, and he offered up a fervent prayer.

When he rose his features were slightly flushed, and I observed an animation in his eyes which was unusual.

He stood for a moment looking in silence at the family, who were great favorites with him, and then, with a martial smile upon his features, suddenly said:

"Would you like me to tell you a secret, my friends?"

"What is it, General?"

"And yet it will be against all military rules."

Expectation was in every eye.

"I am going to attack the enemy to-night."

A flutter ran through the auditory.

"My force is small," he continued with animation, "but it will be doubled by the suddenness of the attack. Shall I prove myself a very bad General by telling you exactly what I design? Well, I am going to flank them on the Martinsburg road, in one hour from this time! You see that unless you can pass my pickets within that time, and warn them, no harm is done by this disclosure. Yes!" he added, with something almost like joy in his face, "I shall attack suddenly with my whole force—I shall drive them back—and our dear old Winchester will not be at their mercy!"

After a few more words, uttered in the same animated tone—I had never before seen him so elated—the General bade them good-night, and we left the house.*

Passing the telegraph office on Loudoun street, he called to the courier on duty there for any dispatches.

"This has just this moment arrived, General."

And a paper was handed him, which he read by the light streaming through the window.

Suddenly I saw his brows knit together, and something like gloom overspread his features. He crumpled up the paper in his hand, dropped it, after his habit, and, growling in the curtest tones, "Very good!" rode on, without uttering another word.

As we approached head-quarters he said curtly, in the stiffest of military tones:

"Major Surry, direct General Garnett and the other commanders to provide the troops immediately with three days' cooked rations, and hold themselves in readiness to move."

* Historical.

7*

I saluted, and Jackson added in the same tone:

"Then ride on to Colonel Ashby—you will find him on the Martinsburg road—and direct him to hold himself in readiness to withdraw his command through Winchester. I wish this movement to be deliberate—I will have no stampeding."

I set off rapidly, and, having transmitted the orders to the infantry commanders, rode on to the front, in search of Colonel Ashby. I had some curiosity to see this officer. During my visit to the First Brigade the conversation had turned upon his character, and I had found my friends quite enthusiastic on the subject. They seemed never to tire in relating his exploits. He was unresting, a sleepless war-machine, ready night and day for a raid, an attack, a battle—any thing, so that it had "fight" in it. While others slept, he was in the saddle. Seen to-day at one point on his swift white horse—to-morrow he would be at another place, sixty or seventy miles distant, inspecting his pickets, gaining information, and seeing that all was well. Utterly reckless in action, and liking most to "come to the sabre," he was represented as the soul of courtesy and kindness. His men idolized him—he was their *beau ideal* of chivalry, and the whole army chanted his praises.

It is not surprising, therefore, that I was glad of an opportunity to make the acquaintance of the Colonel. The opportunity was at hand. In the extensive fields on each side of the road were seen through the darkness the long lines of Ashby's cavalry in line of battle—every man in the saddle.

There was always something especially picturesque and war-like, to my eyes, in this spectacle of cavalry at night, drawn up to await or make an attack. While the infantry sleep, the dark figures on their black horses are watching. Only the clank of a sabre now and then, or the shrill neigh of some impatient animal, proves that the long line, silent there in the gloom, is not composed of phantoms.

But I had no time to indulge in thoughts of the picturesque. I inquired for Colonel Ashby; was directed to a tree, on a neighboring hill, where a small fire glimmered like a star, and soon reached it.

XLII.

ASHBY.

A FIGURE wrapped in a cloak was lying by the small fire, which the chill March night made far from uncomfortable.

I could see, as I approached, that this personage was reading in a small volume, and, as he raised his head, and the firelight fell upon his face, something on his cheek glittered.

As he rose, I recognized my travelling companion on the way to the Valley, who had carried before him the weak beggar-girl, and given me so cordial an invitation to visit him. His beard was blacker and heavier; his face more swarthy; his expression deeply sorrowful. But in the cavalry colonel of low stature, clad in gray, with sabre at side, and wearing a hat with a dark feather, I easily recognized my former companion.

"Colonel Ashby?" I said.

"Yes, sir."

"A message from General Jackson, Colonel. I am glad to see you again, but am afraid you don't remember me."

I drew nearer as I spoke, into the circle of light.

"Perfectly, Captain," he said, with much courtesy. "At first the darkness prevented me."

And, with frank and soldierly grace, he extended his hand, hastily turning aside as he did so, and passing his other hand across his eyes.

The voice of the speaker was profoundly sad; but in his air I observed the same high-bred courtesy and kindness.

In reply to my message, he now said:

"Then the General intends evacuating Winchester? I am sorry we are to do so without a fight, and I received orders to prepare for action in an hour. The General's directions will be observed, Captain—I beg your pardon—Major: I think I can promise that my command will fall back in good order."

"I have no doubt of it, Colonel. I am glad to see you in command of so fine a body of men."

"Yes, they are gallant fellows, but I fear I am no disciplina-rian."

I had thrown my bridle over a bough, and was warming my fingers at the fire.

My host gave me a seat beside him upon his cloak.

"I am afraid I disturb you in your reading," I said.

"Oh! not at all."

"What book absorbed you so?"

"I was reading in the Bible," he said, simply, but with his former sadness of tone; "it is the best resource for the unfortunate."

"Do you class yourself with such, Colonel?" I said. "I should think that, with so fine a command as yours, and your constitutional gayety—which I well remember you showed upon our ride last April—you would regard yourself as any thing but unfortunate."

"My 'constitutional gayety'?" he murmured. "I have none left."

The accent of the speaker, as he uttered these words, was so mournful, that for an instant I did not reply.

"Pardon me," I said, at length, "if I have touched some chord which jars. Had I supposed that my words would wound you"—

"It is nothing," he said, sadly; "but I am much changed since I saw you. I have lost my brother."

"Your brother?—but pardon me again. We will speak of something else."

"It does not pain me," he replied, with settled sadness. "At times it is a relief to speak of our sorrows to a friend—if you will let me call you such, sir."

I bowed with as much respect as sympathy, for the voice of this man went to my heart.

"When I saw you in April, Major," he said, in a low tone, "I had never had any thing to distress me, and doubtless I appeared to you gay enough. I lived at that time near Markham's, with my brother Richard, and we passed our lives together. I had no other friend. You should have known him: he was not a small, plain-looking man, like myself, but tall and imposing, with one eye of an eagle, and a soul that was the very mirror of truth and honor. A braver spirit never breathed—a kinder heart never beat in human bosom. I weary you—but I loved my brother," faltered the speaker, " he was all I had. You see now why I am not so gay as when we met down yonder. I cannot help it—my poor brother is dead."

A flush came to the swarthy features of the speaker, and the fire-light glittered on a tear which trembled in his eye.

"They killed him yonder, on the Potomac," he added, in a low voice, "where his company was scouting. He had only a few men with him, and was overpowered. He would not surrender—l never intend to, Major—but fell back, fighting a whole squadron. In crossing the railroad, his horse fell into one of those openings called 'cattle-stops'—before he could rise, they were upon him; and can you guess what happened?" said the speaker, in a lower tone than before.

"Tell me."

"They beat him to death—literally; riddling his breast with bullets as they did so."*

The tears were burnt up in the fire which blazed from Ashby's eyes as he spoke.

"I came up at the moment," he continued, more calmly, but with gloomy feeling in his voice, "and charged with a few men, killing eleven—but my brother was dead. We buried him on the banks of the Potomac. I am a strong man, but nearly fainted at his grave. Then I came back to my work."

The deep-toned and sorrowful accents died away. I understood all, and realized what a lady afterward said to me—"Ashby is now a devoted man."

He preserved silence for some moments, gazing into the fire; and then, drawing a long breath, as though to relieve himself of some weight upon his breast, made an evident effort to banish his gloom. His former air of gentleness returned, and he said, with an attempt to smile:

"Pardon all this egotism, Major. The unfortunate are too

* Historical

prone to cry out at times, and try to make others share their burden. It is hard to bear alone the weight of that 'perilous stuff that weighs upon the heart.'"

"Your words have affected me deeply," was my reply.

"But I should have spared you this recital. The world would be a gloomy place if every unlucky fellow insisted upon retailing his misfortunes to his friends."

"Sympathy, at least, is something."

"It is much—almost all that is worth living for. Life is not a very gay affair—in fact, I am rather tired of it. But let me cease this unprofitable talk. It would astonish the rough, brave fellows yonder, who think I am laying some plan to entrap the enemy. So we are to withdraw, and without a fight!"

"You will have charge of the rear."

"Of course; and I promise you that, if they press too hard, they shall feel my teeth. But I expected a regular battle. Well, that must come, too, before long."

I rose to go, and said, laughing:

"You are one of the few men I have met with who look forward with pleasure to a battle."

"I have never seen one—I was not at Manassas," he replied, gently.

"It is very poor amusement, Colonel, I assure you."

"But exciting?"

"Too much so."

"Can any excitement be too great?" was his sad reply, as I got into the saddle; "it enables us to forget."

And, saluting me with a movement full of friendly grace, the colonel of cavalry resumed his place by the fire, and recommenced reading his Bible.

XLIII.

"WILL NEVER LEAVE WINCHESTER WITHOUT A FIGHT —NEVER, NEVER!"

WHEN I returned to head-quarters it was nearly midnight.

The General was absent, and ascertaining that he had ridden into Winchester ten minutes before, I followed and came up with him on Loudoun street.

To my brief report, his only reply was, "Good." Then he rode on in silence. I had never seen him look more gloomy and dejected. Supposing that he was going to pay some private visit I said:

"Any thing further for me to do, General?"

He shook his head.

"I will, then, return to head-quarters."

"Wait a moment—we will ride back together."

And turning out of Loudoun street, he stopped before Mr. G——'s again.

"Come in," he said, in his brief voice.

I entered with him, and, as I had expected, found that no one had retired. The announcement of the intended attack upon the enemy had evidently banished sleep from every eyelid.

Jackson advanced into the apartment, looking so cast down that his expression threw a gloom over every face. His heavy boots seemed to drag over the floor; his sabre clanked drearily.

"I have come to tell you good-by," he said, with drooping head.

"Good-by! You are going to leave us, General?"

"Yes, yes, my dear friends," was his reply. "Since I left you, I have received an order by telegraph to evacuate Winchester."

"From Richmond?"

He nodded, and I saw his eye glitter.

"They know best—or think they do."

These words were uttered so quietly, that it was difficult to perceive the sarcasm under them.

"I am ordered to fall back," he continued, with great dejection; "and perhaps it is best. The attack I intended might cost too much. I cannot sacrifice my men."

"Oh, General! you are going to leave us to the Yankees."

"I must.

Jackson's head sank upon his breast. Then it suddenly rose, his cheeks flushed hotly, his eye flashed, and, clutching the hilt of his sabre, he drew it a foot from the scabbard, and, rising to his full height, exclaimed:

"I will never leave Winchester without a fight—never, never!"

At that moment the appearance of the soldier was superb. His tall figure towered above the group, his eyes darted lightning, his huge nostrils expanded like those of a war-horse "snuffing the battle from afar."

But the unwonted excitement did not last long; the color died away from the cheeks, the fire from the eyes. The head of the General again sank, his dejected expression returned, and, driving back his sabre with a clash which rang out harshly in the silence, he said in a gloomy voice:

"No, I must obey orders—I cannot sacrifice my men. I must go without fighting."

And he bade farewell to all, grasping the hands of one after the other.

"Farewell," he said, "and may Providence watch over you."

I bade our kind host and his family good-by in my turn, and, riding with General Jackson, who was silent and gloomy still, returned to head-quarters.*

At daylight, the enemy were in front of the town, and I expected every moment to see Jackson put his army in motion, in obedience to his orders from Richmond, and retire before them.

He seemed, however, to have no intention of doing any such thing. Instead of falling back, he advanced in full view of the enemy, and manned his breastworks on the Martinsburg and

* This scene is historical.

Berryville roads. Had the General changed his mind? Was he going to fight in defiance of orders, and could there be some truth in the views of those who called him "fool Tom Jackson," and declared that he was "crack-brained"? In his immediate front was a force of thirty thousand men, ready to advance and crush his small force of about four thousand; and, instead of taking steps to retire before them, as the bravest general in the world might have done without imputation on his nerve, he seemed determined to fight them, and die where he was.

I scanned the countenance of the General curiously, as he rode along the line of earthworks, to ascertain, if possible, what he designed. But no mask could have been more immovable. His face was inscrutable, and never relaxed its expression of calmness and gravity.

The lines of earthworks now bristled with bayonets ; firing was heard in front from the cavalry skirmishers ; and I expected every moment to see Ashby retire, and a general battle commence.

I was speedily to comprehend, however, the design of all this manœuvring—and from that time, the "crack-brained" theory of the General's character never presented itself to my mind. All at once, at a preconcerted signal, the infantry formed in column, silently withdrew from the trenches, and, moving quietly along the bottom of a sort of ravine in rear of the works, where they were completely concealed from the view of the enemy, took up the line of march *westward*, and *around* Winchester. The "Round Hill," as an eminence in rear of the town is called, was encircled by the long lines of bayonets, still unseen by the enemy—the little army advanced steadily, and, again obliquing, struck into the Valley turnpike, about a mile and a half *south* of the town.

Jackson had evacuated Winchester, and was completely out of the clutch of his adversaries, at the moment when they were preparing to charge him in his earthworks north of the place.

The infantry had thus disappeared—and soon the cavalry were seen falling back slowly, in a long, dark line through the town, their rear skirmishing with the advancing enemy.

XLIV.

A FEAT OF HORSEMANSHIP.

In falling back, Jackson left absolutely nothing behind for his adversary. Every thing was removed, and the laughing infantry greeted with jests and cheers an enormous railway engine, which, drawn by a long string of horses, moved on with the rest.

Jackson remained last, and his critical eyes peered in every direction, to discover whether any thing had been forgotten.

"Is every thing removed, Major?" he said to his chief quartermaster, Major Harman.

"Every thing, General."

"No commissary stores whatever are left?"

"None, General."

"And those broken cars at the dépôt?"

"They can not be moved."

"Burn them, Major."

"I will, at once, sir."

"And the telegraph wire?"

"Is cut, sir."

"But is it removed?"

"No, General."

"Remove it, Major."

Jackson then added: "Take your time. I am in no hurry to leave Winchester."*

Soon, the broken cars were burning, the wire was rolled up and placed in wagons, and the work was complete.

"Very good," said Jackson, when the report was brought to him; and he sat down under a tree, and, folding his hands across his breast, fell quietly asleep.

He had been up all night, and never was able to go without sleep.

The steady approach of the firing now indicated that the enemy

---

* His words.

were pressing Ashby closely, near the northern suburbs of the town. I rode in that direction, and, reaching the rising ground at the head of Loudoun street, where the remains of the old fort, built by Major George Washington, about 1756, may still be seen, encountered the cavalry, falling back in good order before the Federal advance. The rear-guard, under personal command of Ashby, who was mounted on a snow-white horse, was disputing obstinately every foot of ground; the main column meanwhile defiling through the streets, to form in line south of the town.

I had just reached this point, when a sudden rush of the Federal cavalry broke through the rear-guard, and before I knew it, almost, I was by Ashby's side, in the midst of a squadron of blue-coats, banging away with their pistols, and slashing with their sabres. The sweep of Ashby's weapon was magnificent, and he seemed to launch himself from the saddle at every blow. Never had I seen more imperial horsemanship. He and his splendid animal seemed one, and it is impossible to describe his face. It was on fire—the eyes blazed—he looked happy.

I had no time to bestow upon him more than a glance, however. A sabre-cut nearly unseated me, and the blue cordon was all around us, when a determined charge from one of Ashby's squadrons drove back the enemy, and he chased them two hundred yards north of the place.

"Rather close quarters, Major," said Ashby, whose face glowed hotly. "I don't like to be 'crowded '"

And, placing himself at the head of his men, he waved his sword, and cried in a clear, calm voice, strikingly in contrast with his irate appearance:

"Follow *me!*"

Those clear accents seemed to thrill the men. They responded with a wild cheer; and, driving his white horse to furious speed, Ashby burst upon the Federal line like a tornado.

Before that furious onslaught, so sudden and desperate, the enemy's cavalry gave way. Ashby was in front of his line, cutting right and left with the sabre; and when, a few minutes afterward, he came back, his white horse dancing on all four feet, as

the nervous hand reined him in amid a shower of balls, his face
was calmer : for the moment he seemed satisfied.
He continued to retire slowly, and reached the suburbs of the
town. The enemy did not at once move forward. The Confederate cavalry passed through, and it was not until I reached the
southern suburbs that I missed Ashby.

Turning, I saw him seated on his white horse in the middle of
Loudoun street, looking quietly at the Federal cavalry and infantry pouring into the place. It is impossible to conceive any thing
more calmly indifferent than his attitude. He seemed to have
taken his place there to witness some peaceful pageant, and to
regard the advance of the Federal masses, now nearly in contact
with him, with languid curiosity.

All at once, some shots were fired at him, but he took no notice of them. This seemed to enrage the enemy, and a detachment charged him at full gallop, firing as they came.

Ashby waved his hat around his head, uttered a cheer, and
en, drawing his revolver, galloped off, firing as he went.

He had nearly reached the suburbs, when suddenly I saw two
ederal cavalrymen issue from a side street, and post themselves
in the middle of the street to intercept him. I rode rapidly forward to warn him of his danger ; but it was not necessary. He
turned, saw them, and charged the two men, with a glow of unmistakable pleasure upon his features. One fell, shot through
the heart; then, his barrels being all emptied, he seized the
second by the throat.

I then witnessed one of those spectacles which are supposed to
be confined to romances. Borne on at a furious speed upon his
powerful white horse, Ashby dragged his adversary clear out of
the saddle, never relaxed his clutch, and in a moment was beyond
pursuit, still dragging his prisoner by the side of his horse.*

A cheer rose from his men as Ashby released the prisoner, and
coolly looked to the disposition of his command. His face was
again calm; the sad expression had come back; and when he
said, "Well, Major, they are laughing at us yonder, I suppose,

* Historical.

by this time," his voice was as sweet and gentle as when speaking of his dead brother.

<hr>

XLV.

THE "FOOT CAVALRY."

I HAD seen Jackson advance and fight: I was now to see him retreat. The world at large, which judges of every thing superficially, undervalues the art of "falling back;" but it is one of the surest evidences of soldiership. Jackson's method of retiring was cool, deliberate, and extorted my admiration. More than ever, I saw in him those resources which make the great soldier.

Ashby's cavalry brought up the rear, and he had under him a battery of horse artillery, commanded by that gallant young officer, Captain Chew. The roar of these guns was never hushed. It saluted the ears of the infantry, as they lay down in their bivouacs to snatch a few hours of slumber, and was their reveille when they opened their eyes at dawn.

Mingled with the sullen roar of the guns was heard incessantly almost the sharp crack of carbines, showing that the cavalry skirmishers were engaged. The enemy pressed hotly on the rear; but Ashby met them with a coolness and an indefatigable vigilance which defeated all their attempts to throw the army into disorder.

I was much with him in those days, and more than ever admired the great soldier—for such was this man. It was impossible to be with him without experiencing both admiration for his great qualities and affection for him personally. He was truly the flower of chivalry, and was as winning by the campfire as he was utterly fearless in the field. He was one of those men who seem inaccessible to the emotion of fear. I have often seen him sitting quietly on his milk-white horse, gazing from a hill upon the advancing enemy, who poured upon him a storm of balls—when it was impossible to believe, from his appearance, that he realized his danger. I have seen others do this from

bravado—but it did not so impress you in Ashby. He seemed
to be thinking of something else—but at times the spirit of
"fight" came to his face, and he would pace slowly up and
down on his white horse, the mark of a hundred bullets, with
his face turned disdainfully over his shoulder; or rein in his
animal, and, like an equestrian statue, remain in face of the hot
fire, completely motionless.

These scenes were generally followed by a charge, and the
flash of Ashby's sabre, as he led it in person. When he fell
back after such rencounters, he was quieter than ever. A certain
amount of fighting every day seemed necessary to his peace of
mind.

I am not writing a romance, or inventing a hero, worthy
reader. Such was Ashby as he lived and moved before me.

Thus, incessantly fighting with his rear-guard, Jackson continued his retreat up the Valley; and ere long the enemy seemed
to grow weary of the pursuit—their assaults gradually less
determined—finally they stopped. They had fallen back to
Strasburg; thence, as scouts reported, to Winchester; and soon
it became obvious to those who had means of acquiring accurate
information, that the Federal authorities had determined to give
up the idea of an advance by way of the Valley, and concentrate
their forces near Fredericksburg, and on the Peninsula, for an
advance upon Richmond.

Accurate information came on the very day the army ceased
retreating, near Newmarket. The weary troops had scarcely
gone into camp when a courier came at full gallop from Ashby,
who held the front toward Strasburg.

Jackson read the dispatch which he brought with great attention; reflected as much, probably, as half a minute, and then
directed orders to be issued to have the troops ready to march at
daylight.

In their exhausted condition, I thought this utterly impossible
—but at dawn the little army of about four thousand men was
under arms. Jackson rode along the column, looking keenly from
under his faded cap; and then, placing himself at the head of the
troops, took the direction of Winchester.

Without relaxation—stopping for nothing—and at last, accompanied by only a portion of his force, the rest having broken down from the enormous rapidity of the march, he reached, at three or four o'clock on a raw March evening, the little village of Kernstown, within two or three miles of Winchester.

XLVI.

THE VALUE OF TEN MINUTES.

THE troops were so utterly broken down that I did not dream of any further movement that day. The men would stagger, and even fall, if they accidentally placed their feet upon a rolling stone; they lay down in the road at every momentary cessation of the advance; and their haggard faces, more than all else, betrayed the immense prostration of the whole command. Under these circumstances, I did not deem it credible, although Ashby had found the enemy in our immediate front, that an attack would be made that day.   I did not know Jackson.

"Major," he said, with great coolness, "the troops seem somewhat tired."

"Th' are broken down, General."

"But they retain their good spirits?"

'Admirably, sir."

"Well, I am going to attack."

As he spoke, Ashby appeared, approaching at full speed, and soon checked his horse and saluted.

"Any news, Colonel?"

"Very important, General. I have just received intelligence from one of my scouts, who is entirely reliable, that a column of about fifteen thousand men, under General Williams, has passed the Blue Ridge, and is making in the direction of the Rappahannock."

Jackson's eye glittered under his cap, and he moved his head up and down in a way common with him.

"Any thing further, Colonel?"

"I am fighting them in front, and the force here seems larger than we supposed. I think a shell wounded one of their general officers—perhaps my glasses deceived me, however."

Jackson nodded gravely again, looked thoughtfully toward Winchester, and said :

"Continue to press them on the turnpike, Colonel, and send me prompt intelligence of any movement. I am going to attack."

"I am glad to hear it, General—I was afraid the troops were too much exhausted."

"They are very much so—but any delay will give the enemy time to bring up re-enforcements. Besides, the advance of the column under Williams must be arrested."

Ashby bowed.

"You desire me, then, to make a determined attack?"

"I will be glad if you will do so, Colonel. My line of battle will be formed here." Ashby saluted again, disappeared at full gallop, and soon the rapid and continuous firing in front showed that he had attacked with ardor.

Line of battle was now rapidly formed, and, exhausted as they were, the troops were full of alacrity. The force numbered three thousand muskets, and, I think, about four or five batteries.

Jackson was rapidly making his dispositions, when a courier from Ashby announced that the enemy were moving to flank his left. The General's quick nod indicated that he had expected this; and Fulkerson's Brigade, of two regiments, supported by the Stonewall Brigade, was immediately moved rapidly in that direction. Other forces were pushed forward under heavy fire from the Federal guns on a hill in front, and the rattle of musketry on the left soon indicated that the action had begun.

The battle of Kernstown was fought between the turnpike and the North Mountain, on rolling ground, partly ploughed, partly wooded, and the rest overgrown with broom-straw. The fields were divided by worm-fences and stone walls—that ever-recurring feature of the landscapes of the Valley.

Jackson hastened to form his line on an elevated piece of ground, and, calling my attention to a heavy stone wall which extended in front of his left. said :

" Tell Colonel Fulkerson to secure that wall."
I had soon reached the point indicated and delivered my message, which was followed by an instant advance of Fulkerson's
two regiments to gain the desired cover.

I had not arrived a moment too soon. As his line advanced
from the woods into the field, through the centre of which the
wall ran between him and his adversaries, the United States
flag was suddenly seen in the edge of the woods on the opposite
side ; a long surging line of blue coats appeared ; and, like their
opponents, they rushed forward to gain the wall.

The field was several hundred yards in width, and both lines
had a race for the prize. The spectacle was exciting. The
opposing flags flaunted defiance as their bearers rushed on—the
long lines crackled with musketry as they rolled forward—and
for a moment it was impossible to decide which would reach the
wall first. My heart was in my throat—it was a question of life
or death to many a brave fellow that he should gain that cover
—with straining eyes I followed the headlong race.

Suddenly I rose in the saddle and shouted. Fulkerson had
gained the wall when the Federal line was within thirty yards
of it; and, dropping on their knees, the men rested muskets on
the stonework, and delivered a staggering volley in the very
faces of their opponents.

Then rose a wild cheer. I saw the Federal flag go down.
The next moment their whole line broke and retreated, leaving
the ground strewed with dead.

I went to carry the intelligence to Jackson, and found him
leading a charge of his centre, composed of the Stonewall
brigade—a mere handful to be called by the name—and other
troops. It was now obvious that the Federal force in his front
was considerable; and, in fact, it was afterward ascertained to
number eleven thousand men, of whom about eight thousand
were probably engaged. Jackson's force "up" was three
thousand and eighty-seven, of which number two thousand
seven hundred and forty-two were engaged.*

* See Jackson's report.

8

The sun was now declining, and the blood-red rays began to pour their crimson stream upon the woods, and across the fields of broom-straw waving in the melancholy wind. The battle was raging furiously from end to end of the field, and charge after charge was made by the Federal and Confederate lines— each in turn—while the shell from the opposing batteries raced overhead, crashing amid the timber, or descending on the heads of the combatants in iron showers. I never saw a more determined struggle, and the men of the South fought that day with heroic gallantry. To see raw volunteers maintain their ground with such unflinching nerve was a grand and noble spectacle; and the long crash of musketry, rising and falling on the wind, was like the determined and steady fire of veterans upholding upon some world-famous field the destinies of a nation. And they were all Virginians, if you leave out twenty or thirty Marylanders. The men who fought here were the youths of the Valley, in sight almost of their homes. It was this which must have made them stand so obstinately, and charge with that fierce enthusiasm which nothing could overcome. Three times I saw the Federal banner fall; and once, as the long gray line rolled forward, blazing everywhere with musketry, I thought, and still think, that the enemy were on the point of giving way. The victorious Southerners were carrying every thing before them then, when suddenly a fresh Federal regiment, which had been lying down behind a crest, rose up and met them with a yell. They were forced back by this fresh and thoroughly-ammunitioned line. They slowly retired; and I remembered the occurrence afterward, when a Federal officer said that the stand made by one of their regiments " alone saved them."

Thus the battle reeled to and fro upon the bleak fields, and the shades of night began to descend—each line moving still toward the left to outflank its opponents. A sort of fury seemed to inspire the combatants—they fought like tigers. Meanwhile, the thunder of Ashby's guns came in a long, continuous roll from the extreme right on the turnpike, where they were pressing him hard; and on the extreme left the incessant crash of musketry told how fierce the fight was there.

It was at this critical moment, when the opposing lines had grappled breast to breast, that the old Stonewall Brigade, which had borne the brunt of the fight, was seen to waver and retire.

Jackson's eyes darted lightning as he galloped to the spot, and, seizing a drummer boy, he growled :

"Beat the rally!"

The drum rolled, and the line re-formed. The brave Garnett had only ordered it to retire a short distance, as the ammunition of the men was entirely expended, and the brigade was re-formed without difficulty under the hot fire.

But the battle was lost—the enemy's numbers swept everything. They were closing in rapidly on both flanks, and driving the centre. The day was decided.

What the eye saw then by the last light of day was an army falling slowly and sullenly back, with a victorious enemy closely pressing them. Jackson was thus fairly beaten—but here is a strange fact: ·

I was retreating like the rest, when a cavalry-man, crossing the field at full gallop, recognized me, and asked for General Jackson.

" A dispatch from Ashby?"

" Yes, sir."

I seized and opened it. There was just light enough in the sky to read it by.

It was in these words, hastily traced with a pencil :

" GENERAL :—Hold your ground only ten minutes longer. and the enemy will fall back. I have captured a courier from General Shields. His line is ordered to retire.

" ASHBY."

In five minutes I had found Jackson, and given him the note. He was sitting his horse in the midst of the retreating troops, without exhibiting emotion of any sort ; and read the note from Ashby without moving a muscle in his face.

"I thought so," was all he said in his curtest tones, as he crumpled up and dropped the paper. " It is too late."

And he turned his horse's head and rode on with the retiring forces. We were approaching Newtown, about five miles from the field, when the voice of Major Harman, chief quarter-master, was heard in the darkness.

"Where is your train, Major?" was Jackson's brief question.

"Gone to the rear, General."

"Bring it back."

Major Harman bowed and was moving off.

"See that rations are issued to the men—they will camp here to-night."*

And he rode on. Darkness had now fully descended, and the enemy, who had steadily followed, came to a halt. They seemed to fear the presence of reserves—and upon this Jackson, no doubt, counted. He certainly betrayed no sort of intention to hurry away from the dangerous proximity, and the men were soon ordered to halt, build fires, and cook rations. It was a picturesque spectacle—the long lines of twinkling fires far down the turnpike, and the dusky groups laughing and jesting around them.

Jackson sat down by a fire, so near the enemy that we could hear the men talking around their fires. Here he dictated his orders: these directed the troops to move at daylight.

While thus engaged, some intrusive personage, who had strolled up, said:

"A bad day, General."

"I feel very well,"† was the curt response, accompanied by a look which checked all further words. The General then went on munching a piece of corn-bread, which he had taken from his pocket, and giving his orders. Having finished, he picked up an armful of corn which was lying in the road, and, carrying it to a fence corner where his horse was standing, gave it to the animal. Here some rails had been collected and a fire kindled; and saying to Major Pendleton, his adjutant-general, "wake me up at four in the morning, Major," he wrapped himself in his blanket, stretched himself upon the ground, and immediately fell asleep.‡

* Historical.   † His words.   ‡ Historical.

Before daylight he had mounted his horse, and the forces were in motion, retreating up the Valley.

Such was the battle of Kernstown—a hard fight, and fair defeat. " But such was the discipline of Jackson's forces," says General Shields in his report, "that at no time during the fight or retreat did they give way to panic."

XLVII.

THE OFFICER WHOM ASHBY HAD WOUNDED.

I was riding by General Jackson, when he suddenly reined in his horse, and for a moment seemed lost in reflection.

"I do not like to leave my wounded," he said, "and my dead unburied."

He looked toward Winchester, and added, turning all at once to me:

"I wish you would attend to this, Major."

"I any way you indicate, General."

"Well, suppose you try if they will let you remain under a flag of truce. General Shields may consent to it. You can appeal to our friends among the citizens to do what I cannot."

I saluted, and was going.

"Stay, I will give you your credentials."

And, tearing a sheet from his note-book, he wrote in pencil:

"GENERAL:—The bearer, Major Surry, of my staff, is sent to superintend the burial of my dead in the action yesterday, and look after the wounded. I have the honor to request that he may be permitted to pass your lines for that purpose. He will give ary parole you require.

"Very respectfully, your obedient servant,
"T. J. JACKSON,
Maj.-Gen'l Com'd'g C. S. Forces."

"I think that will answer, Major."

"Any further instructions, General?"

"None. I rely upon your good judgment and discretion."

He held out his hand, gave mine a friendly grasp, and, adding, "I shall expect you back soon," rode on toward Strasburg.

I turned my horse's head toward Winchester, and rode through the dim light in the direction of the enemy, whose camp-fires were glimmering upon the hills in front.

Ere long I encountered the dark masses of Ashby's cavalry, drawn up across the road in line of battle to cover the rear of the retreating army. Their commander was in the saddle, on the turnpike, listening for any movement.

"Well, Major," he said, in his gentle voice, "this is rather an ugly business, but we gave them a good hard fight."

"Yes—it is a pity we could not have held our ground a little longer."

"I see you read my dispatch."

"Yes."

"Shields would have fallen back in a few minutes. I *know* this to be so."*

"Well, he is going, instead, to follow us up; but I don't expect to be with you this time."

"Why?"

"I am sent back—if I can get through the Federal line."

And I explained my orders.

"It is day," was Ashby's reply, as he looked up; "you can go to their picket without danger. I will pass you through my own."

And he rode with me through his own picket, until we were in sight of that of the enemy, where, with a grasp of the hand, we parted.

Waving a white handkerchief, I approached the Federal picket, and was halted by the vedette, who passed the word to his officer.

I explained my object to the officer, who was a very courteous person, and, not to weary the reader with the various personages

* His words.

whom I was carried before in succession, was conducted to a house some miles in the rear. Here I found General Shields lying upon a sofa, with his arm in a bandage.

"Major Surry, I believe," was his formal greeting.

"Yes, General."

"From General Jackson?"

I bowed.

"Your object in coming into my lines is to superintend the burial of your dead, and the care of the wounded?"

I bowed again.

"If not contrary to your views, I would be glad to secure that permission, General."

He evidently hesitated, but at last said:

"Well, I shall grant General Jackson's request, sir, though the whole affair is irregular. One of my staff will accompany and assist you."

And he sent an orderly for the officer.

"Were you in the action yesterday, Major?"

"Yes, sir."

"It was a hot affair. I confess I should like to know, as a matter of pure curiosity, what numbers you had engaged."

I began to laugh.

"Oh! that would not interest you, General."

"I see you refuse to tell me. I asked from pure curiosity, and only wished to know if I was right in estimating the force at fifteen thousand."

To this I made no reply.

"General Jackson is a hard fighter," he continued; "and General Ashby, of your cavalry, handles mine rather roughly. I am indebted to him for this wound."

Here the staff officer who had been sent for entered and saluted the General, who instructed him to ride with me to the battle-field, and render me any assistance, returning with me in the evening to his head-quarters.

"Major Surry will not be allowed to communicate with any one," he added, "except upon the subject of his mission."

I bowed, and was leaving the room, when the General said:

176 SURRY OF EAGLE'S-NEST.

"By the by, Major, what did General Jackson think of yesterday's fight? Does he acknowledge himself fairly whipped?"

The temptation was irresistible to fire a parting shot:

"He has some curious ideas about the action, General."

"What are they?"

"He believes, among other things, that, if he had held his ground a little longer, you would have retreated from the field."

"Ah! ah!"

"And even that you had actually issued the order for your line to fall back."

The General uttered a constrained laugh.

"What could have put such an absurd idea in anybody's head, Major? But I am detaining you."

As he spoke, the sound of firing came from the front—the long roll of the opposing batteries.

"I must go there," muttered the General, as I left the apartment.

Accompanied by my elegantly dressed companion, a young officer of the staff, I now rode toward the scene of the late action—the firing in front growing heavier, but gradually receding as we went along.

XLVIII.

THE DEATH-TRENCHES.

A SHORT ride brought us to the battle-field of the preceding day. The scene which greeted my eyes was heart-rending. •

The citizens of Winchester had already been at work, and long trenches had been dug to receive the Confederate dead. They were still busily at work; and near at hand were detachments of Federal soldiers engaged in the same duty toward their own.

The blustering March wind blew, chill and cutting, over the great fields of broom-straw, which gave forth a rustling sigh, like that from some host of invisible mourners; the sky was overcast by a curtain of dark clouds, through which the dim light of day scarcely struggled; and on all sides, to render the depressing influence of the scene complete, were the wounded, the dying, and the dead.

There was one feature of the spectacle, however, which affected me more than all the rest.

With the mayor and citizens of Winchester, there had come forth to the battle-field a number of ladies. Their object was to seek for friends or relatives among the corpses—for Jackson's forces were almost wholly from the Valley; and these mourners now passed from group to group of bodies, trying to recognize some husband, father, or brother among the dead.

As the corpses were brought up, carried by two men holding the feet and shoulders, to be deposited in the death-trench, the veiled figures bent down, peering with deep sobs in the faces of the dead; and, as some relative or friend was identified, a wail would rise upon the air, which sent a thrill even through the Federal officers who were present.

I was standing with my companion, the young staff-officer, near the death-trench, superintending the work, when suddenly a beautiful girl, of not more than fifteen or sixteen, with profuse auburn curls and a figure as fragile as a blossom, rushed forward from the group, and, throwing herself upon her knees beside the corpse of a boy just brought up, burst into such an agony of weeping, that her heart seemed about to break.

"O brother!" she exclaimed, "they have killed you! I thought you were spared! O God, they have killed my brother!"

And with both arms round the body of the boy, whose lips were smiling even in death, she drew the cold face close to her own, and covered it with passionate kisses.

"Oh, I will never see him any more!" sobbed the girl in an agony of grief; "he will never more speak to me! My dear, dear brother, that I loved so! Oh, my heart will break! Brother! brother! Oh, my poor dead brother!"

And, half-fainting on the corpse, she seemed about to expire from excess of grief.

8*

My companion, the young staff-officer, put his handkerchief to his eyes:

"This is terrible, Major," he said.

And stepping forward, ne said to the young lady:

"Don't cry so—you cannot bring him back!"

The girl raised her wet face, over which fell the disordered curls all dabbled in tears; but, at sight of the officer in his elegant Federal uniform, her cheeks suddenly filled with blood, and her eyes flashed.

Rising with a bound almost to her feet, her figure grew stiff and erect as an arrow, and she exclaimed with passionate vehemence:

"What right have you to speak to me! You killed him! But for you, he would be alive to love me now!"

The young officer almost recoiled before this outburst.

"Yes, you killed him!" exclaimed the girl. "Why did your people invade our country, and kill him for defending it! But you will never conquer us! We will never yield. We will shed the last drop of our blood before you shall trample on us!"

As she uttered these words, the girl was superb in her passionate grief and scorn. Her eyes blazed through the hot tears, and the red lips, half-parted, showed the small white teeth close set together. Never shall I forget that face.

She was led away by her friends; my young companion looked after her with a troubled glance, which indicated how much her grief had moved him; and the work of burying the dead proceeded as before.*

By sunset the bodies were all interred—those of soldiers related to families in the vicinity having been removed for private interment—and the wounded were all in hospital at Winchester. I accordingly bade my friend the mayor and his assistants farewell, and returned with my companion to General Shields's head-quarters, where, however, I did not find him. The lady of the house supplied me with a comfortable supper and bed; and on the next day an orderly brought a note from Gene-

* These scenes are historical.

ral Shields, summoning the young officer and myself to Strasburg.

As we approached that place, we encountered the Federal army slowly falling back toward Winchester, and an officer from General Shields informed me that I was free to return to General Jackson.

I rode along the blue line, my gray uniform subjecting me to numerous gibes, and at last found myself alone on the turnpike. From a hill I looked back. Heavy detachments of Federal soldiers were felling trees, dragging them to the road, and barricading the turnpike in the rear of their column.*

XLIX

THE SECOND RETREAT.

REJOINING the Confederate column near Woodstock, I made my report, with which the General seemed well satisfied, and then informed him of the barricades erected in the enemy's rear.

He smiled grimly.

"Then we are not so badly defeated, after all, Major."

"It seems they fear, at least, that you will return."

"I accomplished my object. General Williams has come back, with fifteen thousand men, to the Valley."

"What force did you fight at Kernstown, General?"

"About eight thousand, I think. Scouts report eleven thousand in all at Winchester before the action."

"Well, that gives an aggregate of twenty-six thousand, kept here by an attack from three thousand. I think it was worth what it cost."

And the conversation turned upon something else.

The army continued its retreat until it reached Rude's Hill, a lofty elevation near Mount Jackson, and here it went into camp and rested.

* Historical.

About the middle of April, information came developing the Federal plan of campaign for the coming spring. Richmond was to be attacked from every quarter. General McClellan, with an army of more than one hundred thousand men, was to advance from the Peninsula, between the James and York; General Mc-Powell was to march from Fredericksburg, with forty thousand men, and unite with McClellan's right on the Chickahominy; and in the Valley, not less than three heavy columns were to assail Jackson. General Milroy was to advance from the mountains west of Staunton; General Fremont from the northwest; and, General Banks, from Winchester, straight up the Valley.

Uniting near Harrisonburg or Staunton, these three columns were to drive Jackson before them, pursue him to the low coun-'try, and, joining General McDowell's right, as he had joined Mc-Clellan, encircle the Confederate capital with a cordon of bayo-nets. Then *exit* the Confederacy.

This plan became developed, as I have said, about the middle of April, when Jackson received intelligence that Generals Mil-roy, Fremont, and Banks were all in motion. The first was approaching from Monterey; the second pressing toward Rom-ney; and General Banks was rapidly advancing with a heavy force from Winchester.

"They seem determined to drive me from the Valley, Major," said Jackson, when this intelligence came; "but, with God's blessing, I hope to hold my ground, if not drive them back."

The hope seemed desperate to me—and yet it did not. I had begun to *believe in* Jackson, like his men. In spite of the un-doubted defeat which he sustained at Kernstown, the troops had conceived the very highest admiration for him. Whenever he appeared on his old sorrel, in his dingy uniform, they cheered him wildly; and an officer told me that, on the day after the battle, the men "went crazy about him." *

From Kernstown dated that ardent personal attachment of the troops to their leader—a fact which I never could explain. Many among the officers who had been with General Loring con-

* Historical

tinued to sneer at him as " crack-brained ;" but the men would
not be persuaded. They cheered him obstinately whenever he
appeared.

General Banks now pressed forward. His column reached the
little village of Edinburg; and Jackson broke up his camp at
Rude's Hill, and crossed into Elk Run Valley. Here he could
face all his enemies, and retreat, if necessary, upon Richmond.
But that I knew he intended to do only in the last resort.

L.

THE CHASE AFTER MILROY.

I HAD gone to carry a message to Colonel Ashby, and spent
the night with him on the outpost, when on my return I found
the infantry in motion, and soon discovered that Jackson,
now re-enforced by General Ewell's division from Johnston's
army, was going, with a portion of his army, to attack General
Milroy, who had already crossed the Shenandoah Mountain,
west of Staunton, to form a junction with General Banks at
Harrisonburg.

The column was moved with great rapidity—by railway, partly
—and, advancing steadily westward, reached, on a bright evening, the slope of the Bull Pasture Mountain—the enemy retiring
before them.

Here General Milroy's advance force was met and driven back,
and on the next morning Jackson rapidly advanced into the
narrow defile on the western side of which was the Valley of
McDowell, occupied in force by his adversary.

The battle of McDowell—upon which I shall not dwell long
—was an obstinate struggle for the possession of Sutlington's Hill,
a lofty eminence on the southern side of the gorge, and commanding the valley in which General Milroy was posted.

The quick eye of Jackson saw speedily that this was the
key of the whole position, and he lost no time in hurrying for-

ward his regiments, as they came up, to secure possession of it. Such was the roughness of the ground—a steep mountainside, with huge masses of rock cropping out at every step—that no artillery could be gotten to the crest; and the infantry, even, were compelled to march in single file, winding in and out among the huge rocks of the gorge.

Scarcely had the few regiments thus hurried forward formed a thin line of battle on the hill, when the Federal forces, which had promptly massed in front, were thrown against them, and a furious conflict commenced for the coveted position. A heavy column was first hurled against Jackson's left, but, after a fierce conflict, was repulsed. Then the dark masses were seen to withdraw from that quarter and concentrate in front of the Confederate right. An assault more determined than the first followed, to turn that flank; and in an instant the opposing lines had come together with a crash which resembled the furious roar of a mountain storm. The rattle of musketry and the bellowing of the Federal artillery reverberated from the rocky sides of the gorge, until the ears were deafened, and the opposing lines disappeared in a heavy cloud, which concealed completely the whole struggle.

Suddenly the long-sustained yell, heard from the Southern troops whenever they gained a success, rose clear and ringing from the slope, and then a wind swept back the smoke—the setting sun lit up the scene—and the Federal line was seen falling back, pursued by its adversaries.

This was General Milroy's last attempt. He did not renew the struggle to gain possession of the hill.

With the coming darkness, the battle ceased, and the men lay down in line of battle, ready to advance and attack at daylight.

The enemy did not await the assault. Toward day, the woods in the valley were discovered to be on fire—the flames roared aloft, forming a magnificent spectacle—and when skirmishers were thrown forward, the Federal camps were found to be deserted.

General Milroy had fallen back hastily, to avoid the heavy blow which he foresaw would be struck at him on the return of day; and was soon discovered to be in full retreat toward the town of Franklin.

Jackson rapidly pursued him, and reached Franklin. Here, however, the pursuit ceased. The Federal forces were found posted in a strong position on the mountain spurs near at hand —and again General Milroy set the woods on fire, to conceal his movements. From the dense smoke which rose, darkening the whole horizon, came the dull roar of artillery and the shr‑˙ of shell.

Jackson had accomplished his design of preventing the junction between Generals Milroy and Banks; and to attack his adversary, thus strongly posted amid the mountain fastnesses, was no part of his plan. He accordingly issued orders to the troops to prepare for marching back.

Before this movement commenced, however, a solemn ceremony of prayer and thanks took place in the army.

The scene was imposing. In the wild amphitheatre, surrounded by fir-clad mountains, the little army was drawn up, as though in line of battle, and prayers were offered by the chaplains. As they spoke—the men listening with bent heads, uncovered—the dull roar of artillery was heard in front; and, when the speakers ceased, the solemn thunder of the guns filled up the pauses. Overhead was the bright sun in a blue sky—the muskets, neatly stacked in long rows, shone in the sunshine—soon every man had taken his piece, and the column was ready to march.

Returning over the same road, and repassing the Bull Pasture Mountain, Jackson obliqued to the left, and advanced upon Harrisonburg.

As he approached that place, intelligence reached him that General Banks had fallen back to Strasburg.

LI.

THE ADVANCE.

I WAS riding beside Jackson when he received the intelligence of General Banks's retreat. He had been carelessly glancing, as he rode along, at a copy of a Northern newspaper captured by one of Ashby's scouts; and I saw a grim smile touch upon his features—then fly away.

" The retreat of General Banks is rather curious, after this paragraph, Major," he said.

And he handed me the paper, pointing with his finger to a few lines under the head of " Telegraphic."

It was a dispatch from General Banks to the authorities at Washington, dated from Harrisonburg a few days before, announcing that "the rebel Jackson had left the Valley, and was in full retreat on Richmond."*

I had scarcely finished reading the paragraph, when Jackson said to his adjutant-general, the brave Major Pendleton:

"Major, write an order directing General Ewell to join me, without loss of time, at Newmarket, with his entire command. Say 'without loss of time,' Major."

The order was immediately written and dispatched, and Jackson continued his way, reaching Harrisonburg, and thence pressing forward to Newmarket.

General Ewell promptly appeared at the rendezvous with his strong division, and Jackson met him with great cordiality. He was a man past middle age, with black hair, beard, and mustache, with a thin, erect figure, sparkling black eyes, and a manner abrupt and decisive. The General differed in two features then from his subsequent self. He had not received his severe wound in the knee, and he swore, apparently from inveterate habit. It was hard, afterward, to recognize in the pale, thin invalid, commanding a great army corps, and scrupulously decorous in all his utterances, the bluff, abrupt soldier of the Valley campaign.

* Historical.

" Well, General," he said, " here I am. My division is up."

" Thanks for your promptness, General."

" Banks has retreated to Strasburg."

" Yes."

" And you are about to follow him?"

" I think I ought to."

" By what route?"

" Well, we ought to take the best we can find."

It was obvious that Jackson would not communicate his intentions even to his division commanders. They complained of this more than once; but the reader will remember the words of the General heretofore recorded: "If my own coat knew what I designed, I would take it off and burn it."

On the next day all was ready for the forward movement, now plainly decided upon. Jackson had under him nearly twenty thousand excellent troops, including some additional cavalry; and the reader need not be told that such a man, with such a weapon in his grasp, was not apt to let it remain idle. Orders were issued that every species of baggage should be left behind, even the knapsacks—and the most ignorant man in the forces then knew that Jackson was " stripping for a fight."

At daylight, the long column of infantry and artillery was in motion—toward the '' Newmarket Gap," leading into the Luray Valley.

Ewell's question, so skilfully evaded, was thus answered. Jackson was going to attack his adversary in flank and rear.

Take the map of Virginia, my dear reader, and you will understand Jackson's design more clearly, at a single glance, than from the most labored explanation. You will see that Strasburg, where General Banks had fortified, is eighteen miles south of Winchester, on the main Valley turnpike, and that along the east side of this turnpike runs the Massinutton Mountain. On the opposite side of the mountain—between it and the great wave of the Blue Ridge—is the " Luray Valley," leading to Front Royal, directly on the flank of Strasburg. If Jackson could amuse his adversary by cavalry demonstrations on the main Valley road, while he rapidly advanced down the Luray Valley and gained Front Royal, he might hope to pass that point—inter-pose himself between Strasburg and Winchester—and force General Banks to surrender, or fight his way through to the Potomac.

Jackson was now swiftly advancing to the accomplishment of this bold and vigorous conception. The troops moved rapidly across the Shenandoah, and through Newmarket Gap; pressed forward down the Luray Valley, under a burning May sun; and at nightfall threw themselves upon the ground, completely ex-hausted, within ten miles of Front Royal.

Before daylight, Jackson was in the saddle, and his advance force hurried forward to attack the Federal garrison in the town.

The assault was sudden and decisive. The Federal cavalry galloped pell-mell through the streets, strik::g fire from the pavement, and the Confederates rushed in with cheers, amid waving handkerchiefs and tumultuous outcries of rejoicing from the inhabitants. The Federal forces made a brief stand on the elevated ground beyond, and endeavored to destroy the bridge over the Shenandoah. But they were furiously attacked by the advance force; the bridge was saved; and the army rapidly crossed the river.

Jackson was now directly on his adversary's flank, and a few hours would enable him to reach the Federal rear and cut off their retreat. But the strength of the human machine under this great engineer began to fail—the wheels commenced to creak. The immensely hard march of the two last days, under a burning sun, had filled the road with stragglers, unable to keep up; and those who remained in the ranks were exhausted. To concentrate for battle, and rest his entire force, Jackson ordered a halt; and again, at nightfall, the troops lay down in the roads and fell asleep, clutching their muskets.

LII.

A NIGHT ADVENTURE.

STRETCHING myself on the ground, under a tree, I fell soundly asleep, like the rest; but a little after midnight I felt a hand on my shoulder, and, opening my eyes, saw General Jackson.

"I wish you to ride with me, Major."

I buckled on my belt, threw my cape over my shoulders, and mounted my horse, which stood ready saddled near.

"I can get no intelligence from the front," said the General, as we rode on through the darkness, "but something tells me that General Banks has discovered our presence here, and is retreating."

"It is more than probable, General."

"I am going to see."

And pushing on rapidly over the deserted roads, we came to Ashby's cavalry picket, in command of a lieutenant.

"Where is General Ashby?"

"To the left, on the road to Strasburg, General."

"True. Is there any thing in front of you?"

"Nothing, General—this is the outside picket."

"Good."

And the General rode by the vedette, with the words:

"Don't fire on me as I come back."

I followed, and we rode on some distance in silence.

"Ashby is obeying his orders to keep a good lookout on the road from Strasburg to Front Royal, to prevent the retreat of the enemy in that direction," the General now said, half to himself; "but I think the danger is here."

We rode on in silence, following the country road, now passing through wide fields, now under the shade of forests.

From time to time Jackson checked his horse and listened. At the third pause of this description, we distinctly heard a distant rumbling, resembling that caused by artillery or wagons moving over the hard surface of a turnpike.

"I knew it!" were the quick words of the General; ' but let us be certain."

And, galloping rapidly toward the sound, we reached a kill separated by a narrow valley from the elevated ground over which ran the Valley turnpike.

The sound had become a continuous jarring rumble of wheels jingling of artillery chains, clash of hoofs, and that low shuffling sound which comes from large bodies of infantry in motion. Against the sky, beyond the hill, we clearly made out the long, dark lines of infantry, cavalry, artillery, and wagons. General Banks was retreating upon Winchester.

Jackson wheeled his horse, and dug the spur into his side.

"Come, Major!" he exclaimed, with unwonted excitement, "no time is to be lost!"

As he spoke, the shrill neigh of a horse was heard from a clump of woods on the left, and at the next moment a scouting party of Federal cavalry, moving on the flank of their column, appeared in the road.

"Halt!" was the quick order of the officer at their head, as we darted off.

A sudden volley succeeded; and the carbine balls whistled around.

No response followed the order to halt—then was heard the furious clash of hoofs behind us. The cavalry was in hot pursuit.

In five minutes they were so close that I heard the heavy breathing of their horses.

"Halt! halt!" came again, accompanied by a volley of imprecations from the officer behind.

I replied by firing at him, but without striking him.

It was now obvious that, unless we left the road, we would inevitably be captured, and I said as much to the General.

"Well," was his brief response, in the quick, curt tone which characterized him, "let us leave it."

"Shall we try that stone wall, General?"

"Yes."

I cleared the wall, and the General followed, receiving a volley as he rose to the leap. We had got over, and were in a field but the wall was instantly torn down, and the whole detachment scrambled over, and pressed forward as hotly as before.

All at once a by-road, leading into the woods, appeared in front, and we struck into this at a headlong gallop.

"Halt! who goes there!" suddenly cried a voice in front, which I recognized as Ashby's.

"Friends!"

And, reaching his side, I pointed to the Federal cavalry about two hundred yards behind.

Ashby recognized the General, understood all at a glance, and, by a movement as quick as thought, drew up his small escort on the side of the road, beneath the shadow of the trees.

The next moment the Federal cavalry thundered by, and, as their rear passed him, Ashby gave the ringing order:

"Charge!"

A volley was poured into the Federal detachment, throwing them into the wildest disorder—Ashby charged them sabre in hand—and in three minutes the whole party were captured.

Jackson seemed to have forgotten the whole affair in a moment after the cessation of the firing.

"General," he said, with great animation, "the enemy are retreating rapidly toward Winchester. Get your entire command together, and move toward Middletown, on the left of the main body. Major, is your horse fresh?"

"Perfectly, General."

"Go back and tell my column to move forward at once! I wish General Ewell to advance by the Newtown road—the rest by the way we came to-night. Lose no time! General, get your cavalry here quickly!"

I have rarely seen Jackson more animated. I went at full speed to carry the order, and, at the same moment, Ashby's couriers were seen scattering in every direction to concentrate the cavalry at the point ordered.

The General's directions were promptly sent to the different commanders, and in an hour the whole army was in motion—one column, under Ewell, advancing as ordered, by the road to Newtown—the other directly toward Middletown.

Jackson took personal command of tne latter, and at daylight reached the hill which we had reconnoitred from during the night. The road in front was black with General Banks's army in full retreat. Jackson had struck the columns *in transitu.*

LIII.

JACKSON RETURNING TO "HIS PROPERTY."

ARTILLERY was immediately hurried forward, and a furious fire opened on the column. The scene which followed was striking. At one moment the turnpike was black with the long lines of Federal cavalry and artillery moving rapidly toward Winchester—and then, as the cannon suddenly opened their grim mouths, and the shell tore through the Federal column, the cavalry broke in a panic, scattered in every direction, and the dark figures disappeared like flying phantoms in the woods. Where an instant before had been seen the long dense column, you could now discern only horses writhing in the agonies of death, and the forms of the dead and dying.

The Federal artillery and infantry, which brought up the rear, was cut off, and made vain efforts to defend itself. The guns took position and opened furiously, but Taylor's infantry charged them; they were hastily limbered up, and then were seen thundering, at full gallop, back toward Strasburg, from which place they escaped with the infantry to the western mountains.

Ashby had now advanced with his whole cavalry, and was in hot pursuit of the disordered Federal horse and the wagon train.

The scene which ensued was one of wild disorder. The men stopped to ransack the heavily laden wagons in rear; and the consequence was, that the long trains in front were enabled to make good their escape. Worse still, this delay enabled the Federal commander to organize a rear-guard; and, when Jackson's infantry pressed on, it was saluted with a heavy fire of artillery.

The General was furious, and hot words passed between him
and Ashby—now Brigadier-General, and responsible for the
conduct of all the cavalry.

"But for this shameful conduct," exclaimed Jackson, "General
Banks would have reached Winchester without a wagon train,
if not without an army."*

Ashby made a haughty reply, which I did not hear—and for
many days the rupture between them was not healed.

Driving before him the Federal rear-guard, Jackson now continued to press forward with his infantry—the column moved all
night, fighting at every step—and at daylight on the next morning the roofs of Winchester were seen shining in the sunlight.

General Banks occupied the town, and, finding that he was
determined to make a stand on the high ground in the suburbs,
Jackson made instant dispositions for an assault. Ewell was
directed to attack on the right, from the Front Royal road, and,
taking command in person of his left wing, Jackson threw forward a heavy line, supported by a determined fire of artillery,
and charged the Federal forces occupying the high ground west
of the town.

Nothing stops troops who believe that they are driving before
them a demoralized enemy. The Federal forces made a resolute
stand, and their first line, behind a stone wall, bravely held that
position, although the stones were dashed into a thousand pieces
by round shot. But the Southern line carried every thing before
it. It swept down the slope in front—advanced at a double-
quick across the intervening space, under a furious fire from the
enemy's artillery, and, mounting the opposing slope, charged
the Federal line with the bayonet.

For an instant I could make out nothing through the smoke—
no sound was heard but the dull roar of artillery, and the sharp
rattle of musketry. Then a loud cheer rose from the hill, and, as
the smoke drifted, I saw the Federal forces in full retreat, pursued by their opponents.

At the same moment, wild shouts arose on the right, where

* This expression was afterward used in Jackson's report.

Ewell had been thundering with his artillery. I saw his line sweep forward, with glittering bayonets, driving the Federal infantry from a heavy stone wall and other cover ; and, galloping forward, I entered the town just as the two columns united, and the Federal forces scattered, and hastened in full retreat through the streets.

The spectacle was exciting. The streets were full of men, women, and children, who seemed wild with joy. It is scarcely an exaggeration to say that they appeared crazed for the moment. They ran to and fro, shouting, cheering, laughing—every window waved with handkerchiefs, fluttering in the hands of ladies—and such was the crowd of these latter in the streets that the advance of the Southern troops was actually impeded by them. They seemed to pay not the least attention to the balls whistling around them ; and many persons witnessed, and can testify to the curious fact, that a detail of men had to be sent in advance, to make the groups of girls give way, in order that the platoons might deliver their fire.

Never before or afterward did I see Jackson so much carried away as upon this occasion. As men, women, and children flocked around him, grasping his hand, touching his clothes, and saluting him with cheers and exclamations, his face flushed, his eyes sparkled, and, waving his old cap in the air, he uttered a cheer— the first and last I ever heard from his lips.

Then he pushed ahead of the crowd; followed at full gallop the retreating enemy; and was soon so close that, fearing they would turn and fire on him, I said:

"Don't you think you are exposing yourself too much, General?"

" No, Major!" he exclaimed, "they can't hurt me! Go back and tell the army to press right on to the Potomac!"*

The enemy were pursued for some miles beyond Winchester by the infantry, and then the cavalry continued to harass them until they crossed the Potomac, near Martinsburg.

General Banks was thus driven completely from the Valley, and

* His words.

such was the haste of his departure that he left behind him immense stores, which fell into Jackson's hands. The troops ransacked the sutlers' stores, which their owners had fled and abandoned—and the citizens of Winchester still relate with laughter the story of a fat old Dutchman who lost his all. He knew that Jackson was coming back, he said ; he had heard a horn blowing beyond Fort Royal, then at Middletown, then near Winchester; and this horn said plainly, louder and louder as it came, "Who's been here since I's been gone?" That horn was Jackson's, and he it was who was demanding in his terrible voice who had intruded on his property. So, exit Mynheer in the direction of Martinsburg—from which place he returned after the withdrawal of the rebels, to find only empty boxes in his store-rooms, and to exclaim in despair, with hands uplifted, "Who's been here since *I*'s been gone?"

The Federal troops, who saw all, shared this feeling, that the region around Winchester belonged to Jackson, and that he was coming back to take possession of "his property." More than once I heard that groups of lounging soldiers had suddenly started and risen to their feet when some practical-joke-loving individual exclaimed, "Jackson is coming!"—and one had fallen backward from a lofty stool at this announcement, convinced that the fearful clutch of the blood-thirsty Stonewall was on his shoulder.

That awful cannibal had now come back, made a meal on General Banks, and entered into possession of his property. Unfortunately, however, his tenure of it was to be very brief.

LIV.

A LITTLE IDEA OF CAPTAIN BOGY'S.

BEFORE proceeding with the rapid narrative of the great campaign, of which I have given only the main historic outlines, I shall invite the reader's attention to one of those comic scenes which so often appear amid the carnage of war, and afford him

9

a glimpse of an old acquaintance, wellnigh forgotten, I fear, in
the rush of events and the crowd of personages on the imposing
theatre of the war.

I had been sent to the front with an order from Jackson, and
was returning to Winchester, when, just as I debouched into the
main highway between that place and Martinsburg, I descried a
singular cortege.

A long line of Federal prisoners were marching on foot over
the dusty high road to Winchester, accompanied by a guard of
cavalry; and each one of the blue-coats carried in his arms a
negro child!*

They toiled along through the hot sunshine, carrying the
squalling young Africans, and, as I approached, imprecations
greeted my ears, mixed with laughter from the guard, who
seemed to enjoy intensely the disgust of their late adversaries at
this compulsory dry-nursism.

I was about to ride on, when all at once I recognized in the
commander of the cavalry escort my old acquaintance, Captain
Bogy, with whom I had dined, in company with Johnston, Jackson, and Stuart, just before the battle of Manassas. I knew that
the jovial Captain had joined Jackson with his company when
Ewell re-enforced us just before McDowell, but, in the rush of
official engagements, had not been able to visit him.

Bogy was, if any thing, fatter, rounder, and more jovial than
before. His sabre-belt sunk deeper into his enormous body;
his jackboots were heavier; his face more ruddy, and his smile
still more unctuous.

He recognized me at once, and saluted me with a wheezy,
deep-seated, contagious laugh.

"You see I am going back, Major," he said, "with a few of
the spoils of victory!"

"In the shape of prisoners and contrabands!"

"Yes, that is a little device of mine, and I don't mind saying
I'm rather proud of it. Rather a neat idea, eh, Major?"

"Making the prisoners carry the darkey?"

---

* Historical—but this device was invented by the gallant Captain A——, not by
Captain Bogy.

"Why not? They enticed them away, and were carrying off
a their wagons whole families of these monkey-beings. They
are savage on their General Banks, and swear that it was all his
doing. They charge him with leaving behind his own wounded
to make room in his wagon for the ebo-shins."*

"It is not possible!"

"Don't know; but I know they were carried off in shoals to
Martinsburg, and, as I captured 'em, I thought they ought to be
brought back by the same people who took them there. It must
be a pleasing occupation to tote 'em—they love 'em so!"

And, turning to a sullen-looking fellow among the Federal
prisoners, who carried in his arms an uncommonly dirty, chubby,
and squalling negro baby, Captain Bogy asked, with an air of
great interest, whether he was not "glad to have that close to
his bosom one of the poor down-trodden Africans?"

The reply of the Federal prisoner was brief but expressive:

"D—— the down-trodden African!" he growled. "I wish
the whole concern of 'em was in ——!"

And he mentioned a place unnamable to ears polite.

Bogy burst into laughter, and the baby set up a squall.

"Hug him! hug the little darling to your bosom, my friend!"
said the Captain. "I don't myself admire the peculiar odor of
the African, but there's no accounting for difference of taste!"

And, amid the muttered curses of the burly nurse, who looked
as if he would very much like to strangle his burden, Bogy rode
on laughing.

"General order number one!" he called out as we passed on;
"if any prisoner drops his baby, give him two!"

And, shaking all over, Bogy turned to me and said:

"A glorious campaign, Major! a perfect stifler on Commis-
sary-General Banks!"

"*Commissary*-General?"

"That's the nickname given him by the men. They say that
he is Old Jack's commissary and quartermaster too. Wagons,
rations, sutlers' stores—he has provided every thing."

---

* Such was the charge brought by the Federal troops against General Banks at
the time.

"Very true, my dear Captain, and I'm much mistaken if so old a soldier as yourself has not looked out for his mess."

" *Me!*" exclaimed the Captain. "Oh, I never think of good eating, Major!"

And the Captain chuckled.

"Remember that day I dined with you."

"Was the bill of fare good? Delighted to hear it."

"It was miraculous; and I'll bet you will dine as well to-day."

"No, no, I fear not."

And Bogy sighed.

"Come, confess, my dear Captain, didn't you secure some small, unpretending wagon, which no one else would notice, and yet whose contents were a real Arabian Night's Entertainment?"

Bogy looked modest, and was silent.

"Come! you look guilty! Confess, confess!"

Captain Bogy inserted one finger beneath his hat, scratched his head, and replied, in an innocent voice:

"Well, I *did* get a small, a *very* small wagon, Major."

"I could have sworn it! And now confess again! It was a 'head-quarters wagon.' "

"Well, I believe it was."

"Whose, my dear Captain?"

The Captain looked still more innocent.

"I think it was General Banks's," he replied, with lamb-like simplicity.

I began to laugh, and asked if its contents were satisfactory.

"Eminently so, my dear Major, as you will have an opportunity of seeing, if you will come and dine with me to-morrow. To-day is lost; I have dined on a cracker," and Bogy sighed; "but to-morrow! Ah! that's different! To-morrow I shall really dine! Come and let us reconnoitre the wagon together. I have already tried the brandy; it is genuine Otard: the wine is not so good, and I wish these Yankee generals would cultivate a purer taste. They rarely have what suits my palate. But the sauces are excellent; I have tried them: and the cheese very passable. Come, Major! come! Lucullus dines with Lucullus to-morrow; drop in! I will send you word where to find me!'"

Such was the hospitable invitation of Captain Bogy, and I accepted it provisionally—if I could come. Unfortunately, to anticipate, I was unable to be with the gallant Captain.

I left him riding gravely in front of his cortege, occasionally issuing a stentorian order when the nurses flagged in their march or exhibited symptoms of rebellion at their burden.

That spectacle kept me laughing for many miles.

LV.

THE TRAP

" TELL the army to press right on to the Potomac!" had indicated Jackson's entire programme. He was always in favor of following up his successes, and pressing a defeated enemy remorselessly: his object now was to paralyze, if possible, the entire Federal force in the region. General Banks's column was driven beyond the Potomac, but a force was at Charlestown, and at Harper's Ferry a very considerable garrison. Jackson's column was immediately pushed forward in that direction to finish the work.

We afterward heard that his approach was telegraphed to Washington, and caused such apprehensions there that the Governors of the Northern States were called upon for troops to defend the Capital. It will soon be seen that formidable efforts were meanwhile being made to cut off and destroy this great gladiator, whose movements were so sudden, rapid, and threatening.

To return to my rapid outline of events. General Charles Winder pressed on toward Charlestown with the Stonewall Brigade, opened upon the forces with his cavalry before they suspected his presence, and, driving them before him, reached the vicinity of Harper's Ferry, where, on the next day, Jackson joined him with the main body.

An attack was instantly determined upon, and a regiment was sent to occupy Loudoun Heights east of the place; fire had just been opened; all was ready for the attack, when news came which put an end to further proceedings.

A rumor seemed to come, blown on the wind, that a storm was brewing in the rear, and Jackson entered the cars at Charlestown to return to Winchester.

He had scarcely done so, when a courier rode up at full speed.

" What news?" said Jackson, curtly.

The courier fumbled for his dispatch.

"The enemy are at Front Royal."

" Good!" said Jackson.

"Colonel Connor is cut off and captured."

" Very good."*

" Fremont is at Wardensville.   Here is the dispatch, General."

Jackson read it with perfect calmness, crumpled up and dropped it, and then rapidly wrote an order directing his entire command to return from Harper's Ferry to Winchester.

Having done so, he bent forward, leaned his head upon the back of the seat in front of him, and fell asleep.†

The cars moved on, and in half an hour he awoke.

" Are we near Winchester, Major ?"

" Yes, General."

" I can get there first—I mean to Strasburg."

"The march will be hard."

" Yes, if Fremont is at Wardensville and McDowell at Front Royal, as that dispatch announced."

"I don't like to croak, General," I said, " but it appears to me that if any time is lost we are cut off."

" You are right: that would be unfortunate after capturing such valuable stores.   Only one course would remain for me."

" What is that, General ?"

" To fall back upon Maryland for re-enforcements."‡

We reached Winchester, and the captured stores were hastily loaded upon the wagons.   The enormous trains were then sent forward with the long column of Federal prisoners, twenty-three hundred in number, toward Strasburg, escorted by a regi-

---

> His words.   † Historical.   ‡ His words.

ment of infantry, under the brave Colonel Cunningham, afterward killed at Cedar Mountain.

The army was then rapidly concentrated at Winchester; and without losing a moment, or waiting for the Stonewall Brigade, which had held the front at Harper's Ferry, the column hastened toward Strasburg.

There was something both gallant and grotesque in the spectacle of the men limping along over the hard stones of the turnpike, laughing and jesting as they did so. The oddest remarks came to my ears as I rode along the column, glittering, with its burnished bayonets, like some huge serpent with silver scales, as it undulated in the sunshine. "Old Jack ain't cut off yet," seemed the most popular view of the situation; and the critical condition of affairs seemed to be regarded as a good joke. Soldiers are like children, reader—but for that matter, what men are not? Your emperors, kings, presidents, and statesmen—they are all overgrown children.

Jackson's situation was one of very extreme peril. Two heavy Federal columns were closing in upon his rear, toward Strasburg—that under General Shields from the east, and that under General Fremont from the west. The former is known to have amounted to twenty thousand men, from President Lincoln's order to General McDowell to "move twenty thousand men" on the line of the Manassas Gap Railroad, "to capture or destroy Jackson." General Fremont's force was probably about as numerous.

Thus, without counting the forces at Harper's Ferry, Williamsport, and elsewhere on the Potomac, which would immediately follow upon his rear, Jackson had in his front about forty thousand troops, through which it appeared he would certainly be compelled to cut his way.

His own force was fifteen thousand effective men.*

If he was cut off at Strasburg, this force would speedily be enclosed by a cordon of three armies, under Fremont, Shields, and Banks, amounting to about seventy thousand men.

* Jackson's statement at the time.

Jackson rode at the head of his column, and I could not discern any unusual emotion in his countenance. His astonishing
nerve enabled him to look calmly in the face of peril which
would certainly have excited most generals, however courage
ous.

"Move on with the column," came from the calm lips from
time to time, and soon the towering wave of the Massi
nutton Mountain rose before us. Suddenly firing was heard in
front.

Jackson pushed on and entered Strasburg, when a staff-officer
from 'Ashby galloped up.

" What news?"

" The enemy are advancing, General."

" Fremont's column?"

" Yes, sir. They are in sight.'

" Tell General Ashby to hold them in check as long as possible."

The officer saluted and darted off. At the same moment a
courier appeared coming from the direction of Front Royal.

" Well?" said Jackson curtly.

" The enemy are within three miles, General."

" Infantry or cavalry?"

" Cavalry."

" Good." And turning to me, the General, said : " Present my
compliments to General Ewell, and tell him to attack Fremont's
column, at once."

I was riding off.

" Wait a moment."

I turned my horse's head.

" Tell him to hold his ground until he is cut to pieces."

This cheering order I speedily delivered to General Ewell,
who laughed grimly as he threw his division into line of battle.

I returned to Jackson, who was trying to eat a cracker as hard
as iron, as he sat his horse.

" Major, ride up to the top of the hill, and see if you can se
or hear any thing of the Stonewall Brigade. I intend to sta
here until it arrives."

I rode up and reconnoitred, reaching the hill-top just as the long roll of musketry west of Strasburg indicated that Ewell had engaged Fremont.

As far as the eye could see, the turnpike was deserted. No signs of the missing brigade were seen, and I reported tho fact to Jackson.

"Very good."

And he rode forward to where Ewell was fighting. He was heavily engaged with General Fremont's advance force, which had passed ahead of the main body.

At sight of Jackson, a loud cheer rose from the men, and the line, instead of merely standing and receiving the enemy's attack, rushed forward.

Forgetting every thing else, Jackson galloped on with the line, encouraging the men, and, before the impetuous rush of the Southerners, General Fremont's line fell back.

Jackson halted, and wiped his forehead. As he did so, a courier hastened up with a dispatch from General Winder. The Stonewall Brigade would arrive in half an hour.

"Tell the General to lose no time. I am waiting for him."

"Yes, sir."

"Well, General," he said to Ewell, "we will soon move now. Keep your command well together; I will withdraw in an hour."

In twenty minutes the flag of the Stonewall Brigade appeared upon the hill above Strasburg, and the line of glittering bayonets wound down the declivity. They had made an enormous march, but were at last up; and in an hour, as he had notified Ewell, Jackson put his entire column in motion, just as dispatches from the right and the left announced that the forces under Shields and Fremont were pouring forward, and would soon be upon him.

The wagon train and the prisoners had gone ahead, and the long column of infantry now followed.

Last came Ashby's column of cavalry. As the rear of the column reached the high ground beyond the town, the enemy rushed into Strasburg.

Jackson had extricated himself from the trap.

9*

LVI.

FALLING BACK.

THE retreat which followed was one long battle.

General Fremont was pressing Jackson's rear on the main Valley road; General Shields was hurrying by a parallel route up the Luray Valley, to cut him off at Newmarket.

Jackson had taught his adversaries topography. They were playing against him the same game which had been so fatal to General Banks. That commander's woes had all originated from the unfortunate existence of the Luray Valley. Might not Jackson become the victim of a flank movement by that route, in his turn?

So General Shields hurried by Luray toward Newmarket, and General Fremont followed in his adversary's rear.

Desperate attempts were made to break through Ashby's rear-guard of cavalry, infantry, and artillery; and the Federal cavalry charged with very great gallantry.

They were repulsed by the free use of canister, and by the energy of Ashby, who seemed to delight in the performance of the duty assigned to him.

It was Ashby who fought that long battle I have mentioned, from Strasburg up the Valley. At Woodstock, Edinburg, Mount Jackson—on every hill and in every valley of this beautiful region—he fought, with shell, canister, the carbine, and the sabre.

A certain amount of fighting every day seemed now to have become necessary to the man; and such untiring energy and activity had he displayed, that Jackson, who had long since become as warmly attached to him as ever, placed the whole rear of the army under him.

It was thenceforth in Ashby's power to- order into action as much infantry as he wished; but his cavalry and horse artillery continued to be sufficient.

I was with him nearly all the time during this famous retreat— can never think of it without seeing Ashby on his milk-white horse again—and always his noble form and face rise up and illustrate the page which speaks of those events. I see him as he passed before me then, and shall ever see him.

I loved and admired him as the pearl of honor, the flower of chivalry. But how I should have treasured up every word, and been beside him always, had I known his days were numbered—that even then his last sands of life were running through the glass!

LVII.

ASHBY'S WHITE HORSE.

THE army reached and crossed the Shenandoah near Newmarket: it was Ashby's duty now, when his cavalry had passed, to destroy the bridge behind him.

Having carried him the message conveying Jackson's wishes as to the time and manner of destroying it, I was a witness of the scene which followed.

The wagons, prisoners, and infantry had all defiled over the bridge, the enemy following closely on their rear, and it required Ashby's most vigorous efforts and utmost skill in disposing his cavalry, with the fire of the artillery from the hill south of the river, to keep back the pursuing force long enough to enable every thing to get over. At last, however, this important object was achieved; notice was given that the last brigade was over, and Ashby began to cross with his cavalry and artillery.

A strong rear-guard still faced the on-pressing enemy, skirmishing hotly as they slowly fell back; and under cover of this force, commanded by Ashby in person, the cavalry column and guns clattered over the bridge.

Ashby now fell slowly back with the rear-guard, obstinately contesting every step; and never shall I forget the chivalric spectacle which he presented, mounted on his superb white horse, as fearless and defiant as himself. The swarthy face, with its heavy black beard, glowed witn martial ardor; in the flashing eyes might be read the joy of conflict; and, with drawn abre, on his spirited animal, he resembled some knight of the Middle Ages, asking nothing better than an opportunity to meet all comers.

The rear-guard was finally across, and, ordering the column to move rapidly on and join the main body, Ashby selected eight men, and proceeded rapidly to set fire to the wood-work of the bridge.

In this, however, he was suddenly met by a serious obstacle The timbers were saturated by the recent rains, and it was found impossible to kindle the combustibles which had been collected.

To his inexpressible chagrin, Ashby saw the Federal cavalry coming at headlong speed down the turnpike on the opposite side of the bridge; and in an instant a storm of bullets whistled round the heads of the working party, who exhibited unmistakable signs of "demoralization."

Ashby ordered them, hotly, to attend to the work before them; but the Federal cavalry had now dashed on, and were thundering over the bridge, which had just kindled.

In spite of Ashby's stern and passionate orders, the men ran to their horses, and another volley whistled among them, completing their panic.

In an instant they were in the saddle, and disgracefully fled, without thinking of their commander. I found myself alone beside General Ashby, who sat his white horse with wrathful countenance—half resolved, it seemed, to charge the whole Federal column, and die sword in hand rather than fly.

A single moment only was now left in which to decide upon our course. The enemy were nearly across the bridge, charging with loud cheers, and firing as they came.

"Let us give them a shot at least, Surry," he said.

And levelling his revolver, he emptied, in succession, every barrel, and I imitated him.

Then nothing was left but flight or capture; and an exciting race commenced.

We were pursued by a whole detachment, who followed us with loud orders to halt.

"I am sorry my pistol is emptied," said Ashby, looking grimly over his shoulder; "but if it comes to the sabre, _'ll try to give a good account of some of them."

We galloped on at full speed, followed closely by our pursuers, who were excellently mounted.

"Those must be stolen horses," said my companion coolly. "See that tall fellow on the black—it is a superb animal."

"Which?" I said, laughing, "the man or the horse?"

As I spoke, a bullet grazed my neck, bringing the blood.

"Pay for your jest," was Ashby's reply. "Look out, the whole party are going to fire!"

A volley followed, and the next moment I heard Ashby utter something like a growl.

"Look!" he said, pointing to his horse's side.

I saw that a bullet had inflicted a deep wound, from which the blood was streaming.

"Some one shall suffer for that!"

And the moment for carrying out the threat speedily came.

Weary of the ineffectual chase, the cavalry all stopped with the exception of two, who continued the pursuit, apparently from mere bravado. The time had arrived for Ashby's revenge.

Wheeling suddenly round, his sabre flashing at the same instant from his scabbard, he charged straight upon the two cavalrymen, and with one whirl of his weapon nearly severed the head of one of them from the body. Cut completely out of the saddle, the man fell, inert as a corpse, in the road—and at the same moment a ball from the rear-guard of cavalry, which we had nearly reached, penetrated the breast of the second, who also fell from his seat.*

Ashby then returned his sabre to the scabbard, and coolly rode on to the head of his column.

The infantry had halted, and, on reaching the point where they were drawn up, my companion found that his white horse could go no further. He dismounted, and, gazing in silence upon the noble animal which had borne him safely through so many bloody encounters, seemed as much grieved as if he were about to part with some valued friend.

* Historical.

The wound was mortal, and caressing gently, for a few moments, the arched neck of his favorite, Ashby turned away in silence. The horse was led off by one of the men; and never shall I forget the superb appearance of the wounded charger as he passed along the line of infantry. Panting with his hard run, foaming at the mouth, and covered with sweat—his splendid head carried proudly erect—his eyes full of fire—he seemed inspired with human hatred for the enemy, and to defy them to the last.

I could see in the eyes of the men, as he paced before them with the bleeding wound in his side, how much they pitied and admired him.*

LVIII

I AM CAPTURED.

THE river was passed, Newmarket reached, and Jackson's column swept on to Harrisonburg. His cavalry had destroyed the bridge over the South Fork of the Shenandoah, leading into the Luray Valley; his flank was thus safe still—and soon Harrisonburg was reached.

Thence, without pausing, he pushed on toward Port Republic, where, with his back to Brown's Gap, he could stand at bay, and bid defiance both to Fremont and to Shields. But could he reach that point? On the summit of the southern shoulder of the Massinutton, which here subsides into the Valley, could be seen the fluttering of our signal flags; and these said, "Shields is it sight, and rap'dly advancing toward Port Republic."

All now depended upon the rapidity of Jackson's movements and the resources of his strategy. Pressed in rear by the heavy column under General Fremont, and with that under General Shields rapidly advancing to intercept him, he was in a position of very great peril; and I followed, with absorbing interest, the

* See accounts of this scene in newspapers of the time.

movements of the great gladiator thus encircled by his dangerous foes.

An untoward incident now occurred, however, which threatened to prevent me from taking part in the coming struggle.

We were steadily falling back from Harrisonburg on Port Republic, when the incident I refer to took place. General Fremont was pressing closely on the rear-guard under Ashby, which was incessantly engaged, and having by this time formed a strong personal affection for the great cavalry commander, I was with him whenever I could spare the time from my duties.

I often look back now to those days with a longing desire to live them over again, and hear the friendly voice of the great spirit which has passed away. It was a life all excitement and romance which we lived at that epoch—days of fighting, of incident, of adventure; nights of hasty slumber, in rude bivouac under the forest trees, or of long, confidential talks by the smouldering camp-fire; all day long the crack of carbines, and the roar of artillery keeping back the enemy; and then, with the great soldier who had moved in front of his cavalry, ever ready to come to the sabre, those sad, memorial recollections which are the luxury of friends, who exchange their memories as they fall asleep after or on the eve of battle. Often now those days come back to me—I seem to see his face and hear his voice—and peace, amid friends and in the good old home, seems not so wholly charming as I thought it would be, then. Peace hath her victories and her laurels; but the flowers are not so fresh, nor tipped with such fiery dew, as when they bloom amid the hot atmosphere of war.

I wander from my theme—but those old times beguile me. Again the winds of other days blow on my forehead, and I live in the hours that are dead.

To come to the actual occurrences of that time—I was with the cavalry rear-guard between Harrisonburg and Cross Keys, some miles from Port Republic, at which point the infantry was concentrating, when a dust, rising upon the flank, attracted my attention, and I told Ashby that I would go and ascertain what it meant.

"Take care, Surry," was his reply; "the enemy are close behind us, and you will be captured."

"I reckon not."

"Well, keep a good look-out. The Federal advance-guard is commanded by Sir Percy Wyndham, an English officer, who has sworn, I am informed, that he will 'bag' me. I should be sorry to have him catch one of my friends."

"I defy him!"

And, with that spirit of pride which so often precedes a fall, I put spur to my horse, and went at full speed in the direction of the dust, following a narrow forest-road.

Unfortunately, Ashby's fears were speedily realized. I had not gone a quarter of a mile, when a detachment of cavalry flankers debouched quietly into the road behind me, and, levelling their carbines, ordered me to surrender.

It was the coolest and most business-like affair I had ever witnessed, reader. No ill-bred hurry—no excitement—no "violent language," or unpleasant collision. Within twenty steps of me were twenty carbines, cocked and aimed at my breast—the officer at the head of the men commanded, "Surrender, or you are dead"—and, with bitterness in my heart, I surrendered.

"You are an officer, sir?" he said, riding up.

"I am."

"What command?"

"The Confederate States Army."

"Rather a considerable force in our front, Lieutenant," said the officer, who seemed to be something of a humorist; "send the prisoner, under guard, to Colonel Wyndham."

The lieutenant touched his hat—I remember he was a villianous-looking fellow—and three men separated themselves from the column and took charge of me.

"Kill him, if he tries to escape," said the humorous officer.

The men cocked their carbines, and rested them across their pommels; and, with this pleasing escort, I was conducted, by a winding road through the woods, to a house near the main road, which I had remembered passing on the preceding evening.

Here superbly equipped horses were seen tethered to the

boughs and fences—couriers went and came—and my escort conducted me into the presence of Sir Percy Wyndham, commanding the cavalry advance-guard of the Federal forces.

LIX.

I MAKE THE ACQUAINTANCE OF SIR PERCY WYNDHAM.

I FOUND myself in the plain sitting-room of a small farm-house. On a table were spread maps and papers; and a bottle of wine raised its slender neck, flanked by glasses.

Lolling in a split-bottomed rocking-chair was a tall, fine looking personage, clad in a superb uniform, and wearing a sabre with a magnificently chased hilt, which rattled against fine French cavalry boots, decorated with enormous spurs. The countenance of this officer was ruddy, handsome, and full of pride. His hair was light, long, and worn in curls. It was a military Adonis I saw before me in the person of Sir Percy.

When I entered, he was talking with a sleek personage, clad in citizen's dress, who had on his knees a portfolio, in which lay some loose sheets of paper covered with writing. Upon my appearance, this gentleman seized a pen, dipped it in the ink, and held it poised above his paper, with the air of a man who is going to report a public speech.

" A prisoner, Colonel," said my escort.

The Colonel wheeled round in his chair and looked keenly at me.

" When were you captured ?"

" Half an hour ago."

" You are an officer—a major, I see. What command ?"

" I have already replied to that question."

" To whom ?"

" The officer who captured me."

" Well, sir, you can, no doubt, favor me with a repetition of your reply."

I replied that I belonged to the Confederate States Army.

"Close, Colonel!" here interposed the sleek gentleman ih black, who had hastily scratched away at his paper as this dialogue took place.

"A perfect trap!" exclaimed the Colonel, lolling carelessly back in his chair; "but I have never known a single rebel officer who had not this exaggerated idea of the importance of secrecy in every thing. Now, I make no mystery of my movements—none."

"You are going to 'bag Ashby,' Colonel, and that's a fact,' came, with a laugh, from the sleek personage.

"I swear I will! At least you can tell me, sir," he added, turning to me, "whether you know General Ashby."

"Intimately, sir."

"Ah?" and the Colonel rose in his chair.

"I have been with him throughout the retreat—though I am not attached to his command."

These words seemed to attract the Colonel's attention and excite his interest.

"Take a seat, Major," he said. "I did not hear your name"— "Surry."

"An English name. You Virginians come of the genuine English stock—and ought to fight well."

"We try to do the best we can, Colonel."

"And you do it devilish well, Major. Ashby has given me a world of trouble."

"He will be delighted to hear it, when I get back."

"Ha! but I am not going to part with you so soon, my dear àr. Let us talk a little first."

"Willingly, Colonel."

"I have sworn to capture Ashby."

"Don't you think it is a difficult undertaking?"

"Well, he is cool and watchful enough, but I will get the better if him yet. I thought I had him the other day at the bridge."

"Over the Shenandoah?"

"Yes—did you witness the chase after him?"

"I was with him."

"Ah! then you were tne other officer we ran?"

' Yes, Colonel: but your pursuing party went a little too far."

.' How?"

'Ashby cut down one with his sabre, and the other was
shot."

The Colonel frowned.

" And that's a fact, Sir Percy," said the sleek gentleman, scrib-
bling away. "I saw the bodies as we passed."

"Curse what you saw, sir!" was the growling reply.

"I wouldn't take any thing for that incident, Colonel!" exclaimed the newspaper correspondent—for such he evidently
was: "rapid retreat of rebels, pursued by victorious Union-
ists—bridge burning in their rear—Ashby on white charger, 'retiring' at full gallop—unfortunate fate of two of his pursuers,
who, surrounded by a whole brigade of rebel cavalry, fought
their way nearly out, but were finally killed by treacherous blows
from behind: it will be splendid, Colonel!"

A careless laugh from the Colonel greeted this magnificent picture, and, at the same moment, an officer galloped up and entered.

" Well?" said the Colonel.

"The enemy are falling back again, sir—the road is clear in
front."

"Entirely?"

"Nothing seen, sir, but a detachment of cavalry, commanded
by General Ashby."

"How do you know that?"

"I saw him distinctly through my glass, and know him perfectly."

The Colonel started up.

"Order a squadron of picked men to report to me here, in
fifteen minutes," he said to a staff-officer on the porch of the
farm-house.

Then, turning to the newspaper correspondent, he said:

"Do you wish to secure material for a fine paragraph?"

"I would go through fire and blood to do so!" exclaimed the
correspondent, in a martial tone, and brandishing his pen.

" You like amusement?"

" I am devoted to it, Colonel."

" Well, come with me, and you will see some fun."

" What is your design, Colonel?"

" To bag Ashby." *

And the Colonel twirled his mustache with joyful ardor. A quick thrill ran through me, and, assuming a careless tone, I turned to Sir Percy, and said:

"I really should like to be present at that little affair, Colonel."

" You!"

"I can ride in the rear, under guard, and, in either event, there will be small danger of my escaping."

"In 'either event!' My dear sir, I intend to capture your General Ashby as surely as the sun shines. As you doubt it, have your wish, and come and see me do it."

" And I, Colonel," said the correspondent.

" Of course! You are the historian to hand me down to posterity."

As the Colonel, now in high good-humor, turned away, I saw a grimace upon the countenance of the correspondent. He was evidently a philosopher, and estimated the element of failure in all human affairs.

In ten minutes we were all in the saddle—the Colonel riding at the head of the squadron at a trot, on the straight road to Cross Keys

---

LX.

HOW ASHBY WAS NOT "BAGGED" BY SIR PERCY.

The column had not advanced half a mile when Ashby's cavalry pickets appeared in front, reconnoitring from a hill.

The vedettes held their ground until the column was nearly upon them—when they galloped off.

The same ceremony was repeated at the next hill, and as

---

* His words. See the newspapers of the day, containing the correspondent's letter.

Colonel Wyndham continued to advance without flankers, my heart began to beat and my hopes to rise high.

I knew how dangerous it was to trifle with an adversary like Ashby, and the incautious method of advancing adopted by the Federal Colonel subjected him, I knew, to imminent peril of capture.

In thirty minutes, events took place which fully supported my view of the subject.

Reaching a point where the road traversed some low grounds, between two low ranges of hills on either side, Colonel Wyndham saw in front of him, at the distance of about four hundred yards, a small body of cavalry, which slowly retired as he appeared.

The Colonel greeted the spectacle with unmistakable pleasure.

" Now for it !" I heard him call out to his friend, the correspondent, who had prudently withdrawn to the side of the road.   " Look out for some fun !"

And, placing himself in front of his column, the Colonel drew his sabre, and gave the order to " charge !"

The column rushed forward at the word—but oh ! disastrous event !—occurrence ever to be deplored !—no sooner had the horses of the Federal cavalry-men run thrice their length, than the crest on the right of the road, in their rear, suddenly bristled with sabres—and a squadron, led by Ashby in person, thundered down, and fell, with shouts, upon the Federal rear.   At the same instant, the detachment in front, which had served as a decoy, charged the enemy full tilt—and, caught between this double fire, cut off, surrounded, dumb-foundered, the Federal cavalry-men threw down their arms and surrendered.*

I was recaptured, and now found myself by Ashby's side, face to face with Colonel Wyndham.   The newspaper correspondent had glided into the woods and escaped.

I shall never forget the expression of the Federal Colonel's countenance at that moment.   If ever rage, mortification, and astonishment were depicted on the human face, his displayed them.

* Historical.

When he caught my eye, he glanced at me like a tiger, and turned abruptly away.

Ashby treated his prisoner with that calm courtesy which characterized him, but the Colonel would not be mollified. His face was flushed, his eyes full of lurid light—wrath had mastered him. The few words he blurted out had something savage in them; and when he was conducted to the rear, through the lines of infantry, I heard that his wrath exploded.

Some one among the men greeted him, I heard, with the words: "Just look at the Yankee Colonel!" when his long pent-up anger burst forth like a torrent. His peculiar abhorrence, it is said, was to be considered a "Yankee"—and this was the straw that broke the camel's back.

Ashby captured sixty-four men, if my memory serves me, by this ambush; and these were now sent to the rear.

"Your luck is extraordinary, my dear Surry," he said, "to be captured and recaptured both in one day. I am truly glad to see you again. Come, tell me about it."

I narrated all that occurred, and my companion said, with a smile:

"The worst of all possible habits in a commander is to boast of what he is going to do."

"Especially when he doesn't do it."

And we rode on.

LXI.

ASHBY AMONG HIS MEN.

On the same night, I went to carry a message to Ashby, and found him seated at the bivouac fire, in the midst of a circle of his men, with whom he was conversing like one of their own comrades.

His sword and pistols were buckled around his waist; his horse stood ready saddled near; his swarthy face, with its heavy black beard, shone in the fire-light room was made for me at the fire, my message delivered, and the conversation went on between Ashby and his men.

The scene was striking and picturesque. All around the rude bivouac the horses were picketed to the trees, and beyond the circle of fire-light dusky figures came and went like phantoms. The great tree-trunks rose all around ; the heavy foliage of June drooped above ; and, scattered in groups around the brushwood fire, upon which some rails from an adjoining fence had been thrown, were the rudely-clad figures of the cavalry-men.

It was impossible to discover in Ashby's demeanor toward his men the least consciousness of his superior rank. His manner was the perfection of unassuming simplicity : you would have said that the party were a band of huntsmen, of whom he was one.

A thousand witticisms were uttered—a thousand adventures related. Ashby listened with a smile, and, with "Weil, boys," by way of commencement, took his part in the story-telling. Then some one began to sing.

It was a wild and plaintive air, like the sigh of the wind through the trees overhead, or the low sound of the pines in the breezes of autumn. It commemorated the exploits of Ashby ; and, I remember every verse wound up with the chorus :

> "Strike, freemen ! for your country,
> Sheathe your swords no more,
> While remains in arms a Yankee,
> On Virginia's shore !"

The words were rude and destitute of poetic merit, but the air was wild and touching. The men listened in silence. joining, however, with full voices in the chorus.

When the singer had finished, Ashby rose and said :

" Well, boys, it is getting late, and you had better go to sleep. We may have tough work to-morrow—perhaps to-night."

And he mounted his horse, which one of the men led forward.

" Good night, General," came from the group, who stood up ; and we rode back to a point where a small fire had been kindled by the General's servant for himself and his staff. They were all asleep, and, sitting down by the fire, we talked for a few moments.

Ashby was unusually silent and sad.

"What is the matter?" I said; "has that doleful air we heard put you in bad spirits?"

"Oh! no," was his reply.

"Perhaps it is that owl I hear, with its melancholy tu-whoo. Fie! *mon Général,* to be low-spirited without reason!"

"You may laugh, my dear Surry, but I do feel oppressed to-night. Do you know that a curious fancy has taken possession of my mind?"

"What is that?"

"That my end is approaching--my days on earth numbered."

"Pshaw! this is mere moonshine. You are sick."

"I never was in better health, and my arm was never stronger."

His voice was sadder than ever, as he added in a low tone:

"I have been thinking to-night of my brother Richard."

"And went yonder to dissipate your gloom?"

"Yes."

For some moments he remained silent. Then he said:

"Mine has been a sad life for the last few months. I never got over that blow. Why did this cruel war come to make me miserable? I would cheerfully have given my own poor life— but not my brother's."

"Your own has been worth much to the country—you cannot be ignorant of that."

My companion smiled faintly and shook his head.

"Don't let your friendship induce you to flatter me. I am not much. It would puzzle you to find any sort of accomplishment in me except the art of riding. I believe I *am* a good rider—I ought to be, as I have been in the saddle, riding over the hills of Fauquier, since my childhood; but that is all. I am not intellectual, as Richard was, and I can hardly write at all. As to my soldiership, Surry, I am a mere partisan with good eyes and ears, not an educated officer."

"Is West Point every thing?"

"I confess it does not make a great soldier, but I sadly need training. Well, I have done what I could. Little as it is, it was my best, and no man can do more. I can say, if I fall, 'I gave my country all I possessed.'"

"No one can say more."

"It is my pride to be able to declare as much. I did not go into this war to receive military renown, or gain rank. God knows I would have laid down my life to prevent it. But what could I do? Our soil was invaded; I was a Virginia gentleman; I should have died of shame had I remained at home. For the proud, hard-riding Ashbys to have proved laggards was impossible. So I took my part—and then came that heavy blow which you know of. I confess that it made me bitter, and has added force to many a blow of my sabre. I have killed many. I pitied these people sometimes when my men were cutting them to pieces, but then I seemed to hear a voice in my ears, 'Remember Richard!' The thought made me merciless, and steeled my heart. I have no doubt that yonder in the North they represent me as a bandit and ruffian, but I appeal to my life to confute their charges. I have fought fairly and openly; I have never oppressed the weak, or ill-treated a prisoner. In Winchester, some ladies from the North came to me and said, 'General Ashby, we have nothing contraband in our baggage or on our persons. You can search us.' I bowed to them and said, 'I am a Virginia gentleman; we do not search the trunks or persons of ladies here, madam.' You see I boast—but I am proud to remember that I have never done any thing which was unworthy of my father's son. I have carried on hostilities, in this struggle which my whole heart approves, as a Virginia gentleman should. That consolation, at least, remains."

"And it ought to be supreme."

"It is. I have no self-reproach—no regrets. If I could have done more for old Virginia, I would."

"It is something at least to have lived in the saddle, watched day and night, and risked your life every hour"

"Risked my life? Is that much to risk?"

10

"It is to most men."

"It is not to me."

"I understand —since your great misfortune. But he died like a Southern gentleman, fighting to the last."

"Well, I hope to do so, too."

And, making an evident effort to banish his gloom, Ashby began to converse upon the events of the morning. I drew as grotesque a picture as possible of the confident Sir Percy, and the sleek newspaper-correspondent, to make him laugh, but I could not succeed. His sadness seemed beyond the power of words.

Taking my leave at last, with that grasp of the hand we bestow upon friends in time of war—friends whose faces we may never see again—I mounted my horse, and set out on my return.

Fifty yards from the bivouac fire, I chanced to turn my head Ashby was upon his knees, praying.

LXII.

"VIRGINIANS, CHARGE!"

GENERAL FREMONT continued to press forward from Harrisonburg upon Jackson's rear, while General Shields hastened up to intercept him between Port Republic and the Blue Ridge.

The rear of the army was near Cross Keys, when, as I was riding along with General Jackson, a courier came from Ashby with a dispatch.

Jackson read it, and then, handing it to me, said :

"Major, ascertain what force of infantry General Ashby requires, and see that he gets it."

As I went to execute this order, I read the note. Ashby stated that one or two regiments of Federal infantry were pressing forward incautiously ahead of their column, and that with a small force he felt convinced he could flank and capture them. To obtain General Jackson's sanction of this movement was the object of his note.

I found Ashby on the summit of a hill, pointing out, with

animated gestures, to General Ewell, the peculiarities of the ground, and its adaptation to a battle. He had completely lost all *his* sadness of the preceding night; his swarthy face was full of ardor ; his eyes brilliant with the thought of the approaching contest.

So striking was this animation in every gesture and movement, that, as I passed the First Maryland Regiment, drawn up on the side of the road near at hand, I saw its commanding officer, Colonel Bradley Johnson, point to the two Generals, and heard him say :

"Look at Ashby enjoying himself."*

I saluted and informed General Ashby of Jackson's response to his note. He could have any force he desired.

"Two regiments will do," was his quick reply. "I will take the First Maryland and the Fifty-eighth Virginia yonder—though it is a mere handful. Look at them!" he exclaimed, with his arm extended at full length, "look! they are coming on as if we were chaff to be scattered to the/winds!"

And he pointed out a dark column on the road ahead, tipped with burnished bayonets.

Preparations were rapidly made for the projected attack. Ashby's design was to make a circuit to the right with his infantry, while his cavalry remained in the road before the advancing column, as a decoy ; and at the moment when the Federal infantry came opposite to him, exposing its flank, to make a sudden and determined attack upon it.

But for one of those unforeseen incidents which interpose in all human affairs, this skilful conception would have been crowned with complete success. What defeated it will now be related.

Ashby hastened to the spot where the two regiments were drawn up under arms, and rapidly issued his orders. The troops were concealed from the enemy by the hill, on which the cavalry were drawn up, and there was no difficulty in moving them, without discovery, in the direction proposed.

They were promptly in motion, and, exclaiming, "Come, Surry,

---

* His words.

and see me attack them!" Ashby galloped ahead, followed at a
rapid pace by the infantry.

We had ridden about half a mile, when suddenly the report
of a gun came from a body of woods in front of us, and a bullet
whistled by our heads.

"What can that be?" exclaimed Ashby, riding coolly ahead;
"there can be nothing here."

"Can the enemy have conceived the same plan as yours—and
got thus far?"

"It is hardly possible."

Suddenly, in a dense skirting of undergrowth which ran along
a fence on the edge of the woods, I saw the glitter of bayonets.

"Take care! There is their line!" I exclaimed.

As I spoke, a blaze ran along the fence, and a storm of bullets
whistled around us.

Ashby turned and galloped back to his infantry.

"Forward! double-quick!" was his ringing order, and, rapidly
communicating with the Colonels, he gave his directions.

The Fifty-eighth Virginia was to charge the enemy in front,
while the First Maryland, formed upon its left, was to turn the
Federal right, pour a cross-fire upon them, and then charge with
the bayonet.

In three minutes line of battle was formed, and every thing
ready for the attack.

Ashby placed himself, still on horseback, at the head of the
Fifty-eighth Virginia, which resembled a small battalion rather
than a regiment, and Colonel Johnson gallantly advanced at the
head of the Marylanders on the left.

I shall never forget the appearance of the landscape at this
moment. In front was a wheat field waving with ripe grain,
over which rippled long shadows as the wind swept it; and
beyond extended the heavy foliage of the woodland, mellowed
by the golden light of the calm June evening. The sun was
slowly sinking behind a bank of orange clouds: the serene canopy
of soft azure, touched with gold, stretched overhead. It was
hard to believe that this beautiful landscape, where seemed to

reign the very genius of repose, was about to become the theatre
of a fierce and sanguinary conflict.

That conflict was not delayed. Ashby found his plan of flank-
ing and surprising the enemy completely thwarted · but there
they were before him—they had thrown down the challenge—
and he was not the man to refuse it.

Stern, obstinate "fight" was in his bronze face and sparkling
eyes, as he rapidly threw forward his line toward the fringe of
bushes on the edge of the woods, where the enemy were concealed; and, in an instant, the action commenced.

It speedily began to rage with extraordinary fury. The Fifty-
eighth Virginia poured volley after volley into the undergrowth,
where, lying behind a fence, the Federal line awaited their attack; and from the left was heard the hot fire of the Marylanders, rapidly advancing to turn the Federal flank.

They now saw their danger, and opened a rapid and destructive
fire both upon the Virginians and Marylanders, in front and
flank. The undergrowth blazed with musketry; a continuous
roar reverberated through the woods; and the enemy—the
Pennsylvania "Bucktails," Colonel Kane—met the attack upon
them with a gallantry which proved that they were picked
troops.

Ashby continued to advance on horseback at the head of the
Virginians, waving his sword and cheering them on; and Colonel
Johnson pressed forward, pouring a hot fire into the enemy's
flank. The latter had now gotten so close, and was in so favorable a position for a final charge, that Ashby saw the moment
had come for the bayonet.

At that instant his appearance was superb. He was riding a
bay horse—the same ridden by Jackson at the first battle of
Manassas *—and as he reined in the excited animal with one
hand, and pointed with the sword in his other to the enemy, his
dark face was full of the fire of battle, his eyes blazed, and in his
voice, as clear and sonorous as the ring of a clarion, spoke, as it
were, the very genius of battle.

---

* Historical. This horse was the property of Lieutenant James Thomson, of the
Horse Artillery—one of the bravest spirits of the war.

I think of him often as I saw him at that moment, charging, with unconquerable spirit, at the head of his men.

The Marylanders were almost in contact with the enemy when Ashby ordered the men of the Fifty-eighth to cease their fire, and close upon the enemy with the bayonet.

"Virginians, charge!"* came ringing from his lips, when a bullet suddenly pierced his horse's chest, and, advancing a few yards, the animal reeled and fell.

Ashby was upon his feet in a moment, and, pointing with his sword to the Federal line, now not more than fifty yards distant, continued to cheer on the men—when all at once I saw him stagger. A bullet had penetrated his breast, and I caught him in my arms, just as he was falling.

"You are wounded!" I exclaimed.

"I am done for, Surry," he replied, faintly; then extending his arm, while I saw the pallor of death overspread his features, he murmured:

"Tell my Virginians to press them with the bayonet!"

His head fell back as he spoke, and I laid him on the ground, supporting his shoulders upon my breast.

"I told you—last night—but it is a good death!" he murmured.

At that instant the shouts of the Southerners told that they had driven the enemy before them, and were hotly pursuing them through the woods.

"What is that?" exclaimed Ashby, half rising, with a flush upon his face.

"The enemy are flying."

A sudden light flashed from his eyes, he tried to rise, but fell back in my arms.

"Tell them I died in harness, fighting to the last!" he exclaimed—and, as the words left his lips, he expired.

Such was the death of Ashby, "the Knight of the Valley."

* His words.

LXIII.

CUT OFF.

WITH Ashby seemed to pass away all the splendor, the glory, the romance of the war. I could scarcely realize that the whole scene which I had witnessed was not some hideous dream—some nightmare of the hours of darkness.

Dead?—he who had passed unscathed through so many bloody encounters—who had seemed to possess a charmed life which no enemy's ball or blade could touch? Ashby, the hero of such romantic adventures, splendid achievements, and heroic exploits, dead, like a common, every-day mortal, and never more to lead his men, with flashing sabre, in the charge? The idea seemed monstrous—incredible.

But slowly came the realization of the truth. He was gone—the dauntless cavalier, the noble gentleman, the charming and winning companion. Who could supply his place? Under whom would the horsemen of the Valley fight so recklessly?— and what other leader could inspire them with that spirit which overthrows all obstacles?

I asked myself that question, and then came another thought —where will you find another friend like this pure spirit?—who can take his place with you?

I cannot draw the great outline of this splendid chevalier in my hasty memoirs; some abler hand will trace it—some more eloquent voice speak of his virtues. For me, I loved and will ever love him, as the perfect flower of chivalry. When he disappeared, the bloom seemed to pass away from the summer flowers, the azure from the calm June sky. Brave men were left, and the future was to be as glorious as the past—but, with this gentle heart, this perfect chevalier, seemed to fade the splendor and romance of the fresh dewy morning of the war. Thenceforth, it was a thing of sweat and blood and toil under a burning sky.

I come back to the narrative of events.

The column under General Fremont was now pressing hotly
upon Jackson's rear, between Harrisonburg and Port Republic;
and that under General Shields was hastening rapidly to place
itself between him and Brown's Gap—the avenue of exit from
the Valley. Jackson must retreat, if he retreated at all, by that
Gap, as the panic-stricken citizens had destroyed the bridges
above Harrisonburg; and, if General Fremont could only delay
his adversary sufficiently long to enable General Shields to come
up, the fate of the Confederate commander seemed decided.

From this moment commenced that admirable game of strategy
by which Jackson aimed to crush his adversaries in detail. He
had destroyed the bridge over the Shenandoah at Conrad's Store,
thereby preventing a junction between the two Federal columns;
and, establishing his head-quarters in the town of Port Republic,
prepared, with his main body, to attack General Shields, while
Ewell remained in front of General Fremont, and held him in
check. Shields 'once defeated, Jackson intended to recross to
the west bank of the Shenandoah, re-enforce Ewell, and, falling
upon General Fremont, decide every thing by a pitched battle.

I shall not stop here to speak of General Jackson's emotion
when he received intelligence of the death of Ashby. His opinion
of that officer was afterward expressed in his report. "An
official report," wrote Jackson, "is not an appropriate place for
more than a passing notice of the distinguished dead; but the
close relation which General Ashby bore to my command, for
most of the previous twelve months, will justify me in saying
that, as a partisan officer, I never knew his superior. His daring
was proverbial; his powers of endurance almost incredible; his
tone of character heroic; and his sagacity almost intuitive in
divining the purposes and movements of the enemy."

Such was the epitaph of Ashby, traced by the hand of Jackson.
It will live in the memories of the people of Virginia when
bronze has rusted away and the hard marble crumbled into dust.

Jackson's head-quarters had been established, as I have said,
at Port Republic—with his own division just opposite the town,
on the western bank of the Shenandoah, and Ewell at Cross
Keys, a few miles distant toward Harrisonburg—when, early on

the morning of the 8th of June, a company of cavalry, which had been sent down the Luray Valley, came galloping panic-stricken into the town, announcing the rapid approach of Shields.

The truth of the report was soon exhibited in a manner far from agreeable.

The enemy's advance force of cavalry and artillery thundered into the town; a gun was unlimbered and placed in battery near the bridge over the Shenandoah, so as completely to command it—and Jackson was cut off from his army!

He had hastily mounted, as the few scattering shots indicated the rapid advance of the-enemy; and, as he saw the Federal artillery unlimber at the bridge, his face flushed.

"We are cut off, General!" exclaimed one of the staff.

"Yes!" came curtly from the General, "but I am not going to remain cut off."

And he rode, with perfect coolness, toward the bridge.

I followed, with an internal conviction that the whole party would soon be enjoying an interview with General Shields, as his prisoners.

What followed, took place in the space of two minutes.

Jackson rode straight toward the piece of artillery, whose grim muzzle was pointed so as to rake the bridge in front of it, with every cannoneer at his place.

When he was within twenty yards of the gun, he coolly rose in his stirrups, and called out, in the calmest possible manner:

"Who ordered this gun to be placed here?"

I did not hear the reply of the officer in command of the piece, but he evidently mistook Jackson for some general or colonel of the Federal forces, and approached him with a deferential salute.

"Bring the gun over here!" the General called out.

And, as the men hastened to obey, he set spurs to his horse and darted at full gallop upon the bridge.

The whole scene had taken but a moment. At one instant the colloquy with the Federal officer was taking place—at the next we were clattering across the wooden flooring of the bridge.

I looked back as we went—the cannoneers were running to

10

their gun; they were seen rapidly to load; and then a roar was heard, and a shell screamed over our heads. Another and another followed, so close that we felt the wind which they made; but suddenly we reached ground which afforded cover—and Jackson was safe.*

He still continued his way at full speed, and, reaching the camps of his division, which had been suddenly aroused by the firing, caught his cap from his head, and, waving it, exclaimed: "Beat the long roll!"

The drums rolled; the troops fell into line; and, rushing his artillery into position, Jackson opened a rapid fire upon the enemy in the town.

Taliaferro's brigade now hastened forward; one of his regiments charged across, capturing the gun which had fired upon us; and the enemy's cavalry, with the infantry supports in their rear, hastily retreated from the town, and were pursued down the river.

Such was the narrow escape made by Jackson.

LXIV.

FREMONT CHECKED.

THIS incident immediately preceded the battles of Cross Keys and Port Republic.

I am not writing a history, my dear reader, and I refer you to the "official reports" of these great occurrences for the movements of the various bodies, the names of the regiments and brigades, and the exploits of this or that commander.

I write from memory—and memory is so treacherous! You forget almost all that is "important," and recall only some trifle which chanced to attract your attention. I picked up a black lace veil when we captured McClellan's dépôt at the "White

------

* The gun here mentioned belonged, as I afterward heard, to Captain Robinson's battery, from Portsmouth, Ohio. He was in command at the time.

House," and I remember it perfectly, though I have nearly forgotten that great conflagration. At Fredericksburg, a girl's slipper, dropped in the street as she ran from the enemy's shell, interested me more than the long rows of bullet-riddled houses and the bloody action!

The advance force of General Shields had hardly been driven from Port Republic before General Ewell became hotly engaged with Fremont at "Cross Keys."

Cross Keys is a locality about four or five miles from Port Republic, where a tavern with such a sign used to stand, I am informed. I could only see a stream, woods, and a red hill, upon which our artillery was in position. On both flanks were woods—in front the road approached through open fields.

The enemy advanced and opened a hot artillery fire about ten in the morning, and kept it up for some hours. Then, as though this had grown tedious, their infantry was marshalled in heavy lines, and a furious attack was made upon General Trimble, who held Ewell's right.

He waited until the Federal line had mounted the crest of a hill within close range, and then a blaze ran along the Southern lines, and the crash of musketry followed.

This sudden and determined fire produced a decisive effect. The Federal line gave way, fell back rapidly; and seeing a battery coming into position in his front, Trimble charged it, and chased the whole force more than a mile.

Ewell now threw forward his whole line, attacked with vigor, and the enemy retired before him. They largely outnumbered him, as was ascertained from captured documents, and I could never account for this easy victory until I discovered the composition of the troops. They were nearly all Dutch.

At nightfall, Ewell had driven the enemy some distance, established his lines considerably in advance, and then awaited further orders.

LXV.

EXEUNT OMNES.

JACKSON had returned to his head-quarters in Port Republic, and was up receiving reports and attending to business all night. I never saw him cooler or more collected. Events were rushing on, and the decisive moment had at last arrived, out, instead of becoming flurried and excited, he grew more calm.

His designs now became clearly developed. Orders were dispatched to General Ewell to move his main force, during the night, into Port Republic; leaving a small body of troops only in General Fremont's front: and, an hour or two afterward, Colonel Patton, left in command of this force, came to General Jackson's head-quarters to obtain specific instructions. The ground he was to fall back over, if hard pressed, the Colonel declared to be exceedingly unfavorable for such a movement; and he desired to ascertain exactly the General's wishes.

"Hold your position as long as possible," was Jackson's reply, "only retiring when you cannot maintain your ground. Then fall back slowly, fighting at every step, and, by the blessing of Providence, I hope to be with you before ten o'clock to-morrow."*

The General's design was thus obvious, and I laid down to snatch an hour's sleep, before the attack on General Shields.

I was aroused at daylight. Jackson had already put his forces in motion. The long column defiled through the town of Port Republic, crossed the South River Fork of the Shenandoah on some wagon-bodies sunk in the stream, and soon the firing in front began.

"Come, Major!"

And Jackson rapidly got into the saddle.

"Winder is engaged," he said, as we rode along, "but I am afraid the enemy's force is too great for him."

* His words.

We reached the field, about three miles from the town, just before sunrise, and events soon occurred which fully justified the General's fears.

The river here makes a bend in the shape of a crescent; and the ground thus enclosed was waving with a magnificent wheat crop, glowing in the fair June morning. On the right was an elevated piece of ground—and here the enemy were posted in heavy force.

Their long lines stretched, dark and menacing, across the wheat field; the high ground on their left was crowned with artillery; and the United States flag rippled proudly in the breeze.

The banner of the Stonewall Brigade—the Virgin of Virginia—advanced defiantly to meet it, and, with a roar like thunder from the opposing batteries, the battle began.

The advantage derived by the enemy from the commanding position on their left now became fatally obvious. The ranks of the Stonewall Brigade were torn by a deadly fire of shell and canister; and, taking advantage of this circumstance, the Federal right and centre rushed forward, charged the Southern artillery, and, pouring a destructive fire into the infantry, forced both to fall back in disorder.

The action seemed about to be decided at a blow. The Federal infantry, dark against the golden wheat, was pouring on in one continuous stream, firing as it came; and our artillery went off at a gallop to escape capture.

"Bad, very bad!" came curtly from Jackson, as he hurried to the spot. "Major, tell General Ewell to hurry up; no time is to be lost."

I found General Ewell approaching with his column, and delivered the message. Jackson's order was promptly responded to. Two Virginia regiments were advanced at a double-quick: Jackson placed himself at their head and galloped forward: then came the long roar of musketry, as they suddenly fell with fury on the flank of the triumphant enemy.

Their advance was instantly checked, but the heavy batteries upon the right still raked the field with a fire so destructive that no troops could sustain it. The shell, round shot, canister, and grape tore the ranks to pieces, and it was obvious that, as long as those guns held their position, nothing could be effected.

The Federal infantry, for a moment checked, now re-formed their line, and were evidently preparing for a more determined charge. Soon it came.

The batteries on the high ground redoubled their thunders; the plain was swept as by a hurricane—and then the Federal flag was seen pointing forward, its folds rippling as it came, and beneath it the long line rushed on, with shouts and volleys which seemed to shake the ground.

So determined was this charge that the Southern lines gave back before it—the enemy rushed on—the battle seemed lost.

I was by General Jackson's side at this moment, and never shall forget the stern, immovable resolution of his iron face. The heavy jaws were locked together; the cheeks flushed; from 'the keen eyes lightning seemed to dart.

" Those batteries must be silenced," he said, briefly, to Ewell, who was by his side.

At that moment General Taylor rode hastily up.

" General," said Jackson, in the briefest of tones, " can you take that battery ?"

" I think I can, sir," was Taylor's cheerful response.

" It must be taken, or the day is lost."*

A chivalric flash darted from Taylor's eyes, and, wheeling his horse, he galloped to his command, which had just formed line of battle on the right, near the ground where Jackson stood.

Taylor's sword flashed out, he rose in his stirrups, and, pointing with the weapon toward the Federal artillery, he called out, in his ringing voice .

" Louisianians ! can you take those guns ?" *

A wild cheer rose from the brigade for sole reply.

" Forward, then !" was Taylor's sonorous order.   " Charge the battery, and take it !"*

His line swept forward at the word, on fire with enthusiasm, and, rushing through the tangled undergrowth, was seen the

* His words.

next moment rapidly mounting a slope beyond. The ranks had been broken by the rough ground over which they had advanced, but Taylor was now seen, with drawn sword, in front of them— the straggling lines re-formed, in close order, for the charge—and, steadily, unmoved by the heavy fire poured upon them from the Federal batteries, they continued to advance.

What followed could be plainly seen from the position which we occupied.

Between Taylor and the Federal guns now intervened only a skirt of woods and a little valley. Beyond this valley was the crest, flaming like a crater.

For a moment the gray line did not reappear beyond the skirt of woods. Jackson's face filled with blood. He evidently feared that the men had recoiled in face of the certain death which awaited a charge upon this volcano.

All at once, a ringing shout was heard from the woods; the Federal artillery directed upon the point a rapid and deadly fire —then Taylor's line was seen to emerge from cover and rush down the hill.

The next moment it began to ascend the opposite slope, straight upon the muzzles of the Federal guns. The fire which greeted the charge was frightful. The guns were discharged so rapidly that the sound resembled volleys of artillery; and directly in the faces of the men was launched a tempest of grape, canister, and shell.

The spectacle was sublime; not for an instant did they recoil. The lines were literally hurled back as the iron storm swept through them, mangling and tearing men to pieces—but the ranks closed up again; the shouts of the Louisianians rang, clear and defiant, above the roar; and then they were seen to dash upon the guns, and strike their bayonets into the flying cannoneers.

Taylor had taken the Federal guns whose fire was so destructive, but he was not to hold them without a terrible struggle.

The enemy immediately concentrated a heavy infantry force in his front—charged him with desperation—and retook the pieces at the point of the bayonet.

Taylor fell back—his men fighting desperately ; but suddenly
the retrograde ceased, the opposing lines grappled almost in a
breast-to-breast struggle ; then, with echoing cheers, the Louisianians again rushed forward, and recaptured the pieces.

Three times they were lost and won, in this desperate struggle;
but, at last, Taylor drove back the line in his front sufficiently
far to bring off the pieces.   Then he drew up his shattered command to sustain the final assault upon it.

But his determined attack had changed the whole face of
affairs.   The enemy had been compelled to re-enforce their left
by withdrawing troops from their centre and right, which had
pressed so hard on Jackson ; and this, in turn, enabled Jackson
to move his forces from the left to the right.

Taylor thus found himself fully re-enforced ; his men held
their ground with new resolution ; and the opposing lines rushed
together in a mortal struggle.

It was soon decided.   Attacked in front by Jackson's infantry,
and subjected to a heavy fire from his batteries on the left, the
Federal lines began obviously to waver.   The musketry fire redoubled ; the Southern lines rushed forward with cheers ; and,
giving way in disorder, the enemy retired in confusion from the
field.

They were followed with a heavy fire—pursued for miles—
and, when the infantry were too weary to go further, the cavalry
took up the pursuit.

At this moment a new actor appeared upon the scene.

Suddenly, a furious roar came from the western bank of the
Shenandoah, opposite Port Republic—and General Fremont's
forces appeared upon the elevated ground, and his artillery
opened fire upon the parties engaged in burying the Federal and
the Confederate dead.

It was too late—Shields was defeated, and Fremont could not
cross.   Jackson had ordered the force in his front near Cross
Keys to fall back and burn the bridge—this had been done—and
now General Fremont was subjected to the mortification of seeing his brother general crushed before. his eyes, without the
power of coming to his assistance.

I have always considered this the most "dramatic" scene, as the French say, of the war:

General Shields flying in disorder, hotly pursued; General Fremont gnashing his teeth upon the opposite bank of the river; and Jackson looking calmly on, with the grim smile of the victor.

On the next day, General Fremont retreated down the Valley, and Jackson remained undisputed master of the country.

LXVI.

IN WHICH THE WRITER OF THESE MEMOIRS IS TAKEN TO TASK.

AFTER writing the preceding chapter, my dear reader, I rose, walked to the window, and, looking out upon the tranquil Rappahannock, so vividly in contrast with the hurrying scenes I had been describing, muttered: "It appears to me that my memoirs are becoming a pure and simple history of the war in Virginia."

Now, worthy reader, however noble and dignified the Muse of History may appear in her stately robes, I have always had a preference for the gay little Muse of Comedy, with her caprices, witcheries, and "wanton wiles." She is not half so solemn and imposing as her grave sister, but she is more interesting. If anybody laughs or cries, she finds it out, and tells you all about it—nay, she cries herself with the disconsolate ones, and laughs with the mirthful. There is not a smile or a tear that she will not share—she is the Muse, not of History, but simply of Comedy, you see.

She had been tugging at my skirts all this time, while I have been relating the events of the Valley campaign, and whispering in my ear, "I am growing tired of all these great generals and bloody battles. I wish to hear about some other personages whom you have introduced to me. There is Captain Mordaunt, that mysterious personage; and May Beverley, and Violet Grafton, and others. Where is Stuart, the peerless cavalier, Sweeny,

the banjo-player, Hagan, the giant corporal, and all the rest?
What's become of Fenwick, the serpent, and his cheerful companion, Mrs. Parkins? Has Captain Baskerville been wounded
in any action, and what of Will Surry, of the United States
Army? Are all these personages to be sacrificed upon the
remorseless altars of *History*—are we to have nothing but battles, battles, battles?"

Pardon, gentle muse, for the infliction. True, battles become
weariness. Carnage bores at last; death becomes the normal
condition of things, and ceases to interest. But it was the
great figure of Ashby that enthralled me. Watching the flash
of his bright sabre in the charge, or talking with him by the
camp-fire after the hard-fought day, I forgot all else, and could
see, in all the world, that noble figure only. Hereafter, I shall
leave to the historian the detailed narration of great battles.
When they cross my path they shall not detain me long, gentle
muse!

LXVII.

LEE STRIKES.

THE campaign of the Valley ended on the 9th of June. On
the 26th, Jackson was at Ashland, within sixteen miles of Richmond, rapidly advancing to throw his veteran corps against the
right flank of General McClellan.

I am not going to describe at length, my dear reader, the
great struggle which soon took place on the swampy banks of
the Chickahominy. See the histories. They are detailed, im-
partial, and strictly reliable. There you will discover that both
sides whipped; that General McClellan was utterly defeated,
and yet only " changed his base;" that the great campaign
against Richmond was ended at a blow, and yet that the Federal
army secured a better position for more decisive operations.

All this and more you will learn from the histories, which
never fib. I am only going to record a few incidents.

Jackson received at Ashland a note from General Stuart, addressed, "General T. J. Jackson, somewhere," and his corps continued its advance—now preceded by the cavalry—reaching the vicinity of Old Cold Harbor House on the afternoon of the 27th, just as A. P. Hill recoiled from McClellan's almost impregnable position.

Immediately the veteran legions of the Valley were thrown forward, and the woods reverberated.

Jackson was riding about on an old gaunt bay, peering out from beneath his cap, drawn down upon his forehead, and sucking a lemon. Calling a staff officer to him, he said:

"Major, ride to General Lee, present my compliments, and say that I have closed in on the front and rear of the enemy, and am pressing forward."*

At this moment, Stuart—now brigadier-general—rode up, and a warm greeting took place between the two commanders. The blue eyes of the great cavalier flashed—in his ruddy, heavily bearded face was the joy of the coming conflict.

"Well, General," he said, "you are attacking?"

"Yes."

"My command is ready to cut them off if they attempt to retreat toward Old Church. I have told the men to get ready for tough work."

"Good. What gun is that, General, so hotly engaged in front?"

"One of Captain Pelham's Napoleons; he is a splendid young fellow, and is fighting like a tiger!"

"Yes! There is one of my batteries about to relieve him."

At the next moment a young officer, slender, beardless, modest-looking, and covered with dust, came from the front. His blue eyes flashed, his firm lips gave evidence of an unconquerable spirit.

"This is Captain Pelham, General," said Stuart; "he has fought with one gun that whole battalion on the hill, at point-blank range, for nearly an hour."

Jackson held out his hand, and the young artillerist took it with a low bow, blushing as he did so, like a girl.†

* His words.   † Historical.

The battle had now begun to rage with fury, and, as Jackson rode to and fro, in the great field by the Old Cold Harbor House, courier after courier came and went, bringing him intelligence. His calm expression had not left him; but under his cap rim the dark eyes blazed.

A staff-officer galloped up.

"General Hood directs me to say, General, that his line is enfiladed by a battery of thirty-pound Parrotts, which are decimating his men, and making it impossible for him to advance."

Jackson rose in his stirrups and said:

"Give my compliments to General Hood, and tell him to hold his position. I will silence the battery. Mr. Douglas," he added, to one of his staff, "go back and get fifteen or eighteen guns, attack that battery, and see that the enemy's guns are either silenced or destroyed."*

In twenty minutes a tremendous fire was opened from the left upon the Federal battery, and then Hood's men were seen to rush forward, charging, with loud cheers.

At this stage of the action, I was sent by General Jackson with a message to one of his generals; and only mention the incident to record my first meeting with one whom I afterward knew well—a very brave and remarkable person. I had delivered my message, and was galloping back, when I saw a regiment almost torn to pieces by the horrible fire of the artillery and infantry on the crest in front. This fire was so appalling that the men could not endure it, and were seeking everywhere in the low, swampy ground, for some shelter from the hurricane of canister which swept it.

I regarded it as my duty to attempt to rally the men, knowing, as I did, that, if the line was broken at that point, Jackson's whole position would be seriously endangered; and I accordingly endeavored to induce the stragglers and scattered detachments to rally again around their colors, and charge the artillery, which was flaming in front.

* His words.

This is one of the most disagreeable portions of a staff-officer's duty; for if the immediate commanders of troops—their captains and colonels—cannot control them, it is still more difficult for an unknown officer to do so. It was, nevertheless, my duty to make the attempt, and I did so, but with small results. The stragglers paid little heed to me—every one was "sick," or "wounded," or in equally bad plight. In plain words, the fire was so deadly that they were unwilling to charge in face of it.

Ill success had put me in something like a rage, as, with drawn sword, I galloped up to a man separated from the regiment, and ordered him, in a hot and imperious tone, to rejoin his command.

He turned and looked at me with a cool air of surprise, and, as he had just loaded and capped a peculiar double-barrelled English rifle which he held in his hand, he took deliberate aim at a Federal officer, visible upon a hill near, and fired.

The officer fell, and as the personage with the rifle turned round I had a good view of him.

He was a young man, apparently about twenty-five or six, lithe, erect, and vigorously knit. He wore top-boots, a long blue coat, with a belt, containing a pistol, strapped around his waist; and over his forehead fell a brown hat, decorated with a black feather. His face was handsome and intelligent; his eyes dark and soft; his complexion sunburnt; and his mild-looking lips were surmounted by a delicate black mustache.

There was an air of immovable calmness and repose about this man, even at the instant when he brought down his enemy, which was very striking.

"Did you speak to me?" he said, in a courteous voice, very low-toned and mild.

I was in a rage at my ill success with the stragglers.

"Yes! Join your regiment there! Every man must be in his place!"

"I do not belong to that regiment," he said, as coolly as before.

"To what, then?"

"I am a staff-officer, sir—Captain Farley, of General Stuart's staff."

I saw the error into which my haste and hot blood had betrayed me, and hastened to beg Captain Farley's pardon.

"No harm done, Major," was his smiling reply, in his low, peculiar voice. "I suppose you are trying to get the men up—but you cannot do it. The line here is so thin, and the Yankees in such a powerful position yonder, that nothing can be done without re-enforcements."

I saw the justice of these words, after reconnoitring the Federal position.

"We will whip them," said Captain Farley, philosophically. "I went in with that regiment, as an amateur, the cavalry not being engaged; and have been trying to blow up some caissons, with explosive balls—but have had no luck. I have, however, killed three officers."

And the speaker quietly reloaded his empty barrel with a peculiar-looking cartridge, which he took from a fine English satchel made for the missile. He seemed entirely unconscious of the hail-storm of bullets which hissed around him, cutting twigs from the trees, during this operation; and, as I galloped off, I saw him again taking deliberate aim at an officer waving his sword in front of the Federal line upon the hill before us.*

In consequence of the intelligence I brought, Jackson immediately moved a brigade to re-enforce the line where it threatened to give way; and the battle raged more and more furiously.

Half an hour passed; and then a courier from General D. H. Hill brought a dispatch, saying that he was hard pressed and required re-enforcements.

"Where is the Stonewall Brigade?" asked Jackson, briefly.

"Just behind that hill, General," replied one of the staff, pointing to a wooded acclivity.

"Order it to advance to the support of General Hill."

The officer galloped off, disappeared in the woods, and very soon the long line of glittering bayonets emerged from the foliage—the red battle-flag in front.

Jackson's eyes flashed.

* Historic.

"Good!" he said; "we will have good news in a few minutes now!"*

The Stonewall Brigade rapidly crossed the wide field, plunged into the woods, and then was heard the long, steady, continuous roll of the musketry, as they came to the support of Hill.

From that moment, the battle was a mortal struggle—on the enemy's part, to defend the bristling crest, frowning with triple lines of breastworks; and on the part of the Southerners, to storm and carry the works with the bayonet. The sun slowly sank amid a haze of smoke, dust, and, you would have said, of blood, so fiery was its drapery of cloud.

Jackson was talking with Stuart, his eyes glaring now, and sucking his lemon, when a staff-officer galloped up and said:

"General Ewell directs me to say, sir, that the enemy do not give way in his front."

Jackson rose in his stirrups until his form was as stiff and erect as an arrow. His eyes blazed—his teeth were ground together. Stretching out his hand containing the lemon, he said:

"Tell General Ewell, if they stand at sunset, to press them with the bayonet!"*

General Stuart exclaimed:

"The officer may be shot!—send another, too, General."

"Right!" said Jackson; and, turning to one of his couriers, he said:

"*You* go!"

Major Pendleton, his adjutant-general, that young officer of a courage so splendid, volunteered to carry the message; and soon the roar of guns redoubled in front; then tumultuous cheers were heard, as the Southern line charged.

Just as the sun sank, Jackson's whole line—Hood's Texans before the rest—swept forward in one wild bayonet charge; and, from the fury of the shouts, and the long crash of the musketry, it was plain that the decisive assault was being made.

In a few moments, that electric shout which indicates success rose from the woods, and made the pulses leap.

* His words.

The Southern troops had charged the crest, flaming like a volcano, upon which the enemy were posted—swept them from it with the bayonet—and terminated the struggle.

It was like the conflict between the Titans and the gods of old mythology—but the Titans stormed and took the heights from which their opponents hurled the thunderbolts.

As the sun disappeared, McClellan's forces were in full retreat, pursued by the Southern troops.

Jackson was riding in and out between the guns, still pouring a steady fire—and the glare of the burning woods lit up his flashing eyes as he conversed with Stuart.

McClellan was thus defeated, and in full retreat toward James River. Jackson's corps held the front in the pursuit, and had a hard fight at the bridge in White Oak Swamp.

Then came the desperate struggle of Malvern Hill, which was a bad affair for us. The Federal commander massed his artillery, held his ground until night, and then retreated to Harrison's Landing, under cover of his gunboats.

"Now is the time," exclaimed Jackson, "for an advance into Pennsylvania! The Scipio Africanus policy is the best!"*

No such advance was made. Jackson's supreme military instinct told him that General McClellan was paralyzed—but the authorities at Richmond doubted. Thus the golden moment passed. Soon intelligence came that another Federal army was rapidly assembling north of the Rappahannock.

No new advance upon Richmond, however, was intended—. that army was to protect Washington. The Federal authorities agreed with Jackson. They knew that the Army of Northern Virginia *ought to* advance, and they acted upon the sound military maxim, always to give an enemy credit for intending to do what he ought to do.

But the hour of destiny had passed—the opportunity slipped away. Who counselled this inaction? It is impossible that it was General Lee, for one day after Malvern Hill, Jackson said to an officer:

* His words.

"*I* hear that some persons say General Lee is *slow*. He is *not* **slow.** I have known him for five and twenty years, and he is the only man I would follow blindfold!"*

It was on the field of Cold Harbor that I first saw General Robert E. Lee; and I have never seen a nobler type of manhood than this brave old cavalier—then known to very few—now one of the immortals.

Here is his outline:

Fancy, my dear reader, a man apparently about fifty years of age; tall in stature, erect as an arrow, and with a certain air of simplicity and grandeur in every movement of his person. His hair was gray, like his beard and mustache; his eye clear, penetrating, benignant, and yet full of that latent fire which betrays a powerful organization. His uniform was plain, and somewhat faded—the riding cape, upon his shoulders, evidently an old friend—and his brown felt hat was wholly without decoration. But it was impossible to mistake the general. His calm and collected air; his grave and measured courtesy without abandon; his perfect seat in the saddle, for he had been a cavalry officer— all pointed out the commander-in-chief. I have seen the noblest figures of the war, but none can be compared to that of our old captain. In every movement of his person, every tone of his voice, every glance of his honest eye, was the perfect grace, the sweet and yet stately courtesy of the old Virginia gentleman. Health, happiness, and length of days to our old hero! His glory is beyond the reach of hostile hands; and to-day, ten thousand and ten thousand, who would have died with him, take off their hats and salute him as the flower of truth and honor!

* His words.

LXVIII.

PAST THE RAPIDAN.

JACKSON'S corps had decided the fate of the day at Cold Harbor, as his brigade had turned the tide at Manassas. When he arrived, A. P. Hill was retiring, torn and bleeding—Longstreet unable to advance. The flank attack of the Valley-men decided all.

These veteran troops were now to bear the brunt of battle against a new adversary.

Leaving the hot woods of Charles City, they took up the line of march toward the Rapidan; and soon the long blue wave of the Ridge gladdened their eyes.

Jackson advanced without pausing, and, on the 9th of August, attacked and defeated General Pope at Cedar Mountain.

We had heard the most glowing accounts of this commander— how he had arrived at his head-quarters in a special car, decked out with flags and streamers—how he had penned an order, promising his army that he would never retreat, or seek that " rear " where, he said, " lurked shame and disaster,"* and how he had declared that hitherto he had " seen only the backs of his enemies."

In the midst of the wild plunder of the inhabitants which he permitted, he suddenly met Jackson face to face, on the slopes of Culpepper.

Cedar Mountain was a hard fight, and a vigorous charge drove our left wing back in disorder. But Jackson placed himself at the head of the men—a great shout, " Stonewall Jackson! Stonewall Jackson!" rose—and the enemy were swept back. Then Ewell closed in on the right; the whole Southern line advanced with cheers; and the forces of Pope gave way, and rapidly retreated, pursued by their adversaries.

The troops slept on ground in advance of the battle-field, under the brilliant August moon.

* See General Pope's order on taking command.

Jackson had fought at Cedar Run thirty-two thousand Federal troops, with less than half that number. General Pope concentrated his whole army now in our immediate front, and Jackson fell back.

He was met near Orange by the main body of the army under General Lee.

"Forward!" was now the word; and all was soon ready for a decisive trial of strength with General Pope.

LXIX.

AN ADVENTURE OF STUART'S.

IF the reader will now lose sight of all these great events—the mighty stepping-stones in the history of a nation—and consent to fix his attention upon the personal movements of the humble author of these memoirs, I will conduct him to a distance from the embattled hosts fast gathering on the banks of the Rapidan, and, descending that stream, penetrate with him the wooded country which stretches around the little village of Verdiersville.

I was the bearer of a message from General Jackson to General Stuart, then concentrating his cavalry on the right flank of the army; and I expected to find the commander of the cavalry somewhere in the vicinity of Verdiersville.

Good fortune attended me. I had scarcely reached the point where the Richmond or Antioch Church road debouches into the main highway below Verdiersville, when I heard a voice in the woods trolling lustily a camp-song, of which the jolly burden was—

> " If you want to have a good time,
>   *Jine* the cavalry !
>   Bully boys, hey !"

—and in a few moments Stuart appeared at the edge of the woods with his staff, coming from the south.

I have outlined Colonel Jeb. Stuart, of the First Virginia

Cavalry, with his blue blouse-coat of the U. S. Army, his Zouave cap, and floating " havelock." Let me now give some idea of Major-General Jeb. Stuart, commanding the cavalry of General Lee's army.

Imagine a figure stouter and more athletic than before ; a face fuller and ruddier, and decorated with a longer and heavier mustache and beard ; an eye more laughing, and a voice even more ringing and sonorous. This figure was clad in a gray "double-breasted " jacket, worn open, with the edges folded back and buttoned on each side—the sleeves heavily braided—and with a buff collar ornamented with three stars encircled by a wreath. A gray waistcoat reached to the throat ; top-boots with shining brass spurs extended to the knees; and over the high forehead, with its clear blue eyes, drooped a brown felt hat, looped up with a golden star, and decorated with a black feather.

At the side of this martial figure, which advanced with one leg thrown carelessly over the pommel of the saddle, rattled a light French sabre, balanced on the opposite side by a pistol in a black holster; and, as he came, the gay chevalier played negligently with one of his long buckskin gauntlets, keeping time to his song.

> " If you want to have a good time
> *Jine* the cavalry !"

rung out clear and joyous, echoing through the woods; and then the quick glance of Stuart—he never forgot anybody—had evidently recognized me.

" Hey !" was his laughing exclamation ; " here's our wandering cavalier ! How are you, Surry, and how did you leave old Stone-wall ?"*

" Perfectly well, General, and thirsting for the blood of Pope."

The next moment I had exchanged a grasp of the hand with the General, and my friends on the staff—only a portion of whom were present.

" Who would have expected to find you at this out-of-the-way place?" exclaimed the gay commander. "Some of these days

* Stuart's familiar name for Jackson.

you'll be ambushed by the Yankee cavalry, and then good-by to Surry!"

"I am not afraid. What news, General?"

"None—do you bring any?"

"Only a message from General Jackson." And I delivered it.

"All right," was Stuart's response. "I had thought of that, and Fitz Lee is ordered to this point. I expect him to arrive tonight. Is the army moving?"

"It will advance to-morrow."

"Good!—the cavalry will be in place! And now come on, and tell me all the news. You can't go back to-night. That old house would be a good head-quarters," he added, pointing to a deserted tenement at the mouth of the Antioch road, "but I believe I will go on to Verdiersville. Come, Surry!"

And resuming his sonorous advice to "*Jine* the cavalry!" the General rode on, with the staff and myself.

Passing the little skirt of pine-trees where, I remember, he afterward had his quarters—*al fresco* and tentless, in the cold December of 1863, and when General Lee, riding by, said, "What a hardy soldier!" as he saw Stuart thus bivouacking "under the canopy," in the chill nights—we pushed on, and about nightfall reached the little village of Verdiersville.

"I am going to stop here," said Stuart, drawing rein before a small deserted house, the first on the right as you enter the village from the west. "I ought to hear from Fitz Lee very soon now."

"This is the rendezvous?"

"Yes, and in the morning I shall be in the saddle, ready to advance—if the Yankees don't make a descent and capture us to-night."

"Have they any force in this vicinity?"

"Two or three regiments. They are scouting along the Rapidan at this moment, and may take a fancy to prowl in this direction."

"And you have no force near?"

"None within ten miles."

"My dear General," I said, laughing, "don't you think there is some danger that the Confederacy will be deprived of your valuable services?"

" Well," was his laughing reply, "we can't guard against all the chances of war."

"You ought at least to have a picket out."

" True, but I have only one or two couriers with me, and they are as tired as I am."

" And you are going to sleep here, without even a vedette?"

" I'll risk it."

And lightly throwing himself from his horse, the gay cavalier led him into the small yard in front of the house, threw the bridle over the palings, and, taking from his satchel some ham and biscuits, invited me to sup with him.

The staff imitated him; and when the meal was finished Stuart rose.

" It is singular that I don't hear from Fitz Lee," he said, and, turning to Major Fitzhugh of his staff, he added:

'Major, I wish you would take a courier, and ride back to the mouth of the Richmond road, and look out for Fitz Lee. Tell him to move on, and join me here without delay."

The Major promptly obeyed, and was soon out of sight, followed by the courier. We were not to see him again for many a long day.

" Come, Surry," Stuart then said, " let us get some sleep. I have been riding all day."

And, spreading his riding cape upon the little porch in front of the house, he almost instantly fell asleep. I wrapped myself in my blanket, and lay down beside him.

At dawn, the sound of steps on the porch woke me, and, rising, I saw the General walking bareheaded toward the gate.

" Strange I don't hear from Fitz Lee!" he said.   " What can be the matter?"

At that moment, the distant tramp of cavalry was heard, approaching from the direction of the Richmond road.

" Ah! here he is at last!" exclaimed the General, as the

head of the column appeared through the pines beyond the hill.

Then, as he turned, Stuart suddenly looked again in the direction of the column. It was impossible to make out the figures clearly, but some instinct seemed to warn him that all was not right.

"Captain," he said to an officer near, "ride down the road and see what that column is."

The officer mounted, and spurred toward it.

"It must be Fitz!" muttered Stuart, "and yet"—

At that moment shots were heard in front. The officer who had ridden in the direction of the approaching cavalry came back at a gallop, pursued by a detachment in blue uniforms, firing at him as he ran; and the mystery was solved.

The column was not Confederate, but Federal cavalry; and in an instant they were thundering forward, and had nearly reached the house.

There was no time to parley or to hesitate. The pursuers came on with loud shouts of "Halt! halt!" and in an instant were opposite the house.

I got hastily into the saddle, and finding all egress barred by way of the narrow gate, leaped the palings just as Stuart did likewise.

He had not had time to get his hat or riding-cape. I am not sure even that his horse was bridled, and believe that he rode only with the halter.

At all events, his swift bay cleared the fence in gallant style; and, pursued by furious orders to halt, accompanied with a shower of bullets, we crossed a field, and reached the cover of the woods.

"Quick work!" exclaimed the General, his face fiery hot. "Just look at the rascals!"

And, turning my head, I saw the Federal cavalry-men, who had only pursued the General and his staff a short distance, raising his riding-cape and hat upon the points of their sabres, with shouts of laughter and triumph.

We afterward ascertained that Major Fitzhugh had gone as far as the deserted house I have mentioned, and, after waiting for an hour or two for General Fitz Lee, had lain down on the floor to take a short nap, leaving the courier posted at the mouth of the road, to announce the General's arrival. Instead of General Fitz Lee's column, it was that of a Federal colonel com. manding a brigade. The courier was captured; and when Major Fitzhugh, hearing the tramp of horses near the house, rose *to go and meet General Fitz Lee*, he saw some blue-coats leading off his fine sorrel, which had been tied to a limb. Then they rushed in, seized him, and, after a struggle, made him prisoner, conducting him to the colonel. That officer acquired no information from the Major's rough replies; and, directing him to ride at his side as guide, proceeded toward Verdiersville.

The reader knows what followed. Stuart and his staff retired with more rapidity than ceremony; and the Federal colonel said to Major Fitzhugh :

" What party was that ?"

The Major saw that his general had escaped, and was laughing, overjoyed. He could not resist the temptation of making his captor " feel bad."

"Did you ask what party that was which has just escaped, Colonel ?" said the Major.

" I did, sir."

" Would you like to know very much ?"

" I would."

" Well, Colonel, that was General Stuart and his staff."

The words were like the explosion of a shell.

"Stuart ! That was *Stuart ?* Here—a squadron ! follow that party, and kill or capture them. It is Stuart !"

The squadron rushed forward on the track of the fugitives, and Stuart saw it coming.

" Pshaw !" he said coolly, " they won't come far. But let us get out of their way, Major."

And we galloped on. A few shots came, and we were pursued a short distance. Then, as Stuart predicted, they ceased following us. The General turned his horse. and rode back toward Verdiersville.

"They will be afraid of a trap, and leave the place at once," he said.

The event showed the justice of this surmise. As we came in sight of the small house from which we had retired so precipitately, the Federal cavalry was seen rapidly moving in the direction of the Rapidan.

"They have got my hat and cape," growled Stuart; "but I hope to get even with them."

And we re-entered the village.*

LXX.

THE PURSUIT.

WE had scarcely regained the house from which we had been chased with so little ceremony, when a courier announced that General Fitz Lee was approaching; and very soon his column appeared, the General riding in front.

"General Fitz," as his friends called him, was about twenty-six, of low stature, and with a stout and vigorous person. His face was ruddy and laughing, his eye bright, penetrating, and full of humor. A heavy brown mustache and beard half covered the gay and insouciant countenance. He wore a brown felt hat, looped up and decorated with a feather; a gray dress coat, and elegant cavalry boots, against which rattled his long sabre. "General Fitz" seemed to enjoy the profession of arms—to like movement, fun, and adventure—and was evidently a great favorite with Stuart, who was soon laughing gayly at his late escapade.

Not a moment, however, was lost in following the Federal column. Stuart, who had borrowed a hat from one of his men, took command in person, and pushed after them in the direction of Locust Grove.

"Come, Surry," he said, "you ought to be present when I have my revenge."

* A real incident.

11*

"But what will General Jackson say, if I go scouting with the cavalry? He will think that your adventurous life has demoralized me."

"Not a bit. Come! the army is moving, and we will join it sooner by crossing the Rapidan below."

I only wanted an excuse to yield. The cavalry *had* "demoralized" me. After their gay life, so full of romantic scenes and incidents, the infantry seemed tame.

I followed the General, and very soon we came upon the track of the retreating brigade. Stuart now pushed on rapidly, and an exciting chase commenced. Straight down the old turnpike toward Chancellorsville swept the column, following the fresh footprints of the enemy's horsemen; and soon I found myself once more in that strange country of the Wilderness, where was situated the house at which I had spent the night on my journey from Richmond to report to Jackson, in April, 1861.

All at once, not far beyond Locust Grove, rapid shots were heard from the advance-guard, which had pushed some distance ahead, and Stuart went at a swift gallop to the front.

"Here they are!" he shouted, and, rising in the stirrups, he cried, in his sonorous voice, as clear and ringing as a clarion:

"Form fours!—draw sabre!—charge!"

A yell rose from his column at the words; and on they came, the sabres glittering in the brilliant sunshine.

Then followed, my dear reader, that brief but animated spectacle, called a cavalry fight. Only the enemy did not make a good, obstinate stand; they seemed to aim only at getting off.

Bang! slash!—bang! bang! bang! And we were among them, cutting right and left.

They did not stand long. In five minutes they were running, followed at full speed by the yelling Southerners.

The chase continued as far as the river; and the Federal cavalry-men scrambled down the steep hill toward the ford.

Stuart was about to follow, when a long dark line appeared on the high ground beyond; a piece of artillery "countermarched" at a gallop; and then a puff of white smoke was seen, followed by the shriek of a shell, which fell in the very centre of the pursuing column. Another came, then another; and, under cover of their artillery, the Federal cavalry crossed the river.

Stuart ordered a halt, and, drawing up his column behind a hill, rode forward to reconnoitre. The Federal force on the opposite bank was ascertained to amount to at least a division of cavalry; and finding that an assault was impracticable with the small force which he then had, Stuart at once dispatched orders to his main body, which had not come up, to move on rapidly and join him.

"When they arrive," said the General, "I will show you, Surry, what my men can do in the way of charging across a river in the face of sharpshooters and artillery. I don't intend to let those fellows stop me. 'Do or die' is my motto."

And the General threw himself at full length under a tree, with no trace of ill-humor at his morning's adventure. From the bright surface of his splendid nature the breath of anger quickly passed.

The long chase and the time lost at the river had consumed the day, and the sun now began to decline. Stuart had given up all idea of attacking until the next morning; and, seeing that we were to be detained in our present quarters all night, my thoughts persistently reverted to the fact that I was but a few miles distant from that mysterious mansion in connection with which I had so many curious recollections.

Were you ever haunted by one possessing thought, reader—so that no effort could banish it? In vain did I endeavor to fix my mind upon the events of the day—the chances of the coming campaign—the probable result of the fight on the morrow. Still came back to my mind the obscure mansion where I had met with such strange adventures. Who lived there now? Not Violet Grafton, nor the poor White Lady, who was sleeping under the turf of Manassas. She would never await the coming of her "darling" any more, as on that night of my arrival. And the queenly girl who had loved and cherished her so tenderly was out of the clutches of Fenwick and the harridan, evidently his accomplice—beyond their reach, amid friends who would watch over her.

But was the house in the Wilderness then deserted? Had the human owls and night-hawks left the obscure nest and flown to some other region? Where was Fenwick, the secret foe, spy, plotter, and villain generally? Would a visit to that house and a conversation with its possible inmates furnish any clue to his whereabouts?

These thoughts incessantly recurred to my mind, and at last the temptation to go and satisfy myself by a personal "reconnoissance" became irresistible. I determined to take advantage of the opportunity thus thrown in my way to revisit the place; and availing myself of a moment when General Stuart's attention was engaged—for I wished to avoid explanations—I mounted my horse, and quietly took a road which I was tolerably sure led in the direction of the mansion.

I soon found myself lost in the dense and lugubrious thicket, but from time to time noticed some traces of my former route —then I came to the road which I had followed in April, 1861.

The way was now plain. The house I knew was not a mile distant, and I pushed on over the winding road, between the impenetrable walls of thicket, vocal now, as before, with the melancholy cries of the whippoorwill. Ere long I saw the opening which I had expected; and, as the last rays of the sun disappeared, and darkness slowly descended, came in sight of the obscure mansion on the pine-encircled knoll.

This time I tied my horse to the thicket near the brushwood fence, and ascended the hill on foot, making no sound as I did so.

LXXI.

THE HOUSE IN THE WILDERNESS, AND ITS OCCUPANTS.

THE place seemed entirely deserted, and had about it an inexpressible air of desolation. The gloomy-looking mansion positively oppressed my spirits as I drew near, and—alone thus in the mysterious depths of this melancholy Wilderness—I looked around suspiciously, tried the lock of my pistol, and prepared to defend myself against any foe who appeared.

Why is it that some houses, and even regions of country, thus affect us? There are mansions which seem to smile and welcome us—where sunshine reigns, and all is bright and joyous. Others appear to frown and receive you with averted glances—to bring up thoughts of dark and mysterious tragedies—of blood and murder. "Some hideous crime must have been committed here!" you murmur, as you look upon the sullen walls; you feel that God has cursed the roof-tree, and set his seal upon the place. So with certain regions: they scowl at you, and oppress the heart—and such was this melancholy Wilderness, in which was lost, like a leaf, this gloomy and apparently deserted house.

All at once, however, as I approached, I saw a light glimmer through the closed shutters, and stopped. Something told me that the place was no longer occupied by hospitable women, but by enemies, whom it was necessary to approach with caution.

I carefully secured my sabre in my left hand, so that the weapon could not clatter against the ground, and, silently approaching the house, looked through a chink in the closed shutter, into the apartment from which proceeded the light.

Here is what I beheld in the apartment—the same in which I had held my interview with Miss Grafton and the White Lady:

Seated at the table, half turned from me, was the woman Parkins, in conversation with no less a personage than Fenwick. I saw before me the same grim face and lowering brow. She was unchanged. The eyes, cold, wary, and forbidding, were intently fixed upon her companion.

From the woman, my glance passed to Fenwick. He was the same lithe, muscular, and vigorous figure as before; and his countenance, in which the dark eyes scowled disagreeably, wore the same sneering expression. The man looked as treacherous as a serpent; and the keen flash of the eye showed that he was as dangerous.

He had evidently been drinking. On the table, between the worthies, was a black bottle, and Fenwick held in his hand a half-emptied tumbler of spirit. I saw from the slight color in his sallow cheeks that he had reached that point where men, under the influence of drink, grow voluble, boastful, and defiant —prone to rude jest, and to indiscreet talking.

Something told me that the hand of Providence had directed my steps to this obscure den; and, gluing my eyes to the aperture in the shutter, I preserved perfect silence, and disposed myself to listen.

————

LXXII.

ARCADES AMBO.

FENWICK seemed to be, as I have said, in that condition which induces men to talk of every thing or nothing. There was a defiant abandon in his manner which I had never seen before.

"Come, my dear Madam Parkins," he said, with a harsh and discordant laugh, as he pushed the bottle toward the woman, "you don't drink, my dear. Fill, fill! Let me see your countenance expand under the mollifying effects of this devil's elixir! It will much improve your appearance!"

The woman seemed to take no umbrage at this unceremonious address. She coolly grasped the bottle, poured out some of the spirit, and raised it to her lips.

But I observed that she did not drink. Then I caught a quick glance of her eye, toward her companion. She was watching him.

"We are a jolly pair!" he exclaimed, emptying his glass and leaning back in his seat; "we resemble lovers—eh, my dear creature? We are here all alone and *tête à tête*, with no one to disturb us. We are revelling in the uninterrupted interchange of fond affection, and we never grow weary of each other's society."

Nothing more sneering and disdainful than the air of the speaker, at that moment, can be imagined.

"Come, let us find some method of passing the evening agreeably, my angel," continued Fenwick. "Tell me a little love romance, my dear creature, or sing me a song!"

"Don't you think," said the woman, in her harsh and forbidding voice, "that you had better get away from here?"

"And pray why, madam?"

"The rebels are not far off. You heard the guns this evening."

"Ha, ha!—and so you think, my dear, that Fenwick, the Yankee spy, blockade-runner, and secret agent, had better get off, eh?"

"Yes," was the cool reply, "they say that Colonel Mordaunt is coming here; and if he finds you"—

"Curse him!" suddenly exclaimed Fenwick; "do you think I fear him? Woe to him, if we meet again!"

The woman's face was distorted by a quick sneer, which instantly disappeared, but not without attracting the attention of her companion.

"Aha!" he growled, "you are laughing at me, are you? You are thinking of that scene in the Stone House at Manassas, when I did not stay to fight two well-armed men, Mordaunt and that cursed friend of his, Surry! But I know what I am about, madam. Do you think I am going to meet your Colonel Mordaunt in open fight, instead of taking him unawares?"

"You met him once at Richmond."

A bitter scowl came to Fenwick's face.

"I did," was his reply, "but under a compulsion which I need not explain, my dear madam."

The woman nodded, as if the subject did not interest her, and Fenwick again had recourse to the bottle. I saw his cheeks grow ruddier, and his eyes sparkle. Soon his tongue was loosened.

"I will not tell you about my little arrangement for the benefit of our dear friend Mordaunt," he said, with his sardonic laugh; "but, by way of passing the evening agreeably, I ought to let you know why I don't like that gentleman."

"I know something, but not all; tell me the story," said the woman, who still watched her companion, and evidently lost not a single word.

"You really wish to hear all about that little affair, my dear?"

"Yes."

Fenwick hesitated, and looked with a quick flash of the eye at his companion. It was the last struggle between his cunning and desire to talk.

"After all, why shouldn't I tell you, most amiable Parkins?" he said, with a leer; "my life is a pretty little romance, which will amuse us this dull evening. But are you sure no one besides can hear us?"

"There is not another soul within five miles of this place!"

"Are you certain?"

"Yes."

"Nevertheless, my dear, suppose I make entirely sure?"

And rising, Fenwick walked, with a perfectly steady step, to the door, from which he passed to the front door of the house, which he threw open.

I shrank down in the shadow of the porch, within five feet of him. The darkness concealed me—the door closed—and, hearing the sound of his feet in the apartment again, I returned to my place at the shutter.

Fenwick had resumed his former seat, and prepared himself for his narrative by swallowing another glass of brandy

" You really think it will interest you to know why I don't
fike the excellent Colonel Mordaunt?" he said.

"Yes, I should like to know."

"It will involve a long explanation, my dear one, but there
should be perfect confidence between us. Must I begin at the
beginning, like a romance?"

The woman nodded, and looked at her companion with the
same furtive glance.

Fenwick did not observe it.

"Now for the little romance!" he said.

"I am listening," said the woman.

Her companion leaned back and said:

"Well, my dearly-beloved elderly Parkins, once upon a time
there were two young men about twenty years of age, whose
names, respectively, were Fenwick and Mordaunt. They lived
in Fairfax County, in the State of Virginia, and were a perfect
instance of Damon and Pythias. They could not hunt without
each other, ride without each other, or pass a day out of each
other's society. This heavenly state of things might, no doubt,
have lasted, had not a woman appeared on the scene—one of
that angelic sex to which you, my charming one, belong."

The woman remained silent and impassive.

" Well, this pretty devil, who was to rend asunder the touch
ing bonds of friendship between Damon Mordaunt and Pythias
Fenwick, was a young lady named Carleton—Frances Carleton.
You have never heard of her?"

"Yes, go on."

" With delight, my elderly one. Well, Miss Carleton was the
daughter of an English gentleman, who had come, with his wife,
daughter, and only sister, to America, a few months before. The
sister married Mr. Grafton, a clergyman, of Maryland; the
brother, Miss Frances's father, settled, with his wife and daughter,
in Fairfax County, renting a small estate near Manassas, upon
which stood the picturesque Stone House, in which we recently
had our pleasing little adventure.

"Here Messrs. Fenwick and Mordaunt first knew Frances
Carleton. She was a pleasing young female, with light auburn

hair falling in ringlets around her face, and 'as pure as an angel,' everybody was fond of saying. So Fenwick and Mordaunt immediately fell in love with her, and from that moment grew as cold as ice toward each other. I believe there was some sickly attempt on Mordaunt's part to continue on friendly relations with his old companion, but that gentleman treated his proposition with deserved contempt; and soon events took place which made them open foes. Mordaunt—curse him!—was the handsomer of the two, and possessed a large estate. To make a long story short, he paid his addresses to Miss Carleton, and married her!"

Fenwick grew livid as he uttered these words, and paused.

"That made me his life-long foe!" he added, at length, with bitterness; "that is to say, it made my young friend, Mr. Fenwick! He had heard preachers prate about brotherly love, but never pretended to love the rival who carried off the woman he had been crazily in love with. From that moment he began to hate Mordaunt bitterly, and swore in his inmost soul that he would take vengeance on him. It was not a common, vulgar revenge he aimed at, a duel or affray, ending in mere blows and blood. No! such a thing seemed silly and childish. What Fenwick wanted, my dear madam, was not so much to shed his enemy's heart's blood, as to make his existence one long groan of misery. You, no doubt, feel shocked at this, madam, as you are a woman, but that is the way men hate when they hate in earnest."

"I can understand it."

"Very well—all the better. It will save me from repeating over and over that the amiable Fenwick had a hatred for the respectable Mordaunt so bitter that it stopped at nothing in the way of its gratification. To reach his aim, Fenwick was obliged to have recourse to what is called treachery by fools, but strategy by military men. He did not quarrel with his beloved friend Mordaunt—the coldness between them completely passed away—and very soon young Mr. Fenwick was a regular visitor at the Stone House, where Mordaunt lived with his bride. He had become the 'friend of the family,' you see, madam, and Mrs. Mordaunt had unbounded confidence in him.

" For a long time no opportunity of avenging the affront put on him presented itself to Mr. Fenwick. Mordaunt and his wife were completely happy—and the idea of sowing suspicion or producing any misunderstanding between them was simply absurd. They 'lived in a dream of felicity,' as says the poet, my dear madam; and Mr. Fenwick was compelled to put off his little plan for the benefit of his dear friend Mordaunt.

"Events, however, very soon occurred which seemed to favor his scheme. Mr. and Mrs. Carleton both died, within a few days of each other, and Mordaunt and his wife were left alone together in the Stone House. The only other inmate of the establishment was a most charming, respectable, and excellent person, of the euphonious name of Parkins, who filled the position of housekeeper. Have you ever heard of that lovely creature, madam?" asked Fenwick, with a guttural laugh ; " she was the paragon of her sex."

" Go on," was the response of the woman, who was evidently watching Fenwick closely, and waiting for him to come to something which had excited her curiosity.

" The respectable Parkins," continued Fenwick, leaning upon the table, and looking at his companion with a leer of affected admiration, " was in every way calculated to prove an ornament to her sex, and had only a single failing. Which of us is without his peculiar weakness? That of the worthy Parkins was a love of money, and, not to weary you, my dear madam, with a prosy explanation—Fenwick bought her. He gently insinuated into her not unwilling hand a bank note of the denomination of one thousand dollars, with the promise of more, and lo! the virtuous Parkins was at his orders."

" Go on," was the woman's sole reply.

" With pleasure. Well, with the housekeeper thus bought, one great step was taken toward a little plan Mr. Fenwick had on foot. It had suddenly flashed upon him one day, when he visited the Stone House soon after Mr. Carleton's death, and he heard Mordaunt inform his wife that he would be compelled to go to England to attend to very important claims left by the young lady's father. A charming scene followed—tears, fond

words, remonstrances, embraces, kisses! Curse him!" exclaimed
Fenwick, "I could have killed him where he stood!"

"Why didn't you?" asked the woman coolly.

"For this good reason—that I had a better plan in view.
Listen now, and you shall hear how skilfully the youthful Fenwick set about his little arrangements."

The speaker touched his empty glass to his lips, as if from
habit, looked with a sneer at the woman, and resumed his
monologue.

LXXIII.

MORDAUNT'S SECRET.

"MORDAUNT set out for London. He expected, he said, to be
absent for about two months—then he would return, never more
to leave 'what was dearer to him than all the world, his home.'
Pathetic, you see! I witnessed the parting—they were locked
for about ten minutes in each other's arms—and then the young
lady sank into a chair, sobbing and crying as if her heart would
break. At that moment, with her auburn ringlets around her
face, she looked 'like an angel.' Fenwick, you see, my dear
madam, was the devil lurking near.

"He continued to visit the house, as a friend, during Mordaunt's absence; and the smiles of the young lady nearly turned
him from his purpose. But those smiles became brighter and
brighter as the days rolled by. One day she would be heard
murmuring, 'It is only three weeks now!' Then, 'To-morrow
it is only eleven days!' She was counting the time, you see,
before her husband would return—and Mr. Fenwick grew crazy
with rage at the thought. He would lie awake all night, and toss
and rave at the pictures which his imagination drew of their
meeting—their kisses, embraces, fond words. And all this might
have been his! This was to continue before his eyes—all this
happiness of his rival—when *he* was writhing in agony? He
swore in his heart that he would have his vengeance—and he
kept his oath!"

A gloomy shadow seemed to cross the speaker's face—his eyes flashed.

"Well, madam," he continued, "the plan of Fenwick involved what is popularly known as forgery. He gave his instructions to the excellent Parkins, and then proceeded to carry out his design. One day, Mrs. Mordaunt received a letter from her husband—hand-writing, post-mark, date, every thing complete—announcing that he would be in New York on a certain day; and requesting, for reasons which he would subsequently explain, that she would meet him there. His friend Mr. Fenwick would, no doubt, take pleasure in escorting her, if asked to do so. Indeed—added the writer—he had written to Mr. Fenwick, by the same mail, requesting that he would accompany her to New York, and see to her safety.

"She came with this letter in her hand, and, before she spoke, Fenwick announced the receipt of a letter, requesting his escort for madam. That would have removed all suspicion—but she had none. Her face glowed—she trembled from head to foot with joy and excitement, and was ready, on the next morning, to commence the journey. Leaving the worthy madam Parkins to keep house in her absence, she set out in her carriage with Mr. Fenwick, who kindly consented to drive the small vehicle himself."

The speaker paused and gulped down a mouthful of the raw spirit. It seemed only to make him gloomier and more morose.

"They had a pleasant journey across the Potomac into Maryland," he continued, and stopped one evening at a house where Mr. Fenwick had friends, or, rather, a friend. It was in a remote locality between wooded hills, and well suited to the design he had in view. This was to confine Mrs. Mordaunt, under the old hag—your respectable aunt, madam—until Mordaunt committed suicide, or died of misery; then to release her. Toward the young lady, Fenwick had no ill-feeling—he almost pitied her, and I swear to you he treated her with the deepest respect. It was her misfortune, not her fault, that she was entangled in this network of vengeance!"

He stopped—something like a human expression touched upon the sneering mask: then it fled away.

"Two days after her arrival," he said, relapsing into his cynical coldness, "she gave birth to a son."

"Ah! and did the child live?"

"It died on the same evening."

The woman leaned back in her seat, with a look of unmistakable disappointment.

"Go on," she said.

"Then you are interested in my pleasing little romance," said Fenwick. "Charming—is it not, my dear madam? But I don't think I have entirely explained the plan of my dear friend Fenwick. He was not a blood-thirsty monster, only a man who had sworn vengeance against an adversary. He had none to satisfy against the wife. It was Mordaunt whom he hated—and that note of the value of one thousand dollars, with the promise of more, had been presented, as a small testimony of regard, to the beautiful Parkins, in order to induce her to poison Mordaunt's mind upon his return. The little scheme was all arranged. When he appeared, the skilful Parkins was to rush forward, hair dishevelled, accents heart-broken, and convey the intelligence that Mrs. Mordaunt had deserted her husband's roof, in company with her old lover, Fenwick. It is true that the most devilish ingenuity was necessary to render this credible to Mordaunt—but there was the fact of madam's absence, and Fenwick's also. That gentleman had sold his landed estate—put the gold in his pocket—and disappeared, along with madam.

"You see how every thing tended to deceive Mordaunt; but, in addition to this, some letters were handed to him. One was from his wife—I wrote it—announcing that she was about to leave him for ever, in company with the only person she had ever really loved. The other was from me—I mean from Fenwick, madam—and it contained only these words: 'You were my successful rival. What are you now?' When those letters were given to Mordaunt, he no longer doubted. In one day, they said, he became ten years older. Then he commenced the hunt after the triumphant Fenwick; but that gentleman managed to have his name inserted in a list of passengers sailing for Europe, and saw that Mordaunt received the paper. That took him out of the country—and he did not return for more than fifteen years.

"Thus you will perceive, my dear madam," continued the speaker coolly, "that Mr. Fenwick may be said to have at last secured a very pretty little vengeance. His rival was broken-hearted and in exile—his hate, and it was intense, was for the moment glutted. But, you will ask, what became of Mrs. Mordaunt? My dear madam, did you ever hear of that scourge called *puerperal fever?* The young lady was attacked by this malady upon the birth of her child, and lost her reason. I was sorry," muttered Fenwick. "I swear to you I was sorry, and all was done that could be done. She was sent to a public asylum under her maiden name, and there she remained, uncured, until her cousin, Miss Grafton, now an orphan, discovered her.

"My story's growing rather prosy—eh! my dear madam?" continued Fenwick. "Well, it is nearly done. There was a curious end to all these adventures. Miss Grafton was the exact image of her cousin, Frances Carleton, when she was a young lady—fair complexion, golden ringlets, blue eyes, and all. So what must that admirer of the ladies, Mr. Fenwick, do, but fall in love with her? He met her one day at the asylum—and often thereafter. He formed the design of marrying her. But she was incessantly engaged in her duties as assistant at a school—her father, the clergyman, having followed his wife to the grave, leaving the daughter nothing. Then one day, Fenwick said, 'I will give your poor cousin a quiet home, if you will come and take care of her, Miss Grafton;' and lo! with the sweet Parkins for companion, the two ladies came to reside in the lively mansion we now occupy."

The woman nodded; and her companion coolly went on:

"The plans of Fenwick had thus apparently been crowned with success. His hatred was gratified; his rival miserable and in exile; the young lady whom he loved as the living image of Frances Carleton, the light of his youth, was under his roof. But when was virtue really rewarded? The insane lady never even seemed aware of her benefactor's existence; Miss Grafton had evidently taken up a positive dislike to him; and presto! who should reappear upon the scene but Mordaunt, strong, dangerous, and thirsting for the amiable Fenwick's blood!

"That gentleman put himself to no trouble to meet Mr. Mordaunt, having other affairs to attend to; but fate brought them together at Richmond, in April last year, and they fought, Mr. Fenwick receiving a bullet in his breast, which he purposes some day to return with interest to its owner. Soon afterward, in July of the same year, the rivals met again at the Stone House, near Manassas, when Mr. Fenwick was engaged in the pious task of burying the insane lady, in the spot where she had been so happy. This was in accordance, as you know, my dear madam, with her own request: we took the body there, and, when retiring from the grave, Mr. Fenwick was again assailed by his adversary. And for what? Had *he* made the poor lady lose her mind? Not at all. It was the fever. Had *he* produced her death? No, she was treated with all kindness, for Mr. Fenwick really pitied her, and religiously obeyed her last request.

"Thus you see, my dear madam, Mr. Fenwick was an ill-treated personage. Everybody tries to cut his throat, and Miss Grafton, on your late excursion to Alexandria to attend to some of your affairs there, leaves you on the road, doesn't wait to say good-by, and takes refuge with entire strangers, instead of returning, as she should have done, to this hospitable roof. When Mr. Fenwick puts himself to the trouble of discovering her retreat, and presents himself before her, she draws herself up with the air of a queen, declares that she never wishes to return to this lively abode in the Wilderness, and plainly intimates to him that his visits are disagreeable, his addresses hateful. Yes, *hateful!*" added Fenwick gloomily. "You were right in what you said to me one day—she cannot bear me. And I— I would cut off my right hand to win this girl!"

For a moment there was silence. Then Fenwick broke into a harsh laugh.

"Well, that's the little romance I promised you, respected Madam Parkins!" he said. "Now, do you like it? Is it gay, cheerful, lively; the sort of thing that makes an evening pass delightfully, and puts one to bed in a mood that brings on pleasant dreams? The recollection of these little occurrences is the chief happiness of my existence. You see, I am landless now, and though I manage to scrape together a very respectable income, and have many powerful friends—although they never acknowledge my acquintance in public—I cannot be said to have many sources of happiness except this. It is enough. The thought of Mordaunt wretched and broken-hearted suffices me; and if my little affair with that gentleman has amused my dearest Parkins, I am more than happy!"

With these ironical words Fenwick rose and yawned.

"I am tired with my long ride," he added, "and shall now, madam, bid you, most respectfully, good-night. I must cross the river before daylight at the old place, and be with my friend General Pope by sunrise, if possible. I have intelligence he will be glad to get."

"From Richmond?"

"Yes, we have many more friends, you know, down there, than people think; and even among the employés of the War Department—but I am blabbing secrets. Where are my arms, most excellent Mrs. Parkins?"

"On the mantel-piece."

"I will take them to my room with me, for fear of accidents."

And he made a step toward the mantel-piece.

Before he reached it I had burst open the door with one blow of my heel, and was standing in the apartment, with a cocked pistol pointed at his heart.

"You are my prisoner!" I said. "Move a step, and you are dead."

LXXIV.

THE SNAKE SCOTCHED.

FENWICK recoiled, and made a step to seize his pistol, which was lying in its holster on the mantel-piece. I raised my weapon, directed it at his head, and said to him :

"I give you my word of honor, sir, that if you move another foot, I will blow your brains out."

He became livid, and uttered the hoarse growl of a tiger at bay.

"Who are you?" he cried, with a flash of fury in his blood shot eyes.

"You know me perfectly well, as you have already met me. I see you remember."

"Your purpose?"

"To arrest you."

"And by what authority—yes, sir! by what authority is this intrusion on my premises—this threat with a loaded pistol!"

"By my own. I require no authority to arrest a spy and an infamous wretch. I know you thoroughly. Resist in the slightest degree, and, by heavens! I will lay you dead on that floor!"

Anger faded from the eyes—cunning and treachery took its place.

"I am at a loss to imagine the meaning of this scene, sir," he said, with affected coolness; "you say that you intend to arrest me : where and before whom am I to be carried?"

"Come with me, and you will see."

"How am I to go at this hour of the night? In the morning, if you insist, sir."

"No—we are going to take a little ride to-night. You will accompany me instantly--if you have no horse, you will walk."

He must have seen that no wheedling would avail him.

"I have a horse," he said hoarsely. "I will go and saddle him."

will accompany you."

"Then if I give you my parole, sir, not to attempt to escape?"

"Even if you give me a hundred paroles."

At this last insult his face grew livid.

"Major Surry, you shall answer for this!"

"Ah! you know me, I see."

"I do—you shall know me, too!"

And, grinding his teeth audibly, he left the room. I followed to a small stable behind the house, where a horse stood, and saw him saddled.

"Mount!" I said, "and ride before me down that path."

He obeyed, and we had soon reached the spot where my horse was tied. The woman Parkins had not uttered a single word, nor did she now appear at the door.

I directed Fenwick to ride on my left, and I never removed my eyes from him. With such a man, no precautions were too great.

"Really, sir," he said, as we rode on, "this is a most remarkable proceeding. I am at a loss to understand what brought you into this out-of-the-way place, or induced you to take up the most unfounded supposition that I am a spy."

"I will, ere long, enlighten you."

"Where are you conducting me?"

"You will soon discover."

"I protest again, sir, against your most unauthorized"—

"You will please spare your remarks—I am tired of the sound of your voice. I have heard nothing else for the last hour."

By the light of the moon, which had just risen, I saw him turn livid; and from that moment he said no more.

More than once his quick glance was directed toward me, as though to discover if there were any hope of escape. But a pistol barrel shone in the moonlight—he uttered a sort of growl, and rode on in silence.

Soon the cavalry camp came in sight. I rode to General Stuart's head-quarters, and found him just about to stretch himself upon his red blanket.

"Who is that?" he said

I dismounted and approached, in company with Fenwick.

" Here is a prisoner, General."

" Ah.   Where did you take him?"

" I will tell you."

And, leading the General aside, I told him enough to convince
him of Fenwick's dangerous character.   The revelation which I
had heard of Mordaunt's private history was, of course, not alluded to.

"If Mordaunt says he's a spy," said the General, "the thing
is settled.   There is no better or more reliable officer in my
command.   Can you bring any specific charge against this
man?"

" Only this—that I heard him, with his own lips, declare that
he was going to set out at daylight for General Pope's head-
quarters, with important intelligence from Richmond."

"That's more than enough.   I will embody your statement in
a communication to the War Department, and send him to Richmond in the morning, under guard."

We returned to the spot where Fenwick was standing.

" Well, General," he said, with an admirable affectation of
candor, "I hope you will not authorize this most singular proceeding."

He had addressed himself to the wrong person.   Stuart had
no patience whatever with people in citizen's dress suspected of
disloyalty.

" I am tired," was his brief reply.

" But, General, I have been arrested in my house, without
warning, and "—

" I am sleepy," said Stuart, in tones still briefer.

" I protest, General, with all my power, against"—

" Take this man away, and put him under guard," said the
General.   " Give the sentinel instructions to fire upon him, if he
makes the least movement to escape."

And Stuart yawned, and stretched himself upon his couch.

Baffled, and overcome with rage, Fenwick turned away, and
was conducted to a fire, where he was placed under guard.

"Keep special watch over this prisoner," I said to the guard, "he is dangerous, and will outwit you, if you take your eyes from him for a moment."

"Yes, sir—all right, sir," was the response.

"You have received your instructions?"

"Yes, sir."

"Kill him, if he attempts to escape."

The sentinel tried the lock of his carbine, which clicked significantly, and then laughed.

Unfortunately, I did not pay sufficient attention to another sound which I afterward remembered—the rattle of gold pieces in Fenwick's pocket.

LXXV.

THE NIGHT ATTACK.

I STRETCHED myself beside Stuart, and was soon asleep. We were destined to have a somewhat disagreeable waking.

Half an hour before daylight, we suddenly heard heavy firing near at hand, and started up.

The firing approached with rapidity; the sound of horses at a gallop was heard; and, at the next moment, the picket, in the direction of the river, appeared, retreating in hot haste.

"Look out!" they cried, "the enemy are on you!"

Stuart sprang to the saddle, and, in a moment, his bugle was heard sounding "Boots and Saddles"—then, "To Horse."

He had hardly formed line when the enemy's cavalry came upon him. They had rapidly spurred through the shallow ford. driven in the picket, and, proceeding apparently upon some information, were now charging straight upon Stuart.

"Where is the prisoner I brought last night!" I suddenly ex claimed.

"Escaped, Major," replied a courier.

I darted to Stuart.

"Look out, General! Fenwick has escaped to the enemy, and. no doubt, given full information of your strength and position."

"I'll fight them, if they are a corps!" exclaimed the General, hotly. "Form platoons!"

His sonorous voice was heard above the crack of the carbines. "Draw sabres!—charge!"

And, placing himself in front, Stuart led the charge in person, his sabre gleaming in the moonlight.

Never shall I forget that scene. It was one of the wildest and most romantic I ever witnessed. At least a division of Federal cavalry had attacked Fitz Lee's small brigade, and, for half an hour, nothing was seen but a fierce and determined struggle between dusky shadows—nothing heard but yells, the sharp ring of the carbine, and the clash of the sabre.

It was, altogether, a most mixed-up affair, and I can give no better description of it than by saying that the men seemed to fight each for himself, and without seeing their opponents.

I tried to keep with Stuart—lost him—and found myself in the midst of a hundred blue-coats.

A sabre-blow cut my hat from my head—then my horse was shot, and I felt him stagger. The next moment he fell, carrying me with him, and catching my leg under him.

I was making violent efforts to disengage myself, when a squadron of Stuart's, with the General at their head, charged over me—the hoofs of the horses brushing my very face.

The squadron charged with the sabre, forcing the enemy back, and I struggled to my feet.

A dozen riderless horses were galloping to and fro, mad with terror, and I caught one, and mounted. I had scarcely done so, when Stuart's line was seen falling back, under a heavy fire, and pressed closely by a heavy force, with drawn sabres.

The crisis had come. Day showed the enemy the small force of Stuart, and they were pressing him close.

I was by him, and saw the man "under pressure." His face burned like fire, his eyes blazed, and he looked dangerous. "Do or die" was in every look, and, sword in hand, he fought among the men.

Reaching a good position, he faced about and met them, sabre to sabre. The fight began to rage more furiously than before, and the whole field was filled with the clash of sabres and the ring of pistols and carbines.

In five minutes Stuart would have been forced back and compelled to retire from the field, when suddenly I heard a ringing shout beyond the hill on the left—then a long line of sabres glittered on the crest. A fresh regiment, on spirited horses, burst like a torrent upon the enemy's flank, and in front of them I recognized Mordaunt.

The charge of Mordaunt's column completely reversed the whole aspect of the field. The Federal cavalry recoiled, wavered, and then fell back. Fitz Lee advanced with a cheer in front; Mordaunt closed in with the sabre; and in a marvellously brief space the Federal cavalry were driven to the river.

Suddenly a white cloud, tipped with fire, rose from the opposite bank, and a shell tore through the ranks, overthrowing men and horses. Stuart rode up to Mordaunt, who was advancing with his column.

"Colonel," said Stuart, "do you think you can take that battery?"

Mordaunt laughed, and wiped his bloody sabre on the mane of his superb black horse.

"I can try, General," was his reply, and his face was resplendent. His eyes sparkled—his white teeth appeared under his black mustache: I had never before seen Mordaunt look happy.

Three bounds of his horse took him to the head of his column, upon which two guns were now pouring a heavy fire.

"Forward!" he cried, with a whirl of his sabre. "Follow me!"

And, darting at a gallop down the steep descent, at the head of his column, Mordaunt fell like a thunderbolt upon the rear of the enemy, now retreating rapidly across the ford.

The column did not pause. The platoons splashed into the river, spurred through, and were then seen to mount the opposite slope, charging straight into the muzzles of the artillery, which hurled in their faces a hurricane of canister.

Still the column advanced at a headlong gallop, though wide gaps were visible in the ranks, torn and bleeding from the storm sweeping through them—and still the flash of Mordaunt's sabre was distinguished in front, his powerful black horse mounting the slope with long leaps, which cleared rocks, ravines, and every thing.

The Federal sharpshooters greeted him with a rapid and destructive fire, but were charged, ridden over, and cut down with the sabre. Then a wild cheer arose above the roar of the guns —the Southern column disappeared in the cloud of smoke— the next moment they were seen sabring the cannoneers at the guns, which had been hastily limbered up to be carried off.

It was too late. Mordaunt was in possession of the hill: he was seen to close with the Federal cavalry, in a desperate hand-to-hand conflict—and Stuart, who had risen in his stirrups and shouted as he witnessed the charge, placed himself at the head of the main body, and went at headlong speed to his support.

The ford was passed—Fitz Lee led his column straight up the hill on Mordaunt's left, and in an instant the enemy were furiously attacked in flank. Under this double assault they wavered—the lines broke, and then gave way, followed by the Southerners with triumphant cheers.

The crest was won, and the enemy completely routed.

LXXVI.

AN OLD ACQUAINTANCE.

STUART was sitting his horse upon the crest, when Mordaunt rode up. The General's face was glowing, his blue eyes full of martial fire. Mordaunt, on the contrary, displayed no emotion on his dark countenance, and saluted with military coolness.

"A splendid charge, Colonel!" exclaimed Stuart, grasping his hand. "I see you are of the 'if-you-want-to-take-a-battery-I'm-your-man' sort! I never saw any thing finer."

Mordaunt bowed.

"Every thing depends on the start in cavalry, General, as you know better than I do."

"Yes, yes."

"The men carried the hill easily."

"And your loss?"

"I am afraid it is considerable. The artillery had full play on the column. In the charge over yonder I lost very few."

"And saved the day."

Mordaunt inclined again.

"My men will be proud to hear that you approve of their conduct, General."

"It was splendid. But who is that riding up? Saltoun, or I'm mistaken!"

The words were scarcely uttered when an officer, wearing the uniform of a lieutenant of cavalry, approached at a gallop, and I recognized the young Marylander who had joined us that day in the Valley, at Captain Bogy's quarters.

A slender mustache curled proudly above his handsome, laughing mouth; his eyes sparkled; and from his hat floated gallantly a splendid feather. He sat his horse admirably—and galloped up, holding one hand in his breast.

"We thundered 'em that time, General!" he exclaimed, with a loud laugh. "We took their artillery, drove them, and they are not done running yet!"

"Bully for you!"* replied Stuart, echoing the young man's laugh in a manner which showed that he was a favorite. "So you have got your lieutenancy in the Maryland company?"

"Yes, General, and made the company a speech! I told them 'the despot's heel was on their shore,' and now or never was the time to strike!"

"Good!—see that they do it. But what is the matter with your arm?"

I looked, and saw that the young lieutenant's sleeve was covered with blood.

"I was shot in the charge," he replied, "but it's not much. Only a flesh wound. How are you, Major Surry?"

And, spurring to my side, the gay youngster shook hands cordially.

---

* A favorite expression of Stuart's.

12*

"We are old friends, you know," he said, with a laugh. "I saw old Bogy yesterday, and dined with him. He is looking out for another wagon!"

Mordaunt turned at this movement, and, addressing the young man, desired him to carry an order to his command, then moving upon the road to the Rappahannock. He bowed with soldierly grace, touched his horse with the spur, and darted off at a gallop, his black feather floating in the wind.

"A gay youngster, Mordaunt," said Stuart; "how does he fight?"

"Like a firebrand!" was the reply. "He is as brave as steel, and doesn't seem to know what stopping in a charge means."

"I thought he was made of that sort of stuff from the first. He joined me in the Valley."

"A Marylander, I believe. But here is an officer with a prisoner, who must have something to communicate, General."

The officer approached and touched his hat.

"This man can tell you something about the attack last night, General."

"Well, out with it," was Stuart's reply, addressing the prisoner.

His information was soon extracted. A man in citizen's dress, perfectly answering to the description of Fenwick, had come into their lines toward daylight that morning, and asked for the commanding officer; he could tell, he said, what Confederate force was in front, and how it could be surprised. He was conducted to head-quarters, and half-an-hour afterward the order came to mount.

So Fenwick had brought the attack upon us, as I expected—but how had he escaped? This I learned long afterward. He had bribed his guard with a considerable sum in gold, which he had upon his person; the man could not resist the dazzling coin; and Fenwick had been allowed to glide off, mount his horse, and escape to a point down the river, where he crossed, and entered the Federal lines.

Hence the night attack upon Stuart.

LXXVII.

WHAT I FOUND IN THE SADDLE-POCKETS OF MY CAPTURED HORSE.

BEFORE proceeding with my narrative, I shall call the reader's attention to a discovery which I made on the morning succeeding the encounter upon the Rapidan.

It will be remembered that my hat was carried away by a sabre cut, during the night attack, and my horse killed. I regained my own hat, but mounted somebody else's horse; and when I came to examine the equipments, I found, from papers in the side-pockets of the "McClellan-tree," that the animal had belonged to a Lieutenant Govran, of the Federal Army, no doubt wounded or killed in the engagement. The papers alluded to were chiefly private letters addressed to the lieutenant; and what was my astonishment to find among them one directed in the handwriting of my brother Will!

His letter was gay and rollicking—such as one youngster addresses to another who has been with him at West Point. It announced that the writer had just secured his transfer to the cavalry; had made "a scout" in the direction of White Plains; and had met, at the residence of a lady in that vicinity, a certain Miss Henrietta Fitzhugh, with whom he had fallen desperately in love! In every line of the letter I recognized Will. He was evidently the same jovial, thoughtless, rollicking boy as before; and his letter overflowed with fun, jokes, and rapture about his new flame.

"But what do you think, Tom," he went on, "the little ma'm-selle just turned up her nose at my blue uniform, and would scarcely speak to me. She is not more than sixteen, but she's a perfect tartar, and, as the only way of standing any chance with her, I believe I'll desert, put on a gray jacket, and enlist in old Stonewall Jackson's band. I wouldn't be surprised if I had an opportunity soon. Pope seems blind, and I predict Jackson will be after him soon with a sharp stick. You can't think how

crazy my little *friend,* Miss Henrietta, is about Jackson and
Stuart. She goes into ecstasies about 'em, and made me blue
to think I was fighting against them and old Virginia. Tom, I
would give my right arm if this —— —— war was finished!"
Will's adjectives preceding the word "war" I refrain from
recording.

Such was his letter. It was a curious way of hearing from
one's brother in the United States Army! But there it was; and
I hope I shall not be regarded as having violated "private correspondence."

As I rode along I continued to reflect, not without sadness,
upon this discovery. Has the reader forgotten Miss Henrietta
Fitzhugh? It is probable. But I remembered her perfectly—
her gayety and abandon; her coquettish ways; and the clouds
and sunshine which alternately flitted across the pretty face
of the little witch of sixteen. For Will to have fallen in love
with her, complicated matters terribly. She was passionately
Southern in her feelings; and could not bear the thought of
even speaking to a Federal officer. That of all the maidens in
the whole wide world, my brother should go and place his affections upon this little will-o'-the-wisp!

I put away the letter with a sigh, went to attend to my
duties, and tried to forget the whole affair. But still I kept
thinking of it.

LXXVIII

A GLIMPSE OF GENERAL EARLY.

STUART continued to press the Federal cavalry toward the
Rappahannock; and soon the sound of artillery on the left in
the direction of Culpepper Court-House indicated that General
Lee was attacking in front.

The sound speedily began to recede northward; the cavalry
in our front continued to fall back, and, reaching a lofty hill near
Stevensburg, we could see the infantry column of Pope rapidly
retreating to the Rappahannock.

I hastened to rejoin General Jackson, who was pressing closely upon the Federal rear, and came up with him near Hazel River.

The appearance of the country through which I passed was frightful. I had seen hard fighting up to this time, but never before fully comprehended the horrors of war when conducted upon the principles of Attila. The country was a desert. On every side were the ruins of houses, wantonly burned by the troops of General Pope; the fences were destroyed; the forests cut down; the fields laid waste; and this beautiful land, but recently a scene of peace, plenty, and happiness, was the picture of woe and desolation. The sight of those ruins, from which women and children had fled to escape plunder and insult, gave me the heartache; a weight seemed pressing upon my breast as I passed through this desolated region. I felt for the enemy a hatred a thousand-fold greater than any which could have been produced by blood spilled fairly in open fight, and ten thousand others felt the same.

Jackson hastened forward to the Rappahannock; and all along that river, across which the enemy had retreated, commenced a hot artillery engagement—the Federal forces obstinately disputing the passage of the stream. Jackson was in front, and, rapidly advancing to Warrenton Springs, threw two brigades across, under General Early. This, I think, was on the 22d of August, and on the next day a violent rain-storm produced such a freshet in the river that all the bridges were washed away.

Early's position was now extremely critical. The enemy's main body was in his immediate vicinity, and might attack him at any moment.

I was talking with General Jackson when a courier rode up with a message from Early, that he could not hold his position.

"When did you leave him?" asked Jackson, briefly.

"About two hours ago, General. I had to go to the upper ford to cross."

"Why not swim?"

"My horse is too weak."

" And you are going all the way around again ?"
The courier looked abashed.

My own horse, I informed the General, was' quite fresh, and I would take his message.

" Thank you, Major. Tell General Early that he must hold his position."

" Under any circumstances?"

" Yes."

I saluted, and set out rapidly for the river. It was a perfect torrent; but, pushing my "Yankee horse," much against his will, into the current, I managed to force him through. He scrambled up the opposite bank, and I was very soon in presence of General Early. Tne person and character of this brave officer are probably well known to most of my readers. Fancy a rough, curling head, a pair of piercing eyes under shaggy brows, a cynical smile, a nasal utterance, and the air of one who is afraid of nothing upon earth—there is General Early as he then appeared.

" How are you, Major?" said the General, in his peculiar drawl through the nose. " Any news?"

" None, General."

" The enemy are pressing me here. Did General Jackson receive my message? I sent a courier three hours ago. I will murder him when he returns."

" He received your message, and I came over to bring the answer. General Jackson desires you to hold your position."

" Can't do it."

" The order is imperative, General—to hold your ground under all circumstances."

Early shook his head obstinately, and said, in his slow, deliberate voice, with that indescribable drawl through the nose:

" I have reconnoitred the ground in my front and flanks, Major, and—I'll *be* ——— if I can hold it." *

The General smiled cheerfully as he spoke, and dwelt with evident pleasure and emphasis upon the words italicized. I began to laugh.

* His words.

"Well, General, I have given you the order in General Jackson's very words."

"Oh," was the drawling response, "don't give yourself any trouble, Major, about *that*. You don't understand. I don't mean that I am *not going* to hold this position—I mean I'll be ———— if *I can* hold it. Old Jubal can be cut to pieces as well as any other man!"

And, uttering a low chuckle, the General seemed to contemplate that ceremony of being made mince-meat of with actual satisfaction.

Such was not, however, to be his fate. He was reserved for those hard fights against the great odds of Sheridan; and was to startle Washington with the roll of his drum.

My horse carried me back without accident, and I found Jackson superintending in person the preparations for building a bridge. Heavy details were already at work; the timbers were stretched across; and, just as the enemy advanced to throw themselves upon Early, his column defiled across, the rear-guard hotly engaged with the Federal advance.*

Jackson had a long conversation with Early, and both then rode to General Lee's head-quarters, where they were soon closeted with him. When Jackson came out, he said to me:

"Major, I wish you to ride to General Stuart—you know where to find him—give my compliments to him, and say that I have had a consultation with General Lee, and it is of the utmost importance that a reconnoissance should be made in the direction of Warrenton. The enemy's force and movements are not known accurately—whether they intend to fight here or retreat further. Explain this to the General. If he can cut the railroad in the enemy's rear, so much the better. This might be done near Catlett's. No time should be lost."

"Any thing further, General?"

"Nothing. Don't lose time on the road, Major."

I went in the direction of Stuart, soon found him, and delivered my message.

* Historical.

"Good! I was thinking of that very thing."

And he issued orders which put his column in motion in ten minutes.

"Come on, Surry, and '*jine* the cavalry'!" said Stuart, laughing; "perhaps we may secure our revenge for Verdiersville."

I could not resist—something about Stuart drew me. I ro by Jackson's head-quarters, obtained h's permission, and set out with Stuart on his raid.

LXXIX.

STUART TAKES HIS REVENGE.

CROSSING the Rappahannock above Jeffersonton, Stuart pushed forward with his column, and, passing in the vicinity of Warrenton, made for the Orange and Alexandria Railroad, directly in the enemy's rear.

By this time the sun was down, and, knowing the danger which attends operating with cavalry by night, I supposed that Stuart would go into bivouac with his command and wait for daylight. I said as much, but he shook his head.

"Can't afford the time," he replied. "It is hazardous to move cavalry at night, but I must risk it. Hagan!"

The word was passed back to the escort, and soon the dark-bearded giant whom I had formerly known in the Valley rode forward and saluted. Hagan was unchanged, except that his beard was heavier, his eye more twinkling, his huge mustache more prone than ever to curl with lurking humor. When he spoke, his voice was like the rumble of winds from the caverns of Æolus.

Hagan, I soon learned, was corporal of the guard—in other words, commanded the General's escort. He recognized me immediately, and, putting two fingers to his hat, exclaimed "Major!" in the most military style.

"Hagan," said the General, "do you know this country?"

"Not just along here, General—but I have got two men who do."

"Call them up."

Hagan turned and called, in a thundering voice:

"Snakebug!"

"Who on earth is that?" exclaimed Stuart, with a laugh.

"Only a little pet name, General."

"Well, call the other."

Hagan again elevated his voice, and shouted:

"Moonshine!"

This was more than Stuart could stand. He laid back on his horse, and uttered a "haw, haw!" which exploded like a pistol.

"I will put your friend Moonshine in front of my column, Hagan. He's the very man for a march at night! He shall light the way. Where is he?"

"Here, General," responded Hagan; and, turning round with austere dignity:

"Moonshine!" he said.

"Yes, sir," submissively responded Moonshine, a thin and wiry individual, with a hawk nose and eye.

"Snakebug!"

"Here we are, Corporal," came in gutteral tones from Snakebug, who had the appearance of a gentleman ready to go through fire and storm for plunder.

"Speak to the General!" said Hagan, in a voice of thunder; and Snakebug and Moonshine rode forward. They stated that they knew the country perfectly; and, sending one with the advance-guard, Stuart kept the other.

My friend Corporal Hagan had touched his hat with that military courtesy which characterized him, and fallen back to take command of his detachment.

Stuart now advanced, without pause, although the night had grown pitch dark, and the sky was overclouded. Soon some rain-drops began to fall.

"That's bad," he muttered. "I must hurry up here, or the streams in the rear will be so swollen as to prevent my return."

"Where are we now, General?"

He called to Moonshine, who reported that they were then within about two miles of Catlett's Station.

"I'll go there to-night, at all events," said the General; "move on with the column."

We now advanced in silence, through the black darkness, under a heavy drizzle, which was rapidly changing into a regular rain-storm. It was impossible to see three feet ahead; and the idea of charging headlong over broken and unknown ground, upon an enemy whose position was unknown, did not suggest the most pleasing ideas.

But Stuart seemed to have no doubt of the result. He was as gay and cheerful as ever; and, taking the head of the column, advanced through the black darkness, at a rapid trot, straight toward Catlett's.

"Now for it, Surry!" he said, with animation, as we came in sight of glimmering lights; "out with your sabre, and I'll lead the way!"

"Where!" was my response to the unseen voice.

"Right into the enemy!"

"All right, General; but I'm getting horribly demoralized."

"At what?"

"For fear I shall be charged by some gigantic limb on these trees, and ignobly unhorsed in the very beginning."

Stuart laughed.

"Shut your eyes, and trust to luck! Yonder they are!"

At that moment a scout hurried up, and Stuart recognized his voice.

"Well!" he exclaimed, "here I am, Stringfellow! What intelligence?"

"You are within eight hundred yards of Pope's head-quarters, General."

Stuart uttered an exclamation.

"Press on with the column!" was his loud order. The clatter of hoofs redoubled. Then quick firing was heard from the advance-guard, and the flash of carbines shone in the darkness.

"Forward!" cried the General, drawing his sabre.

Bang! bang! bang! was heard from the advance-guard. They were driving 'in the picket.

Then a loud cheer arose in front.

" Draw sabres!—charge!" came in a ringing shout from Stuart; and, digging the spur into his horse, he went at a headlong gallop straight down the road, followed by his column.

We were approaching the railroad, and the ground became broken, intersected with ravines, and almost impassable. Worse than all, the obstacles were invisible. I only knew by the quick leaps of my horse what we were passing over. On came the column behind ; and suddenly I heard exclamations, a heavy "thud" or two, and the clatter of accoutrements. More than one horse and rider had "gone under," and were rolling in the ditch. The rest, however, pressed on—a sudden volley was fired in our faces—then we were at the tents, from which the Federal officers ran in their night-clothes.

The scene was animated. The fight had commenced, and the whole locality was one maze of quick flashes, accompanied by the sharp crack of carbines.

The men charged straight forward on the railroad ; drove the Federal forces beyond it ; and quickly set to work to tear up every thing, and destroy the bridge near by.

In this latter attempt they were unsuccessful, the rain having wetted the timbers to such a degree as to prevent them from kindling. As the light revealed the forms of the men, destructive volleys were poured into them from the darkness.

I went to witness the bridge burning, but soon galloped back to Stuart, who was in the midst of the fire, cheering on the men. Suddenly an officer rode up to him, said something, and I heard that quick, animated response which always indicated intense satisfaction with the General. He galloped to a tent at some distance—and I saw at once that it was the adjutant-general's. It contained all the " official papers " of the Federal army!—and near at hand, in another tent, was General Pope's coat, with its badge of rank, hastily left by him in his flight.*

* Historical.

As Stuart held it up to the light, he burst into a laugh, and exclaimed:

"Here is my revenge for losing my hat and cape at Verdiersville!"

The important official documents were at once secured, and having accomplished this, so much more than he expected, Stuart ordered the pursuit of the scattered enemy to cease, and his command to fall into column.

Ere long, they were rapidly retiring over the same road by which they had come, to regain the Southern lines before the waters rose in their rear.

"Well, Surry!" exclaimed the General, as we rode along, "what do you think of your raid?"

"I like it, General."

"It is more than a success—far more. Do you know what we found yonder? Those papers are a complete *exposé* of Pope's strength, position, expectations, and designs. He writes that without Burnside he can't hold his ground, and must retreat from Virginia! We know his whole hand now, and can play our cards to suit it!"

"Then you have completely blocked his game."

"It looks like it—to say nothing of capturing the General commanding's coat! Ha! ha!"

And Stuart laughed with the keenest enjoyment.

On the next morning we had re-entered the Southern lines, and General Lee had the captured papers. A few hours afterward Jackson ordered three days' rations to be issued, and his men to be gotten under arms.

LXXX.

FLANKING POPE.

THE long glittering column was drawn up, ready to march. The clothes of the men were in rags, and their feet bare; but their faces were laughing and their bayonets bright.

I rode along the column, and heard upon all sides—who can tell whence the information came?—"Old Jack is goin' to flank 'em!"

That was the exact truth. Jackson left the vicinity of Warrenton Springs, ascended the left bank of the Rappahannock, passed Amissville, and, crossing at the narrow, rock-bound, and forgotten ford at Hinson's Mill, dragged his artillery up the opposite acclivity, and pushed on to the little village of Orleans.

Stuart's cavalry, except one regiment in front, moved on the right of this column, between it and the enemy, keeping off their scouting parties; and, leaving the high road to Barbee's, Jackson struck into the fields, pressing forward through farm gates, and along obscure country roads, toward Salem.

The people greeted the sight of the gray coats with perfect amazement. But it was a joyful surprise. They ran to their doors, full-handed, to welcome and feed the weary troops—on all sides were heard joyous exclamations—and so the column pushed on, weary but laughing, toward Thoroughfare Gap. If it could only reach and pass through that frowning defile before the enemy were aware of the intention, the great *dépôt* of stores, at Manassas, would be at Jackson's mercy.

At sunset Jackson sat his horse, looking at the column as it defiled before him. He had issued orders that the men were not to cheer, for fear of attracting the enemy's attention, and the troops, as they passed before him, only took off their ragged old hats and waved them round their heads. This silent greeting seemed to touch Jackson greatly. The setting sun shone on his face, and the countenance at that moment was resplendent. There was something proud and yet gentle in the brilliant eye, the expression of the lips, and the air of the man, as, sitting his old sorrel in the yellow light, he gazed from beneath his dingy cap—chin in air—upon his followers.

All at once a single cheer rose; and the effect was electric. It ran along the line; the air was split by a great shout; the long pent-up feelings of the troops had burst forth.

Jackson's face glowed; he raised his cap in response, and the cheers redoubled. The men whirled their old felt hats around their heads with wild enthusiasm. With sparkling eyes, and rising in his stirrups as he spoke, Jackson said :

" Who could help being proud of such men as these?"

And, touching his horse with the spur, he galloped on to the front, still pursued by the tumultuous cheering.

The exhausted troops were now halted near Salem, for food and sleep; and knowing that the column would move at the earliest dawn, every man lay down, with his musket at his side, ready to respond to the order at a moment's warning.

I did not lie down ; and now beg that the reader will accompany me on a short ride I took.

LXXXI.

I CHASE AND COME UP WITH A FEDERAL OFFICER.

THE object of my night-ride is probably no mystery to the reader. Salem was near White Plains; and near White Plains was " Elm Cottage."

I had determined to go and reconnoitre in that direction, in spite of the Federal cavalry in our front. Many things induced me to visit the cottage. Was Violet Grafton still there? Had Fenwick again been lurking around the place? I say *again*, for, in his night interview with Mrs. Parkins, he had spoken of his reception by Violet. Had Mrs. Fitzhugh heard from May Beverley? It was that last question which, despite my fatigue, made me get into the saddle.

The ember was not cold. It flamed again at a breath. Do you laugh, good reader, at the love-sick condition of the unfortunate Surry, pining, with a hopeless attachment, for a woman who was to be the wife of another? Alas! love laughs at logic as well as locksmiths—and, though I have not insisted upon speaking incessantly of Miss May Beverley, she had occupied my thoughts on many battle-fields, and bent over me, beautiful and smiling, as I fell asleep by numerous camp-fires ! Such things, I know, never occur in the lives of other men—and of you, beloved.

reader, this fable has never been narrated. But so it was. I tried to cease the immoral proceeding; but I was in love with my neighbor Baskerville's wife—I coveted the property of that paladin and flower of chivalry, as much as ever!

So I went to find whether Mrs. Fitzhugh had heard from her, and incidentally to see Violet Grafton and the rest.

The infantry picket halted me, but, upon giving my name to the officer, I was allowed to pass. The same occurred when I came to the exterior picket of cavalry, and I rode on through the darkness. For half an hour, no sound broke the deep stillness. The enemy's scouts, I suspected, were prowling around, but none made their appearance—and ere long I came in sight of the clump of trees embowering Elm Cottage.

From a distance came the glimmer of a cheerful light; and, pressing forward, I had reached the outer gate, when the neigh of a horse was heard near the house. My own horse neighed in reply; and I was galloping along the winding avenue, when, all at once, the door opened, a flood of light poured through it, and I recognized the blue uniform of an officer of the U. S. Army.

He had taken two rapid steps toward his horse, when I ordered him to halt and surrender.

His reply was a loud laugh, which I distinctly heard; and, turning to utter a few hasty words to some ladies behind him, he ran to his horse.

As he mounted I fired upon him, but did not strike him. A second laugh greeted the shot; and, clearing the low fence, the officer darted off.

I followed, and pursued at full speed, ordering him to halt or I would kill him. His horse was fleeter than my own, and the distance between us was increasing; but suddenly my challenge seemed to produce the desired effect. He drew rein—I approached at full speed—and, levelling my pistol at his head, said:

"You are my prisoner!"

A third burst of laughter greeted me; the figure held out his hand; and I heard, in the familiar voice of Will Surry:

"How are you, brother!"

"Will!" I exclaimed

"Certainly it is Will, and you have given me a devil of a chase!" responded the boy; "to say nothing of that shot, which has spoiled my very best coat!"

And, with a gay laugh, the speaker showed me the collar of his uniform coat, which was pierced by a bullet.

"Good God!—this miserable war!" I could not forbear from exclaiming. "Brother taking the life of brother!"

"Not at all! I never felt better in my life; and my horse, too, is unhurt. I could easily have gotten off; but I recognized your voice, and stopped, to hear the news from home, brother."

These words were an inexpressible relief to me. Then Will was not my prisoner—he had voluntarily stopped, and I was not bound, in honor, to regard him as a captured officer.

In a moment we had dismounted, thrown ourselves upon the grass by the road-side, in the light of the rising moon, and I was answering the boy's ardent questions. They were all about home.

"And so the dear old gentleman is well. And how is Annie—my little pet?"

"Perfectly well."

"And old Carlo! Does he hunt now? How are the ducks on the river? And what's become of Jenny Clayton—at the North still? Pshaw! why ain't she at home? Brother, there's no place in the world like Old Virginia—it's the best of lands, and Eagle's-Nest is the best place in it!"

I could make no reply. There was something inexpressibly sad to me in these questions, from an officer of the U. S. Army.

"I see what you are thinking of," said the boy, with a cloud upon his brow. "I am an enemy—fighting against you. Well, so I am—but I can't help it, brother! I thought Virginia would not secede, and held on to my commission until the fighting commenced—and then I thought it my duty to stay in the army. The devil of it is," he added, with a quick sigh, "that I can't help wishing the South would whip! But I'm going on 'fighting for the old flag'—that's a glorious sentiment—eh?"

He remained for a moment silent and gloomy.

"And to-night," he said, in a low tone, "suppose you had killed me? I wouldn't have cared, but you know it would have broken your heart."

"Indeed it would, Will."

"I say, brother," he said, resuming his good spirits, "don't let us shoot at each other hereafter! War is my trade, but I am not bound to kill you; and as to your shooting me, that would be remarkably inconvenient just at this time."

I could not help catching the contagion of the boy's light-heartedness, and gliding to more pleasant themes.

"The fact is, brother," he said, "I'm dead in love with a little girl not a hundred miles from this place, and being killed would seriously interfere with my arrangements."

"You mean Henrietta Fitzhugh?"

"How in the world did you know it?"

I told him the history of his letter, and he said:

"So poor Tom Govran is wounded or killed. Sorry for him! And you've got my letter?"

"In my valise."

"And know all about my 'flame,' as the poets say! But brother, she's a regular tartar, and will scarcely speak to me. I had just 'dropped' in when I heard your horse neigh, and thought you were a whole squadron, or I wouldn't have run so. But here I am running on about trifles. Tell me all about dear old Eagle's-Nest, and your own adventures? Did you get over your wound soon? Is the old place changed? What does our old mammy say about the war? Does Annie 'love me as before?'"

And the boy ran on in a perfect torrent of questions—all now about 'the old folks at home.' I replied to all—and so we conversed for more than an hour. Under the great oak beneath which we had thrown ourselves, two brothers were talking of home; the gray and blue coats made no difference—the hearts which they covered beat close together. On the heaving arena of war they had found this little spot of firm soil to stand upon and greet each other as they were borne along.

We were talking still when shots were heard upon the right,

13

at the distance of about half a mile; and Will rose to his feet.
There were tears in his eyes, as he said :

"My company is yonder!   I must go there."

"Good-by, Will."

"Good-by, brother!"

A close pressure of the hand—and in a moment he had
disappeared.

LXXXII.

VIOLET GRAFTON'S SECRET.

I RODE back toward Elm Cottage, but was not destined to
arrive as soon as I expected.

My horse had scarcely brought me again in sight of the
house, when I saw a figure standing in the road before me, and,
drawing nearer, recognized Violet Grafton.

In a moment I had dismounted, and we had exchanged a cordial greeting.   By the light of the moon, which had now fully
risen, I could make out every feature and expression of the
charming face—the large blue eyes, with their mild and tranquil
splendor, the innocent mouth, the cheeks upon which two blush-
roses seemed blooming, and the broad fair brow, upon each side
of which fell those closely curled ringlets of bright golden hair.
She was very simply clad, but her figure was exquisitely graceful, with the light shawl drooping from the shoulders.

"I recognized you as you followed Lieutenant Surry," sne
said in her calm sweet voice.

"He is my brother; we have been talking for an hour."

And I related every thing.

"This terrible war!" she said with a sigh.   "Oh, when will it
end?   I am in fear and trembling for my friends in the army,
all the time."

"Perhaps I can give you news of some of them," I said.

"I have very few," was her reply, accompanied by a quick
look toward me, which I did not understand.   I thought she was
about to add something, but she only colored slightly.

All at once, I know not why, I thought of the night ride of the young lady with Mordaunt, before the battle of Manassas, and said:

"You remember Colonel Mordaunt, do you not?"

I was startled by the effect which my words produced. Her head turned quickly, and I could see her become suddenly pale.

"Has any thing happened to him!" she exclaimed in a quick, agitated voice. "He is not wounded!"— I saw that she had not strength to add, "or dead." Her eyes dwelt, with an expression of agony almost, upon my face. That look revealed the secret of Violet Grafton.

"He is perfectly well," was my reply.

She drew a long breath—her bosom heaved.

"I am very glad," she murmured, rapidly regaining her calmness. "I heard something of a battle on the Rapidan, in which his regiment was engaged."

"The report was correct. Mordaunt made a splendid charge in the action, but came out of it entirely unhurt."

She inclined her head, and we walked on toward the cottage.

'My interest in Colonel Mordaunt, perhaps, surprises you," she said in an instant; "but we became very good friends on that night ride from Manassas, before the battle."

"Is it possible? Mordaunt is the coldest of the cold toward your sex."

"Yes, that is true."

I hesitated for a moment, and then said:

"Did you give him his package? Do not think me a prying person, Miss Grafton. I chance to know that those letters were written by his wife."

And I went on to speak of some portions of the narrative which I had heard from the lips of Fenwick.

"I see that you know every thing—even more than myself," was her low reply; "but you are in error upon one point. That package did not contain letters, but a regular journal, written by my poor cousin from day to day—from the moment that she left home until the time when she became insane."

"And from those papers Mordaunt knew all."

She gently inclined her head, and I walked on in silence. I had then been instrumental in convincing Mordaunt of his wife's fidelity and devotion. The contents of that package had lifted from his life, to some extent at least, the deep shadow of misery which rendered the whole female sex abhorrent to him. He knew, from that journal of the poor dead woman, that she had loved him to the last—that he was still her 'darling.' To a man like Mordaunt, writhing under a sense of shame, this conviction, I felt, must be an inexpressible relief.

"It is a happiness to me, Miss Grafton," I said at length, "to know that Colonel Mordaunt has thus been enlightened in regard to this horrible mystery. I will add that he is fortunate too—solitary and unhappy as he may be—in securing your friendship."

"Oh! that is nothing—he is very noble!"

And the telltale cheek again glowed.

"You cannot like him more than I do," was my reply; "he is the soul of honor, and is noted throughout the army for his reckless courage. He is not far off now, and perhaps may have time to call and see you."

I had scarcely uttered the words when hoof-strokes were heard upon the road, and a horseman, followed a few paces in rear by another, was seen approaching. In the foremost I recognized Mordaunt—in the latter, his Moorish servant, Achmed.

Mordaunt recognized us in an instant, and bowed to Miss Grafton with an air of cold, proud courtesy. Then dismounting, he calmly held out his hand to me, and said:

"You don't seem to be afraid of capture, Major. Do you know that you are outside my picket, and very near the enemy?"

"I supposed so," was my laughing reply; "but if Colonel Mordaunt can risk it, I can."

"I shall be busy to-morrow, and came to see my friends here for a moment."

And bowing again to the young lady he walked on—Achmed having taken his horse.

There was a happy light in Violet Grafton's eyes, which no longer left me in any doubt—and I sighed. What evil fortune had made this girl of such exquisite nature place her affections upon that marble statue? It was spring-rose and icicle, sunshine and snow. Would the snow ever melt?

I was asking myself that question, when Violet Grafton dropped her handkerchief. Before Mordaunt or myself could pick it up, Achmed, the young Moor, had bounded to the spot, lifted it from the ground, and pressed it to his lips with a passionate gesture, which betrayed his warm Eastern blood.

As he did so, his face became crimson, his sparkling eyes sank before the cold look of Mordaunt, and, with head bowed submissively on his breast, he approached Miss Grafton, knelt upon one knee, and, with the air of a slave in presence of his mistress, presented the handkerchief. As she took it, his forehead sank lower, he crossed both hands upon his breast, and remained thus with abased eyes, until the young lady passed. He did not see, or dared not take the hand which she held out to him.

"He is asking you to pardon his presumption in pressing your handkerchief to his lips," said Mordaunt, coolly; "the boy is the creature of impulse."

And they walked on. Before reaching the house, however, I thought I could see in the face of the young Moor, who now gravely followed, an expression which accounted for that sudden act. Had I discovered, in one evening, a double secret? Had Achmed ever seen the young lady before?—and what was the meaning of that passionate glance?

And Mordaunt? That mask of ice showed nothing.

LXXXIII.

I AM THROWN INTO CONFUSION BY MISS HENRIETTA

On the trellised porch we met Mrs. Fitzhugh and her gay niece, Miss Henrietta, who uttered many exclamations at my appearance. I merely said that my chase had resulted in nothing, and no further allusion was made to the visit of Lieutenant Will Surry.

The excellent old lady led the way into the house, and insisted upon giving me a good supper. Mordaunt had supped, he said, and he and Miss Grafton remained upon the porch, conversing in the light of the splendid August moon. The Moor remained in charge of the horses—but I could see that his dark eyes were fixed upon Miss Grafton.

During the meal, which was a marvellous and exciting spectacle to the eyes of a hungry soldier, I was amused by the gay sallies of Miss Henrietta, and the delightfully plain-spoken views of Mrs. Fitzhugh. I have stated, on a former page, that the excellent old dame had the habit of saying exactly what she thought upon every subject. If she did not like anybody, she was very apt to say so, and give the grounds of her opinion. I soon found that she did not like Captain Baskerville—upon whom the conversation soon chanced to turn.

Here is how that happened:

SURRY, *with his mouth full:* "Have you heard from the Oak lately, Mrs. Fitzhugh?"

MRS. FITZHUGH, *busily knitting by the fire, while Miss Henrietta pours out:* "Several times, and all are well but May. I believe she is pining away at the idea of marrying that Captain Baskerville. They are engaged, but May can't bear him—and her opinion of him is perfectly just."

SURRY, *with deference and interest:* "Her opinion of Captain Baskerville, madam?"

MRS. FITZHUGH, *knitting more busily;* Yes, she has not a particle of respect for him, my dear. I forget, you are not one of my nephews. May *can't* respect Captain Baskerville, and she can't bear the idea of marrying him. As sure as you sit there, Mr. Surry, that man is a mean person. I never was mistaken in a human face, and I know Frederick Baskerville besides. He always has been mean. He would sell his soul for money, and he don't care a rush for May Beverley or any one else, for themselves."

SURRY: "You surprise me, Mrs. Fitzhugh! I thought Captain Baskerville was rich, and Miss Beverley by no means so."

MRS. FITZHUGH: "Yes, he is rich, but so is May. Her uncle, an old bachelor, who was very fond of her, by his will, when she was fourteen, left her at least one hundred servants; and, as sure as you are sitting there, that is what Frederick Baskerville is marrying her for. His property is almost entirely in land, and he wants servants. May is a fine-looking girl—we are of very good family—and Frederick Baskerville thinks that altogether, with the hundred servants, it is, to speak vulgarly, a good speculation."

SURRY: "Can Miss May Beverley suspect this motive?"

MRS. FITZHUGH: "I believe she does, but she knows Frederick Baskerville, and can't bear him. It is wicked in my brother to insist upon the marriage upon that trumpery idea that he is bound by his word to the elder Baskerville. As sure as fate, Captain Baskerville—I'd like to know where he got his title—will make May Beverley wretched; for he is mean, my dear—excuse me—and not what we old people call a gentleman."

I need not say that the reasoning of this excellent lady appeared to me irresistible. I had never listened to a train of argument which impressed me as more brilliant and conclusive. Perhaps this arose from the fact that our views upon the subject of Captain Baskerville exactly coincided.

I was indulging these reflections when Miss Henrietta, that mischievous young damsel, burst into a ringing laugh, and cried:

"Aunty! you don't know how you are delighting Major Surry!"

"I? How, my dear?"

"Why, he is in love with cousin May!"

Surry feels a profound conviction that he is blushing violently.

"Just look at him!" exclaimed the young witch; "he is coloring like a girl when she is courted."

I tried to laugh.

"How do you know how they feel under those circumstances, mademoiselle, at sweet sixteen!"

"I know well enough!" replied Miss Henrietta with great candor.

Mrs. Fitzhugh had looked up. She now smoothed the heel of the stocking she was knitting upon her knee, and said with perfect quietness:

"I wish May would marry you, Mr. Surry. Why don't you ask her? Your family is very good—like ours—and we should not have a Baskerville connection."

To these excessively plain words I could find nothing to reply, and only attempted a laugh. Miss Henrietta's gay voice came to my relief, and I rose from table.

"I am sorry I teased you!" whispered Miss Henrietta.

"You ought to be."

"Why don't you take aunt's advice, and court cousin May?"

"Absurd; she cares nothing for me."

Miss Henrietta looked at me intently, and said in a low tone:

"Must I offer you some advice?"

"If you please."

"Ask cousin May," she whispered, "if she doesn't care for you; and you will then find one reason why she doesn't want to marry Captain Baskerville!"

There was a whole volume of meaning in the audacious smile, and again I felt that disagreeable sensation in the cheeks which I am informed proceeds from the act of blushing.

Violet Grafton and Mordaunt, however, entered at this moment, and a diversion took place. There was nothing whatever in Miss Grafton's countenance to show that her conversation with Mordaunt had been anything more than that of one friend with another; her face was perfectly tranquil and happy.

Mordaunt took his seat by Mrs. Fitzhugh, and they conversed for a quarter of an hour. He then rose, and said he must return to camp. As he bowed and turned away, I heard the old lady say:

"Violet, my dear, your friend, Mr. Mordaunt, is a very fine gentleman indeed. His family must be very good—like ours."

I laughed, and, informing Mordaunt that I would accompany

him, buckled on my pistol and sabre—articles which Mordaunt
had not laid aside.

Man proposes, only. At that instant rapid hoof-strokes resounded without; Achmed's pistol was fired; and, looking
through the door, we saw a whole company of Federal cavalry
gallop into the grounds.

At their head, as they approached through the moonlight, I
recognized Fenwick.

LXXXIV.

SURROUNDED.

NOT a moment was to be lost, if we intended to attempt to escape. The Federal cavalry-men had seized upon our horses, and
were now rushing upon the house, in pursuit of the Moor.

I never saw Mordaunt look more cool; but, when he recognized Fenwick, a livid light suddenly glared in his eyes, and his
teeth clinched.

As Achmed entered, he advanced two steps and heavily
barred the door. Then turning to Mrs. Fitzhugh, he said:

"We are going to defend the house, madam. Will you retire
to the upper rooms with the young ladies?"

The old lady hastened to obey, followed by Miss Henrietta,
who trembled from head to foot.

Violet Grafton did not stir. The color had faded from her
cheeks, but her eyes were brave and proud.

"Let me stay," she said, in a voice as firm and sweet as it had
been an hour before. "I am not afraid."

Mordaunt took her hand and led her, without speaking, to the
staircase in one corner of the apartment.

Her head fell, a burning color mounted to her cheeks, and
she disappeared just as the Federal soldiers threw themselves
against the door.

"Now, Surry," said Mordaunt, with a sort of devil in his eyes,
"I don't know what you are going to do, but I am not going to
run from that reptile. I mean to defend this house to the last."

13*

"You can count on me."

"Good—I thought as much, comrade. Achmed is armed, and as brave as steel. Is your pistol loaded?"

"Yes."

"Then we have some fifteen shots. It's odds if we don't hurt somebody—then the sabre!"

While he spoke, Mordaunt, assisted by Achmed, dragged a heavy table against the door, and I secured the door in rear in the same manner.

"Open!" cried a threatening voice, accompanied by the heavy blow of a sabre-hilt; "open! you are my prisoners!"

"Come and take us!" was Mordaunt's reply as he cocked his pistol.

"Open, or you are dead?"

"Bah!—we are not children!"

"Who are you?"

"Gentlemen!"

"Officers?"

"What matters it? We are men."

"In ten minutes you will be dead!"

"It will take longer than that."

The reply was a pistol-shot, which pierced the door and struck the opposite wall.

Directing Achmed to reserve his fire, Mordaunt reached the window, took dead aim, and fired. A groan followed, and the heavy sound of a body falling.

"One!" he said, quickly securing the shutters. With another movement he extinguished the only light in the apartment.

He had scarcely done so when a whole volley of bullets passed through the shutters; and then vigorous hands were heard endeavoring to tear them open.

I fired at three paces from the window, and heard a howl from without.

"Two!" was Mordaunt's cool comment. "Keep against the wall, Surry!"

The advice was good. A second volley came, tearing both through doors and windows, from front and rear.

"Open!" howled the voice we had heard before; "open! infernal guerrillas that you are! Open, or in ten minutes I will roast you alive!"

Mordaunt's cool reply was:

"We have the honor to call your attention to the fact that we are not guerrillas."

"What are you, then?"

"I have already informed you. We are gentlemen."

"What is your design?"

"To defend this house, and kill as many of your command as possible."

"Fire!" was the answer in a voice of rage from without.

And a volley crashed into the room.

"Fire again!—tear down the door!"

Another came; then heavy shoulders struck against the door.

"Reserve your fire—it misses, or only wounds," said Mordaunt, "you will soon need it."

Suddenly we heard the voice of Fenwick. He spoke in a low tone, but every syllable reached us.

"Captain," he said, "I know this house well, and I know the man who is defending it. He will stop at nothing, and he has barred the door, so that it cannot be opened. Attack from above, and you will have better luck."

Mordaunt uttered a low growl, and raised his pistol—but lowered it again.

"It is very easy to say attack from above," came in response to Fenwick from without; "but how the devil am I to do it?"

"There is a ladder yonder—and a window at the side of the house. Nothing is easier."

"Will *you* mount?"

There was a moment's silence, interrupted by a sarcastic laugh.

"That was not the bargain," replied Fenwick, coolly; "send one of the men."

"A man there, to mount a ladder," said the captain.

Mordaunt looked at me and laughed.

"That's a small affair," he said; "it will save ammunition to send Achmed with his knife. The poor boy is dying to take part."

In fact, the young Moor had remained erect, silent, and motionless, but his sparkling black eyes betrayed his desire to engage in the struggle.

The sound of a ladder dragged along the ground was now heard—then the noise it made in striking against the wall above.

Mordaunt turned to the young man, and said a few words to him in Arabic, pointing, as he did so, to a long, slender poniard in Achmed's breast. The boy's face glowed; he drew the long, bright blade, and disappeared at one bound up the staircase, moving as noiselessly as a tiger.

"Ready!" came from without; and then was heard the noise of heavy boots ascending the ladder, accompanied by the clatter of a sabre against the rounds.

"Now for it!" shouted the voice of the Federal captain. "You are at the window! Burst it in!"

The steps continued to ascend; the shutters were evidently being torn open; when, all at once, a frightful cry resounded above, and a heavy body was heard falling along the ladder, and striking violently against the ground. The ladder was then heard to crash down—and the next instant Achmed reappeared, wiping his poniard, which was streaming with blood.

With a few words in Arabic, he resumed his former place. As he did so, a volley of oaths resounded without, and one of the men said:

"He's dead, Captain—stabbed through the heart."

"Three!" said Mordaunt, laughing.

He had scarcely spoken when a furious rush was made on the front door, amid a wild outburst of yells and imprecations.

"They will break it down, Surry," said Mordaunt, coolly.

"So it appears—and then, my dear friend, the affair will be pretty well decided."

"One thing will be left, Surry."

"What's that?"

"To die game."

As he uttered the words, the door was burst open, and the assailants crowded the opening—their captain at the head.

For a moment the heavy table checked them—and behind this table stood Mordaunt, pistol in hand, erect and threatening as a destroying angel.

"Surrender!" howled the Federal captain, raising his pistol as he spoke.

Mordaunt did not reply. His arm was extended, as straight as an arrow, across the table—he fired, with the muzzle of his pistol almost touching his adversary's breast—and the Federal captain fell forward, shot through the heart.

For a single instant the assailants recoiled, and I fired at an officer behind, but missed him. The Moor had already emptied all his barrels, and had drawn his poniard.

Suddenly the voice of Fenwick was heard exclaiming:

"Kill the tall man!—a thousand dollars to the man who kills him!"

Mordaunt fired his sole remaining barrel, and I knew from his hoarse exclamation that he had not struck Fenwick.

"Now for the sabre!" he exclaimed, as the table was hurled back, and a dozen men rushed on him.

The overthrown table formed a sort of barricade, and across this now took place a desperate struggle. The men behind were afraid to fire, for fear of wounding their companions; and those in front required all their skill to parry the rapid and mortal blows of Mordaunt, and the deadly strokes of Achmed's poniard.

To "die game" seemed now all that was left for us. But even at that moment, when certain death seemed staring us in the face, I could not suppress a thrill of admiration for the defiant courage of my companion. He fought, thus at bay, amid his crowding adversaries, with the skill and coolness of a swordsman fencing for amusement—and at every stroke with the edge, or lunge with the point, his weapon drew blood.

But we were rapidly forced back; shots fired over the heads of the assailants buried themselves in the wall behind; and, suddenly, the table was broken down and trodden under foot.

At the same moment Mordaunt staggered.

'You are struck!" I exclaimed.

"No—my foot slipped—in the blood!"

And, clearing a circle with a single whirl of his sabre, he placed his hand against the wall—in his fiery eyes the wrath of a tiger at bay—ready to die, but not to yield.

At his side was Achmed, calm yet fiery; and this was the condition of affairs when, all at once, amid the clash of the sabres, shots were heard without, and then the rapid sound of hoofs.

"Charge! and cut down every man!" shouted a voice which seemed familiar; and in an instant the Federal cavalry were charged by a detachment of gray-coats.

In front rode Harry Saltoun, and at his side—Violet Grafton!

She had escaped from the house during the struggle—hastened on foot to the nearest picket—and led the party back to the house, fearlessly riding upon the saddle of a trooper!

In an instant the detachment led by Harry Saltoun were in collision with the Federal soldiers, cutting right and left The blue-coats ran to their horses, and hastily mounted—but, before the whole could do so, a number were shot down or sabred.

Mordaunt rushed through the doorway and mounted his re-captured horse.

"Follow me!" rang out in his sonorous voice.

And, placing himself at the head of the detachment, he charged the retreating enemy, cutting down every man he came opposite.

LXXXV.

THE SINGLE COMBAT.

WE had followed the enemy for more than half a mile, when, all at once, twenty yards in front, I saw Fenwick. He was mounted upon a splendid bay, and wore a pistol and sabre.

Mordaunt had already recognized him, and was pursuing him like an avenging Nemesis, apparently forgetful of all else.

"At last!" I heard him say, with a hoarse growl, through his close-set teeth.

And, without another word, he darted upon his adversary.

Mordaunt's horse, driven on with bloody spurs, made long and desperate leaps—I saw his rider rise to his full height in the saddle—then his weapon passed to his left shoulder, and I knew that he was about to make, as he came up with his adversary, that terrible "right cut" which I had seen him deliver in battle.

The thundering stride of his great black brought him opposite Fenwick. I saw his sabre gleam in the moonlight as it whirled —when, suddenly, Fenwick's horse fell, shot through the body by one of the cavalrymen behind, and Mordaunt's blow passed over the rider's head.

In an instant Fenwick was on his feet, and, as Mordaunt rode at him, fired. The bullet pierced the neck of the black, and he staggered forward—Mordaunt leaping from the saddle as he fell.

Then he rushed upon Fenwick, and they closed, breast to breast, in a mortal struggle.

Absorbed by this passionate encounter, I forgot all else, and checked my horse to witness it.

Fenwick was evidently an excellent swordsman, and I saw that he was brave; but he was no match for his adversary. Mordaunt drove him, step by step, across the road, toward a gigantic oak, which stretched its gnarled branches above, in the moon light—and then, with his back against the trunk, Fenwick could retreat no further.

The moon shone full upon his face—it was distorted by an expression which might have done honor to the mythologic furies. He struck at Mordaunt with the fury of despair—then the combat terminated.

Rushing upon him, with his sabre at tierce point, Mordaunt drove the keen weapon through his breast, and the point was buried in the tree beyond.

Fenwick remained erect—stretched out his arms—and his sword fell from his grasp.

"Die!" exclaimed Mordaunt, folding his arms, and speaking in a tone which it is impossible to describe. "But, before your black soul goes before its Judge, reply to me!"

Fenwick's drooping eyes slowly opened. He looked at his adversary as the bleeding wolf caught in the trap looks at the huntsman—sidewise, with sullen and bloodshot eyes.

"Why did you make my existence one life-long agony?" said Mordaunt, hoarsely. "What harm had I done you, that you should render me thus wretched?"

"I hated you!" came in a savage murmur from Fenwick; and the blood rushed to his lips, as he glared at his enemy.

"Why did you hate me?"

"Because she loved you."

Mordaunt's face grew rigid.

"Enough of that. What brought you here to-night?"

"To carry off the other."

"Violet Grafton?"

"Yes," he gasped.

"And kill me, if you found me there?"

"Yes! hate! hate! hate! eternal hate for you—that—goes with me—I die with that!"—

And again stretching out his arms, Fenwick fell forward, the sword snapping in his body.

At this moment, heavy firing came from the front, and rapidly drew near. Saltoun's detachment, which had pursued the enemy, were evidently returning at a gallop, hotly pursued in their turn—and, in a few moments, the scattered horsemen came in sight, with the enemy on their heels.

As one of our own men fled past us, a bullet pierced his back, and he fell mortally wounded from the saddle.

I seized the rein of his horse, and threw it to Mordaunt, who got into the saddle. Under his energetic appeals the men rallied in a measure; but young Harry Saltoun soon appeared, falling back like the rest.

"It's no go, Colonel!" he exclaimed; "they have more than a regiment, and are pressing me back, in spite of all I can do! Here they are!"

The whole detachment was now seen falling back in disorder before the enemy.

"Steady! shouted Mordaunt. "All right, boys! Re-enforcements will soon be here!"

And, giving a quick order to Lieutenant Saltoun, who galloped off, Mordaunt took command of the detachment, slowly retiring as the enemy pressed him.

This movement was effected with masterly nerve and coolness—at every step the enemy were met by skilfully disposed sharpshooters—and, before Mordaunt had been pressed back half a mile, the force for which Saltoun had gone arrived. It was the remainder of Mordaunt's regiment; and it had no sooner appeared than he placed himself at the head of it, and charged the Federal column, which proved to be nearly a brigade.

An obstinate fight followed, in which neither side gained any advantage—and then a desultory firing ensued. Daylight approached.

Mordaunt and myself had ridden forward to make a reconnoissance with Harry Saltoun, when suddenly the young man was seen to reel in his saddle, and if I had not passed my arm around him he would have fallen.

"What's the matter?" I said, as he raised his head.

"I was shot yonder," he replied, trying to smile as he spoke, "in the charge at the house! It is nothing "

And he fainted.

The bullet had passed through the same arm which had been wounded on the Rapidan, inflicting a painful injury. The sleeve and gauntlet of the young man were drenched in blood; but he had said nothing, followed the enemy, ridden, and brought re-enforcements, and then charged at the head of his company. "It was nothing "— but he had fainted at last.

He was placed upon a litter, and sent back to Elm Cottage, with a note from Mordaunt to Violet Grafton.

Afterward I knew that, in sending the youth there, Mordaunt had a double motive, and performed one of those actions which only great souls are equal to. But one of the worst faults of a writer is to anticipate.

At daylight the enemy retired, and Mordaunt immediately pressed forward.

As we passed the gigantic oak where the bloody combat between Mordaunt and his enemy had taken place, I looked for the body of Fenwick.

It was not visible. The enemy had no doubt carried it off with the rest of their dead, except those at Elm Cottage.

I looked at Mordaunt's face. In the dark eyes was the fierce glare of the tiger who has just torn his prey limb from limb.

LXXXVI.

IN WHICH THE WRITER OMITS A DESCRIPTION OF THE SECOND BATTLE OF MANASSAS.

JACKSON moved again at dawn. So perfect had been the cordon of cavalry pickets and scouting parties between the Southern column and the enemy, that the march was still entirely undiscovered; and reaching Thoroughfare Gap, a few miles west of Manassas, Jackson found it entirely undefended.

Passing through the frowning ramparts of the gorge, he descended upon the great Federal dépôt at Manassas.

He was now completely in General Pope's rear, and directly upon his communications with Washington. The great object of the expedition was to destroy the stores at Manassas, defeat General Pope's attempt to rescue them, and lastly, hold him in check until General Lee arrived with Longstreet's corps. Then, a pitched battle.

Jackson made his dispositions rapidly, and with consummate skill.

Ewell was sent toward Bristoe, a station on the Orange road, about four miles from Manassas, and Stuart then proceeded with his cavalry and Trimble's brigade, in advance to Manassas. The attack was made about daylight, and the troops rushed in, under a hot fire, and were soon in possession of the place.

About seven in the morning, General Taylor's Federal brigade, which had been hurried forward from Washington, crossed at Blackburn's Ford, and made an obstinate attack—but it was too late. Stuart was in the works, and no sooner had the Federal infantry appeared than he opened a sudden and determined artillery fire, which completely drove them back. They were pursued by Captain Pelham, with his horse artillery, and driven in the direction of Alexandria.

This attack had scarcely been repulsed when Ewell received the assault of General Pope, at Bristoe, meeting it with his customary obstinacy. When notified by Jackson that Manassas was destroyed, he slowly fell back, burning the bridge in his rear; and the various columns converged toward the little village of Groveton, near the old battle-field of July 21, 1861, where, with his back to Sudley Ford, Jackson awaited the enemy.

The scenes at Manassas, when the troops marched in, were singular. Enormous stores of every description greeted the eyes of the men, in the government dépôts and sutlers' shanties, and these were seized upon by the starving troops with avidity. I saw famished men, barefooted and in rags, eating lobster salad and drinking Rhine wine.

When Jackson turned his back upon Manassas, nothing was left but a mass of smoking ruins, from which a few straggling cavalrymen disappeared, slowly retiring before the advance of Pope.

By the destruction of these great stores, and the railroad toward Alexandria, which was accomplished by Fitz Lee, General Pope was left without supplies for men or horses. At one blow Jackson had wounded him mortally. If the Confederate commander could only hold his ground now until Lee arrived, a determined attack upon the starved men and animals of his adversary must end in his complete defeat.

Jackson made desperate efforts to hold his ground. His force was under twenty thousand men, and General Pope had his whole "Army of Virginia" in close vicinity, pouring forward to crush the audacious destroyer of his stores.

Jackson did not wait to be assailed. He attacked—and a bloody engagement continued until after night.

Meanwhile, Longstreet was rapidly advancing. Every hour

now counted. Jackson would be attacked on t e next morning
by the whole Federal army. He seemed to have made up his
mind to stand at bay, and fight whatever force assailed him—
leaving the rest to Providence.

It was after night when a courier, who had ridden by a bridle
path over the mountain, reached Groveton, and announced that
General Lee was near the Gap, and rapidly advancing. When
Jackson received this intelligence he drew a long breath, his
brow cleared, and he rose erect in his saddle, as if a heavy weight
was raised from his shoulders.

Soon the thunder of Longstreet's guns was heard reverberating
from the gorge of Thoroughfare Gap, and the enemy's force
there made a furious response, completely raking the narrow
pass with shell and canister.

It was not long, however, before the Federal artillery was
withdrawn at a gallop; Longstreet's men rushed through; and,
as the sun rose, the long glittering lines of bayonets were seen
steadily advancing to take position on Jackson's right.

The line of battle thus formed was an open V, with Groveton
in the angle. Jackson's line—the left wing—was in front of
Sudley Ford; Longstreet's—the right wing—running across the
Warrenton turnpike. Where the two lines joined, a crest bristled
with artillery to repulse the attempt which would probably be
made to burst through, and thus pierce the Confederate centre.

My readers must go to the histories for an account of the great
"Second Battle of Manassas." I cannot enter upon that vast,
desperate, and long-continued combat. The action will always
possess a weird interest, from having been fought upon the identical ground of the first battle—except that the adversaries had
changed positions. It was the Federal forces which now attacked
from the direction of Manassas, and Jackson who stood with his
back to Sudley Ford.

See the histories. The writer of memoirs deals in colors, incidents, and "trifles"—not in the great public events about which
so much is said in "official documents." He would make a fine
"battle-piece" of the great second battle of Manassas, were it
necessary; paint the blue and gray lines reeling to and fro; the

artillery "sweeping like a whirlwind of shot and shell" through
the opposing ranks; and, after reading his "animated description," the reader should find himself in that pleasing condition
of mind when the memory retains only a blurred and confused
idea of dust, smoke, uproar, blood—dead men and horses, breasts
riddled with bullets, color-bearers grasping their flags with forms
torn in two by round-shot—bodies deficient in legs, deficient in
heads, deficient in arms—groans, yells, shouts, cheers: and then
a "glorious victory." A glorious victory is no doubt a glorious
thing; but it is a brutal and bloody affair—this war-making—
under the glory and the laurels.

When the sun set on the third day's fight, the conflict was
over. Pope was defeated, and in full retreat toward Washington; the Federal Capital was in imminent danger; and General
McClellan, in command of the reserve retained for its defence,
wrote, "This week is the crisis of our fate."

Such were the magnificent results accomplished by the great
flank movement of Jackson. That march and what it effected
will always remain one of the most remarkable episodes of military history, and rank with the proudest glories of the great
commander.

There seemed to be something like retributive justice in the
result. General Pope had permitted, if not authorized, the most
flagrant oppression of the poor non-combatants of the country he
had occupied, declaring that he had never seen any thing of his
enemies but their backs.

Now he saw the face of "Jackson's men"—and his star went
down in blood.

LXXXVII.

THE YOUNG SIGNAL-OFFICER.

On the day succeeding this desperate conflict, Jackson, whose
column was pressing toward Centreville, directed me to find
Stuart, and accompany him in a movement which he was making
to the rear of the enemy. I was to ascertain the state of things

in that direction, and return as soon as possible with confidential intelligence from Stuart.

My route led me by the Stone House, which my readers cannot have forgotten ; and I soon came in sight of it. The place was a mass of ruins. The walls had been shattered and overthrown by cannon-balls, the garden torn to pieces in the hot struggle; and, reining in my horse, I could scarcely make out the stunted tree under which the unfortunate lady in white had been buried.

The mansion was a melancholy ruin, charred and blackened— it seemed to typify the life of the woman who had returned to this place, the scene of her former happiness, to sleep the sleep of death.

Had Mordaunt passed near that spot? I asked myself as I rode on; and then a thousand thoughts chased each other through my mind. How singular were the circumstances which had put me in possession of this strange man's history! How sad that record! How surprising had been the combination of events which threw him face to face, on that gloomy night, in this weird spot, with the living image of the woman whom he had loved! I could understand the profound emotion which had mastered the strong man, at seeing thus, as it were, the very face and eyes and hair of Frances Carleton once more there before him, where she had smiled long years before—and understand too the poignant anguish which wrung his heart, when all his fancied wrongs and shame were thus brought back to mind, and traced, as it were, with a pen of flame upon his heart. And then a deeper admiration than before for this proud spirit inspired me—for this man who, burying his grief and distress and bitter anguish, had borne up so bravely, and served his country with a courage and devotion so conspicuous and splendid.

Stuart had pressed on rapidly, and, before I had joined him, I heard the thunder of his horse artillery as he attacked the Federal forces near Fairfax Court-House. Pushing on, I reached the spot, and found the General superintending the fire of the guns, which were commanded by young Pelham, now his chief of artillery.

"All goes well, Surry," said the General, when I had delivered any message. "I am crowding 'em with artillery;* and, if Stonewall doesn't hurry up, there will be nothing for him to do."

"He is coming right on, General."

"And you have pushed on to 'jine the cavalry'! Well, we have had a little affair near Chantilly—captured a whole company of Yankee cavalry. Look! there is the captain!"

And he pointed to an officer mounted upon a magnificent black horse, carrying before him on the pommel of his saddle a brilliant stars-and-stripes flag.†

I looked at the officer and thought I recognized him, but could not remember where I had seen him. A second glance recalled the time and place. It was the humorous personage who had captured me near Cross Keys, and sent me to Sir Percy Wyndham with the laughing order to my guard to kill me if I attempted to escape.

"We recaptured poor Hardeman Stuart's coat, too," added the General, with a sad expression in his bold face. "You remember him, do you not—my signal-officer?"

"Remember him?" I said; "he is one of the best friends I have on your staff, General. It is impossible not to love his gay, frank face, with its blue eyes and chestnut curls. I saw him just before the battle opened."

"Ah?" said Stuart, with the same half sigh.

"Yes," was my reply, "I was riding over to the right, when a dusty figure, without hat or coat, ran out from a house and hailed me. I could scarcely recognize Hardeman, who is the model of elegance, you know, in uniform and appearance. He called out, 'How d'ye, Major!'—shook hands with me—and then told me, laughing, that he had been attacked on the mountain yonder, at his signal-station, and had lost his horse and coat. He said he intended to get another horse and rejoin you."

"Poor boy!" sighed Stuart; "he could not mount himself, and he was too brave and devoted to remain idle. He got a musket, fought with his old company from Mississippi, and was killed."

I felt deeply shocked at this intelligence. Hardeman Stuart

---

* Stuart's expression.   † Real.

had been one of my greatest favorites, and I loved him, as every-body did, for his sweet, frank temper and his gallant spirit.

"Hardeman dead?" I said.   "It is not possible, General!"

"It is true, and the singular thing is that we have just recaptured his new uniform coat."

"His coat?"

"Yes, it was strapped to his saddle, and captured with his horse. This Yankee company of cavalry, surprised at Chantilly, had it.*   There it is."

And he pointed to the coat strapped behind a courier.

"Poor, poor Hardeman!   But he was buried?"

"Yes. Major Von Borcke saw his grave. But we are getting sad. Come, Surry, I am going to withdraw, and, as I expect information during the night, you had better remain until morning. Come with me, and I will provide you with lodgings."

"Willingly."

And I followed the General, who retired just at nightfall.

LXXXVIII.

ONE OF STUART'S "TIGHT PLACES."

THE cavalry soon halted, and lay down in bivouac.

Stuart rode on with his staff through the black darkness; and the sad story which he had just told me gradually disappeared from his mind. This strong and exuberant nature could not long remain gloomy.

Half an hour's ride brought us to a house near Frying-Pan Church, where we halted, and were received with the warmest hospitality by some young ladies, who seemed overjoyed at sight of our gray coats, and the General, who was evidently an acquaintance and favorite. If you recall that evening, fair and charming "friends of the soldier," and this page meets your eye, receive the assurance of the unchanging regard and admiration

* A real incident.

of one person who that night basked in the warm light of your smiles.

If I were writing a romance, worthy reader, instead of my veritable memoirs, what a favorable opportunity would now be presented to make Stuart the hero of a "thrilling adventure!" Contemplate the situation, and observe its dramatic capabilities! Stuart, the bold cavalier, asleep in a remote mansion near the enemy, far beyond his own pickets, without a single vedette out, and liable to be "caught napping" as at Verdiersville. What would be easier than to bring a whole Federal regiment of cavalry down on the gay cavalier, and narrate in the most approved and striking style the manner in which he engaged them single-handed, and overcame them all! If necessary, Colonel Mordaunt or General Fitz Lee might come to his assistance—the ghost of Fenwick might appear—and indeed almost any thing might be made to happen!

The present writer is much too conscientious, however, to indulge in such "weak inventions." No such incidents occurred, therefore they cannot be narrated. Stern devotion to truth compels me to say that, in spite of the fact that we had not a single vedette posted to give warning of an enemy's approach the hight passed away in perfect quiet; the dawn appeared, and with it our fair hostesses, who gave us an excellent breakfast, and bade us God speed.

Do not the prayers of women shield us often? I think so. They prayed with all their hearts in the late revolution, and were angels to us all. The soldiers of the army and the women did their duty; had the rest done likewise, we might have been the founders of an empire!

So we left our smiling hostess and her friends, and again set out toward Chantilly.

Jackson's column was already pressing forward, and when I joined him he was sitting upon the ground, with his back against a tree, his chin upon his breast, his hands crossed over his bosom, fast asleep. The enemy's sharpshooters were firing rapidly near by, but he slept tranquilly.*

* Historical

14

An hour or two afterward he had pressed on and attacked the enemy near Germantown, on the Oxhill road.

There, the beaten army of General Pope, with reserves from Washington under Generals Franklin, Stevens, and Kearney, made a last stand, and fought with desperation to effect their retreat.

The opposing lines were soon engaged, and to the roar of musketry and cannon was suddenly added that of a violent storm. The thunder drowned the noise of the guns, and the drenching rain which poured down threatened to put an end to the action. Jackson was calmly watching the contest, when a courier from one of his Generals came up and brought a message to the effect that the rain had made the powder wet, and his command could not continue the engagement.

" Tell him to hold his ground," was Jackson's reply. "If it makes his powder useless, it will make the enemy's too !"*

The result of the action was completely in favor of the Southern arms, but I did not witness the latter portion of it. I had been sent again to Stuart, who was moving around toward Flint Hill, an eminence north of the Court-House, to occupy it with artillery, and attack the enemy in flank.

I joined Stuart just as he reached a narrow road leading up the hill. It was growing dark, and the storm was roaring down; but the General did not give up his design. Leaving one regiment at the mouth of the road to protect his rear, he advanced with another, and had soon reached the elevated ground above.

Here the brave Colonel Wickham rode back from the advance-guard, which he commanded, and said:

"General, I got near the Cross Roads, and find them heavily picketed with infantry."

Stuart reflected a moment, and then calling " Captain Farley," whom the reader may remember at Cold Harbor, gave him a message to General Lee.

Farley immediately rode back, and in a few minutes shots were heard in that quarter. At the same moment Colonel Wickham again rode up, and reported the enemy rapidly advancing in front

* His words.

Stuart's position was now critical. He was in the midst of the enemy's infantry, which hemmed him in in front and on his right; night had descended, making any cavalry movement hazardous; and there was but one avenue of retreat, the narrow road by which the column had ascended the hill. Now the firing had come from that direction. The enemy appeared to have closed in upon front and rear.

I afterward remembered, with admiration, the coolness and nonchalance of Stuart. He sat with one leg thrown across the pommel of his saddle, drummed idly with his fingers upon his knee, and seemed to be reflecting. It is impossible to imagine greater *sang-froid* than his appearance, at the moment, indicated.*

"Well," he said, at length, "I have accomplished the object I had in view, and we'll go back."

But the march back was in column of platoons, with drawn sabres!

Halfway down the narrow road, now as black as night, firing came from the advance-guard, and then a shout. The column pushed on—shots hissed from the high banks on either side—then the column debouched into the plain.

What was our astonishment at this moment to hear a bugle in front sound the "charge!"

Colonel Lee, commanding the regiment left behind, took us for Federal cavalry, it seemed, and nothing but the presence of mind of an officer, who shouted "Hold!" prevented a bloody catastrophe.

The firing we had heard was directed at Captain Farley, who was also in great danger from his friends.

So much for night operations with cavalry. They are always hazardous. I have recorded this little incident, however, as characteristic of Stuart's coolness and self-possession.

I said to him, long afterward:

"General, you did not seem to think your command in any danger that night at Flint Hill. I thought it in great danger."

* This whole sketch is historical.

"You are right," was his reply, in a low tone, with a short
laugh.   "I tell you, Surry, that was a tight place!" *

LXXXIX.

IN WHICH THE WRITER GETS OVER A GREAT DEAL OF GROUND.

At nightfall Jackson had driven the enemy before him, with
heavy loss, including two of their best officers—Generals Kearney
and Stevens; and at dawn on the next morning the troops
advanced upon Fairfax Court-House.

The enemy had retreated during the night, and the inhabitants
received their deliverers with shouts of joy.

Thus the work was ended for the present upon the soil of Virginia; and General Lee immediately put his army in motion for
Maryland.

Four or five days afterward, the Southern column forded the
Potomac near Leesburg, with the bands playing "Maryland, my
Maryland," and the advance force pushed on and occupied Fred-
erick City.

Maryland did not receive us with arms very wide open; and
few, very few, ranged themselves under the "bonnie blue flag."
But let not that old bitterness make me unjust.   It was the
Union portion of the State which we entered.   In the lower
counties and on the Eastern Shore there was a different population : there they were friends, here they were—neutrals or
enemies.

For the Maryland campaign in all its details, see the histories.
Here is an outline :

From Frederick City, Jackson was sent to make a detour, by
way of Williamsport and Martinsburg, to the rear of Harper's
Ferry, where there were about eleven thousand Federal troops
and a large amount of artillery.   The result is known.   While
General Lee was opposing the advance of McClellan at South

* His words.

Mountain, Jackson was closely investing Harper's Ferry. When he had ringed it round with artillery and opened upon it from every side, the Federal commander lost heart, and surrendered his eleven thousand men and seventy-three guns.

As the place fell, McClellan burst through to its relief. But it was too late. Jackson's heavy arm had fallen. The place was in his hands, and, leaving a portion of his force to hold it, he returned by a forced march to Sharpsburg, where General Lee had concentrated his whole available force to fight McClellan.

You know, my dear reader, what followed. Thirty-three thousand Southerners fought eighty-seven thousand there at Sharpsburg, on a September day, and repulsed, from morn to evening, every assault. These figures are General Lee's for his own force—General McClellan's for that of the Federals. Thus the Confederates fought nearly three to one at Sharpsburg.

Jackson, on our left, sustained the brunt of the attack. See General McClellan's report, where he says his great assault was with his right wing. Had he given way, the result would have been wellnigh fatal. As it was, he drove General Hooker half a mile, and at night was rooted immovably in his first position.

Lee remained in line of battle on the ensuing day, facing his great adversary. General McClellan says that the condition of his own army rendered a renewal of the battle impossible.

On the next morning General Lee recrossed the Potomac, and, crowning the heights with his artillery, challenged them to attempt to cross. The attempt was made, and in an hour the column was driven into and across the river again, with the bayonet.

That was the first and last attempt which was made to follow General Lee.

He collected his straggling and broken-down men, rested and provisioned his army, and, if the season had been June instead of October, would have advanced upon Pennsylvania.

As it was, he rested.

XC.

HAMPTON CHARGES, AND I "GO UNDER."

I DID not witness the greater portion of the events just narrated in brief outline, and for a reason which I will now proceed to give.

At the moment when Jackson's column approached Williams-port, on his march to Harper's Ferry, I was sent back to General Lee, then beyond the South Mountain, with a message.

I found the army in motion by way of Boonsboro', in the direction of Hagerstown, and was informed that General Lee was with the cavalry rear-guard, then retiring from Frederick City, before the advance of General McClellan.

A ride through the Boonsboro' Gap and Catoctin Mountain brought me to the cavalry, and I delivered my message to General Lee, which fortunately required no reply.

Fortunately, I say, for I now found that my horse was completely broken down, and wholly unfit to take me back at once over the difficult mountain road.

I accordingly looked about for an inviting farm-house, the abode of some good Marylander with Southern proclivities, where I could procure a feed, and soon discovered a promising-looking mansion. It was a fine old house, embowered in trees, on the eastern slope of the Catoctin Mountain; and the ample barns seemed to say, "Come, there is plenty here, and to spare." Without further hesitation I rode up to the wide gate, entered a broad avenue, and soon found myself in front of a large portico, upon which a hale old gentleman was standing.

My wants were made known, and I met with the most friendly reception.

"Your horse shall be attended to immediately, sir," was the smiling and hospitable reply. "Come in—come in. These are terrible times, sir—and you must be hungry, too."

My host then called lustily for a servant, who speedily appeared. gave him directions in reference to my horse, and then led the way into the house, where an inviting meal was soon spread by the hands of an old housekeeper. This elderly lady and my host seemed the only inmates of the mansion.

"Terrible times, terrible times," repeated my host. "The enemy seem to be coming right on. General Lee is falling back, is he not?"

I never liked to answer questions propounded by strangers— that should be one of the first principles of a soldier, and much more of a staff officer.

"The army is not far from this spot," I replied.

The old gentleman smiled.

"I see you are prudent," he said; "but your caution is quite unnecessary. I am a Southerner, heart and soul, and have a son in your army."

"I may know him, and be able to give you some news of him, sir."

"It would greatly delight me. I fear something has happened to him, as he has not been here with the army. My name is Saltoun!"

"Indeed! And is your son's name Harry, Mr. Saltoun?"

"Yes, sir—where is he?" asked the old gentleman, with acute anxiety. "You have no bad news to give me?"—

"No, no. He is wounded, but it is a trifle. He is in the hands of friends."

And, giving my name and position in the army, I informed Mr. Saltoun of the young man's wound and present whereabouts. He listened with anxious interest, and, when I had finished, exclaimed:

"Thank God that he is safe."

"He is perfectly so."

"These are awful times, Major," added my good host. "Awful times! We never know whether our sons are alive or dead. Harry is the light of my eyes—all I have left in my old age—and it would break me down if he was killed. So you know him well, and say he is brave—but I knew that. He was always fearless from his childhood; and when the war broke out I could not keep him at home. Do you expect to see him soon?"

I replied that I doubtless should meet him again in a few weeks, on his return to his command—whereupon the old gentleman asked if I could carry him his watch, which he had left behind him.

"He values it greatly," added Mr. Saltoun; "and, if you will take charge of it, he will be greatly obliged to you."

"I will do so with great pleasure, and tell him that you are well"—

"And wish to see him soon," added the old gentleman, heartily. "This is a terrible war—a very terrible war, indeed, sir!"

And the speaker shook his head in a most expressive manner, and, rising, unlocked a mahogany secretary, from which he took a handsome gold watch, set with jewels.

This he intrusted to me, with many cautions against losing it.

"Harry would not mind the mere value of the watch, sir," he said, "nor would I. But he has had this since his boyhood, and attaches a peculiar value to it."

I had just assured my kind host that I would take especial care of the watch, when firing was heard in front, and I rose. My horse was soon brought, and I had scarcely bidden my host good-by, and mounted, when a long column of cavalry was seen to defile by the outer gate, in the direction of Frederick City, and at their head I recognized General Wade Hampton.

I rode out and joined him. For this brave cavalier of South Carolina I had always experienced a very great respect and regard, since the noble stand which he made at the first battle of Manassas; and I had enjoyed the satisfaction of receiving from him evidences of friendship in return. He had changed little. Before me was the same erect and courteous cavalier, with his flowing black mustache, and mild yet brilliant eyes. In his simple bearing, full of suavity and repose, you read no indications of the hard and stubborn spirit of "fight" which, in every encounter, took him to the front, and made him charge. like a private soldier, and "come to the sabre."

I was soon informed of the state of affairs. General Lee was retiring, and General McClellan pressing on. The enemy were already in Frederick City, and their artillery had opened upon the cavalry toward the Catoctin Mountain.

"I am going to charge and capture it, Major," said General Hampton. "Will you see the charge?"

"I would not miss it, General."

And we continued to advance, the enemy's artillery roaring sullenly in front.

All at once, as the head of the column reached the summit of a hill, Frederick City appeared in front, the fields around swarming with the dark figures of the Federal soldiers.

Above the mass rose the white smoke of the artillery, which was pouring a heavy fire upon the Southern rear-guard, falling back before the furious attacks of the Federal cavalry.

Hampton turned and said a few words to the officer commanding his column. He was a young man of twenty-three or four, with sparkling black eyes, raven hair and mustache, and a bearing which showed him every inch the soldier. "Do or die" spoke in the flashing eye, the laughing lip, and the firm clutch of the sabre. Such was the gay and gallant Georgian, P. M. B. Young, whose charge at Fleetwood afterward saved the fortunes of that desperate day, and covered the young cavalier all over with glory.

"Colonel Young," said Hampton, "I am going to charge those guns at once."

"Ready, sir!" was the answer; and, turning to his men, Young ordered:

"Form fours! draw sabre!"

The column was ready—and, sword in hand, General Hampton placed himself at its head.

The admirable serenity of his countenance had not altered in the least degree. Under that courteous and tranquil glance was the stubborn will which would not bend.

A moment's pause; a few rapid orders; a quick clash of steel, as hundreds of sabres flashed from their scabbards, and then, at a steady trot, which, in a few minutes. became a headlong gallop, the column rushed to the charge.

The weight of the column, with Hampton leading, swept away the Federal cavalry in front, as leaves are swept by the wind; and then, amid loud shouts and the incessant crack of carbines, the Southern horsemen closed in upon the very muzzles of the artillery.

The sudden and desperate charge carried all before it. The men received without faltering the storm of canister hurled in
14*

their faces, rushed upon the guns, and in an instant they had
cut down or dispersed the cannoneers serving them.*

The artillery was captured, but in the charge all the horses
had been killed, and it could not be brought off. Nor could the
Confederate column hold its ground. The Federal infantry was
seen double-quicking across the fields, and Hampton was compelled to relinquish his prize and fall slowly back.

As he did so, a hot fire was opened upon him by the Federal in
fantry, and then came the close and menacing roar of their artillery, and the crash of bursting shell in the midst of the column.

Nothing is more disagreeable than to "fall back under fire."
The hurry, uproar, and shouts of the pursuers are thoroughly
disgusting. The enemy now pressed on, and the air was full of
balls and bursting shell. Suddenly I was deafened by a crash
like a falling mountain, within a few feet of me, and my horse,
with one agonized leap into the air, fell writhing in the death
agony. A shell had burst almost on him—a huge fragment torn
through his body, just behind the saddle—the animal lay upon
the road, a mangled and bleeding mass, struggling in death.

All this I saw only some moments afterward. I was thrown,
violently stunned for the time, and, when I rose, found myself in
the hands of the Federal soldiers, who greeted my unlucky
plight, as they still pressed on, with jests and laughter.

A guard conducted me back to Frederick City, where I was
taken before the provost-marshal, and my name and rank recorded. I was then locked up in a filthy den, with many other
Confederates, and, weary with my long ride, lay down on the
bare floor and fell asleep.

A hand on my shoulder waked me. I looked up—the light
of sunset shone on the wall.

"Are you Major Surry?"

"Yes."

"You are wanted."

And my guard opened the door, and led the way out of the prison. Five minutes walk brought us to a handsome house, which I

* Historical.

knew, from the horses before the door and the number of persons who came and went, was the head-quarters of some general. A moment afterward I was in the presence of General McClellan.

XCI.

I EXCHANGE VIEWS WITH GENERAL McCLELLAN.

THE commander of the Federal Army was entirely alone, in a private room. When I was announced, he rose from a table at which he had been writing, and bowed.

He was a man of thirty-five or forty, of medium height, with a well-knit frame, and the erect carriage of the West-Pointer. His countenance was pleasant and attractive, with its frank eyes, smiling lips, over which fell a brown mustache, and broad, open brow. General McClellan was evidently a gentleman by birth and breeding. His smile was cordial, his bearing easy and natural—his whole appearance calculated to win confidence.

"Major Surry, I believe," he said, and I bowed.

"Take a seat, Major. I heard of your capture, and that you belong to General Jackson's staff. He is an old West-Point friend of mine, and a very great man, too—how is he?"

"Perfectly well, General."

"And on his way to Harper's Ferry, I suppose."

The General laughed as he spoke, and seemed to enjoy my look of surprise.

"What an idea, General!"

"And Longstreet," continued General McClellan, "he is an old acquaintance of mine, too. He has gone to Hagerstown?"

I bit my lips. Where did the Federal commander procure this information?

"Let me see," he continued, with the air of a man who is making a calculation. "Jackson ought to be beyond Williamsport by this time—Longstreet near Hagerstown, and Walker in position on Loudoun Heights. If McLaws is a pushing man, he is in possession of Maryland Heights—and Stuart holds Boons-boro' and Crampton's Gap, to keep me off of Harper's Ferry until it falls."

I listened with a sort of stupefaction. General McClellan was describing, with perfect accuracy and entire nonchalance, General Lee's entire programme, as set forth in confidentia orders to his corps commanders. The enemy knew all.

" You do not reply, Major," said General McClellan.

" It is not my affair," I replied, with a gloor and sullenne -hich I could not control.

" But is my information accurate ?"

" Ask some one else, sir !"

General McClellan dropped his tone of banter and said courteously :

" I do not desire to extract any information from you, Major, and it would be useless. The carelessness of one of your gene rals has put me in possession of General Lee's entire plan of campaign, and I play the game from this moment with a full knowledge of my adversary's designs. Look, Major."

And, taking from the table a paper, he handed it to me.

It was General Lee's confidential order of march for the different columns of his army! The copy of the order was directed to General D. H. Hill, and had been left by him, or some one of his command, at Frederick City."*

" It is useless to deny the authenticity of this paper, General," I said, after glancing at it, " and it gives you a fatal advantage."

General McClellan stretched himself in his chair, with the air of a man who wishes to talk, and said philosophically :

"There are very few ' fatal advantages ' in war, Major—and I assure you that, with adversaries like Lee and Jackson, nothing in the future ever seems certain to me. I ought to whip Lee, holding as I do that chart of his designs—but will I ?"

" I sincerely hope not."

"Ah! you are recovering your good humor," laughed the General. "Well I don't know what the result will be, but I

* Historical.

shall lose no time. Jackson is detached, and I shall probably attack General Lee before he comes up."

" He almost always arrives in time, General."

" As at Cold Harbor," was the cool response. " That was a movement worthy of Lee's brain and Jackson's arm. My dear Major, I begin to think that we have got the sound principles, and you the great men."

I smiled—for there was something in the frank voice of the General which produced good humor.

" Do you know, General, that you are challenging me to an argument on the virtue or wickedness of secession»'

" Not at all, not at all. I really never annoy myself with these abstractions. I am a mere fighting man, you perceive, Major, and follow my flag."

" And we follow ours, General."

" Very well ; and I suppose we will have to fight it out. But I trust we shall do so like civilized people and gentlemen. I intend to break down the military strength of the Southern Confederacy, if I can, and overthrow the whole political fabric with the bayonet and cannon. But, I will not adopt for my motto, *Væ victis*, and, now or hereafter, make war upon non-combatants."

" What of the negroes—do you approve of emancipating and arming them ?"

" I am a soldier, Major, and rarely indulge in the luxury of an opinion," laughed the General. " Let the political errors of the Administration be righted at the ballot-box."*

" And when we are conquered--for you are sure of the result, are you not, General?"

" I think that will be the *finale* in the long run. The North is rich, persevering, and more populous than the South."

What would you do with the rebels, in that unfortunate event ?"

" I would proclaim universal amnesty, and say to the people of the South, ' We have fought hard, let us be friends again.' "

" Your views at least are liberal, whatever may be the result."

* His words.

"They are rational, Major. The statesman who cannot look beyond the petty hatreds and rivalries of the present is a ninny. Suppose the Confederacy is overthrown, and the Southern States accept in good faith the result, as a fair decision after a fair fight; suppose they return to the Union, and honestly take the oath of allegiance; is it good sense or puerile blundering—which —to insist upon treating a great, proud nation as a conquered race? It is the civilians who have never smelt gunpowder that believe the South won't fight if she's trodden on. The choice will be between smouldering, eternal, watchful hate, ready to break out in armed revolution again, or an open, frank, and honest union between the South and the North—the herald of greater prosperity and power for all the nation than before. That union will take place, that prosperity be seen in our day. All that is needed is to sweep away the buzzing and stinging insects of the moment, and the new era will commence in all its glory."

General McClellan spoke with animation, and his frank face was turned full upon me. Then, as he caught my eye, he smiled.

"I understand your look, Major," he said; "you think I am counting the Federal chickens before they are hatched, and fore-casting events which will never take place. Well and good— we think differently. We are going to beat you by numbers— forewarned, forearmed. Now let us talk of Jackson. What a surprising career! We thought nothing of him at West Point, and here he is taking the wind out of all our sails. Were you with him in his Valley campaign?"

"Throughout, General."

"That campaign surpasses every thing else in the war."

And the conversation turned upon other acquaintances of the General in the Southern army, about whom he seemed to have much curiosity.

The interview lasted until nine or ten o'clock, the General dispatching such business as came before him with rapidity and decision. I could only ascertain that his forces were pressing forward toward Boonsboro' and Crampton's Gap, and that he intended, if possible, to bring General Lee to an engagement before he was re-enforced by Jackson.

When I parted with the General, he frankly held out his hand and said:

"We are soldiers, Major, and can shake hands on the eve of battle. I regret your capture, but will see that you are subjected to no annoyance. When you see Jackson, present my respects to him, and tell him that I hope to meet him at Philippi."

"I will do so, General. But take care—his embrace is fatal!"

"W will see," was the smiling reply; and so we parted.

XCII.

WHAT FOLLOWED.

THE next morning I was placed, with other Confederate prisoners, upon a train of cars, which came up from Baltimore to a point near Frederick City; and no sooner had I observed the arrangements made for guarding the prisoners, than I resolved to attempt to escape.

The carriages in which we were placed were "passenger cars," with wide windows, quite sufficient to permit the passage of a man's body; and I saw at a glance that, if I could avoid attracting the attention of the infantry guard at the doors, I could pass my body through one of the apertures. Then, as this could only be effected, with any chance of escape, while the train was in motion, I must take the probable results of a heavy fall. That fall might break my neck, or my limbs; but something has to be risked in war; and the horrors of a Northern prison loomed up in hideous colors before my eyes. I resolved to risk every thing.

The train was soon full of prisoners, and in motion toward Baltimore. I made a reconnoissance of my surroundings. Every seat was filled, and the air was so close that many of the windows had been opened. Up and down the aisle between the seats walked a Federal guard, with musket and bayonet. At each door stood another, armed in the same manner.

I shall not further trouble the reader with the difficulties I en countered in the undertaking which I had resolved upon. After all, the design was not so critical or dangerous; and hundreds of prisoners escaped during the war precisely in the manner I did.

Watching my moment when the sentinel's back was turned, and the train was passing through a belt of woods, I passed my body through the open window, threw myself out, and fell violently to the ground.

As I rose, stunned and bewildered, but with no bones broken, a musket was discharged from the train, which had swept on, and a bullet whistled by my head; then another followed, and I heard that grating sound which is made by the iron wheels of a railroad train when the brakes are put on to check it.

It was too late, however. I was far behind, and, hastening into the woods, I went on rapidly, until the railroad was many miles distant.

So far I was safe. What remained now was, to elude the patrols and scouting-parties of the enemy, who would instantly discover my identity from my gray uniform. To avoid all such dangerous people, I plunged deeper into the woods, and, reaching a secluded dell, through which ran a small watercourse, selected a clump of bushes, and, worn out with my rapid march, lay down upon the cool turf to rest.

My intention was to remain thus *perdu* until night, to avoid scouting-parties; and I had begun to think rather ruefully of the tremendous tramp before me, all the way to Leesburg, when I heard the sound of horses' hoofs, and cautiously looked out from my covert.

Two Federal cavalry-men had entered the glade, attracted by the green grass and flowing stream, and in a moment I saw them stop, unbridle their horses, and turn them loose to graze.

The men then lay down in the sunshine, and began conversing idly.

I was within twenty paces, and heard every word which they uttered, but understood nothing. The explanation of the fact is very simple. The newcomers were two stolid young Dutchmen, evidently raw recruits, and they spoke in the genuine guttural of the Fatherland.

In half an hour they ceased talking, stretched themselves prone on the grass, and a low thunder through the nose proved that, overcome by the warm sunshine, and the fatigue probably of a march, they had fallen asleep.

Suddenly, as I gazed out cautiously upon the slumbering Teutons, I thought, "Why not capture these two worthies?" The affair was not difficult. I saw that they had unbuckled the belt around their portly persons, laid their weapons aside, and, if once I was in possession of their pistols, the thing was decided. Why not?—and, raising my head cautiously, I reconnoitred again.

The men were sleeping as sound as the seven champions of Christendom, and I no longer hesitated. Rising without noise, I listened, advanced from the covert, and then with three bounds reached the spot and seized the weapons of the cavalrymen.

The noise woke them, and they started up, but it was only to find a cocked pistol as their breasts. They were my prisoners, and as harmless as lambs.

No time was now lost. I ordered the men by signs to bridle up, and this they did with an air of perfect indifference; they rode Government horses.

By this time I had taken my resolution. Ordering one of the men, as before, to take off his blue coat, I put it on, strapping my own behind one of the saddles, and then directing the other prisoner to mount, I got into the saddle of the second horse, leaving the coatless personage to make his way back as he could to his command. I set forward rapidly, with my mounted prisoner toward the Potomac.

We travelled all that night, meeting no one—were chased the next morning by a Federal scouting-party, but outran them, and finally I reached and crossed the river at Leesburg, and was once more within the Southern lines.

Does the reader regard this adventure as indicative of "dash," "nerve," &c., &c., in Major Surry? Not at all. There was no more difficulty in capturing those men after once securing their arms, than in letting them finish their nap. They were conscripts, riding Government horses, and averse to fighting, much preferring prison-life and regular rations.

I delivered up my prisoner and his horse to a quartermaster at Leesburg, and then rapidly made my way toward the Valley— Harry Saltoun's watch still safe upon my person.

Crossing the Shenandoah, opposite Hillsboro', I pushed on; heard that Harper's Ferry had fallen; and, still continuing my way, reached the Potomac near Sharpsburg at sunset, to find General Lee's defiant lines still facing the enemy after the tremendous struggle of that memorable day.

XCIII.

WHERE AND WITH WHOM I SUPPED ON THE NIGHT OF THE BATTLE OF SHARPSBURG.

THE spectacle which met my eyes as I reached the field was imposing.

Before me was a picturesque valley, hemmed in upon the east by the wooded ramparts of the South Mountain, and traversed by the winding current of the Antietam. On every eminence rose farm-houses, now standing boldly out, now embowered in trees. The light green of nearly ripe corn, the deeper green of clover, and the russet-brown of ploughed land, over which the shadows came and went, made up a landscape which must have been charming only the day before.

Now it was torn, dismantled, and swept bare by the besom of war. All day the opposing battalions had charged backward and forward through those smiling fields; from behind those peaceful farm-houses, now crowded with the dead and wounded, sharpshooters had delivered their hot fire; the corn was trampled under foot; the ground ploughed up with shot and shell; the whole face of nature desolate.

On the elevated ground extending on both sides of the Antietam were drawn up the hostile lines which all day long had wrestled to and fro in one of the bloodiest combats of history. Connecting them was the small bridge over the Antietam which had been the occasion of a struggle so desperate, of which General McClellan had said, "Tell General Burnside to hold the bridge! The bridge! always the bridge! If that is lost, all is lost!"

It was lost, and the battle with it. On the left, Jackson had held his ground with that stubborn and unconquerable resolution which accomplishes every thing. Stuart had driven back with his artillery under Pelham the advance to turn Jackson's flank; the sun had set, the conflict was over, and all was well.

General McClellan had attacked and been repulsed. That meant defeat.

Passing along the lines of weary but laughing troops, cooking rations at their camp-fires, I found General Jackson busily masticating a cracker by his fire, and reported the cause of my absence.

"Your escape was truly providential, Major," he said. "We have had some hard fighting in your absence, but have held our ground here. With five thousand fresh troops I think we could have driven the enemy from his position, and defeated him."

In this opinion I afterward understood that General Lee coincided.*

The General then proceeded to give me some account of the action, and I afterward found that General McClellan's report fully coincided with his opinions. The Federal commander had massed his forces under Hooker against the left, where Jackson was posted, and the failure of the attack in that portion of the field decided the fate of the day. The fighting was desperate, and our loss terrible—as was that of the enemy, I afterward discovered, especially in officers; but at nightfall Jackson occupied the ground which he originally held.

"Our friend Stuart has performed invaluable services to-day," said the General, warmly; "he is a very great soldier! And that youth, Pelham! You know him, do you not?"

* Historical.

"Intimately, General.

"He is a very remarkable young man. He commanded to-day nearly all the artillery of the left wing of the army, and I have never seen more skilful handling of guns. It is really extraordinary to find such nerve and genius in a mere boy. With a Pelham on each flank, I believe I could whip the world!"*

These words delighted me. In the hurry of my narrative I have not spoken of the warm friendship which existed between myself and the noble young Alabamian; but, with every fight in which I witnessed his superb and headlong courage, his coolness, dash, and stubborn persistence, my admiration for him had increased.

An hour after my arrival, Jackson sent me with a message to Stuart, all his other staff-officers being absent on duty.

I found the commander of the cavalry lying under a tree, on his red blanket, by the camp-fire, laughing and talking with his staff. His enormous physical organization never seemed to break down; at all hours, in all weather, under every fatigue, Stuart was the same superb war-machine, which nothing could affect.

He laughed heartily at the narrative of my escape, and said:

"You ought to get our friend Joyeuse" (the sobriquet of a member of his staff) "to write your adventures. Well, we have had a jolly time here, and nearly whipped them. Pelham has covered himself all over with glory!"

Two Major-Generals had thus chanted the boy's praises, and those Major-Generals were called Jackson and Stuart!

After a few more words I rose and bade the General goodnight.

"Long may you wave!" was his gay reply, as he stretched himself upon his blanket; and I rode back through the darkness. Stuart had spoken in ardent terms of Pelham, but he had not referred to his own reckless gallantry, his obstinate stand when Hooker tried to turn our left, and, his headlong gallop on his beautiful "Lady Margaret" across the front of a Federal regi-

* His words.

ment, who, recognizing his high rank, poured a murderous volley into him at the distance of fifty yards!

He had passed unscathed. The fatal bullet was not moulded then, which struck him at the Yellow Tavern.

A quarter of a mile from Stuart's bivouac, I passed a battalion of artillery, grimly frowning toward the enemy, from the rising ground where it was placed in battery, and, when I asked who commanded it, the reply was "Pelham."

Ten paces further I found him seated by the camp-fire among his men, and laughing gayly with a young Federal officer, who was munching a cracker.

As I approached, the officer turned round. It was my brother Will!

In an instant he had risen, and with all the ardor of a boy thrown his arm around my neck. A hundred exclamations of delight followed, a hundred questions were asked. Will seemed positively overwhelmed with joy.

His presence was soon explained. A company of Federal cavalry had charged Pelham's guns that day—Will had led them—and one of the cannoneers had coolly swept the young lieutenant from his saddle with a sponge staff.* When his company retreated, torn to pieces by Pelham's canister, Will had remained in the hands of his enemies.

In the commander of the horse artillery, however, he had soon discovered an old comrade. He and Pelham had been intimate friends at West Point, just before the war, and they met each other with a shout of pleasure.

Seated by the camp-fire, they had exchanged a thousand jests and recollections, interspersed with boyish laughter.

"Well," said Pelham, as he stood by the fire, after shaking hands with me, "that's what I call romantic! I thought that *my* meeting with Will was curious, but here he finds his brother."

"And the best brother you ever saw!" laughed Will, "if he is a rebel! I wish I was in the Southern army."

* Fact.

And, passing from laughter to sighs, the boy looked gloomy.

"Stop all that talk, Will," said Pelham. "And that reminds me that we have had no supper. We live splendidly in the Southern army generally—pheasants, woodcock, champagne, and Havana cigars, for regular rations! But the commissary seems to have forgotten us to-night. Suppose we go over to that house yonder, and get something better than hard tack."

"All right!" was the gay reply of Will as he rose.

"First, however," said Pelham, with mock solemnity, "I will take your parole, lieutenant, not to communicate directly or indirectly with the inhabitants of that house."

"Oh, bother! Jack," was the reply; "I intend to ask for a drink the very first thing!"

"That is only reasonable," returned Pelham laughing. "Come on, Surry, go with us."

It did not take much persuasion to induce me to do so, and ten minutes' walk brought us to the house—a plain but elegant mansion, evidently the residence of a gentleman.

I was still absorbed in talking with Will—interrogating him, replying to his questions, exchanging a hundred laughing or sighing recollections—when Pelham was heard exclaiming in a low tone:

"Glorious! they are just at supper!"

And he beckoned to me to come to the window and look.

Through a vine-clad window, I saw a gentleman and his family at supper. There was something familiar in the face of one of the young ladies, but I could not see her very distinctly. I soon had a better opportunity. Pelham had gone and knocked, and the old gentleman rose and came to the door.

As soon as he saw us he evidently comprehended the object of our visit, and very courteously invited us to come in to supper.

We entered, and what was my surprise to see Will suddenly run forward, and, with all the abandon of a boy, throw his arms around the young lady whose face I thought I had recognized!

The embrace was followed by an astounding explosion in the way of a kiss—and then a grand tableau! The young girl blushing to the whites of her eyes, a second damsel standing primly erect, the old gentleman utterly dumbfounded, the old lady holding up her hands, and a pretty little girl of about ten, with a quantity of bright curls, looking with eyes of wild amazement at the spectacle.

Every historian owes his reader an explanation of whatever is obscure. The meaning of all this scene will be better understood if the kind reader will turn back to the chapter headed, "I chase and come up with a Federal officer." In my conversation with Will on that occasion, he said: " *What's become of Jenny Clayton? At the North still? Pshaw! Why don't she come home?*" The young lady before us was Miss Jenny Clayton, a remote cousin of ours, from Virginia, who had been Will's sweetheart when they were children. Her father, a timid man, of lukewarm feeling toward the Confederacy, had sent her to the North to be educated; she had come to visit a schoolmate, the daughter of Mr. Curtis, our host—and so we all met!

A few words explained every thing, and the old gentleman laughed heartily.

"Come, sit down, sit down, gentlemen!" he said to Pelham and myself. "I am what you call a 'Union man,' but I am not a churl on that account."

And he hospitably busied himself in heaping up our plates with smoking "viands"—see the novelists. "Viands," on the present occasion, meant beef hash, hot bread, milk, butter, coffee, preserves, and that succulent edible called "apple butter."

That hash! that "apple butter!"—that gorgeous, magical supper!—memory still returns to it, and dwells upon it with the fond and lingering tenderness of a lover who remembers the bright hours of his happiness!

At last we rose, casting eloquent glances, illuminated by smiles—each at each.

Will sat down by Jenny Clayton, who was soon running on with him in the gayest manner, and Pelham had drawn to his side the pretty little fairy with the curls, who—astounding event!—declared herself an inveterate rebel!

"That is true," said the old gentleman, laughing. "Carrie can't bear her own people, and runs to all the gray-coats."

"But I don't like your flag," said the little girl, "it looks so bloody!"

And she shook her head sadly, looking with her great blue eyes, half covered with golden ringlets, at Pelham. That gaze was met by Pelham with a long, sad, yearning look, which I could not understand. The penetrating eyes had grown soft, the laughter of the lips disappeared, an expression of longing tenderness relaxed the features of the young soldier—and, without seeming aware of what he was doing, he drew the child toward him.

His arm encircled the slender form, his lips were pressed to hers in a long, lingering kiss; and then, as he turned aside his head, I saw tears in his eyes.

"You are the very image of a little sister I have," he said, in a low voice, "far away in Alabama."

The words were drowned in the laughter of Will and Miss Jenny Clayton, who seemed to have become better friends than ever.

When finally we rose, and bade our hospitable entertainers good-night, I thought that Miss Jenny Clayton had quite succeeded in effacing the image of Miss Henrietta Fitzhugh.

I have remembered this evening ever since; but nothing dwells more clearly in my recollection than that kiss bestowed by Pelham on the child, and the tender words he murmured as he pressed her to his heart.

That night Will slept by my side at General Jackson's headquarters, or rather we spent the night together, talking of old days, and friends at home. Why should I record that conversation of two brothers? It would scarcely interest the reader. The chill winds of the September night, fanning the embers of the camp-fire, bore away the words.

On the next day, as I have said, we remained in line of battle facing the enemy, defying General McClellan to renew the attack. On the day after, General Lee was on the south bank of the Potomac—leaving only, growled the New York *Tribune*, "the *débris* of his late camps, two disabled pieces of artillery, a few hundred of his stragglers, perhaps two thousand of his wounded, and as many more of his unburied dead—not a sound field-piece, caisson, ambulance, or wagon. He takes with him the supplies gathered in Maryland, and the rich spoils of Harper's Ferry."

Will was back to his command. To spare him the tedium of a prison, I had succeeded in having his name added to the list of Federal prisoners captured at Harper's Ferry, and released upon parole not to serve until exchanged. With a close pressure of the hand we had parted.

Such had been, from first to last, my experiences of the " Maryland Campaign."

XCIV.

FALLING BACK WITH STUART.

WE spent the beautiful month of October in the Valley.

What is it makes these sad memorial days so charming? What influence descends upon the heart and brings back all the years that are dead—their smiles and laughter, all their happy faces, the mirth and revelry, and joy? Not the fairest May that ever shone, with budding leaves and flowers and grasses, moves me like those slowly gliding hours, which take the golden splendor of the woods, the azure of the sky, the glitter of the sunshine for their drapery, and, filling heart and memory with the dear dead faces, it may be, of friends long gone into the dust, serenely lead us to the " days that are no more."

Is this life of dreams among the fading glories of the rich October woods " unprofitable?" Profit!—forever profit! What is real in this world except your reveries and dreams, O friendly reader? What secret of happiness is greater than to follow your illusions? Life is so short and dull that there is little in it worth our notice, save its illusions!—so cold and sad that I, for my part, wonder we are not all dreamers!

But the narrative of Surry halts by the way. *Marchons!* To horse and away, whatever reveries beckon!—whatever dreams enchain us!

Still, as we pass, let us cast a lingering glance, O kindly reader, on the gorgeous tints of autumn all along the wooded shores of the Opequon and the Shenandoah, gliding, with a musical murmur, to the bosom of the Potomac; on the old hall yonder, with its gay back-ground of many-colored foliage; and upon the smiling fields, over which the " Yankee cavalry" will soon be sweeping.

A parting glance at the fair panorama—a pressure of the hand exchanged with all the kind good friends who have made the days so pleasant—and then " to horse!"   For General McClellan is moving; his great adversary is hastening to intercept him on the Rappahannock; the days of idleness and " sweet do-nothing" yield to day and night marches, and the shock of battle.

At the end of October, Jackson followed Longstreet, and approached the little village of Millwood.   Stuart had already crossed the Blue Ridge, to guard the gaps, as the army moved—and I accompanied him, by Jackson's permission, to capture, if possible, a better horse than that of my Dutch prisoner.

From that moment it was fighting, fighting, fighting!   We charged a heavy picket at Mountsville, and dispersed or captured the whole party of about seventy-five.   Then the column pushed on to Aldie.

As we mounted the hill—bang! bang! And, driving on, the head of the column, Fitz Lee's brigade, ran into Buford's cavalry, about five thousand in number.

This was a species of hornet's nest, which buzzed in a manner more exciting than agreeable.   Stuart fell back with his small force to the hill above, and, receiving intelligence that another column was closing in on his rear, opened with his horse artillery upon the enemy, and quietly withdrew, by a friendly cross-road, to the town of Middleburg.

At Mountsville, the officer commanding the picket, from the First Rhode Island, was wounded, and his watch taken in charge by a staff-officer.   Months afterward it was returned to him by the hands of Captain Stone, a Federal prisoner.*

* Real.

So we marched into Middleburg, where a bevy of fair girls came forth to meet the gallant Stuart, in a state of crazy joy at seeing the gray-coats, and the black feather of their favorite chieftain. Did the bold lips press some rosy cheeks without having them withdrawn? If so, will anybody blame the maidens? Not I.

Thereafter, still fighting, fighting, fighting! At Mountsville, at Union, at Bloomfield, at Upperville—everywhere fighting. Here Colonel Wickham, that gallant cavalier, ever leading his men in the charge, was wounded; and, more than once, the guns of Pelham were in imminent danger of capture.

I admired now, more than ever, the splendid genius for artillery which this mere boy possessed. There is a genius for every thing—Pelham's was to fight artillery. He was born for that, and found his proper sphere in command of Stuart's guns. With what unyielding obstinacy he fought! with a nerve and courage how gay and splendid! No part of the ground escaped his eagle eye—no ruse could deceive him. He fought with the ardor of a boy and the stubborn obstinacy of gray hairs. Rushing his guns into position upon every hill, there he staid until the enemy were almost at the muzzles and were closing in upon his flanks. Then, hastily limbering up and retiring, under a storm of bullets, he took position on the next elevation, and poured his canister into the advancing columns as before.

Stuart slowly retired before the enemy, fighting at every step, until he reached the high ground below Paris. Here Pelham posted his artillery on the slope of the mountain, at sunset, and before these frowning war-dogs the enemy halted.

Meanwhile the whole command, except a trifling rear-guard, had moved toward Piedmont, to guard the trains then falling back.

You see, my dear reader, I am not writing a series of "romantic incidents," for I have introduced a wagon-train, the antipodes of romance. But this mention of the cavalry-train recalls one of those "trifles" which, I have warned you, I remember more vividly than all else.

Stuart and his staff retired at nightfall to the little village of

Paris, where, after partaking of an excellent supper, we all came to a halt before the old wooden tavern, facing the main street, at the eastern terminus thereof. The house was bare and deserted, but a fire was speedily kindled in the fireplace, and pipes were produced by the staff.

The General was stretched upon a bench, and seemed in the depths of despair.

"What is the matter?" I asked.

"Well, a blunder has occurred in the movement of my column toward Piedmont, and my trains are in great danger."

"That's enough to make any one blue, I confess, General."

"As indigo," was the reply, in the tone of a man who has lost his last friend. And the General sank back, knitting his brows.

As he did so, something was said which produced a laugh—and, to my great surprise, Stuart joined in it heartily.

"You are very gay for a man who has the blues," I said.

"Well, the fact is, Major," was his gay reply, "I am so blue to-night, that I have to laugh to keep up my spirits, you see!"*

And, throwing himself back, the General laughed again, yawned, and immediately fell asleep. My own eyelids were just drooping, when a cavalry-man rode up and waked the party.

"Well, what news?" asked Stuart, yawning.

"Major Wooldridge says the enemy are advancing, General, and that you had better get away from here."

The General indulged in another yawn. stretched his limbs, and buckled on his sabre.†

"I believe I will go and see old Stonewall," he said.

The staff were soon ready; and mounting our horses, we turned their heads toward Ashby's Gap.

We had scarcely emerged from the little village, and began the ascent of the mountain road which leads through the Gap, when

---

* His words.

† In conversation with me, Colonel Surry said, with a laugh, that he knew this and many other scenes of his memoirs would appear too trifling and unimportant for record. "But I am tired of the noise of great battles," he added, "and amuse myself by travelling along the by-ways of my subject, and picking up the 'unconsidered trifles.'"

rapid firing came from the rear, and then the clatter of hoofs was heard upon the street of the village.

"They are crowding Wooldridge," said the General, "but he is one of my best officers, and will take care of himself. Come on, Major, we are losing time."

And we pushed our horses into a rapid trot, which soon brought us to the river. Fording at the spot which I so well remembered on my hard ride from Manassas to Winchester in July, 1861, we went on to Millwood, and found General Jackson in his tent, under the trees of a forest near, reading his Bible, from which he looked up with a smile of pleasure as Stuart entered.*

Before daylight Stuart was again in the saddle and travelling rapidly toward Front Royal, to cross at the first gap he found unoccupied by the enemy, and take command of his column. I was with him.

XCV.

WHICH CONTAINS A VALUABLE MORAL REFLECTION.

THE last words of the last chapter are easily explained.

I was a short day's ride from May Beverley, and I could no longer utter those rebellious words, "I will not look again upon her face!"

Alas for human resolution! However hard the iron, there is a fire that will melt it!—however obstinate a man's will, it yields to the smile of a girl! I had sworn not to go near May Beverley, and I was hastening to see her once more, as fast as my horse would carry me!

Moral:—Never trouble yourself by making good resolutions when the eyes of a woman are mixed up with them!

I had easily procured twenty-four hours' leave of absence from General Jackson, who evidently was in no haste to leave Mill-

* General Stuart spoke of this incident more than once.

wood; and setting out with Stuart, who had been joined by Hampton's Brigade, passed through White Post and Smoketown, and entered Manassas Gap.

Beyond this gorge in the Blue Ridge was The Oaks, a little off the track of the advancing enemy.

"Who are you going to see, Surry?" said Stuart, as, having ridden ahead of the cavalry, we wound along the mountain road toward Linden.

"Going to see, my dear General?" I echoed. "Why, the manner in which your cavalry is handled."

Stuart laughed.

"'Sweet Evelina! dear Evelina!'" he sang; "is her name Evelina, Surry, and where does she live?"

"Pshaw, General! Your suspicion is enormous! But I now remember there *is* a friend of mine in his region."

"Aha! I thought so! I wish I could go with you."

"She would be delighted to see you. You know all the girls are crazy to 'follow your feather.'"

"You make me gloomy—to think what I miss. Well,

> "If you get there before I do,
> Oh! tell her I'm a-coming too!"

And, as we came to a point where we had to separate, Stuart cried:

"Success to you, Surry, and long may you wave!"

With these words the gay cavalier put spur to his horse, and galloped on to catch up with Rosser.

I rode on rapidly toward The Oaks, which soon rose before me, on its wooded hill.

From beyond came the clear crack of carbines, and from time to time the thunder of Pelham's guns, as he fell back slowly before the advancing enemy.

XCVI.

A DREAM OF AUTUMN.

AGAIN at The Oaks! How many stirring scenes had I witnessed, what vivid emotions had been mine, since first I ascended
the steps of this old portico in April, 1861!

Then I was a gay and ardent youth, on fire with the coming
conflict, and revelling in dreams of glory and romance. Now I
was a weary, dusty soldier, with clanking sabre, dingy uniform,
and a settled conviction that the thing called war was a hard
and disagreeable affair—not at all a splendid series of adventures.

I had seen much, felt more, reflected most of all—and here I
was within ten feet of her smile, the sheen of her hair, the
haunting splendor of her eyes! Oh, glory, fame, the long result
of war!—what are all these when a girl looks at you, laughing
with her eyes, and, blushing, murmurs :

"You have come at last!"

An hour after my arrival at The Oaks, I had answered all
Colonel Beverley's questions—agreed with him upon every subject—and was walking with May Beverley across the hills. Very
soon we lost our way.

There are moments when, in losing our way, we find all that
is worth having in this world of disappointments, sorrows, and
regrets!

The afternoon was dreamy and memorial. The affluent glories
of the splendid autumn burned away; and on every side the
forests blazed with crimson, blue, and gold—slowly fading now
into the russet brown of winter. The mountain slopes were
magical in their vivid coloring; and you would have said the
banners of all nations flaunted in the dreamy atmosphere. The
sky was like the blue eyes of a girl, when, opening from bud to
blossom, she expands into the perfect flower of womanhood ; the
limpid waters of the streamlets near lapsed away as sweetly as the
"murmur of a dream;" and over all the scene of shining stream,
and deep blue sky, and azure mountain, drooped the mellow

haze of the mild Indian summer, rounding every outline, soften-
ing every tint, and making of this lovely region a bright Arcady
of love and poesy and dreams!

Such was the scene amid which I wandered with the woman
I had loved so long; and, like some magical influence, it melted
deep into the hearts of those who gazed upon it. All the silver
spangles of the ocean rippling in the wind, all the glitter of the
stars, the murmur of the waves, the perfume of the breezes, and
the dreamy splendor of the sky seemed here to mingle into one
supreme and perfect whole of love and joy and beauty!

Only, yonder, not a mile away, is heard the thunder of the
guns as Pelham drives the enemy back; and ever it draws
nearer—that grim sound which seems to desecrate the tranquil
landscape.

May Beverley does not seem to hear it. She is sitting now
upon a mossy rock, beneath a little pine; and, looking down,
with cheeks suffused in blushes, plays with the tassel of her belt,
or with an autumn flower, which she has plucked beside the
rock. The other hand—once she strove to withdraw it, but the
effort had been soon abandoned. It trembled slightly, but rested
in the clasp which encircled it.

The pine-tree listened doubtless to the murmurs, mingling
with the whisper of its tassels as the low breeze stirred them on
that mild memorial afternoon.

Did it hear a woman whisper, as her head sank on the bosom
of a man who held her in his arms, clasped to his heart—hear
her murmur with a face full of tears and blushes:

"Yes! from the moment when you lay before me, pale and
motionless, in the wood, that day!"

"And never forgot me—never lost sight of the poor soldier,
living only for you?"

"Never! never!"

O pine-tree, never whisper what you heard or saw! There
are things which the cold world laughs at, makes it cynical jest
of, and so desecrates.

Yet who shall dare to laugh at the spectacle of a proud and
beautiful girl, long fettered by a hateful contract, shuddering at

a loathsome union with a man she despises - who shall laugh when she gives way to her heart, and, falling weak and over come into the arms of one who has loved her long and dearly murmurs, "Take charge of my poor life—direct my fate—I have loved, and love you only!"

That was the confession which came in a murmur from the beautiful lips of the proud May Beverley, and she made it amid the thunder of the guns, her face hid in my breast, heart beating against heart.

XCVII.

THE AWAKING.

WE had returned to The Oaks: the young girl had disappeared upstairs: I was having a "private conversation" with Colonel Beverley.

A few words will place upon record all that is necessary to a comprehension of these memoirs.

My host listened in silence and with evident pain to my avowal and demand of his daughter's hand. When I had finished, he shook his gray head sadly, and seemed too much moved to speak. Then he leaned over, took my hand, and said in his brave and loyal voice:

"My dear young friend—for I am very much older than yourself, and may call you so—you have given me more pain in the last ten minutes than words can express. You ask of me what it is out of my power to grant—my daughter's hand. I appreciate the sincerity of your feeling, and doubt not that my poor child is equally in earnest, and would to God I could consent to your union! To have for my son the son of my oldest and dearest friend, would be an inexpressible delight to me; it is almost beyond my power to deny you, but I must. My honor is pledged. I am bound irrevocably by a promise to the dead—Frederick Baskerville's father; and I must add that my child is also bound by her promise to that young man. She must adhere

15*

to her pledge, and I to mine. Our hearts may break, but at least the honor of the Beverleys will remain untarnished!"

The old man's cheeks flushed, his eyes filled with tears.

" Would to God," he exclaimed gloomily, " that I had cut out my tongue, severed my right hand, before I uttered and recorded that promise! I am no admirer of young Baskerville: had I known what his character would become—but this is idle! Do not think hard of me, Major Surry! this marriage must take place; let us end this painful interview, it is almost more than I can bear!"

I rose. What is it that a proud man does when his heart is breaking? I think he remains calm and quiet, resolved not to shrink or bend, though the thunder smite him.

I went to my chamber to get my arms. On the staircase I met May Beverley. She glanced at my pale face, and said:

"Papa has refused you?"

" Yes."

The color mounted to her beautiful face, and her head rose erect as that of an offended duchess.

" I will never marry that person!" she said naughtily.

Then her head sank, and she burst into tears.

Captain Baskerville would have been displeased had he seen where the young girl's head then rested; but then, Captain Baskerville's views or opinions were not important. This woman was not yet his property.

Her lips were pressed to my own, and this is all that was said in ten minutes:

" I love you!"

"I will never marry him! no, never, never!"

" And if there is any hope for me?—I shall be far away."

"I will send you a flower like this!"

And taking from her bosom an autumn primrose, the blushing girl held it out to me, remained a moment sobbing in my arms, and then disappeared.

Ten minutes afterward I had left The Oaks.

XCVIII.

HOW PELHAM FOUGHT HIS HORSE ARTILLERY

I TURNED my back upon The Oaks with a heavy heart, and the solitary ride I was about to take back over that ground, traversed so gayly in the morning, appeared inexpressibly dreary.

I had reached a lofty hill at some distance from the house, when the last regiments of cavalry appeared falling slowly back, and Pelham's guns were seen bringing up the rear. On the long column of pieces, caissons, and mounted cannoneers, the red light of the setting sun was streaming splendidly, and in front was seen the slender form of Pelham, with his smooth, girlish face, and his brave, gay smile. The crimson light illuminated his figure, and fell around him like a glory.

I would have avoided him, for I was in no humor then to speak with anybody; but his first words as he recognized me gave me something like a thrill of satisfaction.

" How are you, old fellow?" was Pelham's friendly greeting. " Where did you come from? You are just in time. We are going to have a thundering fight here before night!"

And he grasped my hand with that cordial, kindly manner which made him so many friends.

" Ah!" I said, " are they pressing you?"

" Yes, in heavy force."

" You don't seem in a hurry."

" Well," was his reply in a tranquil tone, " I don't like to be hurried, but they'll be here by the time I get into position yonder."

And he pointed to the next hill.

" The boys are in splendid spirits," he added gayly; " listen!"

In fact, the horse artillery were singing at the top of their voices :

> " Ain't you—ain't you—happy?
> Anchor by-and-by!
> Ain't you—ain't you—happy?
> Anchor by-and-by!
> Stand the storm, it won't be long!
> Anchor by-and-by!"

There was something stirring in the jovial voices, and Pelham's face lit up as he listened.

"There never were better cannoneers!" he said; "they will fight the Yankees to the very muzzles of the guns!"

As he spoke, a French song resounded—a gay and lilting air —and he began to laugh.

"That's my 'Napoleon detachment,'" said Pelham; "and Dominic the No. I. is leading."

All at once, above the voices, was heard rapid firing from the small rear-guard, and a cavalry-man came on at full gallop, with the intelligence that the enemy were pressing forward rapidly to charge the guns.

Pelham rode quietly to a point near, from which he could get a better view; then he suddenly came back like lightning, and ordered:

"Forward! gallop!"

The column of pieces moved at the word, broke into a gallop, and, thundering across a flat, mounted the opposite hill.

Pelham was beside them, and they were instantly placed in battery, and opened fire.

It was not a moment too soon. A heavy force of Federal cavalry had charged the rear-guard, broken through it, and were now seen advancing at a headlong gallop to charge the pieces.

All at once, the bronze war-dogs of Pelham opened their grim mouths, and a storm of solid shot tore through the Federal ranks, overthrowing men and horses; and this was succeeded, as they still pressed on, by a deadly fire of canister.

At the same moment, Gordon, that brave and noble North Carolinian, one of my best friends, charged them at the head of the "Old First," and, had it not been for a stone wall and ditch, would have swept them back at every point. As it was, his horses floundered in the deep ditch, the sharpshooters behind the wall poured in a destructive fire, and Gordon was forced to fall back to the hill.*

* See his report.

The fine face of the North Carolinian was flushed with rage; his eyes glared; he could ill brook such a repulse.

Pelham met him with a calm smile:

"Don't annoy yourself, Colonel," he said, "they won't ride over me."

And, turning to an officer, he said coolly:

"Double-shot all the guns with canister."

As he spoke, the enemy, who had rapidly re-formed their .ine, charged straight upon the pieces.

Pelham sat his horse, looking coolly at the dark column as it swept upon him. He did not move a muscle, but his teeth were clinched beneath the thin lips, and the blue eyes blazed. The enemy were suffered to advance within less than a hundred yards of the guns, when Pelham rose in his stirrups, and in his ringing voice shouted:

"Fire!"

The ground shook; a huge cloud for an instant obscured the scene; then, as it drifted, the Federal ranks were seen to break in disorder and retreat, leaving the ground strewed with their dead.

"All right!" said Pelham, coolly. "Reload with canister.

The cannoneers sprang to the pieces, and they were soon ready again. But the enemy did not seem willing to renew the charge. They dismounted a heavy line of sharpshooters, advanced, and taking advantage of every species of cover, were evidently preparing to close in upon the guns.

The bullets now began to fly thick and fast. Pelham sat his horse motionless, and gazing at the advancing line.

"They will make a rush directly, Surry," he said coolly, "and I'll show you how my boys will mow them down."

"They do seem determined to come to close quarters."

"Why don't they do it, then? They are after something I don't understand. What is it?"

The reply came from our rear. Suddenly a loud cheer was heard directly in rear of the guns; and a regiment, which the enemy had sent round through a clump of woods, charged the pieces at full gallop.

"Action rear!" Pelham shouted, darting to his guns; and two pieces were whirled about, and opened upon the charging column. The fire raked the enemy with deadly effect; and they wavered for an instant. Then they re-formed, and came on again head-long. At the same moment the line of sharpshooters in front charged at a run, right up to the muzzles of the guns.

We were surrounded; and from that moment the fight became desperate. Pelham was everywhere, cheering on the men, with his drawn sabre flashing in the last rays of sunlight—and as that blood-red light streamed on his slender figure, and countenance all ablaze with the fire of battle, his appearance was grand.

The boy-artillerist was in his proper sphere—fighting his guns to the very muzzle, determined to die where he stood, or drive the enemy back.

More than one of the dismounted Federal cavalry charged up to the mouths of the pieces and were hurled back, torn to pieces with shell or canister; and, as each deadly discharge swept their enemies back, the cannoneers uttered triumphant shouts, in which might be discerned the fierce joy of fighting which these veritable war-dogs experienced.

Suddenly above the thunder of the guns resounded the loud, imperial *Marseillaise,* sung with a species of ferocious roar by the men of the "Napoleon detachment," as they worked the guns, driving back the charge upon the rear.* There was some-thing in the voices of these men inexpressibly defiant and deter-mined—-the martial chorus rang out splendid and triumphant; it seemed to say, "Come! we will die here, where we stand!"

Above them, on his horse, towered the form of Pelham, and his voice made the men grow wild.

Never have I seen such a fight. It was an episode from the wars of the Titans—the conflict of the giants and the thunder-bolts.

The force in front was swept back, decimated, and completely routed. As they gave way, Gordon charged and drove them with the sabre. At the same moment the force in rear was seen to recoil.

* Historical.

Then was presented a spectacle which made the heart leap, and brought a fierce cheer from the men.

Right down on the enemy's flank burst a column of Southern cavalry, and then followed the quick work of the sabre. A desperate combat followed—but it did not last ten minutes. The enemy gave way—the Southern horsemen pressed them, cutting right and left; and as the scattered Federal cavalry darted over the hill, I saw in front of their pursuers the tall form of Mordaunt.

At every sweep of his heavy sabre a man was cut out of the saddle; and not until he had struck their main body did he sheathe his weapon and slowly retire, with a firm and defiant front, which the enemy made no attempt to charge.

"Well, Pelham," he said, as he rode up, "you have had pretty hot work, but I think they have got enough for the present."

And he grasped the hand of Pelham, whose face blushed proudly.

When I took the hand of Mordaunt in my turn, something wet and clammy attracted my attention.

"It is only blood," he said, laughing grimly; "there is a good deal on my hands."

The fighting was now evidently over for the day. Night had come, and the enemy would not attempt to renew the attack before morning.

I woke to the consciousness, as the artillery limbered up and prepared to move on, that I was mounted on a weary horse, with night and a journey of about thirty miles before me. I was thinking of the dreary ride, when, all at once, the voice of Mordaunt said:

"Come and sup with me, Surry—we are not far from my house, and I must go there for an hour or two, to get some papers."

To this I agreed, especially as the place was on my route. Pelham bade me farewell with a laugh.

"Tell General Jackson that we are all right, Surry!" he said; "and come and see me soon."

With a pressure of the hand I parted with the brave boy, and he rode on.

As the horse artillery took up the line of march, I heard the cannoneers again strike up the lilting chorus:

"Stand the storm, it won't be long!
Anchor by-and-by!"

XCIX.

I DELIVER UP HARRY SALTOUN'S WATCH, AND MAKE A DISCOVERY.

MORDAUNT had gone to give an order to his second in command, relating to the movements of the cavalry during his brief absence, when I was hailed by a laughing voice near me, and young Harry Saltoun rode up, with one arm in a sling, and held out his hand.

He looked thin and pale, but his eye was as laughing, his smile as gay, and his bearing as gallant as ever.

"How are you, Major?" was his easy greeting. "Delighted to see you again! Just to think of my missing the whole Maryland campaign!"

"Your wound kept you away?"

"Yes—at that glorious Elm Cottage! Did you ever know kinder people?"

"They are charming."

"I believe you."

"Did you like your young nurse? I believe she took especial charge of you?"

Harry Saltoun's face colored suddenly—it was a veritable blush which came to his cheeks.

"Oh, yes," he stammered, "we became very good friends. But tell me about Maryland. How sorry I am I did not go with the cavalry boys! They passed right by my father's—near Frederick City."

What did that sudden blush mean? Had Harry Saltoun

fallen in love with Violet Grafton, to whom he had carried Mordaunt's note, soliciting her good offices for the youth, when he was wounded?

"You ought to have found out our house," he continued, laughing, "and made the old gentleman supply you with rations. They beat the Confederate article, I tell you!"

"I can testify as much from personal experience," was my reply, and, informing the young officer of my visit to his father, I drew from my breast and gave him his watch.

At sight of it he exhibited the most unmistakable pleasure.

"Thank you, Major!" he exclaimed; "you have done me a real favor! When I left Maryland I left this behind, and, as I have always worn it, I felt as if not having it would bring me bad luck."

"Take care, or some Yankee will get it."

"Never—I will die first. I never have been captured yet—for, you see, I take care of myself!"

"That is no doubt the reason you left Elm Cottage?"

"Precisely! No sooner did I hear that McClellan was advancing than I fell back in good order, and here I am!"

The boy's laughter was like a cordial, and almost made the gloomy Major Surry smile.

"And you left all well?—your fair nurse and everybody?"

"Perfectly."

And again, at the utterance of that word "nurse," Harry Saltoun blushed unmistakably. The thing was perfectly plain.

"Well, Major," he said, "good-by, now! Thank you again for bringing my watch. There is Colonel Mordaunt calling to you. Did you ever see or read of a more splendid fellow in a charge? His men adore him—and I would rather have him say to me, 'Well done!' than get another grade from the War Department."

With these words the gay youth saluted with the easy grace which characterized him; and, joining Mordaunt, I rode with him toward the mountains.

354 SURRY OF EAGLE'S-NEST.

C.

ACHMED

A SHORT ride brought us to Mordaunt's house, buried in the depths of the woods, and, dismounting, we entered the same apartment, decorated with book-shelves, pictures, and tiger-skins, in which I had held my first interview with the singular man, who from a stranger had become a friend.

On the table lay the identical copy of Hugo's " Les Miserables " which I had noticed before. The same agate eyes glared at me from the tiger and leopard skins—the same Arab horsemen hurled their javelins or wielded their ataghans in the pictures.

On the threshold appeared Achmed the Moor, in his picturesque costume, bowing low at sight of me, and a few words in Arabic evidently announced supper.

It was spread in an apartment decorated with old mahogany furniture and long rows of family portraits, doubtless those of Mordaunt's ancestors. The dames and caveliers, in yellow lace, and doublets loaded with embroidery, looked down sedately upon their swarthy descendant in his gray uniform, with its braided sleeves—on his brown hat, black plume, and heavy sabre.

The supper was excellent, and was placed upon a service plain but rich. Mordaunt scarcely ate any thing, contenting himself with a light meal and some bitterly strong coffee, after which he lit his short, black meerschaum, and led the way back to his library. I had eaten nothing. The depressing events of the day had told upon me.

As I now, however, fixed my eyes upon Mordaunt, whose martial figure was stretched in a leathern chair opposite me, the reflection came, " What is your disappointment, compared to the misery which this man has suffered? what right have *you* to complain of a mere ' cross in love,' when you see before one who, in spite of suffering which would break the hearts of most men, retains his calmness and endures his agony without complaint?" The immense trial which Mordaunt had thus met and overcome by his iron resolution came to my memory, and the sight of his stern, brave face was like a tonic, giving me strength again after a moment of prostration.

Of that dark passage in his life I had never spoken to him; nor did he know that I had plucked out the heart of his mystery. I shrank from letting this proud spirit suspect my knowledge of ʰis history, and had never breathed a syllable to him of my adventure with Fenwick.

"You no doubt remember this apartment," said Mordaunt. "I have not been here for more than a year, but it remains as I left it. See, Hugo's 'Les Miserables,' which I remember we discussed, is lying there open at the page I was reading."

And he pointed to the volume.

"I see—it is a story we never finish quite in this life,-Mordaunt."

"Ah! you philosophize, my guest!" he said, with his grim smile, "and you are right. The history of 'The Wretched' is that of humanity, and it is rather long, as I once before said."

What an infinitely mournful book that is! What a pathos! What a genius! Beside it, with all its tedium and surplusage, how small all other books of the epoch seem!"

"You are right," replied Mordaunt; "but in a strong man the death of the old galley-slave would be unnatural. Look, here are the lines in which the author sums up his drama."

And, taking the volume, he read aloud:

"Il dort. Quoique le sort fût pour lui bien étrange
Il vivait. Il mourut quand il n'eut pas son ange:
La chose simplement d'elle-même arriva,
Comme la nuit se fait lorsque le jour s'en va."

"If all men died when they lost those who were their good angels," he said, "what a grave-yard the world would be! The man who is strong bears his woe in silence—if he is wronged, he avenges himself!"

And I saw a stern, hard look in the swarthy face of Mordaunt. I knew he was thinking of Fenwick, and that his fierce spirit returned in thought to that scene near Elm Cottage. Then his face cleared up; he resumed his tranquillity, and said:

"But we are touching too much upon philosophy, Surry. Let us get to someting more cheerful. You were talking this evening with young Saltoun."

"Yes; he is a splendid boy."

"As brave a fellow as ever drew sabre. He has just returned to his command."

"And left his heart behind, if I am not mistaken, at Elm Cottage—has he not? I break no confidence—he has told me nothing, and I speak to his friend—but he is evidently in love with Violet Grafton."

Mordaunt turned his head quickly, but immediately became as calm as before.

"Ah! you think that, do you?" he said in a low tone.

"Yes," I replied.

"Well," was the cool response of Mordaunt, "he will make her a very good husband."

"You think she will marry him!" I exclaimed.

"Why not?" came as coolly as ever.

"You astonish me, Mordaunt! Violet Grafton marry this gay youngster! Why, he would never suit her."

"My dear Surry," was the cold reply, "do you think that women, when they love, inquire if the individual in question will 'suit them?' You are a novice if you think so, or imagine that like takes to like! This young man, Harry Saltoun, is what the French call the 'flower of the peas'—all life, gayety, and sunshine. Miss Grafton is tranquil, pensive, and serious. There is your marriage made at once!"

And Mordaunt smiled; but I could see that there was little gayety in his dark face.

"Well," I said, "perhaps you know best; but there is another circumstance which threatens to mix itself up with the affair."

"What is that?"

"The love of your *protégé* Achmed for the same person."

"Ah! you have observed that, too! You are discerning."

"It was made perfectly plain that night when he picked up

the young lady's handkerchief, and by his burning glances directed toward her afterward."

"Well," said Mordaunt indifferently, "I don't think Miss
Grafton will ever unite herself with this young leopard; but she
would not thereby debase herself."

"Is it possible that you think so, Mordaunt? Miss Grafton
marry your servant!"

"Achmed is not my servant—he is my friend. He is the son
of a sheik, and, in his own country, ranks as a nobleman."

"Still he waits upon you."

"Yes, as a son: he does not follow me for gain, but from affection. You look incredulous—stay! I will give you a proof of
what I say."

And reaching out his hand, Mordaunt touched a small bell
upon the table, which gave forth a single ringing note.

Almost instantly the door opened without noise, and the
young Moor stood before us.

Mordaunt coolly drew from his pocket a heavy purse of gold,
and, emptying its glittering contents upon the table, said some
words to Achmed in a language which I did not understand.
The effect which they produced was remarkable. The youth
turned pale, and his lip trembled."

"I informed him," said Mordaunt to me, "that I had no
longer any need of his services, and offered him that gold as a
parting gift."

Then turning to Achmed, he uttered a few additional words,—
like the first, in Arabic. This time the effect was more remarkable than before.

Achmed trembled in all his limbs, his face flushed, tears rushed
to his eyes, and, falling upon his knees before Mordaunt, he
bowed his face in his hands and burst into bitter sobs, mingled
with accents so beseeching, that, ignorant as I was of the language in which he spoke, I could not possibly misunderstand
them.

"He prays me, by the memory of his father, and the grave of
his mother," said Mordaunt coolly, "not to make his life
wretched by banishing him from my presence. I am his life, the

poor boy says—without me, he will die. I offer him money, when he would pour out his heart's blood for me!"

Mordaunt made no reply to the Moor in his own tongue; and this silence seemed suddenly to arouse all the pride of the son of the desert. He rose to his feet; folded his hands across his bosom, and, letting his head fall, uttered a few words in a tone so proud and calm that it was plain he would say no more.

" He says," explained Mordaunt, " ' It is well. Kill me! The son of Barach will not disgrace his blood—he does not fear death! Kill me! I will never leave you!' Are you satisfied, Surry?"

" Yes," I replied, filled with admiration by the proud and resolute countenance of the young Moor; " he is a noble boy, and you are happy in having so devoted an *attaché* ! "

Mordaunt uttered a few words in Arabic, and again the boy threw himself upon his knees, but this time with extravagant indications of joy. Seizing Mordaunt's hand, he covered it with kisses, and his eyes, as he raised them toward the face of his master, were resplendent.

At a word from Mordaunt he retired, with a step as proud and graceful as that of a young lion in his native desert; and, turning to me, Mordaunt said :

" You see that the boy is disinterested."

" Yes, I no longer doubt."

" But I do not mean that he would be a proper mate for a young lady of Virginia. Miss Grafton appears to me to have made a much more rational selection in Lieutenant Saltoun—if such be her selection—I know nothing. He is a gentleman, and there is no braver officer in this army."

The words were uttered with perfect coolness—not a muscle of the proud face moved; and, knowing Violet Grafton's secret, I could not suppress a sentiment of deep sympathy for the beautiful girl. To have placed her affections upon Mordaunt, that stern and haughty spirit, and to have done so, as his cold reference to her probable marriage showed, with so little probability of inspiring him with a similar feeling! I thought I saw impending a tragedy as sorrowful as any in Hugo's volume.

From the fit of moody silence which these reflections occa-

sioned, I was aroused by the voice of my host, who rose and informed me that he must return to his command, which was moving on. Would I not accompany him, or spend the night at his
house?

These offers I declined, alleging my short leave, and at the
door we mounted, to go different ways.

With a grasp of his strong hand, Mordaunt bade me farewell;
and, touching his powerful horse with the spur, disappeared at
full gallop in the darkness. My own road led in the opposite
direction, and, gaining the Gap, I passed through, crossed the
Shenandoah, and by sunrise reached General Jackson's head-
quarters near Millwood.

CI.

IN A CARRIAGE WINDOW.

MILLWOOD is a pleasant little village, dropped like a bird's nest
in the midst of smiling fields and the foliage of noble forests.
The region around is charming—all flowers and pretty faces.
So at least it appeared to that bird of passage, Surry, who lightly
touched and went: but not so quickly as to miss seeing the bright
eyes of maidens, true as steel in blood and heart and soul to the
cause of the South.

McClellan had advanced, but Jackson had halted. While the
Federal commander was streaming toward the Rappahannock,
Jackson remained idle near Millwood. What did it mean?
did not know then, but now all is plain. With that dangerous
foe upon his flank, and in a position to strike his rear, McClellan
advanced with doubt and fear. Who could tell at what moment
the formidable Stonewall Jackson would put his column in motion, hasten through Ashby's Gap, and strike the Federal rear,
while Lee attacked in front?

General McClellan, however, continued to move southward,
Lee everywhere facing him, when suddenly his head went to the
block, and General Ambrose Burnside reigned in his stead.

Thus made his final exit from the stage the greatest of the Federal commanders.

"Off with his head!   So much for Buckingham!"

The days passed on, but we lingered still in this lovely land, the Valley of the Shenandoah.   Slowly the glories of the autumn faded.   The russet brown of winter came, and the trees, of late so beautiful with their variegated trappings, began to be denuded by the chill blasts preluding winter.   But still the sunshine slept serenely—dim, memorial, and pensive—on the yellow woods; the wild geese made the far depths of the November heavens musical with their plaintive cry; and any one given to revery and dreams might have found still in the noble forests haunts full of quiet beauty, starred with wild autumn flowers, where hour after hour would glide by silently, and no sound would be heard but the murmur of the Shenandoah, flowing to the Potomac, its eternity.

This land and this people Jackson loved more than all the rest; and there was not a face that did not glow with pleasure, or an eye that did not look brighter at his coming.   His corps was full of young men from this very region—the Second Regiment, indeed, was almost made up of brave youths born here—and their mothers, sisters, and cousins constantly visited the camps.

With these, the famous General was an enormous favorite. All the world admired his great achievements, but the people of the Shenandoah Valley looked upon him as their own especial hero, their great defender and beloved chieftain.   Not the strong men only, who had estimated coolly his grand military genius, nor the matrons who had recognized in him the perfect type of Christian manhood—it was the girls who, more than all, grew wildly enthusiastic about the shy, retiring General Stonewall, in his dingy old coat, his faded cap, his heavy boots—a figure so unlike the young, flashing military heroes of the imagination!   I was riding with him in the neighborhood of Millwood one day, when we passed a carriage full of young girls; and I remember how one of them looked at the famous soldier.   As he approached, the maiden leaned through the window, her cheeks glowing, her eyes sparkling, and, ever as General Stonewall came, leaned

further still and further, with the same long, ardent gaze, "all
her soul in her eyes," until that look, as if by some irresistible
magnetism, drew his eyes to her glowing face. What would you
give to be looked at in that manner by a Virginia girl, good
friend? I think it would be better than to have a " brown-stone
front " on Fifth or any other avenue.

Jackson caught the flashing glance of the admiring eyes, colored slightly, saluted, and rode on, followed bv those sparkling
eyes. At least she had seen him!

From the woods below Millwood the General moved his head-
quarters to a picturesque spot called " The Glen," near an old
house known as "Saratoga." Here, for a brief space, the white
tents glittered on the greensward in the sunshine, and the quiet
scene was full of couriers, noise, hoof-strokes, rattling sabres, and
floating plumes.

Then all this passed away. The tents disappeared. and silence
again reigned in the secluded glen of " Saratoga."

Jackson was on the march.

The Federal army, under its new commander, General Burnside, had continued to advance toward the Rappahannock. Soon
vigorous attempts were made to cross the upper waters; but
everywhere the blue column found in its path the serried ranks
of Lee. To cross the river in face of the great captain was a
hazardous affair; and Burnside changed the direction of his
march, and turned the head of his column toward Fredericksburg.

When he reached the heights on the Rappahannock opposite
that town, there was General Lee still facing h im.

Such was the condition of things about the 1st of December,
when any one who had been in the woods which cover the long
crest of hills along the Massaponnax, near Fredericksburg, might
have heard an echoing shout which rang for miles, and seemed to
indicate the reception of some joyful intelligence by the men of
Longstreet.

The long-continued cheering was succeeded by the glitter of
bayonets, the tramp of Jackson's veterans.

He had marched from Millwood up the Valley, passed the

16

Massinutton and Blue Ridge at Newmarket and Thornton's Gaps, descended from the mountains, and, traversing Orange, followed the plank road through the Wilderness to the woods of the Massaponnax.

Taking his position on the right of Longstreet's corps, Jackson prepared for another conflict ; and it soon took place.

His presence meant combat and victory.

CII.

FROM THE HILLS OF THE MASSAPONNAX.

THE region around the hospitable old town of Fredericksburg is charming in the spring and summer. Even when I saw it first, at the end of fall, it was beautiful and attractive.

Come with me, worthy reader, and, instead of giving you an " official account " of how the great battle was fought, I will point out to you some features of the landscape.

We are standing on the long wooded crest which sweeps from the Rappahannock above, in front of the old town, and sinks into the plain near Hamilton's Crossing. In front of us is an extensive " bottom," traversed by a run, very deep, and with precipitous banks. Behind these banks the Federal infantry are going to take refuge from the Southern shot and shell. Beyond flows the river, and upon its southern bank you see the white spires and old-fashioned houses of Fredericksburg, soon to be torn by cannon-balls. Look now to the left. Yonder is Marye's Hill, which the Irish Brigade is going to charge with reckless gallantry, strewing the ground with their dead, as the merciless canister is hurled upon them ; and below the hill, the low stone wall where Barksdale will re-form his line when the enemy cross ; and Generals Cobb and Cooke will fall at the same moment—one of them killed, and the other dangerously wounded.

Along the crest, from Marye's Hill eastward, you see the embattled lines of Longstreet, flanked with cannon. On his right, extending to Hamilton's Crossing, is the corps of Jackson, bristling with artillery, posted upon every hillock, especially above the crossing, where the battalions of Walker wait, ready to sweep the plain, when General Franklin rushes forward to turn Lee's right and drive him back.

Still further to the right you see the extensive plain which stretches along the Massaponnax, emptying below into the Rappahannock. The level roads are skirted by deep ditches and long rows of beautiful cedars. In those ditches the Federal sharpshooters are going to crouch, within one hundred yards of the muzzles of our cannon, and pick off the cannoneers in spite of all the canister which sweeps above them, tearing through the cedars.

In the woods beyond, Stuart's cavalry will be drawn up, ready to take part in the battle, if the Southern flank is turned; and in the great field on Jackson's right, Stuart will mass his artillery, and—debarred from charging with his horsemen by the yawning ditches—show, by the stubborn, daring, and invincible handling of his pieces, that, if he were not the most famous of all cavalry commanders, he would be one of the greatest of artillerists.

One feature of the landscape we have not yet noted—the heights beyond the river yonder. That house upon the hill, where the banner of the stars and stripes is rippling in the wind, is "Chatham"—and some Federal general has taken it for his head-quarters. Those blue specks upon the northern bank are "Yankee pickets." See that blue horseman riding along the crest—it is an officer reconnoitring.

On the 11th of December—was it not?—the great struggle began.

At daylight, the Federal pioneers, as busy as beavers, were heard putting together the pontoons, in the fog, opposite the town; and, in spite of a rapid fire from Barksdale's brave Mississippians, who held the town, the bridges were built, and a column was thrown across.

Barksdale retreated, fighting from street to street; and soon the thunder of artillery began. Shot and shell raked the streets of the town, tearing down the chimneys and riddling the houses; but Barksdale held his ground—and it was not until an overpowering force of infantry assailed him that he doggedly retired behind the stone wall beneath Marye's Hill.

All day the unfortunate town was heavily bombarded. More than one hundred guns was fired every minute.

As night descended, the glare of burning houses, set on fire by shell, lit up the landscape; and the sullen roar of an occasional gun seemed to indicate that the ire of the assailants was not sated.

That bitter December night the roads were full of women, many of them with bare feet, who carried in their arms their infants. They had hastily fled, and, in the corners of fences, or beneath the bleak winter trees, shivered till morning.

When the sun rose, the Federal army was drawn up upon the southern bank.

General Lee had made no movement to prevent them from crossing.

————

CIII.

"IT IS WELL THIS IS SO TERRIBLE—WE WOULD GROW TOO FOND OF IT!"

BEFORE dawn on the morning of the great conflict, Jackson was in the saddle, and, joining General Lee, rode to the right to reconnoitre.

He was dressed, on this day, in an entirely new suit. His overcoat was dark blue, lined with red; his cap blazing with gold lace; his uniform-coat, which Stuart had given him in the Valley, flaming with its new brass buttons.

The troops scarcely knew him, and, when he had passed one of his regiments, a soldier was heard to say:

"*That* finely-dressed officer Old Jack? No, *sir!*"

Below the Crossing we met Stuart, and the three generals rode down the "stage road," to reconnoitre. The enemy were already advancing through the fog, and very soon the whiz of bullets indicated that the Federal sharpshooters had descried the dusky figures.

Stuart gave an order, and a piece of artillery was seen moving across the field to the right. Soon its thunders were heard, and a Federal battery in front replied.

The three generals now rode to the top of the hill above Hamilton's Crossing. From the right came the steady and continuous roar of the single gun—under Pelham—sent thither by Stuart. About three batteries, a few hundred yards in its front, had opened upon it; and an enfilading fire was raking the field from thirty-pound Parrotts across the river. But Pelham fought on.

General Lee looked in the direction of the fire.

"It is glorious to see such courage in one so young," he said.

And, in his official dispatch, he immortalized the young Alabamian by speaking of him as "the gallant Pelham." To be the sole officer below the rank of Major-General mentioned by Lee —and to be called " the gallant Pelham!"

That is better than a scrawl from any war department!

As the dense fog lifted, and the sun shone through it, the dark Federal lines rushed forward across the plain, and charged Jackson's front with desperation.

They were met with a murderous fire of musketry; the guns on the crest above opened all at once their iron mouths, and the battle began to rage with fury.

The column which assailed the right wing, under Jackson, numbered fifty-five thousand men, under Generals Franklin Hooker, and others—see their reports. At Sharpsburg, McClellan decided to overwhelm Lee's left, and was met by Jackson. At Fredericksburg, General Burnside decided to flank and drive back Lee's right, and found Jackson in his way.

If that assault had succeeded, Lee's right would have been turned, his line forced back, and the enemy would have stormed his position.

It failed. Jackson met it with his first line. This was broken' through, and he met it with his second, which completely repulsed the assault. D. H. Hill's reserve was not engaged.

Jackson's whole force in the fight was less than fifteen thou sand.

This battle was a remarkable one. The Federal troops fought hard, but apparently without heart. At one time they seemed about to carry the hill—but those who had rushed up the slope were driven back with the bayonet.

Meanwhile Stuart, in the great field beyond the Crossing, was fighting about thirty pieces of artillery, with desperation. Pelham commanded under him, and fought like a veteran of a hundred battles. Behind the woods, near by, the long line of cavalry waited to take part in the action if the right was turned.

Jackson had just brought up his second line to repulse the enemy, who had broken through his first, as I have said, when I was sent to General Lee with a message.

I found him on the eminence in front of Longstreet's line, now known as "Lee's Hill," and was much impressed by his perfect calmness, as I have everywhere been. As I turned away after delivering my message, loud cheers came from the right, and, looking across the plain, I saw the Federal line rapidly falling back, hotly pursued by Jackson's troops, firing volleys as they rushed forward.

General Lee's face filled with blood, and his eye flashed. Turning to one of his generals, who stood near, he said, as he drew his old riding-cape around his shoulders:

"It is well this is so terrible—we would grow too fond of it!"*

Those deep-toned words still ring in my ears.

When I reached the crest above Hamilton's Crossing again, I found Jackson directing the fire of his artillery on the slope of the crest. I had never seen him more thoroughly aroused. His cheeks were flushed, and his eyes glowed. The murderous fire of shot and shell which swept the crest from the crowding batteries of the enemy in front seemed to produce no effect upon him, although men and horses were falling every minute.

* His words.

As I made my report, a shell crashed through a caisson, with in twenty yards, and it blew up with a noise like thunder. Jackson did not move a muscle.

"Major," he said, in his brief accents, "present my compliments to General Stuart, and tell him I am going to advance and attack with the bayonet precisely at sunset. I wish him to advance his artillery as far as possible, and continue the fire. Desire him not to fire too much to the left—he may injure my men."*

I found Stuart in the great field, swept by a tempest of shell, superintending the fire of his artillery.

The ditches in his immediate front were full of Federal sharp-shooters, who kept up a galling fire upon the cannoneers, at close and deadly range. A bullet had cut off a lock of Stuart's hair and as I was speaking with him two others struck his saddle and military satchel.

When I delivered my message his face glowed.

I was about to ride off when a courier galloped up from General W. H. F. Lee, I think, and said something which I did not hear.

Stuart's blue eyes flashed.

"Tell the General all's well," he said, "and that I am going to crowd 'em with artillery!"†

As I rode back, expecting at every instant to be hurled from the saddle by the round-shot which swept the plain, I saw the sun poised like a ball of fire upon the woods, and then to the right and left, from Jackson and Stuart, came the redoubled thunders of the charge. The artillery was charging as well as the infantry, and the dusky plains, upon which the shades of night began to descend, became the scene of a desperate and sanguinary struggle.

It was soon decided. As night fell, the enemy retreated from Jackson's front, and Stuart pushed forward, "crowding 'em with artillery," as he had promised. Soon only a sullen gun at intervals replied—darkness descended, and the bloody fight had ended.

* His words.   † His words.

In front of Marye's Hill, the Federal assault had been re pulsed, as upon the right—and though for some reason which I never could clearly understand, Jackson did not make his intended charge with the bayonet and drive the enemy into the river, the victory was none the less perfect.

General Lee had here thrown into action—counting the forces fighting in every portion of the field—less than twenty-five thousand men in all. Against his right alone, the enemy had thrown a column of fifty-five thousand men, under one of their ablest generals—as the testimony of General Burnside before the Committee of Investigation shows.

Why was a force so considerable unable to drive Jackson from his position? I know not—I only know that they did not.

When the sun went down upon the battle-field, General Lee regarded the attack as only the prelude of a more determined assault on the next morning—his repulse of the Federal forces a mere incident of the drama.

He had achieved a complete victory.*

CIV.

PELHAM AND JEAN.

Night had fallen, and the weary troops slept on their arms, awaiting the more decisive attack which they expected on the next day.

Along the narrow and winding road which led in rear of the line of battle from Hamilton's Crossing to General Lee's head-quarters, near the Telegraph road, couriers came and went, bearing dispatches or orders.

Jackson was up during the whole night; and about midnight an orderly woke me, to say that the General wished to see me. I immediately repaired to his tent, and found him busily writing —his candle having been carefully shaded, so as not to throw its light upon the eyes of a friend who that night shared his bed.

* The incidents of this chapter are all historical.

Before the General had finished the sentence which ne was writing, the sound of horse's hoofs was heard without, and the orderly came to say that an officer wished to see him.

" Come in," was the reply.

And a young officer entered, and saluted.

" General," he said, "I am sent by General Gregg, who was mortally wounded to-day, to say on his part, that in a recent letter he wrote you, which you considered disrespectful, he had no intention of wounding your feelings, but was actuated solely by what he believed to be the good of the service. He is now dying, and begs your forgiveness."

The young man again saluted, and waited hat in hand.

. Jackson rose quickly, and his face exhibited strong feeling.

" Tell General Gregg I will be with him immediately," he said ; and, summoning his servant, he ordered his horse to be saddled at once.

As soon as the animal was ready he mounted, and, making a sign to me to follow him, rode rapidly, guided by the young officer, to General Gregg's head-quarters.

Dismounting hastily in front of the tent occupied by the wounded soldier, he entered it alone—upon this interview I felt that no one should intrude. I only saw, as the tent-flap fell, a pale face, some bleeding bandages, and a weak hand held out, as Jackson, with flushed face, hastened to the sufferer's side.* Then the canvas fell.

What took place on that dark night, between the great leader and the noble soldier who did not wish to die without his forgiveness? I know not. But, when Jackson at length came out, there were traces of tears in his eyes, and for some time he rode on in silence. As he went on through the darkness, I saw him more than once raise his right arm aloft, with that singular gesture habitual to him, and look upward, with lips moving. He was praying for the friend about to die.

At last he seemed to banish these gloomy feelings, and by an effort of the will return to the hard routine of business.

* Historical.

16*

"Major," he said, "I wish you to ride to General Stuart's
head-quarters, and request him to send Major Pelham to me. I
have special need for him to-night, and I beg you will not return
without him."

I saluted, and immediately set out for "Camp No-Camp," the
head-quarters of Stuart, on the Telegraph road, near General
Lee's quarters.

I was there informed that Major Pelham had not yet returned
from the field, and that I would probably find him at the bivouac
of his horse artillery, somewhere in the fields beyond Hamilton's
Crossing.

This was somewhat discouraging, as an additional ride of
three or four miles on a freezing cold night was before me; but
it had to be taken, and, wrapping my cape around my face to
shield it from the bitter wind, I rode on and soon reached the
Crossing.

Across the bare bleak fields, which had been so lately swept
by a hurricane of shell, glimmered the dying light of camp-fires;
and after much delay I succeeded in finding the spot where Pelham's artillery had camped—that is, halted the pieces, and built
fires of rails.

Around one of these fires, which threw its ruddy glare on the
grim cannon near, and the weary horses tethered to the wheels,
was a group of rudely-dressed men, among whom I recognized
Antonio, Rossini, Dominic, and other members of the "Napoleon
Detachment," which had fought their Napoleon, singing the loud
Marseillaise, that day of the attack near The Oaks.

In the centre of the group I saw Pelham—the fire clearly
lighting up his slender figure and beardless face. He was kneeling upon one knee and supporting upon his breast the bleeding
form of a boy of fifteen, who had been nearly torn to pieces by a
fragment of shell, and was evidently dying.

The poor boy was plainly suffering agonies from his mortal
wound, which a surgeon had rudely bandaged; and his exclamations in French and broken English were touching.

"*Jesus Seigneur!*" he exclaimed, in heart-rending accents, as
I drew near, "I suffer!—how I suffer, *mon capitaine!*"

And raising his head, which rested upon Pelham's breast, he gazed on the young officer's face with a look so helpless and appealing, that the quick tears started to my eyes.

"Try to bear it, Jean," said Pelham, in a low voice, "you are among your friends—you know we love you "—

There he broke down, and, turning away his head, uttered a sob. The rude cannoneers around looked grimly on, silent before the scene.

"Oh! to die!" murmured the wounded boy, sinking back in Pelham's arms, "to die, and I so young! What will mother say?—*ma mère!*—it will kill her! You, too, *mon capitaine!*" he added sobbing, "you, too, will be sorry for the *pauvre Jean,* will you not? I followed you from Alabama—I have fought with you in so many battles!—and one day—hold! I die with that at my heart, *mon capitaine!*—one day you said to me, '*Brave Jean!*' Yes, you said that—did you not?"

And, half rising from the earth, the boy threw back his head, and clung with both arms around Pelham's neck.

"You called me *brave*—it is enough!" he murmured. "Tell *ma mère* I fought like a good soldier, *O mon capitaine!*—that you were satisfied with Jean! He dies loving you—the *brave of braves*—his dear, his only friend! When you go back to our home in Alabama, tell them all, that Jean fought under you, and did his duty. '*Brave Jean!*' you said. *O mon Dieu!* I suffer so—but—and—I die—in your arms, *mon capitaine!*"

The head fell back, and the pale lips uttered their last sigh. But, even in death, the boy's arms clung around Pelham's neck —his face rested on his bosom.

The rough group stirred and murmured.

"*Grand Dieu!*—he is gone!" muttered the swarthy Antonio.

"*Il est mort!*" echoed Rossini, making the sign of the cross.

Pelham gently unclasped the cold arms of the boy, and laid the stiffening form upon the grass. His face was wet with tears, and, when some of the men spoke to him, he waved them off with his hand.

For some moments he stood gazing into the fire, from which his glance would turn toward the body of Jean.

"Poor boy!" he murmured, passing his hand across his eyes, "he loved me.   There was nobody braver!"

There he stopped. But in a few moments he had mastered his emotion, and turned to me.   I delivered my message, and, after giving directions for the burial of Jean, Pelham called for his horse.

"Poor Jean!" I heard him murmur again; "what can I say to his mother when I go back to Alabama!"

All at once he went to where the body of the young cannoneer was lying, and, stooping down, cut off a lock of his light, curling hair, and carefully placed it in his breast-pocket.

"It will be something," he said.

And he mounted his horse and rode with me back to Jackson's head-quarters.

I recall still, and could easily repeat, our conversation as we rode on through the darkness; but all do not take that loving interest in Pelham's memory which I do.   Every word he uttered then, and always, is engraved upon my memory, and I recall, with a sad and longing sense of loss, a feeling of bereavement which nothing can satisfy, the hours I passed with him—his voice, his eyes, his smiles.

We reached Jackson's head-quarters, and Pelham was received with that cordial pressure of the hand which the General bestowed upon those who were favorites with him. I knew the opinion which he had formed of Pelham, from their first meeting on the day of Cold Harbor, and now saw that Jackson had a higher regard for him than ever.

His object in sending for the young artillerist was a proof of this.   He wished him to direct and superintend. in person, the fortification of his line for the next day's battle; * and, as soon as he had possessed himself of the General's views, Pelham energetically applied himself to the work. Heavy details were placed at his orders; he superintended and directed the work throughout the night, without further orders; and at dawn the task was finished.

* Historical.

When Jackson inspected, in the morning, the defences which had thus arisen like magic, he said to General Stuart, who accompanied him :

"Have you another Pelham, General? If so, I wish you would give him to me!" *

Those works saved hundreds of lives during the cannonade, which soon began ; but they were not to have their value tested by a charge of the enemy's infantry. That attack of the preceding day had been the decisive assault, and the Federal forces could not be brought up again. General Burnside directed a second attack, but his ablest and most determined major-generals went to him and protested against the order, declaring that the troops could not be induced to make the assault—their *morale* was destroyed. See the testimony of General Burnside.

All day on Sunday and Monday the dense masses of the Federal army remained in line of battle on the Southern shore of the Rappahannock, their bands playing, their flags floating, their artillery in position for a renewal of the assault.

On Tuesday morning they had disappeared.

Thus ended the campaign of 1862.

CV.

RECOLLECTIONS OF "CAMP NO-CAMP."

WE spent the winter of 1862 at Moss Neck, an old mansion on the crest of hills which stretches along the Rappahannock, several miles below Fredericksburg.

Jackson's sojourn there will form a pleasant chapter in that life of him which, sooner or later, will be written by a competent person.

He occupied first a small outbuilding—a sort of office—hung round with pictures of race-horses, game-cocks, and terriers tearing rats. One day when Stuart came to see the General, he said:

* His words.

"I intend to have a drawing made of this room—game-cocks terriers. and all—and label it, *"View of the head-quarters of the famous Stonewall Jackson, showing the tastes and propensities of the individual!"*

At these jests of the great cavalier, Jackson always laughed heartily. He had conceived a very great regard and affection for Stuart—as a cavalry officer, he ranked him above all others in that arm of the service.

Does the reader remember that fine cap worn at the battle of Fredericksburg, with its band of gold lace? It was soon denuded of its decoration. One day a little girl admired it, and. drawing her to him, Jackson tore off the rich braid. placed it like a coronet upon her curls, and enjoyed the delight which his gift occasioned the child.

But these traits of the illustrious soldier will all. some day, be delineated fully. I am not writing a life of General Jackson. but the memoirs of Lieutenant-Colonel Surry.

"Lieutenant-Colonel Surry?" I think I hear the reader exclaim: "Is there not a slight mistake?" Not at all, may it please the worthy reader. About this time General Jackson was made Lieutenant-General; his staff went up one grade; and it seemed good to the War Department to send Major Surry the appointment of Lieutenant-Colonel and A. A. G.—than which rank he never got any further during the war.

So, after all that hard marching of the year 1862. we were resting. It had been a memorable year, full of the thunder of artillery, the crash of small arms, the clatter of sabres, the cheers, yells, shouts, and groans of adversaries closing in the breast-to-breast struggle—and I think that both sides were glad to rest. It had been the first decisive trial of strength upon the whole great arena of Virginia; and the opponents seemed to have exhausted themselves. On the Federal side, scarcely a single commander who had met Jackson remained. Generals Banks, Shields, Fremont, Milroy, Pope, McClellan, and Burnside had all disappeared. The baton had dropped from their hands—their heads fallen—they had vanished from all eyes, and the smoke of disaster and defeat. Lee and Jackson still stood immovable on the banks of the Rappahannock.

Had the country been as resolute as the army *and the women*, the red battle-flag would float there still, instead of drooping yonder, furled, with no hand to give it to the winds—furled and dragged in the dust of defeat, but glorious forever!

During the winter I spent some days, on furlough, at Eagle's-Nest; and whom should I meet there but a youth named Charles Beverley—evidently intent on the capture of Miss Annie Surry!

Charley's regiment was encamped not far from Port Royal, and I strongly suspect that the youth was frequently absent from roll-call, without the shadow of permission! He seemed to think, however, that his hours at Eagle's-Nest more than counterbalanced "extra duty" in the way of punishment—and I soon saw that Annie had made up her youthful mind.

They are married now, reader, and Charley is a model husband. So they vanish!

About the same time came the news of Will's marriage with Jenny Clayton! That young lady had captured him—as Annie had captured Charley—and a gilt-edged note, with a request for the pleasure of our company, came by flag of truce, through the lines! Will had written on it: "How are you, brother? I am bagged at last!"—and he wrote the other day that Jenny was the pearl of her sex.

But I am getting ahead too fast. Let me return to the old days, and recall some of the faces and scenes which illustrated them.

I was often at the jovial head-quarters of Stuart, on the Telegraph road, a few miles from Fredericksburg. His flag had been erected in a great field of broom-straw, sheltered by a thicket of pines from the chill northwest winds; and against the evergreens shone the white tents of the General and his staff. In front of the head-quarters was a beautiful little "Whitworth" gun of burnished steel—slender, delicate, and graceful as a girl. Above stretched the arms of a great oak. The horses were picketed beneath the pines, or in rude stables.

Couriers came and went. The red battle-flag fluttered in the frosty breeze. From the large tent in the pines came the sonorous voice or the ringing laughter of Stuart, that "flower of cavaliers."

In my visits I constantly saw something new in this man to admire and love. He had the gayest humor, the warmest heart, and the most generous temper. He possessed the rough cavalry tendency to jests and practical jokes: would tease you, if he could, upon any subject, and raise the laugh at your expense without hesitation:—but you were welcome to " strike back," and as roughly as you could. It was give-and-take with the trenchant swordsman, and you could not offend him. Writing busily at his desk—then rising to walk up and down and hum a song—lounging idly upon his bed spread on the ground, and playing with his pets, two young setters he had brought in front of him on his saddle, when he fell back from Culpepper—laughing, jesting with his staff—so passed the hours of winter with the brave cavalier at " Camp No-Camp."

When weary of work or talk, he would mount one of his horses, " Lady Margaret " or " Star of the East," and set off to serenade some lady—taking Sweeny along, with his banjo.

For Sweeny was there!—Sweeny in all his glory—with a new " Yankee banjo," the spoil of some captured camp, which he forced to give forth now the gay songs of Dixie!   It was " The bonnie blue flag," and " We are the boys that rode around McClellan," and " I wish I was in Dixie," which Sweeny played and sang, with his sad and courteous face unmoved by the mirth; and these were always succeeded by " Sweet Evelina," " Faded Flowers," " I lay ten dollars down," and the " Old Gray Hoss "—perennial favorites with the denizens of " Camp No-Camp."

You can see the worthy Sweeny—can you not, my dear reader ?—sitting there at the corner of the fireplace in the large tent, his banjo on his knee, his fingers flying over the strings, his foot keeping time, and only the ghost of a smile upon his face as he advises you, "if you want to have a good time," to " jine the cavalry!"

And look! at the door yonder! Is not that gigantic figure, with the flowing black beard, our old friend Hagan—*Corporal* Hagan no longer, as his braid of a lieutenant shows! It is Hagan, now lieutenant of the escort, and behind him are the keen faces of Moonshine and Snakebug, couriers—with the hawk look, keener even than Captain Bogy's for wagons, spoils, and plunder generally. Hagan advances, salutes the general and company with rigid military respect, and is soon engaged in parrying the thrusts of the general's wit. He relates as a pleasing incident—with lurking humor in his eye and a voice like low thunder—how Moonshine, in an absent moment, appropriated Snakebug's blanket; how Snakebug recovered his property in his friend's absence, and accidentally bore off Moonshine's boots, thereby "getting the dead-wood on Moonshine;"—and then Hagan shakes all over with merriment, the general laughs, Sweeny's banjo roars, a negro dances a breakdown, amid shouts of applause, and the cavalry headquarters are in a state of perfect enjoyment.

There too was Pelham, now Stuart's chief of artillery; and Farley, the celebrated partisan of South Carolina, one of his aides.

Stuart! Pelham! Farley! How many memories do these words recall! As I murmur them I seem to hear again the accents of the noble voices; to press the friendly hands—to greet the dear dead comrades sleeping their last sleep!

Pelham, the brave, the true, the kindly, gentle spirit—I never knew a human being of more stubborn nerve, or shrinking modesty. His blue eye never fell before the stare of peril, but often when you spoke to him. His color never faded in the hottest hours of the most desperate fighting; but a word would often confuse him, and make him blush like a girl. A native of the great State of Alabama, he had the warm blood of the South in his young veins; but I think he had come to love Virginia and the faces here with a love as warm as that of her own children. Virginia certainly loved him, her boy defender; but it was impossible to know him and not love him. In that light blue eye was the soul of truth and chivalry. The smooth, boyish face was the veritable mirror of high breeding, delicacy, and honor.

I never knew a comrade more attractive—with a more delightful gayety, naturalness, and abandon. Quick to resent an insult,
or to meet defiance with defiance, he was never irritable, and
had the sweetness and good-humor of a child—suspecting nothing, and fearing no offence. His modesty did not change after
Fredericksburg, and when the whole army rang with that magnificent compliment paid to the boy by the commander-in-chief,
in calling him "the gallant Pelham." His spirit was too proud
and noble to be touched by arrogance. He was still the modest,
simple, laughing boy—with his charming gayety, his caressing
voice, and his sunny smile. On the slightest provocation, the
smooth cheeks were covered with the blush of diffidence. He
never spoke of his own achievements; and you would not have
known, had you been with him for a whole month, that he had
ever taken part in a single action. In Maryland, an old farmer
looked at his beardless face, his girlish smile, his slender figure,
and said to General Stuart, "Can *these boys* fight?"

And yet this "boy," so young in years, was old in toils, in
marches, in hard combats, and desperate encounters. That light,
blue eye had looked unmoved upon the bloody scenes of the
first Manassas, Williamsburg, Cold Harbor, the second Manassas,
Sharpsburg, Fredericksburg, and those stubborn fights in which
Stuart's cavalry—unknown almost to the infantry—were constantly engaged. This boy had fought his guns, at both battles
of Manassas, till the enemy were at their very muzzles; had held
his ground with one Napoleon, at Cold Harbor, against the hurricane of shot and shell poured on him from the batteries near
McGee's house; had commanded all the artillery on the left at
Sharpsburg; held the ford at Shepherdstown, driving back,
hour after hour, the heavy masses of the enemy; and at Fredericksburg had fought with that stubborn persistence, that unconquerable nerve, which made the silent and unexcitable commander-in-chief exclaim:

"It is glorious to see such courage in one so young!"

Such was his record—such the career of this shrinking
youth, who blushed when you spoke to him. Stuart loved him
like a brother, and after his death, when I was speaking one day

of him, the tears came to the eyes of the great cavalier, and he turned away, unable to utter a word. He is dead now; his voice will never more be heard—his laugh never sound again. He was nothing to you, it may be, good reader—you never heard of him, perhaps; or his name was only that of a brave boy who fought his guns with dauntless courage upon many bloody battle-fields. To me he was more. It was a friend of my heart that passed away when Pelham fell—a comrade whom I loved, and who loved me. When he passed from earth, amid that thunder of artillery which he loved, the world somehow seemed drearier, and the sunshine not so bright. The song of the birds was mu_sical no more; the glory of existence seemed to fade; Pelham was dead, and there was no one left to take his place!

Observe how my memory leads me back to those old days, and makes me linger in the haunted domain of the past—reviving the gallant figures, listening again to the brave voices, and living once more in the bright hours that are dead!

But what is left to us poor "paroled prisoners," except memory? Leave us that, at least, as we look upon the red battle-flag, drooping from its staff, after so many splendid victories; leave us this poor consolation of recalling the grand figures and bright hours of the past!

Stuart, Pelham—both are dead now; and Farley, too, has passed away, the bravest of the brave. I never saw his face before the war, nor until the spring of 1862; but often I had heard of a young man in the Army of the Potomac who had made himself famous by his fearless scouting, his cool self-possession in the hottest hours of battle, and his long, solitary expeditions into the enemy's lines. I figured to myself, as I heard of his strange adventures, his desperate combats, a rough, unpolished partisan, with the instincts of a tiger and the manners of a bear; but when I came to know him upon General Stuart's staff—here is what I saw:

A young man of twenty-five or six, of medium height; athletic, but graceful figure; soft dark eyes, low musical voice, and girlish gentleness—there was Farley. He wore a sort of surtout of dark cloth, around which was buckled constantly a belt containing his pistol; handsome cavalry boots, and a brown hat with a black feather.   Sometimes he donned a splendid suit of Federal blue—shoulder-straps and all—captured in the head-quarters of General Casey at " Seven Pines ;" but this was only by way of amusement.   His horse, his arms, his boots, his saddle, his belt, his gauntlets, his hat—all were captured.   He lived on the enemy—despoiled them of all he needed : he had no commission, drew no pay, and was poor, like all of us ; but he wanted nothing.   The enemy supplied him.

When he needed any thing—a horse, a pistol, an " officer's McClellan saddle "—or when the repose of head-quarters had become tedious—he set out by himself, or with a small detail of men, upon a private raid.   Somewhere beyond the Rappahannock he was sure to find the enemy ; and he was as certain to attack them.   The bang of revolvers, the clash of sabres, the cheer of defiance—then Farley retired, laughing in his silent way, with his horses, arms, and saddles.   He came back looking better satisfied ; and waited for the next occasion.

But I am lingering too long.   The memory of this brave and gentle cavalier leads me back to those old days when I knew him.   At " Camp No-Camp " I first became his friend.   It was impossible to imagine any one with a sweeter temper or a more winning address.   The soft dark eyes were full of gentleness and candor ; the smile upon the lips, shaded with a black mustache, was charming ; and the low, measured voice like music to the ear.   Often we wandered over the great fields of broom-straw sighing in the winds of winter ; and in these walks Farley told me all his life.   It was a brave, true heart which thus unfolded itself before me ; and under this modest exterior were the finest traits of the gentleman.   As the old chivalric poetry came sometimes from his lips, and he repeated—

" Gayly bedight,
A gallant knight
Rode on through sun and shadow "—

he was himself the ideal of that gallant cavalier.   Modest, kindly, brave as steel, and devoted to the South, his death was another gap in the lives of those who loved him—a loss which nothing can supply.

Do I weary you, kind reader, with my memories of Stuart, Pelham, Farley, and those days long gone into the dust? I have done. It was the recollection of the hours I spent at "Camp No-Camp," with Stuart, which beguiled me. When these men passed away, with all their smiles, their laughter, their gay voices and brave faces, something like a shadow seemed to fall upon the landscape. I mourn them yet; and sometimes think a portion of my heart is buried with them yonder, where they sleep in peace—dead on the field of honor.

CVI.

I GO WITH STUART TO CULPEPPER.

ONE day in March, when I visited General Stuart's head-quarters, I found him buckling on his sabre and pistol. The black satchel, in which he carried official papers, was already on. His face was serious and earnest.

"My dear General," I said, "I am such a good staff-officer that I not only never ask any questions, but never even form a desire to know any thing. It is permitted, I hope, however, to make a simple remark, and I beg leave to say that you appear to me to be going somewhere."

"You are the model of an aide," was Stuart's reply, "and such virtue ought to be rewarded. I won't tell you where I am going, but, if you are willing, I will take you with me."

"That is a fair proposition."

"You accept?"

"Certainly—but there is my General, who must be consulted."

Stuart went to his desk and wrote a line, calling for a courier as he did so.

The courier appeared at the moment when the General finished.

"Does that express the idea?" asked the General.

And he handed me the paper. It was addressed to General
Jackson, and contained only these words:

"MY DEAR GENERAL:
  "Will you lend me Colonel Surry for three or four days?
                          "Your friend,
                                    "J. E. B. S."

  "It has the military brevity of *Veni, vidi, vici,* General."
And I returned the paper, which was intrusted to Moonshine,
scout and courier, for delivery to General Jackson. In half an
hour—for our head-quarters were now within a mile of Stuart's,
on the Massaponnax—Moonshine returned with the answer. It
was indorsed on the note, and in these words:

"MY DEAR GENERAL:
  "Certainly.
                          "Your friend,
                                    "T. J. J."

  "The General beats me in brevity," was Stuart's comment;
and he put on his riding-cape.
  "Which route are we going?" I asked.
  "We are going to take the train."
  "Ah! the train!—you say the train?"
  "There, you have asked no less than two indiscreet questions,
Mr. Model Staff-Officer!"
  "But your staff, doubtless, know your route?"
  "Not a bit, Surry—they stay here."
  "Ah! Then you make a stolen march?"
  "Come and see."
And we mounted and set out for Hamilton's Crossing, where
—sending back my horse by a courier—I took the cars with
Stuart.
  On the same evening we had travelled by Hanover Junction,
Gordonsville, and Orange, to Culpepper Court-House.
  In front of the tavern, upon his gray mare " Nelly," we found

STUART AND I GO TO ᴜULPEPPER. 383

General Fitz Lee—a gallant figure, in full war-harness, with flowing beard and mustache, laughing face, and eyes sparkling with gayety beneath his brown hat and ebon feather.

Behind him was Pelham, quiet, smiling, wearing his little artillery-jacket, with red collar, and seated upon a huge artillery horse, his knees drawn up by the short stirrups.

" Well, Fitz! what news?" was Stuart's greeting, as he shook hands with General Lee.

" Just heard from Randolph,* who is on picket at the bridge. Averill is opposite Kelly's Ford.

" What force?"

" About three thousand."

Stuart leaned over.

" What *effective* have you?"

" About eight hundred," was the reply.

" Good," said Stuart, "that will do."

And they entered the tavern together.

I had shaken hands with "General Fitz," and was talking with Pelham, who had been in Culpepper for several days on a visit of inspection.

The "Stuart Horse Artillery" had grown from a battery to a battalion, with such officers as Breathed, Henry, McGregor, and others—perfect tigers in a fight, and men after Stuart's own heart.

I never knew Pelham to be more gay. He spoke of the "jolly times" he expected to have in the coming campaign, and seemed to look forward to the storm of battle, ready to burst forth, with all the ardor of a lover who sees the approach of his mistress.

His blue eyes sparkled; his lips were wreathed with smiles; his voice was gay; his jest and laughter incessant.

" Now Stuart has come, we'll have it!" was his exclamation.

" There never was another man like Stuart, Surry!"†

" Poor boy!" said the General to me a month afterward, " he loved me very much!"‡

---

* Captain of the " Black Horse."   † His words.   ‡ His words.

CVII.

THE LAST CHARGE OF PELHAM.

AT dawn we were aroused by the intelligence that the enemy were crossing the Rappahannock and making a determined attack upon the small force posted in the rifle-pits.

Stuart had laid down without taking off his clothes or arms. He was speedily in the saddle—General Fitz Lee having sent him a horse. I had procured one from Pelham, and we were soon riding rapidly in the direction of Kelly's Ford.

As we passed Fleetwood Hill, where the great battle of the 9th of June was afterward fought, and approached Stevensburg, the dark column of Fitz Lee was seen moving steadily through the gray of morning in the direction of the Rappahannock; and, riding on to the head of the column, Stuart joined the General.

The firing from the river in front was now rapid and continuous.

" They have crossed," said Stuart anxiously. " Who commands the force in the rifle-pits, Fitz?"

I did not hear the answer. I only heard the words " reenforced last night."

As he spoke, the firing ceased, as if by magic.

In the dim light I could see Stuart knit his brow.

" They are captured as sure as fate!" he growled.

The words were soon verified. A cavalry-man galloped up, and, to Stuart's quick demand of " What news?" replied in great excitement :·

" The enemy are across, General—at least ten thousand! The men in the rifle-pits are all captured!"

" Where are you going?" said Stuart gruffly.

" To find my company, General."

" Here is a company you can join."

And he pointed to Fitz Lee's column, in which the straggling cavalry-man reluctantly took his place.

" Now, Fitz," said Stuart coolly, " there is only one thing to do—to fight them.   We'll drive right at Averill, and find who is the best man."

General Fitz Lee received this suggestion with a gay laugh.

"That's what I am going to do," was his reply.

The column moved on steadily; the day slowly dawned; and as we approached Kelly's Ford we came upon the enemy, drawn up on the southern bank of the river, not less than three thousand in the saddle.

General Fitz Lee immediately made his dispositions for attack. I say General Fitz Lee, for Stuart had notified him that he would not assume command as long as every thing went on to his satisfaction.

As the sun rose, the spectacle presented was imposing. Ranged in long lines, face to face, were seen the opposing lines of cavalry, drawn up for the charge; and, as the masses moved to their allotted positions, the heavy tramp of hoofs, with the occasional notes of the bugle, alone broke the stillness.

In face of the three thousand cavalry of Averill, the eight hundred of Fitz Lee presented a painfully diminutive appearance. The array of force against the Southerners seemed overwhelming—but never have I seen troops more animated and eager for the fray. The eyes of the men sparkled; they clutched the sword-hilt with an evident intention to make every cut bring down its man; and when Stuart and Fitz Lee appeared, riding along the lines, a wild burst of cheers rose, saying, as plainly as any language, " We are ready! Give the word!"

It was given.   Suddenly the ringing bugles sounded the "Charge!" and Lee and Stuart, with drawn sabres whirling round their heads, led the line in a headlong charge.

In a moment they had burst upon the enemy, drawn up behind a ditch and heavy stone wall ; the carbines were cracking, and the bitter struggle began in all its fury.

It was to last from morn to night—from the rising to the setting of the sun.

I cannot describe it in its animated details; some other hand must chronicle the splendid gallantry of the little band of Lee, fighting nearly four to one ; and tell, too, with what dash and courage Fitz Lee led his men.

17

"It was like a little dog jumping at the throat of a big mastiff!" said an old farmer afterward, in describing the action; and all day long the plucky bull-dog, small, but "game," made those leaps, bringing blood from his huge adversary's throat.

As the hours wore on, the struggle became desperate. From their cover behind the stone walls in their front, the enemy poured a deadly fire into the Southern horsemen ; but the obstacle was hurled down, the horses driven over with the spur, and the battle raged, hour after hour, with varying fortunes, in every portion of the field.

The enemy's great numbers told at last, however. They opened with their artillery—massed their column in front of our left, and, throwing all their weight there, turned the flank, and forced Fitz Lee back.

He retired, fighting obstinately at every step, the enemy pressing on in triumph. But they could not throw his line into disorder. Instead of scattering, the horses, who had been more or less broken into detachments, now concentrated, and, showing thus an obstinate and determined front, Fitz Lee continued to fall back, under the fire both of carbines and artillery.

All at once, from an eminence in rear, was heard the thunder of Pelham's guns; and the shells, racing over the heads of the cavalry, burst in the enemy's line, throwing it into disorder, and checking its advance. Fitz Lee continued to retire, until he reached a body of woods, on the summit of a hill, with open land in front; and here he massed his cavalry, formed line of battle, and prepared to fight to the last.

The sun was now sinking, and the great orb, balanced like a ball of fire upon the woodland, seemed to be bathed in blood. Throughout the whole day, the little force had virtually held its ground; and now, seeing that Averill continued to advance, Fitz Lee determined to attack him.

In our front was a great field intersected by fences; but these were of wood, and could be torn down. On the high ground beyond was the Federal artillery. As far as the eye could reach, extended the dark masses of the Federal cavalry, motionless in line of battle.

Our bugles sounded the charge, and slowly the Southern line advanced—then it broke into a trot—then, at a wild gallop, and with defiant cheers, it burst upon the enemy.

From that moment the action became mad and desperate. The men discarded the pistol and carbine, and had recourse to the sabre. In an instant they had torn wide gaps in the fences, swept through, and were fighting hand to hand.

Fitz Lee and Stuart were in front, fighting like private soldiers. Their presence gave new vigor to the men, and a better fight was not made in the war.

Stuart was leading on the men when Pelham galloped up and made some report in relation to his artillery. I understood in an instant what had brought him—he could not stay in the rear with his guns : he burned to be in the charge.

As he turned away, a regiment swept by, right down upon the enemy, and Pelham's sabre flashed from its scabbard.

At that moment his appearance was superb. His cheeks were burning; his blue eyes darted lightnings ; from his lips, wreathed with a smile of joy, rang "Forward!" as he cheered on the men.

For an instant he was standing erect in his stirrups, his sabre flashing in his grasp ; for a moment his proud voice rang like a clarion which sounds the charge—then I saw him hurled from the saddle, under the trampling hoofs of the horses.

With a single bound of my horse I reached him. He lay with his smiling face turned upward, his eyes closed.

A shell had burst above him ; a fragment struck him upon the head--he was gone!

Gone at the moment when, before the headlong charge of Lee, the men of Averill gave way ; gone at that supreme instant when the long, hard day was won, and the baffled enemy were hastily retiring across the Rappahannock! That spectacle was denied the heroic boy—but he died the death he wished—and is yonder, where the brave and true and faithful are rewarded!

At night the enemy were retiring, "badly hurt," as Stuart telegraphed. He added : "We are after him. His dead men and horses strew the roads."

Before morning, Averill, with his three thousand horsemen, thus defeated by the eight hundred men of Lee, was rapidly retreating beyond the Rappahannock: a complete victory had crowned the Southern arms.

But the death of a boy more than balanced this supreme success. At midnight Pelham's lips had uttered their last sigh. His noble spirit was beyond the stars—

> "Malice domestic, foreign levy, nothing
> Could touch him further!"

CVIII.

THE SPRING FLOWERS OF INCOGNITA.

SUCH was the hard battle of Kelly's Ford, and such the death of Pelham.

The body of the young artillerist was carried back to Culpepper Court-House, and laid in its shroud, amid the sobs of women and the tears of bearded men. That cold, pale face was all that was left of one who had lived and died for Virginia and the South.

I was looking at the pallid face, upon which a smile lingered, as if death had come to him a welcome guest, when a suppressed sound behind me attracted my attention, and, turning round, I saw Stuart standing near, gazing, with eyes full of tears, upon the dead boy's face.

With a measured step, his black-plumed hat in his hand, he approached the body; looked long and silently upon the smiling face; then, stooping down, he pressed his bearded lip to the marble brow.

As he did so, the breast of the great cavalier was shaken; a sob issued from his lips, and a tear fell on the pale cheek of Pelham. Severing from his forehead a lock of the light hair—as the boy had severed one from the head of poor Jean—he turned away; and as he did so I heard, in low, deep tones, which seemed to force their way through tears, the single word—

"Farewell!"

It was Stuart's last greeting, on this earth, to the spirit of Pelham—soon to meet his own again where the roar of battle never comes.

On the day succeeding the battle, Stuart sent this dispatch to Richmond:

"The noble, the chivalric, the gallant Pelham is no more. He was killed in action yesterday. His remains will be sent to you to-day. How much he was beloved, appreciated, and admired, let the tears of agony we have shed, and the gloom of mourning throughout my command, bear witness. His loss is irreparable." *

"He fell, mortally wounded," wrote Stuart afterward, in a general order, "with the battle-cry on his lips, and the light of victory beaming from his eye.

"His eye had glanced over every battle-field of this army from the first Manassas to the moment of his death, and he was, with a single exception, a brilliant actor in all.

"The memory of 'the gallant Pelham'—his many virtues, his noble nature, and purity of character—is enshrined as a sacred legacy in the hearts of all who knew him.

"His record has been bright and spotless—his career brilliant and successful.

"He fell, the noblest of sacrifices, on the altar of his country!"

Such was the wreath of fadeless laurel laid by Stuart on the grave of Pelham—the young, the noble, the immortal! His life had passed like a dream of glory—and Stuart wept beside his tomb! Nor was that all. Tears were shed for the dead boy which the world did not see—there were sighs breathed, far away, which the world did not hear! I heard one, as it passed on the winds of spring, from the orange groves of the South—and the reader shall hear it too.

Some months after the death of my dear, good friend, I wrote

* To Mr. Curry, M. C., from Alabama.

and published, in a Southern journal, a paper upon his character and career. It was nothing—a mere sketch—the hasty lament of one comrade for another, as he passes on. My name was not printed with the sketch—and yet the authorship was in some manner discovered. In the spring of 1864, I received a note, in the delicate handwriting of a young lady, from Georgia, and this note contained a small bunch of flowers—heartsease, violet, and jessamine—tied up with a tress of hair.

The note lies before me, with its faded flowers—here it is:

"For the sake of one who fell at Kelly's Ford, March 17th, '63, an unknown Georgian sends you a simple cluster of young spring flowers. You loved the 'gallant Pelham,' and your words of love and sympathy are 'immortelles' in the hearts that loved him. I have never met you, I may never meet you, but you have a true friend in me. I know that sad hearts mourn him in Virginia, and a darkened home in Alabama tells the sorrow there. My friendship for him was pure as a sister's love, or a spirit's. I had never heard his voice.

"Your name is ever in my prayers! God bless you!

"N'importe."

Such was the note of an unknown Georgia girl, which accompanied the flowers bound up with her hair. Does any one laugh, and mutter "romance!" "extravagance"? I salute and honor her who wrote those words—they are the true "immortelles" on the grave of Pelham. I have "never met her, I may never meet her," but it is something for a poor soldier to have the prayers of a pure heart ascend for him! Not in vain, it may be, O fair Incognita! have those prayers been breathed for the unknown Virginian who, again to-day, in the hours of a sad peace, as yonder, amid the thunder on the Rapidan, reads your words of friendship, in their delicate tracery, and presses your flowers and your hair to his lips. The soul that you loved is gone from earth—never more in any future wars will his blue eye flash or his clear voice ring; but it is something, if yonder, where his spirit hovers, he can know that his memory is immortal in your heart.

Do not weep for him—it is we that remain "in the land where we were dreaming" who deserve your regret. Shed no tears for Pelham! His death was noble, as his life was beautiful and beneficent. Fame crowned his boyish brow with that amaranthine wreath, the words of our great chieftain Lee; and he died, as he lived, amid hearts who loved him as the pearl of chivalry and honor. The "gallant Pelham" cannot pass from the heart or the memory of the people of the South—but there is something which his brave spirit would be touched and thrilled by more than all those laurels which enrich his tomb.

It is the tears of Stuart, as he murmured, "Poor boy! he loved me very much!" and the prayers of this "unknown Georgian," who had "never heard his voice!"*

CIX.

THE ADVERSARIES.

THE advance of Averill was the prelude of the coming campaign.

General Hooker, known as "Fighting Joe Hooker," had superseded General Burnside in command of the Federal army, and every thing pointed to a determined and vigorous renewal of hostilities at the earliest moment which the season permitted.

What was the comparative strength of the opposing columns facing each other on the shores of the Rappahannock in the month of April? Here are the facts—I place them upon record for the historian:

The Federal army, according to the printed statement subsequently of Major-General Peck, U. S. A., numbered one hundred

---

* Colonel Surry showed me the note of the young lady here referred to. The writing is very delicate, and the flowers tied with a tress of auburn hair. He said that this little incident had sensibly touched him, and that he would have acknowledged the receipt of the note if the young lady had given him her name. As it was, he feared she would think him very cold. Some day, however, they might meet, and she would discover her mistake.

and fifty-nine thousand three hundred men. General Lee's force did not quite reach thirty-five thousand. The bulk of Longstreet's corps had been sent to Suffolk, on the south side of James River, for subsistence. All that was left was Jackson's corps, and about ten thousand troops from Longstreet's.

When the April sun began to dry the roads and render the movement of trains and artillery practicable, General Hooker confronted General Lee at Fredericksburg, with a force more than four times greater than that of his adversary.

Such were the conditions under which the great collision, in the first days of May, was about to take place. The enormous disproportion between the opposing forces, you may possibly declare, good reader, must be established by something better than the statement of an obscure officer of the C. S. Army. Be it so. Let my words go only for what they are worth now, when the theory is obstinately and persistently urged by ten thousand journals, of a certain class, that we of the South were overcome, not by numbers, but by superior generalship in the Federal leaders—superior fighting in the Federal troops. The day will come when every secret will be brought to light; when the torch of truth shall illuminate every hidden recess of this misty epoch, and defy the power that tries to extinguish it. When that day comes, the South will have full justice done to her; her victories over enormous odds will be traced to their true origin—a nerve and courage which only numbers could overwhelm. Then the world will understand the meaning of the words—" It was impossible for us to conquer—we have struggled !"

CX.

THE NIGHT-HAWKS FLOWN.

About the middle of April I was sent with a confidential message to General Stuart, who had broken up his head-quarters at " Camp No-Camp," and transferred them to the neighborhood of Culpepper Court-House.

This' mission was far from unwelcome to me; for the brilliant sun of April, after the dreary days of winter, had the effect of the bugle-note that sounds to horse. The wooing airs invited to active movement and adventure; and, strapping behind the saddle my single blanket, in its oil-cloth, I set out, gay and joyous, for Culpepper, taking the road by Chancellorsville and Ely's Ford on the Rapidan.

Do you think the words "gay and joyous" rather curious as applied to a discarded lover? Was it natural that the personage who had bidden a long farewell to the only woman he had ever loved, and never expected to look upon her face again—was it natural that this unhappy personage should be "gay and joyous" under any provocation, and not pass his whole existence tearing his hair and exhibiting other evidences of the gloom which wrapped his soul? Alas! human nature is a poor affair after all, I think! Men will not sigh always—broken hearts mend slowly; or, rather, should we not say that hope never completely deserts us? Was it the April sunshine, the grass starred over with the first pale flowers—what was it, that said, "Do not despond—it is better to laugh than be sighing!"

In this gay and philosophic mood I set out on my journey, and, following the Mine road by Tabernacle Church, struck into the main highway, and reached Chancellorsville. Scarcely glancing at this old brick edifice which had then never been heard of out of the immediate vicinity, I turned to the right toward Ely's Ford and soon found myself in that country of dense thickets—the famous Wilderness—in whose depths stood the lonely house I knew so well.

As I rode on, the bearing of the country told me that I could not be far from this house; and, yielding to a caprice which I could not resist, I turned my horse's head in the supposed direction of the place, and, after half an hour's ride through narrow bridle-paths, came upon the spot.

Leaping the low brush-fence, and ascending the knoll upon which the house stood, I checked my horse before the door, and hallooed. No reply came, and, dismounting, I opened the badly-secured door, and entered.

17*

The place was deserted. There was no trace of a human being; but all at once a sound from beneath my feet, as it were, attracted my attention, and I saw, protruding from a flight of steps which led into a cavernous region beneath, the head of an old black hag, with blear eyes, gray hair, twisted into kinks, and toothless mouth, from which issued a sort of growl.

The growl demanded what I wanted, and, when I asked if any one but herself was at home, another growl conveyed the information that no one but herself lived there.

"Where is Mrs. Parkins?"

"Gone this long time," from the hag.

"And Mr. Fenwick?"

"Dead."

These words terminated the interview, for the head of the old hag disappeared; and, having nothing further to detain me, I issued forth and remounted my horse.

So these night-hawks had disappeared—dead or gone to other regions. Like some poisonous exhalation, they had vanished before the gay sunshine, which poured upon me now as I continued my way toward the Rapidan.

Crossing at Ely's Ford, I pushed on by Stevensburg, and in the afternoon reached General Stuart's head-quarters, near Culpepper Court-House.

CXI.

HOURS AT "CAMP PELHAM."

THE picturesque head-quarters of General Stuart are before my eyes as I write these lines.

They were situated upon a wooded slope west of the little village, and great trees extended their arms above. Under a "fly"—that is to say, the canvas cover of a tent—were the General's desk, chair, and couch spread on the ground. In a clump of pines near by the couriers had pitched their tents *d'abri.* Beyond were the horses, picketed among the trees. In front of the head-quarters, on the grassy knoll, beneath the great trees, the blood-red flag of Stuart flickered like a dazzling flame in the April sunshine—a veritable "giant of battle" rose, the General's favorite flower.

Here at "Camp Pelham"—for so Stuart had called his head-quarters—I spent two or three days; and I now recall them as among the most pleasant I have ever passed. The smile of Pelham and the glad light of his friendly eyes no longer shone amid the group; but others were there—Farley, with his low, musical voice, his narratives of wild adventure; and Channing Price, that brave and lovely spirit, with his frank, young face, his charming manner, and his smile like sunshine—a sunshine which, alas! was soon to disappear, as the voice of Farley was to be silenced, in the lurid smoke, amid the tragic roar of the fast-coming conflict.

Pardon me, reader, if I linger as before among these good companions—if I dwell for a moment on the days spent at "Camp Pelham," as at "Camp No-Camp." As I go back to those times, again the blood-red battle-flag floats proudly in the dazzling sunshine—again I hear the ready laughter, or the sonorous voice of Stuart, as he sings at his work—again the eyes of Farley, Price, and that brave spirit Fontaine, doomed like his comrades, shine upon me and bring back the hours that are gone!

But at that time all was joy and merriment. Our old friend Sweeny played his banjo gayly, making the woods of Culpepper ring, like the pine thickets of Spottsylvania, with the "Old Gray Hoss," and "Sweet Evelina," and "Jine the Cavalry;" Hagan went and came, with huge hand smoothing down his mighty beard; and more than once came bevies of fair girls from the adjoining village, to sit beneath the trees, and laugh with the General, while the red flag rippled, the bugle sounded gayly amid the trees, and Sweeny's banjo filled the air with its uproar.

It was the poetry of war—this life of the cavalry on the outpost—the romance of the hard career of arms. I have forgotten many hot conflicts, but remember still those gay days at Camp Pelham, in the spring of 1863.

Stuart was never in higher spirits, or in finer trim for fighting, and more than ever I admired this immense war-machine, this hair-trigger organization, ready day or night to meet the enemy. It was all the same to him whether the day was brilliant or drenched in storms—he was what the Duke of Wellington called a "two o'clock in the morning man," ready at any moment, and his spirits defied the atmosphere. That gayety and superb *abandon* never left him—war seemed mirth, and he delivered his great blows with laughter. One morning during my visit, a report came that a regiment of Federal cavalry had crossed near Kelly's Ford, and Stuart hastened down in person. As he approached the point, an officer came to meet him at a gallop, and announced that they were drawn up on the Southern bank.

"Well," was his answer, with a laugh, as he rode on, "tell Colonel Beale to lick into 'em, and jam 'em right over the river!"*

Did you ever hear of a more unromantic or "undignified" order, reader? It is just what Stuart said, and the order was obeyed—the enemy forced to hastily recross.

One word more in regard to this great cavalier. There were many silly persons who believed him frivolous, because he laughed easily, and said that he neglected his work to dance and amuse himself with young ladies. Most stupid and unjust of calumnies! A more enormous capacity for work, a more sleepless vigilance than Stuart's cannot be imagined. His daily toil was incredible, his concentration of every faculty upon the task of guarding the line of the Rappahannock unrelaxing. Not an avenue of approach was left unguarded—scarce a picket was unvisited by him. Day and night he was ready.

That he thought profoundly, and saw deep into the future, a single opinion, expressed to me about this time, will show.

"The next battle will be fought near Chancellorsville."†

Such was the far-seeing prediction of a man who was thought by many to be frivolous. His daring was proverbial, his name illustrious; but, besides the troops who fought under and idolized him, there were only two men in the Southern army who ap-

---

* His words   † His words.

preciated him—regarding him as a born master of the art of war.

But the names of these two men were Lee and Jackson.

CXII.

THE SUMMONS.

GOING back to my narrative, from which the recollection of this illustrious figure has diverted me, I proceed to record an event enforcing very powerfully the good philosophy of hoping against hope.

I was about to get into the saddle and set out on my return to Fredericksburg, when Stuart, who had bidden me good-by, suddenly said :

" By the by, there is a letter for you, Surry." And he looked among the papers on his desk.

" A letter, General."

" Yes, brought last night by one of my scouts from over the river. Oh, here it is !—and in the most delicate female handwriting !"

I extended my hand, recognized May Beverley's writing in the address, and tore open the letter.

It contained not a syllable ! But there amid the scented folds of the paper was a flower like that which she had taken from her bosom at our parting, with that promise ! This talisman meant " Come !" and I think the blood must have rushed to my face as I gazed upon it, for suddenly I heard a tremendous burst of laughter from the General.

" Good !" was his exclamation, when he could catch his breath ; " here's our sly Surry getting letters full of flowers from young ladies, and blushing like a girl to boot ! Look, Farley !"

And I found myself the centre of laughing faces, all enjoying my confusion.

" Pshaw !" my dear General, I said, as I put the letter in my

pocket, and uttered a sort of laugh which redoubled the mirth;
"you are eternally suspecting something. I am sure you have
got a dozen letters like this in your desk there."

"Do you think so? But they never made me blush as yours
does you!"

"That arises from the fact that I rarely receive such; this is
merely from—a friend."

"Well! as my scout goes back to-morrow, you can send an
acknowledgment before you set out for Fredericksburg, to your
—friend."

"Thank you, General, I don't propose to set out for Fredericksburg this morning."

"Indeed!"

"I have changed my mind. Will you lend me a courier and a
slip of paper?"

"Certainly—what for?"

"I am going to telegraph to General Jackson for two or three
days' leave of absence—to make a scout beyond the Rappahannock."

At this statement Stuart threw himself upon his couch, and
uttered a laugh which threw his previous performances completely in the shade.

There are moments, however, when it is difficult to tease people: when a man is radiant with happiness, the hardest of all
tasks is to annoy or irritate him. So, having sent off my dispatch to the Court-House, whence it would be transmitted to
General Jackson by telegraph, I submitted myself to the tender
mercies of Stuart, with whom teasing was a passion.

A few hours afterward I received from General Jackson the
leave asked for, and, on the same evening, set out for The
Oaks.

Shall I add another illustration of the fun-loving propensities
of Stuart? As I mounted my horse, he called in a jovial voice
for Sweeny; that worthy at once appeared, with his banjo
under his arm; and, as I rode down the hill, the voice of the
great musician—under the prompting of Stuart—was heard
singing to the banjo:

"Sweet Evelina, dear Evelina!
My love for thee
Ne'er shall grow cold!"

The General's laughter rang out—the staff joined in, and then the triumphant banjo began an uproarious chorus, above which rose the words:

"If you get there before I do,
Oh, tell her I'm a-coming too!"

"Good-by, Surry!" came in the jovial and sonorous voice of Stuart; "success to you, my boy! and long may you wave!"

CXIII.

THE DEFIANCE.

I HAD scarcely ridden half a mile when I heard a voice behind me, and, looking back, descried Captain Farley coming on at a gallop.

He soon caught up with me, his eyes beaming, his white teeth shining under his delicate mustache, his dark plume floating in the breeze of the April evening.

"I couldn't bear the idea of your making your little scout alone," he said, laughing, in his subdued way, "and, if I don't intrude, I will go with you."

"Delighted to have you, Farley," was my reply. "I hate to ride all day with no company but my own thoughts."

"Well, then I'll go with you, and we will try and scare up some game beyond the river."

I laughed, and said:

"I have two objections to that."

"What are they?" he asked with a smile.

"In the first place, I shall be glad if they don't scare up me; and, secondly, my present scout is of the most peaceful character. To-day, I have no sort of enmity toward anybody, not even Yankees."

Farley laughed the low laugh of the scout.

"I understand!" he said; "but perhaps we will come across the bluebirds nevertheless, and bag some."

With these words he rode on by my side, a gallant figure in his dark surtout, his brace of pistols, his drooping hat with its black feather.

We conversed of a hundred things, which do not concern this narrative, and I need not record the conversation. It was our determination to cross the river that night opposite the little village of Orleans; but, unfortunately, Farley's horse cast a shoe, and began to limp so badly that it was absolutely necessary to seek for a blacksmith.

While we were looking out for some friendly citizen to direct us, a light glimmered in front, on the banks of the river—for the night had descended—and suddenly we came upon a cavalry camp, and were halted by a picket.

"Whose regiment?" I asked.

"Colonel Mordaunt's," was the reply.

"Good. Where are the Colonel's quarters?"

We were directed to a tent in a thicket near; and, stretched upon his cloak beside a camp-fire, we found Mordaunt. Opposite lay Achmed, the Moor, wrapped from head to foot, and sound asleep.

Mordaunt greeted us with military hospitality, and he and Farley were evidently old friends. The result of a consultation on the subject of horse-shoes was rather discouraging, as there was no shop near, and we finally accepted Mordaunt's invitation to spend the night. One of his men, he said, should have the lame horse ready shod by daylight.

For an hour we talked upon indifferent subjects. Then, declaring that he was sleepy, Farley wrapped himself in his blankets, lay down by the fire, and his long breathing soon indicated that he was asleep.

Mordaunt did not seem inclined to follow his example. He remained stretched upon his cloak, his head resting on his hand, and gazed thoughtfully into the fire.

As he thus lay at full length before me, his face and form lit up by the ruddy flame, he was the picture of a cavalry-man.

His athletic figure, hardened by the active life of the outpost, was all muscle; his swarthy cheek bore the traces of sun and wind and storm; his dark eyes had that proud and penetrating expression which may be read in those of the mountain eagle. I looked with a species of curious interest upon this powerful physique, this broad brow, and firm l'p fringed with its raven mustache; it was strength in repose, there before me in the person of this silent man, who had found in the shock of battle apparently the solace for that grievous wound inflicted upon his heart.

But, as I looked more attentively at my silent companion, I thought I could discern the traces of unwonted emotion—suppressed by that iron resolution of his, but not so completely as to be wholly undiscoverable upon his swarthy features. There was a strange light in the dark, proud eye—a slight color on the cheek, which evidently proceeded from some hidden emotion. Mordaunt was plainly thinking of something which absorbed him strangely.

This revery at last became so profound that he seemed to lose the consciousness even of my presence—and, muttering some words which I did not hear, he drew from his bosom a paper, small and delicate, such as women write upon, and read it attentively. As he did so, a deep flush came to his bronze face—his eyes flashed—then, as he raised his head, his glance met mine, fixed curiously upon him, and he suddenly seemed to realize my presence. The paper was coolly replaced in his bosom; he drew a long breath; the color faded from his cheek—he was bronze again.

At the same moment the sound of hoofs was heard on the bank of the river, and the quick " Halt!" of the picket.

" Friends!" was the reply; and, as Mordaunt rose, the sounds drew nearer, and then ceased.

The rattle of a sabre indicated that some one was dismounting; and at the next moment the figure of Harry Saltoun appeared in the circle of fire-light.

The young man advanced with measured tread, saluted with cold ceremony, and said in tones of freezing formality:

"I have come to make my report, sir."

"Make it, sir," was Mordaunt's reply in a voice as cold and formal as that of the young Lieutenant.

The latter then proceeded, in the same voice of stiff official coldness, to make his report.

As I listened, I more than once asked myself if this rigid military automaton with the repelling manner, the measured and gloomy accents, the pale face and set lips which seemed at times to suppress with difficulty the temptation to break into a sneer— I asked myself if this could possibly be the gay and joyous Harry Saltoun, so full of life and buoyancy and laughter—this statue, which growled in speaking, and menaced him whom it addressed, with those lowering eyes!

But Mordaunt exhibited no evidence of surprise, and listened in grave silence.

When the report was finished, he said simply :

"It is well, sir. Return with your company to the regiment, and send your prisoners under guard to corps head-quarters."

The young Lieutenant made a stiff salute, but did not move.

"I believe you heard my order," added Mordaunt in a freezing tone.

"I did, sir," was the cold reply, "and it will be promptly obeyed. I only solicit, before leaving Colonel Mordaunt, his reply to a single question."

"Ask it," returned Mordaunt.

"When will he accord to me that meeting which he has promised me ?"

The words were uttered without a change in the accents of the young man—it is impossible to imagine any thing more cold and proud than his address.

To my extreme astonishment, Mordaunt did not give way to the least displeasure at this singular demand. I expected an outburst, but none came.

"In four days from this time," he said, "I will give you an answer to that question. Be content—what is deferred is not lost. You have my word, sir."

The young man saluted—retired without uttering a word—and I was again left alone with Mordaunt.

"This scene appears rather extraordinary to you, Surry, beyond any doubt," Mordaunt now said to me, with perfect coolness; "but I am a perfect Quixote in some matters, my dear friend, and I am acting like the Knight of La Mancha on the present occasion. One of my curious fancies is, that a gentleman has no right to refuse satisfaction to his opponent because that opponent is beneath him in rank. On such occasions the question of rank disappears—it is gentleman against gentleman, and this boy is such."

"And you are going to fight Harry Saltoun!" I exclaimed.

"Exactly," was the cool reply of Mordaunt.

"On what quarrel, in the name of heaven!"

"Really, I can't tell you, Surry," was the careless answer, "I can only inform you how it came about. Do you care to listen —it will not detain you ten minutes."

"Let me hear all about it, Mordaunt."

"Well, our young friend here, Lieutenant Saltoun, has some grievance against me which he obstinately refuses to divulge. I observed the traces of bitter hostility in his manner toward me, for the first time, a few days since. In making a report to me, his bearing was so offensive that I called his attention to it, and he replied in a manner which made it necessary to arrest him. In twenty-four hours I sent an order for his release, believing that some momentary fit of passion had betrayed him into this grave military offence—but no sooner had he been relieved from arrest than he came to me and said, with the eyes of a wild animal about to spring: 'You are the colonel of this regiment, and I am a subordinate—but you are a gentleman also, and I am your equal. If you choose to arrest and punish me for insubordination, do so! If you hold yourself accountable to me, in spite of the stars upon your collar, meet me and give me the satisfaction which one gentleman owes another whom he has outraged.' Those were the exact words, Surry," continued Mordaunt coolly, "and you can understand that they touched my weak point—probed it to the quick. At once I resolved to meet this defiance as man to man—no one shall insult me with impunity—but, first, it seemed to me only reasonable that I should ascertain the grounds of this fancied outrage. Can you conceive that my young Orlando Furioso positively refusea to tell me ?"

"And you are going to engage in a mortal encounter upon grounds as irrational as a hot-blooded young man's simple invitation !" I exclaimed.

A grim smile came to Mordaunt's face.

"You have not heard all," he said. " What I have told you is only the preface."

" Go on—what more ?"

" The most entertaining part is to come. When my young thunderbolt informs me that the ground of his dissatisfaction with me must remain undivulged, I reply, 'That is somewhat extraordinary, Lieutenant Saltoun: you are determined to cut my throat and yet you refuse to afford me the poor satisfaction of knowing why you are resolved to perform that operation.' Whereupon comes his reply, as hot as fire, and in these words: 'Do you call yourself a gentleman?' 'I have been considered such,' I answer, with the tiger in me suddenly becoming developed. 'I ask,' he said, coolly, yes, with a voice as steady as a rock, Surry, 'I ask, because people say that there is something in your history which won't bear investigation—a mystery which may involve an infamy!' Those were his very words, my dear Surry," said Mordaunt, with a flash of the eye which boded no good; "and, not content with this, he uttered the name of a woman whom I formerly knew! Well, when Lieutenant Saltoun did me the honor to thus allude to my private history—to suggest that positive infamy might lie *perdu* beneath the mystery of my past life, and to pronounce a name which recalls to me only bitter recollections—the words which he uttered accomplished his object as effectually as a blow could have done it! I went up to him where he was standing—we were quite alone— and said to him, 'Lieutenant Saltoun, you have formed a tolerably just estimate of your man, and know how to strike. You shall answer for those words with your life. But don't arouse me further now. Go and cool off, sir, and then come back, and we will arrange the terms of the meeting you desire.' He bowed when I said that, and went away—and the meeting to-night is the first which has since taken place between us."

I could find no words of comment upon this most unfortunate affair; and, after a moment's silence, Mordaunt added:

"I would have arranged the whole affair to-night—it would require a few moments only—but I have just received a letter which makes my absence for about four days absolutely necessary. I have thus been obliged to defer this meeting with our fiery friend—on my return he shall have his satisfaction."

CXIV.

MORDAUNT'S MOTIVE.

THE deep voice ceased, and I remained buried in reflection. What possible origin could there be for this bitter hatred of Harry Saltoun's for Mordaunt—the man he loved and admired the most in all the world? I remembered that declaration of the youth in the preceding autumn, that he would rather have "Well done," from the lips of Mordaunt, than another grade— and now all this love and admiration was changed into hate so bitter that blood must flow to satisfy it!

All at once the thought of Violet Grafton came to my mind, and, turning to Mordaunt, I said:

"Have you visited Elm Cottage recently?"

"More than once this spring," was his reply; "my scouting expeditions regularly take me in that direction."

"And you have seen Violet Grafton?"

"Certainly," returned Mordaunt, coolly; "she is living still with her friends there."

"And Lieutenant Saltoun has doubtless called too?"

"Yes, I was assured that he had frequently staid with them when out scouting."

"Then the whole affair is plain, Mordaunt," I exclaimed, " and the mystery is explained at once."

"What can you mean?"

"I mean," was my reply, "that Harry Saltoun is in love with Miss Grafton, and has taken up the fancy, from some cause, that you have injured him with the woman whom he loves!"

Mordaunt's brows contracted, and for some moments he preserved a moody silence, gazing steadily into the fire.

"That is a curious idea," he muttered; "strange that it never occurred to me. And yet"—

"Remember, Mordaunt, how the young man blushed when speaking of the young lady who had nursed him when he was wounded—remember how her very name flushed his cheek; then think of these regular visits which he has since paid to Elm Cottage; lastly, think of the gossip and tittle-tattle which such affairs occasion, and the great probability that you have been represented to him as his rival."

"As his rival!—I!" said Mordaunt; "what an idea! An old bear like myself the rival of this glittering young gallant!"

And, under the cool accents of the speaker, I thought I discerned the traces of bitter irony and melancholy.

"You are right, Surry," he added, in a calmer tone; "something of that description is probably mixed up with the affair. But what imaginable grounds for such a supposition can my conduct have afforded?"

"Simply that you are Violet Grafton's friend. That is enough in the eyes of the old women, male and female, to make you her suitor."

"Yes, they are a plague—these male and female women; they thus make trouble, and will not understand what I have done."

"What you have done?"

"Shall I tell you, Surry? I am not of that class who are fond of making confidences—but I wish to retain your good opinion, friend. Well, do you remember my meeting with Miss Grafton at Manassas?"

"Certainly."

"I rode with her that night, and she did me a great service: I need not refer to this point further, except to say that through her instrumentality I gained possession of a packet of papers, more valuable to me than all the wealth of two hemispheres!"

Mordaunt paused, his face flushed ; then he went on as calmly as before :

" I had long avoided women, having, doubtless, little to attract them, but it was impossible to converse with Miss Grafton without discovering that she possessed a very exquisite character—a soul all goodness and sincerity. My cold manner did not seem to repel her—she resolutely refused to observe my bearishness, and when we reached Elm Cottage we were almost friends. Not to weary you out, however, I will come to the point of all this talk directly: something like an honest friendship sprang up between this young lady and myself; and during the autumn of the year 1861, while I was stationed near Fairfax, I visited her more than once. The consequence of further acquaintance was a stronger regard for her than ever; and, as I think that human friendship should be 'clothed in act,' as says the great English poet, I sought for some means of benefiting Miss Grafton. She was an orphan, without a permanent home, simply the guest of the hospitable lady of Elm Cottage ; and I thought that the best service I could do her was to throw in her way some true-hearted youth who would love her, and, marrying her, give her a home and that happiness which she deserved."

" I understand!" I said ; "you found the opportunity in August last year, when we were going to Manassas."

" Yes. I had long observed young Saltoun—known him in camp and seen him on the field—and I know that a braver and truer boy never drew sabre. You see I am magnanimous," said Mordaunt with a melancholy curl of his proud lip ; " I praise my *rival* and my personal enemy ! Well, this is no less true of him, if he does intend to make me fight ! I have never known that boy to do a mean action, to shrink before peril, or to act in any manner not becoming a gentleman. At this very moment, when I think he hates me bitterly, I would trust him with my life ; I would sleep by his side, though he were awake with a poniard in his hand! Well, I am prosing. I knew that this young man was the son of a rich Marylander, and in every manner calculated to make Violet Grafton happy as her husband. He was wounded that night, could go no further; then I conceived the project of sending him to be nursed by Miss Grafton at Elm Cottage, and gave him a note to her, commending him to her good keeping.

"I tell you this to clear myself of all reproach, friend. I did it from a good motive—none was ever better. And now you can understand the falsehood and malignity in representing me as young Saltoun's rival. Nor rival only! I am plotting secretly against him with Miss Grafton; injuring his character; 'outraging' him, he says, and my blood must flow for it!"

Mordaunt ceased, the prey apparently of bitter and conflicting emotions.

"My life is an unhappy one, Surry," he added, gazing into the fire. "I thought that upon my tombstone might have been at least written, with the applause of all, 'He lost all but honor'— yet, it seems, that this, too, is to be denied me. I am to be regarded as a hypocrite and base traducer of the youth I called my friend!"

There was something so proud and melancholy in the accents of the speaker, that his words went to the heart. More than ever I admired the great wealth of magnanimity and sincerity which lay concealed beneath the cold exterior of this man. Did he love Violet Grafton all that time, too? It was more than probable, as his fits of moody abstraction during the progress of his narrative seemed to indicate. And she—did she love him yet? Or had the youthful attractions of Harry Saltoun driven the dark eyes of Mordaunt from her heart? I knew not; but I thought I saw that she was the sole oasis in the desert of Mordaunt's life—the sunshine under which his cold and arid heart had burst, for a moment, into bloom, soon to have its leaves strewn to the winds by the remorseless hand of that fatality which seemed to make his life unhappy, and thus hold him to his hard, stern work with the sabre.

"I have listened to your explanation, Mordaunt," I now said, "and, more than ever, recognize you in what you have done. It is truly a monstrous thing that this boy should take up such a fancy as he seems to have done, and force you, by his insults, to meet him in mortal combat. There must be an explanation before you fight. But what was that other insult which he uttered —that 'name of a woman'—not Miss Grafton's—which was a part of his offence?"

Mordaunt's brow was suddenly overshadowed.

"I will tell you another time," he said, moodily. "Enough for to-night."

"As you will," I replied; "but, meanwhile, in all this fancied rivalry and conflict between you and Saltoun, what becomes of that boy, who loves the young lady too?"

And I pointed to the prostrate form of Achmed, wrapped from head to foot in his long, Moorish *burnous*, on the opposite side of the camp-fire.

Mordaunt gazed at the sleeping form in melancholy silence for a moment, and then said:

"True—that is something I had not thought of. Yes! the boy loves her passionately now; he worships the very ground she walks upon—and there is no hope for him. This handsome youth—this stranger, you see, Surry, with his laughing eyes, quite overcomes us all—the moody Mordaunt, and the Moor, too! Well, Achmed and I will return, doubtless, after the fighting here is done—if we live to see it end—and spend the rest of our days in the desert."

"You are going back to Europe?"

"If I live—a somewhat uncertain condition. And why not, my dear Surry? I have no family, no ties here in my native country. I am a mere estray—a leaf on the current. Why should I not drift with the stream, and let it carry me where it will? Here I am hemmed in by convention. If I try to make a young girl happy, at some cost, too, to myself—but we'll not speak of that—the gossips buzz, and misrepresent my motives, and even blacken my fair fame as a gentleman. It is not so yonder. In the desert all these voices die away. On my horse, with my arms by my side, I am free—perfectly free! I can go

18

where I will, act as I fancy—and the wind which sweeps the sand never whispers what I say or do—for the eye and ear of the Almighty alone sees and hears in the desert. Yes, I think I will go back with Achmed—the East is the land of lands, and we will bury there all the trouble we have felt in this."

Mordaunt rose as he spoke, and looked out into the night. The dark, proud eyes, full of fire and melancholy, seemed endeavoring to plunge into the darkness. Then he banished, by an obvious effort, the bitter thoughts which absorbed him, and said, with his habitual calmness:

"You are going over the river in the morning, Surry?"

"Yes, to see some friends."

"Well, I have a little journey to make, too? If you return this way in four days from this time, I hope you will stop again and see me."

"I will certainly do so."

"Well, now let us get to sleep, my guest. You must be tired after riding so far."

And Mordaunt made room for me on his cloak.

In half an hour I was sound asleep.

CXV.

SHOWING THAT, THOUGH YOU KNOW WHEN YOU SET OUT, YOU DON'T KNOW WHEN YOU WILL ARRIVE

WHEN I awoke, soon after daylight, on the next morning, Mordaunt was nowhere to be seen; but Achmed was standing by the fire.

As soon as I opened my eyes, he saluted me with his calm and graceful courtesy, and, with a movement of his hand, called my attention to a small camp-chest, upon the lid of which smoked an appetizing breakfast. Mordaunt had, as usual, fulfilled all the rites of hospitality; and Farley was soon speaking in high commendation of the bitterly strong coffee. Hurrying through with the meal, we got into the saddle—Farley's horse having been fitted with four excellent new shoes—and then we set forward.

Crossing the river at Hinson's Ford, we pushed on through the morning sunlight, and, passing Orleans, found ourselves among the hills of Fauquier, at that time constantly scoured by scouting parties of Federal cavalry, bent on the capture of the formidable Mosby.

"Now, Surry," said my smiling companion, "we had better agree upon a programme. I have come across the river upon a little private scout, as head-quarters began to grow tedious—and I intend to pitch into the first Yankees I see, and have some sport. I don't expect you, however, to do so," and his low laughter followed, "for, from the General's jokes, I suppose you are making a scout of a different sort, and are not in the humor for any other."

"That is a good long speech, and I have heard you without interruption, Farley," I said, laughing. "Suppose, however, we wait until the moment comes, and leave circumstances to decide."

"Good! that is right. I think it will come pretty soon, as that man in Orleans said a party of Yankee cavalry were scouting around near Barbee's."

Before we had reached Barbee's the truth of this report was shown in a manner quite unmistakable. I was riding carelessly along, when the low voice of Farley uttered the single word "Hist!" and he immediately spurred his horse into a clump of pine bushes on the side of the road.

I followed, and we had no sooner ensconced ourselves behind the screen of verdant tassels, than the tramp of hoofs was heard beyond a hill in front, and, in a few moments, a squadron of Federal cavalry appeared upon the crest, and steadily approached.

"This is just what I want," whispered Farley, bending over his horse's mane, and looking through the second-growth pines "I am going to fire upon them, Surry, and run them off."

The thing seemed to me impossible—ignorant as I was of the science of scouting—and I said so; but Farley laughed, in his low, confidential voice, and replied.

"I know this sort of game better than you do, old fellow!
I'll bet that they run at the first fire!"

"From two men?"

"So you are going to take a hand."

"Certainly, if you open the ball. I'll never desert a comrade,
Farley; but I wouldn't be captured for worlds at the present
moment—and I am getting awfully demoralized!"

"You are right! Just take that path yonder, and you will be
out of reach in ten minutes."

"And leave you?"

"Oh, I am used to them! and they know me so well that a
price is set on me."

"If you are going to fire on them, now is the time."

"You stay?"

"Certainly."

"Good! then we'll open with a real volley—ten barrels, one
after the other; and, if they crowd us, we will fall back in good
order to the woods yonder!"

Farley's face glowed as he spoke; his eyes danced; his lips
were smiling. He was evidently in his element, and enjoyed the
prospect of the approaching collision.

It soon came. The squadron of blue-coats was now within
fifty yards, marching in columns of twos, preceded by their
captain, an officer with a bushy black beard; and, cocking his
pistol, Farley levelled it over his horse's head, whispering:

"Wait till I give the word!" He waited until the column
was directly opposite, and then, shouting "Fire!" aimed at the
officer, and discharged barrel after barrel of his revolver. I
imitated him, and the sudden attack threw the column into the
wildest confusion. Taken completely by surprise, and wholly
ignorant of the force opposed to them, they scattered upon every
side; and it was several moments before the voice of the commanding officer could be heard.

He shouted to them in a violent rage to rally, exclaiming,
"Charge the bushes! Fire on them! Charge!" and under
his rapid orders, the disordered column rallied, and poured a hot
fire into the bushes where we were standing.

" That won't hurt us!" said Farley, as the bullets whistled around. " I've got a loaded revolver yet, and we'll try them again!"

As he spoke he drew the fresh weapon, and fired barrel after barrel into the cavalry.

They had, however, discovered by this time the insignificant number of their assailants, and, instead of charging straight into the bushes, the officer in command ordered the party to deploy and surround the spot, so as to cut off our retreat.

" Now comes the tug," said Farley in a low voice. " We'll fall back, so as to face them as they come."

And he galloped toward the wood he had pointed out to me, I following.

Before we had gone fifty steps a rapid fire was opened upon us from the rear ; and suddenly I saw Farley's horse go down. At the same instant a ball inflicted a mortal wound on the animal I was riding, and I found myself dismounted.

By this time the enemy had closed in upon us, and the air was full of bullets hissing around us, and cutting the twigs from the pines, or whacking against the trunks. Farley was shot three times through the hat, and *eight* times through the skirts and collar of his coat.* I was untouched—but in ten minutes we were surrounded and captured.

It is impossible to describe the rage of the Federal commander when he discovered that he had been thus audaciously attacked by two men only. He stormed and swore at us in a manner so frightful that I thought he was about to issue an order for our instant execution by the bullets of the men. Fortunately, however, he became somewhat calmer, in consequence of this proceeding—the safety valve of oaths had " let off the steam"—and, wrathfully assuring us that we would be treated as bushwhackers and guerrillas, he directed us to march in rear of the column, now again in line.

This we accordingly did, but our slow pace impeded the advance, and we were finally mounted upon two horses, taken from citizens—to which our saddles had been transferred.

* Historical. The whole is a real adventure of Farley's.

As we thus went on, under guard, I had ample opportunity to realize to the fullest extent my ill fortune. Was ever any thing more unlucky? An hour before, I had been within a few miles of the woman whom I loved more than all the world beside—I was going to hear that musical voice once more, bask again in that golden smile—and now I was a prisoner, in the hands of the enemy, doomed probably to languish for months to come in some Northern prison! At that moment, I think I would have embraced any opportunity, although involving almost certain death, to make my escape; but the thing was quite impossible—on every side the scowling blue-coats, with cocked carbines, made the attempt desperate.

CXVI.

THE WOES OF BASKERVILLE.

This was the rather depressing condition of affairs, when, late in the afternoon, the column, which had made a circuit through the country, reached the neighborhood of the Pignut Mountain, west of New Baltimore.

Here they halted in front of a large and elegant mansion, and, accompanied by a portion of his command, the captain of the troop strode up to the door.

; What was my astonishment to see no less a personage than Baskerville appear upon the threshold in irreproachable citizen's costume, of black and white, without a particle of gray anywhere about him—Baskerville, smiling, winning, the soul of hospitality and politeness to his visitors.

This warm reception, however, did not seem to make much impression upon the Federal officer.

" Your name is Baskerville?" he said roughly.

" Yes, Captain," was the smiling reply.

" You are an officer in the Rebel army?"

" Oh, by no means," came from the other, whose manner

became still more suave. "I had at one time a temporary connection, in a subordinate capacity, with the Rebel forces, Captain"—he said *rebel!*—"but it was merely as an amateur! The fact is, I could never enter cordially into the treasonable schemes of the rebels. I am a good Union man upon principle, Captain."

"Then you have no objection to taking the oath?" asked the black-bearded worthy.

"Oh, not the least! I will take it with pleasure!"

"Are you a Virginian, Mr. Baskerville?" said the Federal officer coolly.

"Yes, Captain."

"Born in this State?"

"Yes, Sir."

"Your family and friends are all here?"

"All, Captain!"

"And some are in the service?"

"Nearly all of them."

"Then, in my opinion, Mr. Baskerville," returned the growling worthy, "you are a sneak, and I won't trust your oath! I have no opinion of you 'Union men,' who profess so much loyalty, and can't find it in your hearts to go either with us or with your native State—all because you want to save your crops and horses and bacon, and *don't* want to risk your valuable skins! There may be some of your class who are obliged to take the oath against their feelings, from family circumstances—but I don't consider you one of them. I won't trust you, sir! We want fresh horses!"

And, making a sign to the troops:

"Gut the whole place!" said black-beard.

It is astonishing how rapidly and completely this order was obeyed. The troops scattered, and soon reappeared leading about a dozen beautiful horses.

Baskerville's face was the image of despair, as he saw his splendid horses thus about to be carried off; but his troubles were not ended.

"Now I want something to eat for myself and my command,"

said the Captain. "Be quick with it. I am going to move on!"

Baskerville obeyed this imperative order, and we could see through the window a costly mahogany table covered with dishes, containing hams, cold beef, bread—every edible; and the dishes were flanked by decanters of wine and brandy.

A motley rout threw themselves upon these viands; demolished the meats, guzzled the liquids, and smash after smash of china told the story of Baskerville's woes.

"They are playing the very devil in there!" said Farley, laughing. "It is rather hard treatment for a good Union man!"

"Where are the prisoners?" I now heard the Captain shouting; "bring them in with the second relay!"

And we were conducted into the house. The scene was striking. In a magnificent apartment, with rich carpet, elegant furniture, and many pictures on the walls, the Federal officer and his myrmidons were seated around the great dining-table covered with the refuse of their repast—"broken meats," half demolished loaves, and empty decanters. All were devouring the substance of Baskerville with greedy mouths, the long ride having whetted every appetite; and over this wild crew presided the Federal captain, laughing, jesting, with a flushed face, which betrayed an intimate acquaintance with Baskerville's liquids.

"Bring in the prisoners, d—n 'em," said the Captain, "and let 'em eat. We don't charge extra at this hotel."

And we were conducted to the table.

Suddenly my eye met Baskerville's, and I shall never forget his expression. Was it wrath, shame, confusion—what? I know not, but it was not agreeable. I could not despise this man more thoroughly than before, but I pitied him.

He did not utter a word during the whole scene, and soon he was rid of his unwelcome guests. We rose—neither Farley nor myself had touched a mouthful.

"Fall in there!" shouted the Captain, walking unsteadily to the door. "I am going to move on."

Then, turning to Baskerville, he said, with drunken gravity:

"Let me advise you, my friend, to go into the Rebel army again. I won't have the pleasure of dining with you then; but no matter: you will be in a more creditable place than at home!"

With these words, the speaker strode out, mounted unsteadily .nto the saddle: and the column again began to move.

Looking back, I saw Baskerville standing in his front door, with a face full of rage and anguish—and I have never seen him since.

The squadron moved now toward New Baltimore, but night all at once descended, and the Captain, who rode on with a rather sleepy air, ordered a halt.

In a few minutes the men had broken ranks, dismounted, and picketed their horses to the trees of the secluded glade in which the column halted; and it was evidently their intention to spend the night there.

An hour afterward the men had cooked and eaten their rations; the pickets were established, and the weary cavalry-men wrapped themselves in their blankets, and began to snore.

Farley and myself had been placed under guard, but not otherwise confined; and now lay side by side for warmth, under a large oak, near a smouldering camp-fire.

Within three paces of us a dismounted cavalry-man walked to and fro, with measured tread—his carbine in his hand—prepared to obey to the letter, apparently, the order which he had received, to kill us instantly if we made any attempt to escape.

CXVII.

I MAKE THE ACQUAINTANCE OF A FAMOUS CHARACTER.

IF you will turn, my dear reader, to the famous history which has immortalized the name of Cervantes, you will find that the characters of the drama, whenever they fall into difficulties, are accustomed to bewail, in pathetic paragraphs, their unhappy

18*

situation, and thus arouse, as far as possible, the interest and sympathy of the reader.

Had I the genius of the great soldier and historian, I might here dwell on the most unfortunate chance which had thus dashed all my hopes, and extinguished, "at one fell swoop," all my rosy dreams of soon meeting May Beverley again. But alas! I am only a humdrum ex-lieutenant-colonel and A. A. G., drawing the outline of my life—not a dramatic writer at all. Thus I am compelled to request the kind reader to place himself, if possible, in my situation, and to imagine how I felt. I proceed to relate what ensued.

Farley and myself lay down, but, in spite of the long ride we had taken, from dawn to dark, felt no disposition to sleep. My companion at first remained so quiet that I thought he had fallen asleep; but a few moments afterward I found that this was far from being the fact. Turning sluggishly over, as a man does when changing his position during slumber, his lips were placed close to my ear; and, in a whisper so low that the low singing of the fire almost drowned it, he said:

"Don't go to sleep—I am going to escape. Don't answer—listen!"

The guard turned and approached; then, with measured step, receded. He had evidently heard nothing.

"As soon as every thing is perfectly quiet," Farley whispered, in the same low tone, "I will give the signal and spring upon the sentinel. He will resist, and his carbine will go off in the struggle—but I will wrench it from him; it is a repeating rifle, and then let the first man who attempts to stop me look to himself!"

I turned over, as Farley had done, and whispered:

"Give the signal when you are ready."

He moved his head slightly, and then lay perfectly still, with his eyes closed; but I could see that he was looking from under the lids at the sentinel.

One by one all the noises of the camp subsided—the horses ceased stamping—nothing was heard but the measured tramp of the sentinel.

As he turned his back in one of his rounds, Farley rose suddenly on his elbow and looked about him.

Not a movement among the recumbent figures greeted this manœuvre, and, as the guard turned, Farley was again apparently sound asleep.

Once more the sentinel approached; remained a moment stationary beside the fire, warming his hands; then he turned his back once more on his round.

No sooner had he done so than Farley exclaimed "Now?" and rose to his feet. With a single bound he was on the sentinel, and clutched his weapon, while I caught him by the throat.

What we had anticipated took place. The carbine went off in the struggle, and in an instant the camp was aroused, and we were completely surrounded. Farley darted into the shadow of the trees—I followed—and we commenced running; but everywhere foes started up in our path, and the moment had evidently come when we must surrender or die.

At that instant there suddenly resounded in our very ears the sharp crack of pistols; and, before I could realize the source from which the sound issued, a wild cheer rang through the wood, and a party of cavalry-men, in gray coats, rushed into the camp, trampling over the Federal soldiers, who were seen running to arms.

What followed did not occupy ten minutes. A scattering and aimless fire came from the Federal cavalry-men, half of whom were only partly awake; and then, at the ringing order of a slender individual, mounted on an iron-gray mare, they threw down their arms, and offered no further resistance.

The slender personage leaped from horseback, by a camp-fire burning beneath an oak, and, as he did so, I had a full view of him. He was a man apparently about thirty years of age, of middle height—thin, lithe, vigorous, and as active in all his movements as a wildcat. His face was entirely beardless; his hair light; his lips thin, and wreathed with a satirical smile, which showed his brilliant teeth; his eyes gray, sparkling, and eternally roving from side to side. This personage wore a plain gray suit, and a brown hat with a golden cord; his only arms were two pistols in his loose swaying belt of black leather, clasped over a red sash.

"Well!" he said, in brief, quick accents, as the prisoners wer⌐ ranged in a line by the fire, "how many horses?"

A sergeant touched his hat, and said:

"I think there are about sixty, Major."

"How many prisoners?"

The sergeant counted rapidly.

"Fifty-five, Major."

"Where is the commanding officer?"

"Here I am," growled our friend, the black-bearded; "whom am I to surrender to?"

"To Mosby," was the reply of the slender individual, with a keen glance of his gray eye.

At the name of the formidable partisan, every prisoner turned quickly and fixed his eyes upon the speaker. Mosby was evidently their bugbear, and they expected, doubtless, to be shot without ceremony, so persistent had the Northern journals been in representing the partisan as a ruthless bandit.

Mosby's thin lips curled satirically. The evidence of interest betrayed by his prisoners seemed to amuse him.

"See that these men are entirely disarmed," he said to a lieutenant, "and then have their horses brought. I am going back."

As he spoke, his eye fell upon myself and Farley.

"Who are these?"

Farley advanced, and, with a smile, held out his hand.

"You don't recognize your old friends, Mosby?"

"Farley! Is it possible?"

"Yes, and this is Colonel Surry, of General Jackson's staff."

I had the honor of being stared at by the prisoners when the name of Jackson was thus uttered, as Mosby had been.

He saw it, and laughed.

"Glad to recapture you, Colonel," he said; "as we ride back, I will get you to tell me your adventures. Captain Mountjoy!"

An officer of erect and military carriage, calm expression, and dark eyes, penetrating but sad, advanced at this summons, and made the military salute.

"Captain, see that the prisoners are mounted and—but you are as white as a sheet, Mountjoy!"

"Only a little scratch, Major!" was the reply of the officer with a smile, but as he spoke his form tottered.

Mosby caught him as he was about to fall, and turned with a savage glare in his eyes toward the Federal captain, at whom he shook his clinched hand.

"This man is worth the whole of you!" he growled, "and if he dies!"—

Mountjoy opened his eyes, and rose erect.

"It was only a little faintness, Major," he said, smiling. "What order did you give?"

"Richards will see to it, Mountjoy," was the reply. "Can you ride?"

"Without difficulty, Major."

And he turned toward his horse.

"Hold on a minute," said Mosby; and, untying the red sash around his waist, he bound up the bleeding arm of Captain Mountjoy, and then assisted him to mount.

"That is one of my best and bravest officers," he said, as he came back. "But we are losing time. I am going to move back, gentlemen; take such horses as you like."

In ten minutes the column of cavalry was moving on, with the mounted prisoners. Farley and myself rode in front with Mosby.

He laughed at the narrative of our mishaps, and I found him a most agreeable companion. Perfectly simple and unassuming in appearance and address, Mosby was not in the least like the ferocious bandit which the correspondents of Northern journals had represented him to be; and it was hard, indeed, to realize that the laughing personage, with the beardless face and careless carriage, riding at my side, was the redoubtable chief of partisans—the terror of the Federal invaders.

"My dear Major," I said, laughing, as we rode on, "you are not at all like the bloody wild-boar of the Yankee newspapers.

I think I could meet you in the woods of 'Mosby's Confederacy here, without the least fear of having my throat cut or my pocket picked by you or your gentry—things which our blue-coated friends yonder evidently expected."

Mosby laughed.

"That is easily explained," he replied. "When my men capture or destroy an army train, the Federal generals are crippled —they get into trouble at head-quarters—and they defend themselves by making me out a robber and bushwhacker, instead of a chief of partisans."

"That is probably the origin of the whole thing."

"Undoubtedly. Why am I a 'bushwhacker,' Colonel? I am regularly commissioned by the Confederate States War Department as major of cavalry; I command regularly enrolled troops; and I carry on open warfare, under the Confederate flag, and wearing Confederate gray. Why am I a robber? It is a part of my duty to capture all the war material of the enemy I can, including greenbacks, which are used in Loudoun and other border counties by our Government, and the want of which makes the unpaid Federal soldiers dissatisfied. I have captured millions, and I am poorer to-day than when I entered the service."

"Which certainly pays badly."

"It pays me well in other ways. No man ever had better friends than I have in this region and the Valley, both of which I have tried to defend. I intend to fight for the possession of the country to the last; and, if the Confederate cause goes under, I will be the last to lower my flag."

"Long may it wave over 'Mosby's Confederacy,' my dear Major! and may you always appear upon the scene at a time as lucky as to-night!"

Thus, in talk about many things, the night passed. At sunrise I parted with the gallant Mosby, and Farley, who decided to remain and go upon another scout with him. The horse I rode was Mosby's parting present to me.

On the same afternoon I came in sight of The Oaks.

CXVIII.

WHICH SOLVES THE WHOLE MYSTERY.

I APPROACHED the old mansion with mingled sensations—a hundred conflicting surmises and emotions.

What was the meaning of that summons from May Beverley? Was her engagement broken off? What could have produced a consummation so devoutly to be wished? Not Baskerville's Union opinions. They were fully known to Colonel Beverley, but had not induced him—fiery as his Southern feeling was—to refuse compliance with his promise. He had regarded his word to Baskerville's father as binding, despite these proclivities of the young man: and thus I was completely at sea for an explanation of my apparent good fortune.

Such was the puzzled frame of mind in which I approached The Oaks; and, as a man condemned to death, but hoping for a pardon, rushes to the prison door to learn his fate, so now the unfortunate Surry, burning with suspense, put spur to his horse, and rapidly ascended the grassy hill, upon whose slopes the fresh spring grass and the first flowers of April were beginning to peep forth.

The eyes of a girl had seen the rapidly approaching figure from the window of her chamber, I afterward knew; and as I entered the wide hall, she stood before me, as bright and beautiful as a vision of the spring.

Before, the beloved form had glided onward by my side like a dream of autumn—some dear illusion of the fading days when the fingers of the wind strip, one by one, the leaves from the trees, the blooms from the rose, the glory from the landscape of the mountains. Now she stood before me—with her violet eyes, her chestnut hair, her form as tall and flexible as the water-flag upon the margin of the Shenandoah. No longer like a dream— no more an illusion; but warm and loving, with the deep, fond blushes, and rosy smiles of a Virginia girl—far better, to my thinking, than the fairest forms of Dreamland!

" You sent for me ?"

" Yes."

"Kiss me first, May !"

Did the old portraits look down laughing, with their curious eyes, at the spectacle of a woman in a man's embrace? I think, sometimes, that these " old people " see the drama of to-day as they saw the tragedy or the comedy of the past ; that they hear the sighs or the laughter, see the smiles and tears—are not dead at all, but ever present with us!

No one but May Beverley had seen me arrive—all the rest were busy somewhere—and, in a moment, we were seated upon the portico, and she was showing me some papers—with a deep flush in her cheeks.

As I am growing old now, my dear reader, and like to " come to business," I proceed to lay before you the contents of these highly interesting documents, without further delay. You will see that they solved all those puzzling questions which I had been asking myself upon the road, in a manner—see the novelists—" as curious as it was unexpected."

Here is Document No. 1, in the handwriting of Baskerville— with all the italics preserved :

" BASKERVILLE VILLA,
"*April* 15*th*, 1863.

" MISS BEVERLEY :

" For some time now it has been plain to me that our engagement is *distasteful* to you, and that you wish to be released from it. Considering the fact that you gave me *ample encouragement*, and never, until you met with *a person whom I need not name*, showed any dissatisfaction at the prospect of becoming *Mrs. Baskerville*, I might be justified in demanding the fulfilment of your engagement. But I do not wish to coerce the action of any young lady, *however my feelings may be involved*, and I scorn to take advantage of a compact made *in good faith* by my late father and myself. I therefore *release you from your engagement*.

" Hoping that this will meet your approbation, I request that you will return *the bracelets*—turquoise—the *diamond ring*, and a *breast-pin*. In concluding, Miss Beverley, I am willing to bury *all animosity*, and to be your friend—and if I can serve you in any way, it will give me pleasure. I hear that the Union soldiers have carried off all your servants, which must be *a heavy blow* at this time—and as I know personally the officer commanding in this district, I may be able to get some of them back for you. If agreeable to you, I will make the attempt—but *not otherwise*.

"Please reply by the bearer, who has orders to wait until he gets an answer.

"I am

"Yours respectfully,

"FREDERICK BASKERVILLE."

There is Document No. 1. Here is Document No. 2—of which the young lady had kept a copy:

"THE OAKS,

"*April 16th,* 1863.

"MR. BASKERVILLE:

"I received your note. Thank you, sir! If I could have induced you to write that letter by kneeling before you, I should have knelt to you.

"I am not angry at the terms in which you address me, or the accusations you bring against me. But do you think it was manly, sir, to charge me with bad faith, and with 'encouraging' you? I was almost a child when I formed that engagement—years ago I repented of it, but you would not consent to have it terminated. You availed yourself of my father's point of honor in adhering to his word, and you cruelly refused to release me from a contract which had become absolutely hateful to me, until—shall I tell you when, sir? You had determined to force me into this revolting marriage, and remained so determined until—my property was gone. You compel me to tell you that, sir—I know your motive as perfectly as though you had expressed it in the plainest language.

"Your information in regard to the loss of the servants left me by my uncle, is entirely correct—not one is left—no, not one, sir. I am absolutely penniless; and papa, I believe, owes a great deal of money—so my portion of The Oaks will be absolutely nothing. You see, sir, I am poor—very poor.

"Do not give yourself any trouble about the servants, I beg. I am afraid the institution of slavery is unscriptural, and nothing could induce me to receive them back. Poor things! they did not know the trouble they caused me, and, doubtless, cannot understand my heartfelt joy at seeing them safely under the protection of your friend, the 'officer commanding in this district.'

"I return the bracelets, ring, and breast-pin, with some other little articles, which are your property.

"You are willing, you say, to bury all animosity, and remain my friend. Yes, a thousand times, sir! Thank you for your letter, Mr. Baskerville! I am your friend for life.

"MAY BEVERLEY."

There is the "correspondence," my dear reader. What is your opinion of it? For my part, I would rather charge three tiers of breastworks, manned with infantry, and flanked by cannon, than receive such a letter from a woman like May Beverley. The serene contempt of the production, and the entire absence of any thing like anger, would have made me rage, I think.

After reading Baskerville's letter, I had an ardent desire to go and cut that gentleman's throat. After reading the young lady's reply, I experienced a good Samaritan inclination to seek him and bind up his wounds. Why should I force a quarrel on this best of friends, who had so completely fulfilled my most cherished wishes? Why should I find fault with those little hasty expressions which escaped him in the heat of composition? Under other circumstances, I might have vented all my spleen upon the *affiancé* of Miss Beverley; but Baskerville no longer figured in that character—another individual occupied that relation to the young lady—and that individual was too well satisfied to mar the festive scene with blood.

I had just finished reading the young lady's letter when a step behind me suddenly attracted my attention, and Colonel Beverley, erect and smiling, issued forth and pressed my hand.

" I see May has shown you that very discreditable and insulting letter, and her reply," said the old gentleman smiling.

" Yes, Colonel ; and I hope it changes every thing ?"

" Completely !"

And the old cavalier laughed heartily, as a young lady, with a face all smiles and blushes, flitted through the door, and disappeared.

CXIX.

IN WHICH MAY BEVERLEY PASSES AWAY FROM THIS HISTORY.

HAVE you never observed the fact, my dear reader, that there is nothing more stupid, in books or life, than happiness ? It is the trials and sufferings of the characters which interest us in romances—the dear, delightful misfortunes of our friends which render real life so cheerful and attractive.

Observe, as a proof of this latter statement, that as long as Lieutenant-Colonel Surry pined away for love of a young lady who was affianced to another, his ill fortune excited the sympathy of his friends; and the young ladies everywhere, who knew his sad predicament, exclaimed with tender voices, " What a pity !" But just as soon as every cloud passed away, and he became engaged to Miss Beverley with the full consent of her parents, all this sympathy disappeared : no more interest was taken in him, and his friends gushed out in tender commiseration of the woes of some other ill-starred lover.

So it would be with those unseen friends who will read their humble servant's memoirs. They would not be amused by the picture of tranquil happiness : the blushes and murmured words would appear insipid—the stream, no longer broken into silver ripples by the obstacles in its bed, would glide on tamely and without a particle of " the picturesque."

So to horse! and back across the border! Other events await us. Hooker is about to advance—Stuart is in the saddle—and perhaps, as we cross the Rappahannock again, we shall know where Mordaunt has been journeying.

Yet ere you shake your bridle-rein, and bid farewell to the good old Oaks, gentle reader—see, standing there in the April sunshine, that slender form, as graceful as a flower of the gay spring forest: that girl with the waving chestnut hair, which the sunlight turns to gold; the violet eyes of a blue as deep and tender as the glad sky overhead; with the lips half parted and as rosy as carnations; the cheeks full of blushes, the bosom heaving—look at May Beverley, and tell me whether this little Virginian flower was not worth the trouble which it cost a friend of yours to place her in his bosom?

I thought so then, when she was the little blossom of " The Oaks "—I think so still, when she is the queenly rose of " Eagle's Nest," with a young flower-garden blooming all around her.

CXX.

DIABOLISM.

I REACHED the banks of the Rappahannock without further accident, and, crossing near Orleans, came in sight of Mordaunt's camp again, as the sun was sinking behind the Blue Ridge.

Near the tent stood Mordaunt's powerful black horse, covered with the foam of a hard journey, and as I dismounted, Mordaunt issued forth, his uniform soiled with dust, apparently from the same cause.

But I did not look at his uniform. The proud face riveted my regard. Never have I seen upon human countenance a more resplendent expression. Mordaunt's eyes were fairly radiant, and his swarthy face glowed with passionate joy. There was no mistaking that look. Here was a man whom some great good fortune had made for the moment entirely happy.

"Good!" I exclaimed with a laugh. " Here you are, with the
air of a general who has just whipped the enemy, and cut him
to pieces, after a desperate struggle."

"Ah?" was his reply with a dazzling look; "do you think so,
Surry? Am I then so gay?"

" You are positively radiant, my dear Mordaunt! Come, tell
me all about it!"

"About what, my dear, fanciful Surry? Upon my word,
you make me think, as I look at you, that one of my old maxims
is more than ever true."

"What is that?"

"That when we are happy ourselves, the whole world seems
to be as fortunate, and every face beams with smiles!"

"Pshaw! Mordaunt—stop all that talk. Your eyes are really
dazzling—you laugh at any and every thing. Explain! explain!"

"I really have not time, Surry, even if I had any thing to tell
you."

"What! are the enemy advancing?"

"No, but I have an engagement. I am waiting for a gentleman who has an appointment with me in half an hour from this
time."

"Ah? Can you mean—?"

"Our young friend Harry Saltoun? Certainly: you remember
my promise to him?"

"And this evening he is to meet you here?"

"Precisely—and hold! yonder he comes, before the hour!"

As Mordaunt spoke, the young officer was seen approaching
from the river; and very soon he had reached the spot where
we stood. Dismounting, he approached with a firm tread, and
saluted in turn both Mordaunt and myself. His air was grave,
stern, and resolute—his face gloomy and rigid—his eyes steady
and determined, but without menace. He seemed to feel that he
was near the accomplishment of his object, and was resolved to
go through with the work before him, without passion or any
thing like a scene.

Mordaunt greeted him with grave and stately courtesy, bowing low in reply to his salute. As they thus stood facing each

other—the youth with his slender figure, his elegant proportions, his classic face, and collected look—the elder with his tall
and athletic form, his face of bronze, and his proud and noble
glance—I thought that they were the most magnificent types
of youth and middle age which I had ever met with.

"You are punctual, Lieutenant Saltoun," said Mordaunt, in the
same grave and courteous tone; "it is the politeness of kings
and of gentlemen."

Saltoun bowed, but said nothing.

"Will you come into my tent, sir?" continued Mordaunt.
"Before making the arrangements which we have agreed upon,
I wish to say a very few words to you."

The young man's face exhibited a gloomy surprise at these
words, but he simply inclined his head, and, entering the tent,
sat down.

"Will you do me the favor to be present at this interview,
Colonel Surry?" said Mordaunt, as I made a step toward my
horse; "I particularly desire it, and request Lieutenant Saltoun
to agree to my wishes."

The young man slightly inclined his head—his eyes had never
relaxed their steady and gloomy expression—and I followed
Mordaunt into the tent.

He unbuckled his belt and laid his arms upon a desk, then
leaning his head upon his hand, he said, after a brief silence, and
in the same grave tone, as he gazed with a strange expression at
the youth:

"Before proceeding to make arrangements for the meeting
which you wish, Lieutenant Saltoun, I beg that you will listen to
a few words which it becomes my duty to pronounce. I am thirty-
eight years old, sir, and thus many years your senior. I have
seen in my time the death of many human beings, here and in
the old world. I do not like blood, and especially shrink from
myself shedding it: hence, I am compelled, sir, by my conscience—even though I offend against every rule of the code—to
ask that you will give me, as gentleman to gentleman, some
explanation of your motive in thus defying me to mortal combat."

He paused, and for an instant silence reigned. Then, in a cold and gloomy voice, just touched with a sneer :

"Is it necessary to explain what an insult means, Colonel Mordaunt?" said the young man. "I choose to offer you a defiance, and you choose to accept it, as I expected. Therefore, you fight!"

"I must fight!" exclaimed Mordaunt. "And for a word, a groundless taunt, I must kill you!"

"Are you about to break your word, sir?" exclaimed the young man with a fiery glance. "Beware, sir!"

"Do not threaten me, Lieutenant Saltoun," was the grave reply; "you ought to know that my nerves are steady, my repugnance to this meeting not the result of timidity, but of genuine and conscientious feeling. If you think me unreasonable, let our friend—the friend of both—Colonel Surry—decide. I will abide by his decision."

Mordaunt turned to me as he spoke, and finding myself thus appealed to, I said :

"There cannot be a moment's doubt of the propriety of Colonel Mordaunt's request, Lieutenant Saltoun, and I certainly think that you are bound to afford him this simple satisfaction before you meet him, for the ease of his conscience. I declare to you, upon my word as a man of honor, and the friend equally of both, that I regard your compliance as imperative *in foro conscientiæ.*"

These words seemed to produce the desired effect upon the young man. His face flushed—a flash darted from his eyes.

"Be it so," he said. "I fight because Colonel Mordaunt has outraged me—yes! has struck me mortally—to the very heart!"

And something almost like a groan tore its way through the set teeth of the youth.

"I fight because he has made me wretched by his baseness—has offered me a mortal insult by his action toward those I love! —because but for him I would not be here with a broken heart, an aimless life, a future dark and miserable!"

Not a muscle of Mordaunt's face had moved, but his eyes, as he gazed at the flushed face of the young man, were resplendent.

" You mean that I have thwarted you in your affection for Miss Grafton!" he exclaimed.

"I have not the remotest reference to Miss Grafton!" was the stern reply; "there is something more beneath this black affair than the love of a girl! There is more than rivalry, Colonel Mordaunt—there is infamy!"

And with eyes which fairly blazed, the young man drew from his bosom a paper which his moist hand clutched with savage earnestness.

" You demand an explanation of my grounds of quarrel!" he said; "you ask why I hate you, and intend to drive a bullet or a sword's point through your heart! Well, you shall know, sir! You shall not die in ignorance. Read! read, sir! There is the the record of your infamy!"

And, trembling with passion, the young man held out the paper, which shook in his stern grasp.

Mordaunt took it from his hand, leaned back in his chair, and with not a trace of anger, but an air of unmistakable astonishment, perused its contents.

As he did so, I could see a blush come to his cheek, his eyes flashed—then grew calm again. When he had finished reading the paper, he turned back, evidently examining the handwriting, then he handed it to me, murmuring:

"He is not dead, then!"

The paper was in these words, written in a bold and vigorous hand.

"VIRGINIA, *April 15th*, 1863.

ˣ LIEUTENANT SALTOUN:

" An unknown friend, who takes an interest in you, writes these lines, to put you in possession of facts which it is proper you should be acquainted with.

" Listen, sir. You think yourself the son of Mr. Henry Saltoun, of Maryland. You are wrong. Your father and mother are both dead—the victims of one man's ceaseless hatred and persecution—following them to the very brink of the grave. Would you know the facts in connection with them, and with **your life**? Listen:—Your father, whose name you shall one day know, lived near Frederick City, and was married, when he reached the age of twenty-one, to a young lady whom he had met in Virginia. Before he made her acquaintance she had been pleased with a young Mr. Mordaunt—now Colonel Mordaunt, of the Confederate cavalry—who loved her, but had never avowed his love. Under these circumstances, your mother, then a girl of only seventeen, was justified in accepting the addresses of your father, and did accept them. They became engaged—were married—and the happy pair went to live in Maryland.

"Now mark what followed. Your mother had broken no faith with young Mordaunt—not a word of love had ever passed between them—but no sooner had her marriage taken place, than Mordaunt conceived a violent hatred against your mother and father, charging the former with deception, and the latter, who was merely a common acquaintance, with treachery. Possibly you know Colonel Mordaunt personally—if so, you can understand that, in a man of his violence of passion, hatred was soon succeeded by the desire for vengeance. Not only did that thirst possess him, but his whole life soon became absorbed in plans to wreak his hatred upon the happy couple. To achieve this end, it was necessary to use caution and stratagem; and very soon everybody was speaking of the touching friendship which existed between Mordaunt and your father. Mordaunt paid long visits to his successful rival; played with him for large sums; lent him money whenever he wished it; and was apparently the best friend of the family.

"In a year or two, the consequence of this fatal intimacy was seen. Your father was a gentleman of the noblest character, and the most liberal disposition—indeed generous to a fault, and utterly careless in money matters. Mordaunt never asked for the sums which he had won at cards—he took a note for the amount, without looking at it, apparently. He never demanded repayment of money lent—but he had your father's bonds. All went on as smoothly as possible, not a cloud obscured the friendship of the two intimates—but, one morning about two years after the marriage, Mordaunt asked for payment of the sums due him. A frightful mass of debt at once stared your father in the

19

face, and he saw that he was utterly ruined if Mordaunt forced payment—but there could surely be no fear of that! His good friend Mordaunt loved him too well to thus ruin him—it was impossible that he could have the heart to press his claims—so he laughed and asked for time. Mordaunt grew stormy, and in a moment the smiling friend was a Shylock. ' Pay what you owe me!' was his unchanging reply; and even when the poor, sick wife—soon to be your mother, sir—went to Mordaunt and besought him to have mercy, he refused. The person who related these events declared that she knelt to him, and that he spurned her; but this is probably exaggerated.

" Mordaunt's vengeance was now about to be sated. He acted promptly. Your father's estate was sold to satisfy a deed of trust upon it, which his enemy held—other claims swept away every vestige of property which the young married pair owned —and in the freezing winter of 1844, your father and mother were driven fom their home, and forced to seek refuge in an almost roofless cabin in the neighborhood. Here they lived with an old negress who had followed their fortunes, and now slaved for them—but soon her care was not necessary. Your mother, broken-hearted, and worn to a shadow by distress or exposure to the chill blasts of winter, died in giving you birth ; and three weeks afterward your father followed her. Before his death, however, he had an interview with Mordaunt, who now occupied the house in which he had formerly been a guest. Your father went to beg—yes, to beg—a small pittance for his infant son—yourself; went in rags, and humbly, to his former friend; and that friend rose from his wine, to go out to the door where the beggar—your father—stood, and refuse, insult, and strike him. When your father sprang at him, and caught him by the throat, it was the *negroes*, Mordaunt's servants, who hurled him through the door, and slammed it in his face!

" I have nearly done, sir. The rest may be soon told. Your father followed your mother, and you were left a helpless infant, with no friend but the old negress—with no friend, but with an enemy. More than one threat of Mordaunt against you reached the old woman's ears, and fearing the power and cunning of this implacable man, the old negress one night took you in her arms, walked many miles to the house of a rich and childless gentleman, whose excellent wife was known through all the country for her kindness; and at daylight you were deposited at the door of Mr. Saltoun, and duly discovered by his wife.

"You know the rest. You were brought up as his son, but must have suspected more than once, from some careless speech or reference, that you were not such. When the war broke out, you entered the Southern army—and a strange fate has thrown you with the murderer of your father and mother.

"Such is your real history. You may say that this statement comes from an unknown source, and may be false throughout. Be it so. The writer of these lines must rest under that imputation, for to sign his name here would subject him to the vengeance of the man whom he has exposed. He may even know my handwriting, and I would beg you not to let it meet his eye. One proof of the truth of what I utter I can afford you. Go to Colonel Mordaunt—look him in the eyes—say, '*What has become of Frances Carleton?*'—and mark his face as you speak. Anger brings a flush to the cheek—the consciousness of infamy, a deep pallor. If he turns pale at that name, you can form your own opinion.

"Mordaunt is the murderer of your father and your mother— the name of the former you shall one day know. I reveal this mystery, because you ought to know it, to guide your action after the war. At present you cannot fight Colonel Mordaunt— he is your superior, and would punish you for even proposing such a thing, unless you offer him such an insult as will arouse his hot blood.

"Of that you must be the judge. Be cool, be cautious, but remember your wrongs!

"A Friend."

There was the letter. I dropped it in a maze of wonder. What hand could have framed this web of incredible ingenuity —of diabolical falsehood? The father of lies himself might have envied the consummate skill of the secret enemy who concocted this story—and, after reading the contents of the paper, I remained in a state of stuyid astonishment until I was aroused by the voice of Mordaunt.

"You see I did not kill him, after all, Surry," he said; "and this letter is his great blow in return for my lunge that night!"

"Fenwick!" I exclaimed; "did Fenwick write that?"

"Yes—it is in his handwriting, and here is the date: not a fortnight ago. But we will speak of this hereafter. I have something else to occupy me now."

And, as he spoke, Mordaunt looked at young Harry Saltoun, who remained cold, silent, and threatening.

That glance sent a thrill to my very heart, and filled me with vague and trembling emotion. What did it mean? I knew not, but I knew that it was as rapid and dazzling as the lightning itself.

CXXI.

WHERE MORDAUNT HAD BEEN, AND THE RESULT OF HIS JOURNEY.

When Mordaunt spoke, his voice was grave and measured; but his eyes had still that proud and brilliant light in them—not for an instant did it change.

"Lieutenant Saltoun," he said, looking steadily into the cold and haughty face of the young man, " in this whole affair you are the victim of a plot so deep and infamous, that no one but a devil, in human shape, could have framed it. Your lip curls with incredulity, and some scorn, I think—you naturally suspect that I am going to defend myself, to offer explanations, to acknowledge some things, palliate others, and endeavor to escape the wrath of the son by smoothing over my treatment of the father. Not at all, sir—I have not the least intention of doing any thing of the sort. That father, you believe in, never had any existence. I was never, in my life, near Frederick City, until I went there at the head of my regiment, last year; your

mother's name *was* Frances Carleton—and that is the single
grain of truth in this mass of devilish falsehood!"

Mordaunt's voice sounded deep, sonorous, and rejoiceful, even
when he uttered the name of the woman he had loved. There
was not a trace in it now of the gloom and reluctance which
he had once shown in pronouncing it. Some greater emotion
seemed to have swallowed up every other.

"Give me your attention, Lieutenant Saltoun, and you, my
friend," he added, turning to me. "I design nothing less than
to narrate my whole life—to conceal absolutely nothing. Then,
when I have done, you shall sit in judgment upon me and my
career—decide in what light I deserve to be regarded—and
then, if I am to fight in this quarrel, why, *pardieu!* I will fight!
Yes, to the death!"

What was it that made Mordaunt's face, his voice, the very
carriage of his person, as he spoke, so animated, proud almost
resplendent? I looked and listened with a sort of wonder.

"Of every word I utter, you shall have the proofs!" he continued. "Oh! be not afraid! You shall have a legal affidavit,
if that is necessary, for every incident! Listen, then. and do
not interrupt me, until I have finished my relation!"

Then, without appearing to observe the astounded looks of
Saltoun, or my fixed regard, Mordaunt deliberately—with
scarcely a change in his voice—related what I had heard from
the lips of Fenwick, on that night in the Wilderness. From the
journal of the poor, betrayed wife, he had learned almost every
thing—he had guessed the rest.

For more than two hours the deep voice resounded—the narrator continued speaking without interruption. During this time,
Harry Saltoun's face turned red, then pale, at times—he had
leaned forward unconsciously with a fixed light in his eyes—
some vague conception seemed rising slowly like a midnight
moon upon the darkness of his mind.

Mordaunt continued his narrative to the very end, described
the burial of his wife on that night at the Stone House near
Manassas, and then spoke of his bitter years of exile, spent in
looking for his enemy, and then in fighting among the Arabs, to

drown his wretchedness. Then a few words were given to his
life in Virginia, his career in the army, and his meetings with
Fenwick, whose authorship of the letter was distinctly shown.
Lastly, he returned, all at once, to the subject of his wife's ab-
duction, and said, in a low voice, which trembled slightly, in
spite of every effort which he made to control it :

"The son, born thus, during my absence, did not die—he is
alive, and well, at this moment!"

"Alive!" I exclaimed; "and have you discovered him?"

"Wait, Surry! Let me proceed, step by step. It is a train
of events I am narrating—hear me without interruption. This
time I am going to give you written vouchers for my statements
—here they are."

And Mordaunt drew from his breast a leather case, from which
he took and placed before him, on his desk, two or three
papers.

"The first I shall show you," he continued, "is a note from
Miss Grafton, received a few days since. Read it aloud, Surry."

I took the paper—it was the same which Mordaunt had drawn
from his breast as we conversed beside the camp-fire, four days
before—and read the following words:

"ELM COTTAGE,
"April 19th.

"COLONEL MORDAUNT:

"I have just had a visit from <i>Mrs. Parkins</i>, and she has made
some astonishing disclosures, of the deepest importance to you.
She declares that you have a son now living, and, before she left
me, I succeeded in discovering that you will be able to learn all
about him by visiting a Mrs. Bates, near Frederick City, Maryland, who is in some way connected with this mysterious affair.
I think that Mrs. Parkins went to Maryland to inquire into this,
with the design of obtaining a reward from you—but she has
now left Elm Cottage, and I do not know where you will find
her.

"You ought to know this without delay—your heart has been
very heavily tried, sir.

"This is sent by one of your men, who staid last night.

"Your friend,

"VIOLET GRAFTON."

"When that paper reached me," said Mordaunt, speaking with an effort, "I procured four days' leave of absence, and went to Maryland."

"You found the woman!" I exclaimed.

"Yes, and here is the result."

He handed me, as he spoke, another paper, which I grasped with eagerness, and read rapidly.

It was an affidavit from Mary Bates, of Frederick County, Maryland, that, some time in the winter of 1844, a gentleman named Fenwick had stopped at her house, with a lady whose name the affiant did not discover—that the lady had, on the night of her arrival, given birth to a son—been attacked by puerperal fever—lost her reason—and was removed, the affiant always understood and believed, to a private asylum, by her companion, Fenwick. The son was taken by Fenwick, a week after his birth, as affiant afterward discovered, to the house of a gentleman some miles off, and left at his door, with nothing to identify the child's parentage, unless there was some private mark upon a watch which had belonged to the lady, and was placed around his neck by her, in a lucid interval, when she recognized her child. This watch had been left upon the person of the infant, affiant knew, and was still in his possession, unless Fenwick removed it after taking the child away.

The gentleman at whose door the infant was thus left, affiant stated, was named Saltoun——

I dropped the paper, and looked at Harry Saltoun. He was as pale as death, and trembled in every limb. By a mechanical movement, he drew from his breast the watch which I had brought from Maryland. Mordaunt seized it, and touched a spring in the handle—the case flew open, and in a private compartment I saw an exquisite miniature of Mordaunt—younger and fresher-looking, but a wonderful likeness still—under which was cut in the golden surface, the words: "*For my own Frances.*"

Mordaunt pointed to it—his cheeks flushed, his eyes sparkling—and said, in a voice of inexpressible tenderness :
"That is the likeness of your father, Harry—this watch his
wedding present to your mother!"

As he spoke, Mordaunt opened his arms, and the young man
fell sobbing on his breast.

CXXII.

BOOTS AND SADDLES

By noon on the ensuing day I was again at "Camp Pelham."
I hope that the reader approves of the summary style of
narrative—the convenient elision of all those scenes which are
either too dull or too full of emotion to admit of description.
What writer is equal to the task of painting the meeting
between a father and the son who has been lost to him for nearly twenty years—who dare intrude upon that sacred mystery of
parental love, melting the soul of iron, convulsing the face of
bronze, and bringing tears to those fiery eyes that scarcely ever
wept before?

Nor have we time to pause at every scene—for we are living
over again an epoch crowded with vicissitudes, adventures,
emotions, treading on each other's heels. In the days of peace,
dear youthful reader, you hang around Inamorita, and lay siege
to her in form. But in war you press hands, smile—kiss, it may
be—then to horse, and she is gone! In peace, you follow your
friend's body to the church and the cemetery, where you stand
uncovered during the solemn service—in war, you see him fall,
amid the smoke of the conflict, you groan out "Poor fellow!"
but you are carrying an order, and you never see him more. A
sigh, a tear, a last look at his face—he has dropped out of life,
and the drama roars over him—you forget him. War hardens!

Listen! there is the laughter of Stuart as he welcomes us.

We are again at "Camp Pelham," and the red battle-flag flaunts

In the April sunshine as before, couriers come and go with jingling spurs, officers with clanking sabres—that gay cavalry sound —and there is the bugle sounding the "stable call" from the camp near by! As its loud triumphant music rings in the wind, it seems like a summons to the field of battle—where soon it will sound now, for the days of conflict hasten.

Stuart greeted me most cordially, asked with deep interest "how I had left sweet Evelina, dear Evelina?" and then introdued me to a tall and very courteous officer, wearing the uniform of a brigadier-general, who was attentively examining a map of the surrounding region. General William H. F. Lee— for the officer was that gentleman, a son of the commanding general—saluted me with cordial courtesy, and the conversation turned upon a variety of subjects. I don't intend to record it. my dear reader: if I set down every thing that was said in my hearing, during the late war, what a huge volume my memoirs would fill!

There are ten words of General William H. F. Lee, however. which shall here be recorded. I had spoken of the passion some generals seemed to have for fighting upon any and every occasion—with or without object—and General Lee replied:

"Colonel, I would not have the little finger of one of my brave fellows hurt unnecessarily, for all the fame and glory that you could offer me."*

That would make a good epitaph on an officer's tomb—would it not, my dear reader? But I trust that a long time will elapse before the brave and kindly heart which prompted the utterance will need a tomb or an epitaph!

"Well, Surry," said Stuart, "the ball is about to begin. Hooker is going to advance."

"Ah!"

"Yes, look out for your head!"

"He is going toward Chancellorsville this time, is he not, and General Lee will fight there?"

Stuart made no reply.

* His words.

19*

"I merely ask for information," I said, laughing, "as Chancellorsville seems to be the strategic point; is it not, General?"

"You can't prove it by me!" was the gay reply of Stuart, in a phrase which all who knew him will remember his fondness for.

"Well, I see you intend to seal your lips, General. At least you can tell me whether, in case I remain a day longer, I shall have your cavalry as an escort to the Rapidan."

"Ah! you are preparing the public mind for falling back, are you? Wait and see!"

"Well, I accept your invitation, General. Oh! I forgot. Miss Evelina sent her warmest regards to you—provided I did not tell you her name!"

"Out with it! Who is she?"

"Her name is Incognita, and she lives in Dreamland. She sent you this bunch of flowers, with the message that she wishes she was a man, that she might follow your feather!"

Which were exactly the words of Miss May Beverley at our parting.

Stuart laughed, put the flowers in his button-hole, and said:

"A man! I'm much mistaken if you are not very well satisfied with her as she is. Well, give my love to her when you see her, Surry, and tell her I mean to be present at her wedding!"

The promise was carried out; and, although she blushed then, May boasts to-day that she kissed the "flower of cavaliers."

But I anticipate. Stuart had hardly uttered the words above recorded, when a courier came in in haste, and handed him a dispatch. He read it, and, turning to General W. H. F. Lee, said:

"General, get your men in the saddle. Hooker is moving!"

CXXIII.

IN WHICH BOGY, MOONSHINE, AND SNAKEBUG ALL "GO UNDER."

STUART was in the saddle before daylight, and his head-quarters disappeared as if a wind had blown them away. " Camp Pelham " was no more.

As we passed through the Court-House, en route for the Rappahannock, Farley was seen rapidly approaching, and very soon he was in eager, confidential conversation with Stuart. I afterward ascertained that he had penetrated the Federal camps, procured important intelligence, dogged the enemy as they moved, and, crossing the river in the midst of their cavalry column, which he was enabled to do safely by wrapping his oil-cloth closely around him, reached General Stuart in time to put him in possession of most valuable information.

As we approached Stevensburg, a little village to the right of Brandy Station, the long, dark columns of Stuart's main body of cavalry were seen drawn up in line of battle in the fields.

General W. H. F. Lee came to meet us, and his report no longer left any doubt of the situation.

Hooker was moving with the Fifth, Eleventh, and Twelfth Corps of his army, by way of Kelly's Ford, and had already crossed; General Sedgwick,* as prisoners reported, was ordered to cross simultaneously at Fredericksburg with the First, Third, and Sixth Corps, to hold Lee in check there; and General Couch, with the Second Corps, was opposite Banks's Ford, below Chancellorsville, ready to cross and unite with Hooker, as soon as he had passed the Rapidan. As we subsequently ascertained, General Sedgwick had orders, as soon as the main column crossed above, to return to the northern bank of the river at Fredericks-

---

* When I came to this name, in reading the MS. of these memoirs, Colonel Surry said : " I remember a *bon-mot* of General Sedgwick about Stuart, which I have on good authority. One day, when he was speaking of the Southern generals, he said: 'Stuart is the very best cavalry officer that ever was foaled in North America !' "

burg, march up the stream, cross over at United States Ford opposite Chancellorsville, and unite, like Couch, with Hooker.

Then the whole Federal army would be safely across the Rappahannock directly upon General Lee's flank; and that commander must retreat upon Richmond, or fight upon ground selected by his adversary.

At the moment when I went, in company with Stuart, toward the Rappahannock, this design was not developed: but the work before the cavalry was plain enough. Hooker's infantry column was supported by a heavy force of cavalry, under General Stoneman—destined, as we soon found, to strike at the Virginia Central Railroad, near Gordonsville; and to check, if possible, this dangerous movement, was a main part of Stuart's task. The remainder was to hang upon the front and flanks of the infantry, harass their march, and impede, in every manner, their advance, until General Lee was ready to meet them upon his own ground.

Such is a brief and rapid *résumé* of the situation. From the generalization of the historian, I now descend to that description of scenes and incidents which is the province of the memoir writer.

Stuart took command of his column and advanced toward Kelly's Ford, where Hooker had already crossed.

As the sun rose, we could see from a hill the dense masses of Federal infantry crowding the banks of the river—their heavy parks of artillery ready to move—and their glittering cavalry drawn up in line of battle. It seemed a veritable invasion of Attila. The task of breaking to pieces that mighty war-machine, bristling with cannon, bayonets, and sabres, appeared almost hopeless. Soon it began to move, to the resounding music of the magnificent bands; and, above the hum of the multitude and the roll of the drums, rose the clear and ringing blasts of the cavalry bugles.

Did you ever see three army corps in motion, my dear reader? It is a splendid spectacle, and you take a peculiar interest in it when you know that they must be met and driven back at the point of the bayonet!

Again I recognized that day in Stuart, as I had often recognized before, the splendid faculties which indicate the born master of the art of war. An eye that took in at a glance every trait of the ground; a coolness in making his dispositions, so perfect that it resembled apathy; but a recklessness, when once engaged, which many would call rashness—there is what I saw in Stuart. He handled his command as the perfect swordsman grasps his trusty weapon, ready to parry or strike; and as he rode on to the front, the exclamation of the men, "There goes old Stuart, boys! it's all right!" indicated that confidence in his generalship, which many an arduous and trying scene had impressed them with. They saw before them the guiding mind, and saluted it, as I did. In the stout young cavalier, so gay and boyish upon ordinary occasions, these fiery spirits recognized their master; and the cheers which greeted him as he went on to the front, said plainly: "We are ready to live or die with you!"

In fifteen minutes after Stuart's arrival, his advance had struck the enemy; and in front of the dismounted sharpshooters I saw the tall form of Mordaunt, as, riding slowly up and down, amid a storm of bullets, he cheered on the men.

"Look at Mordaunt yonder—always at the front!" said Stuart.

And, humming a song,* he rode down to the line of sharpshooters, which had now become hotly engaged.

"Well, Mordaunt," he said, "how are things going? Can you hold your ground?"

"For half an hour, General—not longer. They are bringing up a heavy force to attack me, and I suppose I shall have to fall back."

"Don't retire until you are forced to. Who commands the sharpshooters yonder on your right?"

"Lieutenant Saltoun.'

* Colonel Surry expressed to me his fear that these descriptions of General Stuart's personal habits would be regarded by many, who did not know their accuracy, as the product of the writer's fancy. I can myself testify, however, to their fidelity, having had the honor of seeing the great cavalier in many battles, and of witnessing his peculiarities.

"He's made of the right stuff. Look! he is advancing!"

In fact, Harry Saltoun, by which name I shall continue to call him, was seen pressing forward in front of his line, amid a hail storm of balls, waving his sabre, and cheering.

Stuart galloped toward him, and was soon at his side.

"How goes it, Saltoun!"

"Glorious, General!" exclaimed the youth; "we are driving 'em!"

As he spoke, a bullet passed through his hat, and he burst into a laugh.

"Look, General!" he exclaimed, "the rascals have spoiled my best hat!—but we've spoiled some of their blue coats!"

A loud hurrah from the sharpshooters resounded as he spoke, and, as the enemy fell back, a column of cavalry, sent by Stuart, swept down, at full gallop, upon their right flank, and threw them into wild disorder.

We galloped to the point, and found the column in possession of a long train of wagons, which had moved by a parallel road toward the front; and the men were now seen striking their teams with their sabres, to force them into a gallop, and so secure the prize. Others, however, had yielded to the passion for plunder, and, as I came opposite a fine wagon, evidently belonging to some general's head-quarters, I saw our old friend, Captain Bogy, dart toward it like a hawk swooping at a fat chicken. At the same moment, Moonshine and Snakebug, couriers at head-quarters, who had scented the plunder, also appeared upon the scene—and, leaping from their horses, plunged, head foremost, into the wagon. Bogy followed, or rather led them, intent on booty; and then, what I saw was this—three bodies, half concealed under the canvas covering, and six legs, kicking in the air, as the bold raiders rapidly rifled the rich contents of the wagon.

Saw plainly—but saw for an instant only! Fast approached the relentless and implacable fate!

Even as Bogy's fat legs kicked the unresisting air; even as Moonshine's hands were seen transferring valuable articles to his capacious pockets, and Snakebug's form was disappearing wholly

In the wagon, at this interesting crisis came the hand of
Destiny !

A line of Federal infantry swept forward at a double-quick ;
a tremendous volley resounded ; and, as I fell back with the
cavalry, I saw rough hands grasp the fat legs of Bogy—sharp
bayonets prick the astonished backs of his co-laborers—with one
fell rush the blue stream roared over them—and Bogy, Moonshine, Snakebug yielded and "went under," never more to reappear in this history.

They were "game to the last"—those brave, heroic spirits !
They stuck to their great principle even in that hour of peril—
their principle that "Yankee wagons" were made to be plun-
dered, and that every good Southerner ought to "go through"
the same, wherever found, or perish in the attempt !

CXXIV.

THE LAST OF FARLEY.

THE hard work had now begun, and, in every portion of the
field, Stuart was obstinately opposing the advance of the enemy
—sending dispatch after dispatch, as the morning wore on, to
General Lee.

The enemy continued to press him back, as their heavy masses
surged forward, but he fell back fighting over every foot of
ground, and inflicting very serious loss upon them.

During the movement, Stuart was everywhere, cheering the
men, holding his line steady, and animating all by his splendid
gayety and courage. In the dazzling blue eyes you could see the
stubborn will that would not bend—the steady flame, which
showed how dangerous this man was when aroused. In front
of his sharpshooters or charging at the head of his column, as
he met, sabre to sabre, the on-coming enemy, Stuart resembled,
to my eyes, the incarnate genius of battle.

But I hasten on in my narrative. I cannot describe the

master-movements of the great commander of the Virginia cavalry—vindicating here, as on many another hard-fought field, the supreme genius for war which lay beneath that laughing eye, that boyish manner.   I do not even think of Stuart now, when I go back to those days—my memory dwells with a lingering and sorrowful glance upon the form of one who there, in that unknown skirmish, gave his young life to his country.

By the side of Stuart, in the thickest of the fight, was Farley; and never have I seen, upon human face, an expression of enjoyment more supreme than on the young South Carolinian's as he rode amid the bullets.   The soft, dark eyes, habitually so mild and gentle, flashed superbly at that moment; the mobile lips were smiling—the whole face glowing and resplendent with the fire of battle.   As he galloped to and fro, pointing out to Stuart every movement of the enemy—the position of their batteries, which now had opened with a heavy fire of shell, and the direction taken by the cavalry, moving on the flank—his eyes flamed, his cheek burned hot.   Never have I seen a more perfect model of a soldier.

"There they come, General!" he exclaimed, as a dark line was seen advancing on the left, in order of battle.   "Oh! if Pelham were only here!"

Suddenly, the fierce rush of a shell filled the air with its unearthly scream—a crash, accompanied by a low cry, succeeded—and Farley's horse was hurled to the ground, a crushed and bleeding mass, which writhed to and fro in a manner frightful to see.

Beside him lay the young man—already dying.

The shell had struck him upon the side of the knee—torn off his leg—and, as we hurried to him, he was gasping in the agonies of death.

"Farley!" exclaimed Stuart, leaping to the ground beside him, "look at me, Farley!"

The eyes, over which the mists of death were creeping, slowly opened—a flash of the old fire shone in them—and, half extending his arms, the dying officer murmured:

" Send me home to my mother !" *

Then his head fell back. He was dead.

Stuart gazed at him for an instant, with a flush upon his face
—muttered something in a low, deep voice—and then, making a
motion to some cavalry-men to take up the body, slowly got into
the saddle again.

As he did so, I heard him murmur :

"Serving on my staff seems fatal !"

More than ever was the truth of this shown afterward :
Price, killed at Chancellorsville ; Fontaine, at Petersburg ;
Hardeman Stuart, Pelham, Turner, and others gone before
them ! And now, Farley had passed away, in the very opening
of the fight !

The leg of the young man, which had been torn off by the
shell—boot and all—was placed beside his body in the ambulance ; † and, that evening, I bent over him, and looked into the
cold, pale face, with thoughts too deep for tears.

Pelham—Farley—who would die next ?

"Farewell !" I could only say, as I got into the saddle to
avoid capture by the advancing enemy, "farewell, brave Farley !
Somewhere yonder, past the sunset and the night, I hope to
meet you, and see your smile again !"

CXXV.

THE ABDUCTION.

A SHOWER of balls hissed around me, as I rode on with the
rear-guard, falling back toward the Rapidan.

I was at the side of Mordaunt, who commanded the rear, and
he slowly retired, in obedience to orders, showing his teeth, as
the enemy pressed him, at every step. Near by was Harry
Saltoun, covered with dust, but " gay and happy " as before.

" A tough business, keeping these fellows back, Surry," said

* His words. † Fact.

Mordaunt, coolly. "I don't like this part of a soldier's work falling back in face of an enemy—nor do the men like it."

"You are right."

"The genius of the South is for attack. We do wrong in not invading."

"And Jackson agrees with you."

"That is a great compliment to my understanding, for your general is 'the foremost man of all this world!'"

The sun was disappearing now, and the enemy proceeded more cautiously. Mordaunt had much less trouble in keeping them back—his command retired slowly in column of fours, ready to meet any assault with the sabre—and we talked.

"I have one or two things to tell you, Surry," Mordaunt now said, as he rode on; "and first, do you know that we made a curious blunder in imagining that there was any love-affair between Harry and Miss Grafton?"

"Ah?—and yet I remember what he said one day to me—how he looked."

"After that fight above Barbee's, was it not?—last November?"

"Yes; when I uttered the name of Miss Grafton he colored to the eyes."

"Are you certain?"

"Perfectly."

"See how treacherous is the memory, Surry! You did not pronounce that name at all, my friend—you spoke of his "nurse," under the impression, doubtless, that, in compliance with my request made in that note when Harry was wounded, Miss Grafton had nursed him."

"Did she not?"

"No—he has told me all, not only what took place at Elm Cottage, but even his conversation with you."

"What took place?"

"He was nursed during his illness by another young friend of ours."

"You mean—?"

"Miss Henrietta Fitzhugh."

"Is it possible! Now I see it all. How very stupid I was to thus jump at my conclusions!"

"Not at all. Your supposition was the most natural in the world, and it was mine also."

"Well! well! So the youngster has gone and fallen in love with that little witch, has he?" I said. "I might have known that he would—she just suits him—and you see, after all, Mordaunt, I was right in declaring in our talk together at your house, that there was very little probability of any love-affair existing between him and Miss Violet."

"I confess that you were right and I was wrong," replied Mordaunt.

"So Harry is a victim to Miss Henrietta's bright eyes; and she—does she love *him?*"

"At least they are engaged to be married," said Mordaunt.

"Good!" I laughed. "Everybody seems about to be married these times! And so that is what you had to tell me, Mordaunt?"

"Only a part."

And the face of the speaker became overshadowed. For some moments he preserved a gloomy silence, then he said:

"What I have now to inform you of, friend, is far less agreeable. Violet Grafton has disappeared from Elm Cottage."

"Disappeared! What do you mean, Mordaunt?" I exclaimed.

"I mean exactly what I have said, Surry. The young lady is gone, and no one can tell whither, except that her route led in the direction of Maryland. There is even something worse. Her companion was the woman Parkins!"

And Mordaunt's face grew cold and threatening as he spoke.

"Listen," he said; "a few words will explain every thing. An hour after you left me on your return from beyond the river, one of my men who had been scouting toward Manassas, and stopped at Elm Cottage on his return, brought a note to me from Mrs. Fitzhugh, inquiring whether I knew any thing which could take Miss Grafton to Maryland, and asking the character of this woman Parkins. The note informed me that the young lady had set out several days before, in the direction of Maryland, travelling in a small vehicle driven by that woman; and, in spite of all Mrs. Fitzhugh could do, she had not been able to extract from Miss Grafton the object of her journey. She maintained complete silence upon every thing connected with it—only declaring that she was compelled by a sense of duty to go."

"Good heavens, Mordaunt!" I said, after listening to this statement; "as sure as fate, that devil Fenwick is at the bottom of this scheme."

"You are right," muttered Mordaunt, and I could see his face grow pale, his eyes flash. "There is no manner of doubt about it. And to think that I was yonder—perhaps within a few miles of her—perhaps passing in front of some den in which she was a prisoner! Surry!" he exclaimed, hoarse with passion, "when I next encounter that man, I swear by all that is sacred, that I will never leave him until I see his black heart's blood gushing out before my eyes, and his face cold in death!"

There was something ferocious in the tone and look of Mordaunt, as he spoke—he breathed heavily—his brow was covered with icy sweat.

"You understand, now," he said more coolly. "The young girl is in his power at last—the victim of some devilish plot—and I am here, chained at my work—I cannot go to her succor. But, if God spares my life, I will be by her side before many days. Then I'll settle my account with that human devil, once for all!"

"And you could do nothing when that news reached you! You could only rage and submit!" I exclaimed.

"No—something is done," was his reply. "I have sent Achmed to Elm Cottage, to strike the trail and follow wherever it leads."

"Achmed! Did you make a good selection?"

"Yes. I see you do not know the boy. He is like a sleuth-hound in pursuit of his adversary; and, if any thing can be discovered, he will discover it. Besides, he has an additional motive besides his love for me—you know what I mean?"

"Yes, his love for the girl."

"That will spur him on, night and day; and, if any trace of her route is left, he will discover it. He set out in an hour after I received the note from Mrs. Fitzhugh, and by this time he is following like a bloodhound on the trail."

Mordaunt's information plunged me into deep and gloomy thought. Once more that cunning and unscrupulous foe had thus risen to the surface, from that ooze of darkness in which he had been concealed so long—again, Fenwick was actively pursuing his love and vengeance, in spite of that sword-thrust, which would have put an end to any other human being—pursuing his aims, too, with a cunning and success which he had never before equalled? Truly, the sleepless enmity of this secret foe was something supernatural almost—partaking of the implacable ire of the mythologic deities! What would be the result? Would the lion yield to the serpent—the eagle be pierced to the heart by the vulture? Would Mordaunt's life be made dark at the moment when the discovery of his son had changed his whole nature, and come like a burst of sunshine to light up his gloomy life?

"It is impossible!" I murmured; "the Almighty would not permit such an enormity!"

An hour afterward I had left Mordaunt to join General Stuart again, having first received a promise from him that, if any intelligence reached him in relation to Miss Grafton, he would send me word. When I pressed his strong hand, the nerves were as firm and collected as ever—but upon his swarthy face I saw the ineradicable traces of love, and approaching vengeance.

Rejoining Stuart on the road to Raccoon Ford, I found him giving orders to General W. H. F. Lee to fall back with his column in the direction of Gordonsville, to protect the Central Railroad from Stoneman's great cavalry raid. How vigorously and successfully this work was accomplished is known to all. With a small and half-armed body of cavalry, mounted upon broken-down horses, Lee met, repulsed, and drove back to the Rapidan the great force of Stoneman. With any thing like an equal body of cavalry, he would have cut off and captured the whole command.

Before midnight I had crossed at Raccoon Ford with Stuart, and we were galloping toward Chancellorsville.

Hooker had passed the Rapidan at Germanna Ford, and was hastening on in the same direction.

CXXVI.

HOOKER IN HIS DEN.

THE events which I have just narrated took place on Wednesday, the 28th of April, and on Thursday morning the advance corps of the Federal column from Kelly's Ford was in line of battle near Chancellorsville.

Sedgwick had also crossed at Fredericksburg, to hold Lee in check there ; and Jackson had drawn up his corps to meet him.

On Thursday evening, however, it became apparent that General Sedgwick's movement was merely a demonstration to cover Hooker's main advance above, and Jackson was ordered to leave one division at Fredericksburg, and with the rest move rapidly toward Chancellorsville.

The order of General Lee directed him to "attack and repulse the enemy." To carry out this order, he had about ten or fifteen thousand men. General Hooker had about one hundred and twenty thousand.

Jackson moved at midnight, on Thursday, toward Chancellorsville, and at daylight reached the Tabernacle Church, within a few miles of the place, where he was joined by a division and two brigades under Anderson, which had fallen back before the enemy from the Rappahannock.

As soon as he received this re-enforcement, and all was ready, Jackson formed line of battle across the plank-road leading through the Wilderness, and steadily advanced to assail the enemy.

Hooker's position was almost impregnable. He had rapidly thrown up heavy works fronting west, south, and east, with the Chancellorsville house behind the centre—and in front of these defences the thickets of this strange country had been cut down, so as to form a bristling abatis, and prevent all approach. Beyond this abatis was the dense, tangled, impassable undergrowth, penetrated only by a few narrow roads—and these avenues were commanded by the grim muzzles of artillery.

Hooker was a veritable tiger in his lair—Lee would attack at his peril—and Jackson soon found that he could not drive his adversary from this formidable stronghold. His advance came speedily in contact with the enemy's works, and a hurricane of shell tore through the ranks, inflicting considerable loss. To advance and charge the works was absolutely impossible—the thickets were impenetrable—and, after carrying on a desultory warfare for some hours, Jackson gave up the attempt to assail Hooker from that quarter, and waited for the arrival of General Lee.

The commanding general arrived at nightfall, having left only a small force to hold the heights of Fredericksburg; and Jackson and himself were speedily in consultation. The condition of affairs was critical. Longstreet's corps was at Suffolk, below Richmond, and Lee had less than thirty-five thousand troops with which to attack an enemy numbering one hundred and fifty thousand, behind impregnable earthworks. And yet that attack must be made—Hooker must be driven from Chancellorsville, or Lee must retreat.

It was under these circumstances that Jackson suggested an attempt to turn, by a swift and secret march, the right flank of the enemy west of Chancellorsville, while another column attacked in front. Colonel Pendleton, the chief of staff, informed me that this suggestion was Jackson's—and it was adopted by General Lee.

On the same night, every preparation was made for the movement.

Amid the weird shades of the Wilderness, the two formidable adversaries were now about to close in a breast-to-breast conflict.

CXXVII.

THE WING OF THE DEATH-ANGEL.

EVERY incident of that period is now engraved upon my memory in characters which no lapse of time can efface. I had reached the most tragic moment of a bloody epoch—the great figure I had followed so long was about to disappear amid the lurid smoke of battle—and, going back in memory to those hours, I recall every event, every word, every glance, to be treasured up forever in the depths of the heart.

It was the night preceding the great flank-march which was to overthrow and break in pieces the strength of Hooker. Jackson weary with his hard day's fighting, and his long and anxious consultation with General Lee, stretched himself flat upon his breast, by a camp-fire, beneath a tree, and seemed about to fall asleep.

Looking at him, I observed that he was lying upon the bare ground, and I called his attention to the fact, telling him that he would certainly take cold.

"I reckon not, Colonel!" was his reply. "I am used to it. I am really tired out, and have left behind my oil-cloth and blankets."

"Then take my cloth and cape, General. I insist that you shall use them."

"No, I really cannot think of such a thing!" was his courteous reply; but I insisted, declaring that my English saddle-cloth was quite sufficient to protect me from the damp of the ground—and at last the General yielded.

He lay down on my "Yankee oil-cloth," and I threw over him my gray cape. Then, spreading my felt saddle-cloth near the fire, a few feet off, I lay down in my turn, and began to reflect —chiefly, I think, upon May Beverley, though at times upon the fate of poor Farley.

During this time, I thought that General Jackson was asleep, and, in moving the logs on the fire to make the blaze brighter.

die so carefully, in order not to awake him. As I was thus
engaged, I heard him say in a tone of unusual softness:
"I am not asleep, Colonel—you do not disturb me."
"I thought you were asleep, General."
"No, I have been thinking—as you seem to have been—and
cannot close my eyes. Something tells me that we will have a
hard struggle to-morrow; and many of my brave fellows are
now sleeping their last sleep, I fear."
He sighed, and gazed thoughtfully into the fire.
"This is a cruel war!" he said, in a low voice. "Why was
it ever forced upon us?—as it assuredly was."
"Our Northern friends differ with you on that point, General."
"Well, we won't discuss it—but I never should have taken
part in it, if I had not regarded it as just and holy in its aims.
God tries the heart, Colonel—I pray that He will try mine, and
yours, and the hearts of all, and, if there be any sin of ignorance or evil intent, may He pardon us!"
"Amen, General."
"We are very poor and weak," continued the speaker; "very
hard and sinful. May he make pure our hearts within us, and
guide us in all life's journey! Without his favor, Colonel, we
are miserable indeed! What is fame, or riches, or glory, without
his favor? You have heard me called eccentric, I doubt not,
Colonel; and do you know, at Lexington the young men called
me 'Fool Tom Jackson.' Yes, 'Fool Tom Jackson,'" he
added, in a soft, musing tone, "and all because I made prayer
and religious exercises my main occupation. I thought I was
right, and acting rationally. It was better, I believed, to secure the favor of my Maker than to receive the plaudits of
men. So I prayed, Colonel, instead of laughing—thinking that
time was short and eternity long. I thought of heavenly things,
and the favor of my God, more than of what I wore, what
I ate, how I walked, or the opinion men had of me—and for this
I was called a fool!"
Again, the low voice paused—the speaker seemed to be reflecting.
"I went into this war," he continued, "because God permits
20

us to defend our native land and protect it from outrage. He had given me animal courage, and so directed my steps that I had learned the art of war at West Point—thus my duty, I thought, was plain. I have done what I could for my dear old native State—if I was wrong, may He forgive me! But I do not believe I erred. It was duty no less than pleasure to fight for the land I loved. And how I have loved it! There is not a foot of Virginia soil that is not dear to me—not a river, a stream, or mountain that is not sacred—and more than all, I have loved the town of Lexington, and the beautiful valley of the Shenandoah! I had reason for that. Never had a man better friends than I have there in the Valley of Virginia— from Winchester, the centre of that warm-hearted, brave and patriotic people, to Lexington, where I hope to rest when I die. The love of these good people is my greatest consolation in life —and I love them much in return. I have fought for the women and children of the Shenandoah Valley, Colonel, and I am ready to die for them!"

"You know how they regard you, General—but I hope you will not soon be called upon to give them so great a proof of your affection as by dying for them."

"Who knows, Colonel? War is uncertain—battle dangerous You or I may fall without an instant's warning."

"That is true, General—all things may happen—even the Confederacy be overthrown. We are now at the year 1863. Who knows but that in 1864, or 1865, the Federal Government will be able to bring such overwhelming numbers into the field, that we shall be obliged to succumb to those numbers, in spite of all our efforts."

"God only knows the future, " was his reply; "and He will direct."

"I trust in his goodness, General, with all my heart, and be-lieve, as you do, that all He does is for the best. But it would be hard to understand His almighty purpose, if our over-throw is permitted. Think what the result will be—the loss of all that precious blood—absolute poverty—perhaps military domination! And worse—far worse than all!—we shall have fought, and bled, and fallen, all for nothing! We shall have inaugurated a Revolution—struggled for years—and all to hear, as we return to our desolate homes, the bitter taunt, " You were fools to have defied the enemy—you have gained nothing and lost all "—

—" But honor!" exclaimed Jackson. "No, Colonel! you are wrong—a thousand times wrong! Suppose we are conquered—suppose the South does fail—I declare to you that, should I live, I will not regret for one instant this struggle ; not the blood, the treasure, the failure—nothing! There may be persons who fight for fame or success—I fight for my principles! I appeal to God for the purity of my motives—and whether I live or die—whether the South falls or conquers—I shall be able to say, ' I did my duty!' "

The earnest words died away, and silence followed.

" Well, I keep you awake, Colonel," said Jackson, after a long pause ; "and I expect we shall need all our energies for the scenes of to-morrow. This country is terrible, and the enemy are in a magnificent position—but we must fight them!"

" The disproportion of force is frightful."

" Yes, truly discouraging ; but God has blessed us, Colonel, upon many similar occasions, and in Him I trust."

" Take care of yourself in the battle, General. You expose yourself terribly."

" Not unnecessarily, I hope, Colonel ; and, if I fall, there are many brave souls to take my place. Let us not fear the enemy, my friend ; he can do us no harm. It is God we should love and fear—if He is with us, man can do nothing to hurt us. I may fall to-morrow—it is hidden from me—God knoweth—but, if I raise my heart to Him, what are bullets and wounds? Beyond this world of struggle, uproar, and passion, there is a ' land of calm delight,' where sorrow never comes, and the King of Kings and Lord of Lords reigns in His majesty. Oh! to see His face! to hear from His lips, ' Well done!' May those words be heard by both of us, my friend! Then, as we look back upon this troubled life, wars and rumors of wars will appear like a dream, from which we have awakened in heaven!"

The speaker ceased, and said no more. In half an hour I heard his long, regular breathing. He was asleep.

For some time I lay awake, gazing at the recumbent figure of this celebrated man, whose august words had just resounded in my ears. It was hard to realize that the plainly-clad form before me was that of a born hero and master of men. As I took in at a glance the dusty cavalry boots, the dingy coat, the old battered sabre which lay by his side, and the faded cap which had half-fallen back from his broad brow, edged with its short dark hair, it was only as a weary, hard-worked soldier that Jackson appeared to me.

Now I know that I looked upon the one man raised up by God in many centuries—upon one of the immortals!

CXXVIII.

UNDER THE SHADES OF THE WILDERNESS.

I was aroused about midnight by the voice of the General, and found him sitting by the fire, reading a note which a courier had just brought him from General Lee.

As he did so, he coughed slightly, and I soon discovered that he had risen during the night, and, fearing that I would suffer for want of my riding-cape, thrown it over me, thus leaving himself exposed.*

"I thought you would be cold," he said, smiling gently, as he saw me looking at the cape; "and I am glad you have had a good nap, Colonel, as I shall have to get you to ride for me."

"Ready, General."

And I buckled on my arms. My horse was already saddled and standing near.

The General then gave me a message to Stuart, who was making a reconnoissance over the route which Jackson would advance by, on the next morning; and, having received

* Historical.

instructions where I would probably find Stuart, I set forth on my mission.

The night was calm and clear. The moon, only half obscured behind light drifting clouds, poured her mellow radiance upon the weird landscape through which I rode; and from time to time the plaintive cry of the whippoorwill was heard in the tangled thickets, beyond which Hooker awaited Lee. The scene was still and melancholy—the silence almost oppressive. No sound came from the opposing armies; and, as I went along the narrow and winding road through the thick bushes, the footfalls of my horse were the only interruptions of the oppressive silence.

All at once, however, as I approached the Brock road, leading from Spottsylvania Court-House to Ely's Ford, I heard the quick "Halt!" of a cavalry vedette, and the click of his carbine as he cocked it,

"Friend!" was my reply, and "Advance!" came from the vedette, who awaited me weapon in hand.

"Who are you?"

"Colonel Surry, of General Jackson's staff. Where is General Stuart?"

The vedette turned to an officer who had ridden up.

"Lieutenant, here is an officer looking for General Stuart."

"Who is it?" asked the voice of Harry Saltoun.

"A friend of yours, Lieutenant."

And we shook hands.

"Any thing stirring?"

"Nothing, Colonel—all as quiet as a mouse. General Stuart is a mile ahead. I will send a man with you."

"And Mordaunt?"

"Making a reconnoissance on the road to Ely's Ford."

"Good luck, Harry Mordaunt!" I said, pressing his hand.

And I rode on with the guide. Half a mile further, another vedette halted us. Stuart had omitted, as usual, no precautions. Every footpath was picketed.

"Where is the General?"

"On the Orange road, where it joins the Germanna plank,

sir. Orders a.e, not to ride upon the planks; the Yankees are near there."

"All right."

And, sending back the guide, I rode on until I struck the Orange road, turned to the right, and, avoiding the planking, upon which the hoof-strokes of a horse could be heard a great distance in the still night, drew near the spot where the Germanna road debouches into the main highway.

As I did so, the stifled hum of voices, and the occasional neigh of a horse, from the more open thicket, indicated the presence of cavalry; and soon I saw the dark masses, the men dismounted, but waiting beside their horses.

Two hundred yards further I found Stuart.

He was standing under a tree, with his arm thrown over the mane of his black mare "Lily of the Valley," and the animal had turned her head, and gazed at him with her large, intelligent eyes. Stuart was speaking in a low tone to an officer, Captain Breathed, of his horse artillery

"Look out, Surry!" said Stuart, as he gave me his hand; "don't talk too loud; the enemy's pickets are yonder, within a hundred yards of us."

"All right, General."

And I shook hands with Breathed, whom I knew intimately: no braver spirit ever fought a gun, or went foremost in the charge.

"Well, General," he said, in a low tone, as he mounted his horse, "I understand. I am to keep only a few yards behind the line of sharpshooters as they advance;* but, if I see an opening, I'm going ahead."

"Good. I know you'll do what you say, Breathed. Get every thing ready."

And, as Breathed rode cautiously away, Stuart asked if I had any orders.

"A message, General, in reference to the movement in the morning. Your cavalry, you know, will move in front and on the flanks."

* Breathed's orders.

And I gave him the message intrusted to me by Jackson.

"Good!" he said; "that is exactly what I designed doing. My force is small, but it will do the work."

And Stuart ceased speaking, and listened.

"They are working yonder like beavers," he whispered; "suppose we go a little further and listen."

We advanced cautiously on foot, in the shadow of the trees, and came within sight of the dusky figure of a Federal vedette, posted on the road in the moonlight.

"Listen!" said Stuart; and, bending down, he put his ear to the ground.*

I imitated him, and the quick blows of pickaxes and rumble of spades were heard from the direction of Chancellorsville.

"They are throwing up defences on their right," whispered Stuart, as we went cautiously back to where his horse was standing.   "I am afraid Jackson will find the attack tough work."

As we reached the tree where we had left our horses, a dispatch was handed to Stuart, which he read by the light of a single match shaded from view.

"I was right," he said; "Mordaunt reports that the enemy are throwing up works across the road beyond Melzi Chancellor's."

"Where is Mordaunt, General?"

"About a mile from here."

The idea suddenly struck me that he might have heard something of Violet Grafton, and, as no reply was necessary to my message, I determined to go and find him.

"I wish to see Mordaunt for a moment, General.   Will I find you here when I come back?"

"Probably—unless there is some movement."

"Good."

And, taking Mordaunt's courier with me, I rode in the direction which he indicated—following the narrow and winding bridle-path of the Brock road, skirted with dense thickets.

---

* Colonel Surry stated to me that he had seen General Stuart perform the same manœuvre on the night of the second battle of Manassas.

It was the very route I had passed over in April, 1861.

Half a mile from the Plank road I came upon a column of cavalry, and at the head of it, on horseback, and wrapped in his cloak, I recognized Mordaunt.

CXXIX.

THE RETURN OF ACHMED.

MORDAUNT greeted me with a warm grasp of his strong hand, and I asked, at once, if he had heard any news of Violet Grafton.

"Nothing whatever," was his reply, in a gloomy tone. "Achmed has not returned."

"Has he had time?"

"Ample time."

"I hoped to hear something, but fate seems against us!"

I had scarcely spoken, when a carbine was fired within two hundred yards of us, by the picket, in the direction of the river.

"Attention!" came from Mordaunt; and the sleepy men rose erect in their saddles.

"What can that mean?" muttered Mordaunt. "Some stray scout prowling around, probably."

Hoof-strokes were now heard from the direction of the firing, and two men came up, with another between them.

"Well?" said Mordaunt.

"A prisoner, Colonel."

"You fired at him?"

"Yes, sir, but he came straight on, without taking any notice of it, and surrendered."

Suddenly Mordaunt uttered a quick exclamation, and, in another moment, I understood the origin of it. The prisoner—almost wholly disguised by an oil-cloth poncho—was Achmed.

In an instant Mordaunt had hastened to him, and was bending over, eagerly, in the saddle, listening to the Moor, who spoke rapidly, in Arabic, and with obvious excitement. He wrapped his black poncho more closely around him as he spoke, gesticulated with his hands; and, as the moonlight fell upon his dark face, close to Mordaunt's, I saw that his eyes were blazing.

Mordaunt exhibited an agitation which even exceeded that of his companion. His cheeks flushed, then turned pale—his eyes filled with blood—and, when Achmed handed him a paper, which he read by the moonlight, I heard his teeth grinding together.

Suddenly he turned to me.

"Surry! you know this country?"

"Yes."

"Where is the house at which you stopped on your way—where you first saw Violet Grafton?"

"Within two miles of this spot," I replied, with a sudden thrill of the nerves. "Why do you ask?"

"Can you guide me to it?"

"Yes."

"Come on, then! Come! the game is run to earth!"

And, hastily summoning his second in command, Mordaunt gave him rapid instructions for his guidance, in case any movement took place in his absence—then he put spur to his horse and set out, at full speed, in the direction I indicated. Achmed followed.

"This is the road?—you are sure?" exclaimed Mordaunt. as he went on at full gallop.

"Yes," I said. "Keep straight on. But what has happened?"

"Here is the whole—Achmed has ferreted out every thing. That expedition to Maryland was all a ruse of the she-devil who carried the young girl off! After her departure, Mrs. Fitzhugh discovered, in her room, where she had probably dropped it by accident, the paper which Achmed gave me to-night—and do you know what that paper was, Surry?"

Mordaunt's eyes fairly blazed, as he glared over his shoulder.

20*

"It is an incredibly accurate forgery of my handwriting, Surry; and in it I state that I am wounded—suffering —languishing for some friend to nurse me—will Miss Grafton throw aside all rules of convention, and come to the succor of her poor, wounded friend! That is what betrayed her into the hands of this born devil and his drab; nor did the cunning of Fenwick—for he it was who again committed forgery to ruin me—nor did his cunning stop here. In that note, I beg Miss Grafton to con ceal from every one the object of her visit. I am ashamed, I am made to say, of the request I make—evil tongues may slander her—will she not, therefore, keep her journey entirely secret, not even informing Mrs. Fitzhugh of its object!

"Do you understand?" added Mordaunt, as his powerful horse still cleared the ground with long leaps. " The forger feared that I would come, or some friend of mine, and find the treachery thus practised! The whole affair must be concealed! —and that concealment was secured—would have been perfect—but for the accidental loss, by Miss Grafton, of the forged paper. Now for Achmed! He followed on the trail to Maryland, and soon found that, after going a short way, they turned southward, and travelled toward the Rappahannock. He tracked them along their entire route—found they had crossed at a private ford, so obscure and unknown that it was wholly unpicketed —and then, for the first time, he lost them in the Wilderness here. He succeeded in passing through the centre of the Federal army, disguised by his poncho—has pushed on with his information—and your mention of Fenwick, in connection with that house which you stopped at, affords the clue to the whole. Violet Grafton is a prisoner there, in the power of Fenwick?"

"You are right," I said; "let us lose no time. We are now within a quarter of a mile of the house."

CXXX.

LOVE AND DEATH.

MORDAUN ' struck the spurs into his horse as I uttered these words, and the powerful animal thundered on over the dark and narrow road, between the walls of thicket rising, in the dim moonlight, upon either side.

I led the way, and, as before, on that night of April, just two years before, when I passed over the same ground, the whip-poorwills cried in the thicket—the owl's unearthly screech was heard from the tangled depths—and the scraggy arms of the gnarled and stunted black-oaks resembled goblin hands about to clutch the nocturnal intruders on this land of mystery, and bear them away into the weird recesses of the Wilderness.

Mordaunt never relaxed his headlong speed, and the quick pants of his black charger were ever at my ear, driving me onward. But I was as wild with anxiety almost as himself. The thought, that Violet Grafton was a helpless victim in the hands of the monster who had entrapped her, drove me like a goad. With bloody spurs I forced my weary horse to his utmost speed, trembling, as I went on, with a vague apprehension of some monstrous outrage, some unspeakable infamy.

Mordaunt was half a length behind me, sweeping on like an incarnate fate. Wrapped in his dark cloak, upon his horse, as black as night, he resembled the wild huntsman of the German legends, following close upon his prey.

" Are we near the place !" he said, hoarsely, at my ear.

" Yes—yonder it is !"

" I mean to kill him, this time, Surry ! Not the wealth of both hemispheres could buy his blood of me, or make me spare him !"

" And I won't plead for him !"

" It would do no good ! Is that the place ?"

" Yes, we have arrived."

And, leaping the low brushwood fence, I spurred up the hill, closely followed by Mordaunt and Achmed. The face of the

Moor, as the moonlight fell upon it, wore a wild and splendid look, such as no words can describe. Call it the ferocity of the tiger, the thirst of a panther for the blood of the wolf. The fierce blood of the desert-born flamed in that regard, and made the countenance glow as though the glare of a great conflagration were upon it.

In three bounds our horses reached the house, through the shutters of which a light glimmered. Mordaunt was on his feet in a single instant, and had rushed to the door!

With one blow of his ponderous shoulder he burst it nearly from its hinges—it flew open; and, at the same moment, a loud explosion was heard, and a bullet whistled past me.

At a bound I reached the door of the apartment, which I knew so well—and here is the scene which met my eyes:

Fenwick, pale, emaciated, with eyes bloodshot and sunken, standing erect in the centre of the apartment—pistol in hand; and, in one corner, Miss Grafton, with dishevelled hair, trembling and sobbing, as she endeavored to tear herself from the iron arms of the woman Parkins, who was trying to drag her away.

Such was the scene which a single glance took in. Then to that pause succeeded the roar of the lion bounding on his prey. Mordaunt, sabre in hand, sprang straight at Fenwick, and, in another instant, the sharp point would have pierced his heart. But the blood of his bitter foe was not to be shed by his own hand. Suddenly, a slender form passed him at a single bound; a gleaming poniard was seen to rise and fall; and Fenwick fell, pierced through the heart by the dagger of Achmed.

As he staggered and fell, a loud explosion was heard, and Achmed uttered a low cry. In falling, Fenwick had fired his pistol, and the ball had passed through Achmed's breast.

Fenwick rolled on the floor, the blood spouting over the hilt of the poniard, which remained buried in his breast. Then, with a last convulsive effort, he clutched a chair, rose erect, and with clinched hands, raised above his head, exclaimed, looking at Mordaunt:

"You conquer!—I die!—but beyond the grave—in death as in life—hate! hate! hate! to all eternity!"

As the words left his lips, the glare faded from his bloodshot eyes; his hands, madly clutching at the air, fell powerless; a bloody foam came to his lips; and he fell at full length, dead.

Within two paces of him, Mordaunt was holding in his arms the dying form of Achmed, whose head was resting on his bosom.

A few low words, in Arabic, to which Mordaunt replied with something like a groan—then the young Moor's face was illuminated with a radiant smile, and his eyes turned toward Violet Grafton. The woman Parkins had disappeared.

Dragging himself along, Achmed reached her feet, and, taking one of her hands, pressed it closely to his lips, murmuring some faint words, as he did so, in his native tongue.

"He says he is happy, for he dies for you!" exclaimed the deep voice of Mordaunt, as he stood with arms folded across his heaving bosom.

Achmed seemed to understand that his words were explained, and, again pressing a long, lingering kiss upon the girl's hand, fell back, with the pallor of death upon his face.

She caught his fainting form, and, for a moment, he was clasped in her arms—his head rested upon her bosom.

His eyes opened, and he saw her face wet with tears, as it bent above him That spectacle made his pale cheeks flush, his eyes glow for the last time on earth.

Turning faintly toward Mordaunt, with a glance of unspeakable affection, he murmured some words, and stretched out his hand.

Mordaunt grasped it, with a strange tremor in his stalwart frame; and, with his other hand, Achmed took that of the girl, and pressed it to his heart.

As he did so, a smile of unspeakable happiness lit up his face; his lips uttered a faint murmur ; and, falling back in the arms of the woman whom he had loved, he died, with his head upon her breast.

CXXXI.

THE LAST GREETING BETWEEN STUART AND JACKSON.

HERE my memoirs might terminate—for the present, if not forever. All the personages disappear, lost in the bloody gulf, or have reached that crisis in their lives when we can leave them.

But one scene remains to wind up the tragedy—another figure is about to fall, as the mighty pine falls in the depths of the forest, making the woods resound as it crashes to the earth. The hours drew onward now when the form of him to whom all the South looked in her day of peril was to disappear—when the eagle eye was to flash no more, the voice to be hushed—when the hero of a hundred battles was to leave the great arena of his fame, and pass away amid the wailing of a nation.

Come with me, reader, and we will look upon this "last scene of all." Then the curtain falls.

At daylight, on the morning succeeding the events just narrated, Jackson put his column in motion, and directed his march over the same route which I had pursued on my way to find Stuart. At the Catherine Furnace he was observed and attacked by the advance force of the enemy, but, pushing on without stopping—his flank covered by the cavalry—he reached the Brock road, and, finally, the Orange plank-road.

Here I joined him at the moment when General Fitz Lee, who commanded the cavalry under Stuart, informed him that, by ascending a neighboring eminence, he could obtain a good view of the enemy's works. Jackson immediately rode to the point thus indicated, in company with Generals Fitz Lee and Stuart; and the works of Hooker were plainly descried over the tops of the trees.

The whole was seen at a glance, and, to attack to advantage, it was obviously necessary to move further still around the enemy's flank.

"Tell my column to cross that road," Jackson said to one of

his aides; and the troops moved on steadily until they reached the Old Turnpike, at a point between the Wilderness Tavern and Chancellorsville.

Here instant preparations were made for attack. The force which Jackson had consisted of Rodes's, Colston's, and A. P. Hill's divisions—in all, somewhat less than twenty-two thousand men—and line of battle was immediately formed for an advance upon the enemy. Rodes moved in front, Colston followed within two hundred yards, and Hill marched in column, with the artillery as a reserve.

Jackson gave the order to advance at about six in the evening, and, as the sinking sun began to throw its long shadows over the Wilderness, the long line of bayonets was seen in motion. Struggling on through the dense thickets on either side of the turnpike, the troops reached the open ground near Melzl Chancellor's—and there, before them, was the long line of the enemy's works.

Jackson rode in front, and, as soon as his lines were formed for the attack, ordered the works to be stormed with the bayonet.

At the word, Rodes rushed forward—the men cheering wildly —and, in a few moments, they had swept over the Federal earthworks, driving the Eleventh Corps in wild confusion before them. The woods swarmed with panic-stricken infantry, in utter confusion; artillery galloped off, and was overturned in ditches, or by striking against the trees. At one blow the entire army of Hooker, as events subsequently proved, was entirely demoralized.

Jackson pressed straight on upon the track of the flying enemy; and I soon discovered that he was straining every nerve to extend his left, and so cut off their retreat to the Rappahannock. Unavoidable delays, however, ensued. The lines of Rodes and Colston had been mingled in inextricable confusion in the charge; officers could not find their commands: before advancing further, it was absolutely necessary to halt and re-form the line of battle.

Rodes and Colston were, accordingly, ordered to stop their

advance, re-form their divisions, and give way to Hill, who was directed to take the front with his fresh division, not yet engaged.

Before these orders could be carried out, it was nearly nine o'clock at night, and the weird scene was only lit up by the struggling beams of a pallid moon. On all sides the scattered troops were seen gathering around their colors again, and forming a new line of battle—and soon A. P. Hill was heard steadily advancing to take his place in front, for the decisive attack on Chancellorsville, about a mile distant.

Such was the condition of things, when General Jackson, accompanied by his staff and escort, rode in advance of his line down the road toward Chancellorsville, listening, at every step, for some indications of a movement in the Federal camps.

When nearly opposite an old wooden house, in the thicket by he roadside, he checked his horse to listen; and the whole cortege, General, staff, and couriers, remained for some moments silent and motionless, gazing toward the enemy.

From the narrative of what followed I shrink with a sort of dread, and a throbbing heart. Again that sombre and lugubrious Wilderness rises up before me, lit by the pallid moon; again the sad whippoorwill's cry; again I see the great soldier, motionless upon his horse—and then I hear the fatal roar of the guns which laid him low!

Jackson had halted thus, and remained motionless in the middle of the road, listening intently, when, suddenly, for what reason has never yet been discovered, one of his brigades in rear, and on the right of the turnpike, opened a heavy fire upon the party.

Did they take us for Federal cavalry, or were they firing at random, under the excitement of the moment? I know not, and it is probable that the truth will never be known. But the fire had terrible results. Some of the staff were wounded; others threw themselves from their horses, who were running from the fire toward the Federal lines, not two hundred yards distant; and Captain Boswell, engineer upon the General's staff, was killed, and his body dragged by his maddened horse to Chancellorsville.

As the bullets whistled around him, Jackson wheeled his horse to the left, and galloped into the thicket. Then came the fatal moment. The troops behind him, on the left of the road, imagined that the Federal cavalry were charging; and, kneeling on the right knee, with bayonets fixed, poured a volley upon the General, at the distance of thirty yards.

Two balls passed through his left arm, shattering the bone, and a third through his right hand, breaking the fingers.

Mad with terror, his horse wheeled round and ran off; and, passing under a low bough, extending horizontally from a tree, Jackson was struck in the forehead, his cap torn from his head, and his form hurled back almost out of the saddle. He rose erect again, however; grasped the bridle with his bleeding fingers; and, regaining control of his horse, turned again into the high road, near the spot which he had left.

The fire had ceased as suddenly as it began, and not a human being was seen. Of the entire staff and escort, no one remained but myself and a single courier. The rest had disappeared before the terrible fire, as leaves disappear before the blasts of winter.

Jackson reeled in the saddle, but no sound had issued from his lips during the whole scene. He now declared, in faint tones, that his arm was broken; and, leaning forward, he fell into my arms.

More bitter distress than I experienced at that moment I would not wish to have inflicted upon my deadliest enemy. Nor was my anxiety less terrible. The lines of the enemy were in sight of the spot where the General lay. At any moment they might advance, when he would fall into their hands.

No time was to be lost. I sent the courier for an ambulance; and, taking off the General's military satchel and his arms, endeavored to stanch his wound. While I was thus engaged, I experienced a singular consciousness that other eyes than the General's were intently watching me. I can only thus describe the instinctive feeling which induced me to look up—and there, in the edge of the thicket, within ten paces of me, was a dark figure, motionless, on horseback, gazing at me

"Who is that?" I called out.

But no reply greeted my address.

"Is that one of the couriers? If so, ride up there, and see what troops those are that fired upon us."

At the order, the dark figure moved; went slowly in the direction which I indicated; and never again appeared. Who was that silent horseman? I know not, nor ever expect to know.

I had turned again to the General, and was trying to remove his bloody gauntlets, when the sound of hoofs was heard in the direction of our own lines, and soon General A. P. Hill appeared, with his staff. Hastily dismounting, he expressed the deepest regret at the fatal occurrence, and urged the General to permit himself to be borne to the rear, as the enemy might, at any moment, advance.

As he was speaking, an instant proof was afforded of the justice of his fears.

"Halt! surrender! Fire on them, if they do not surrender!" came from one of the staff in advance of the spot, toward the enemy; and, in a moment, the speaker appeared, with two Federal skirmishers, who expressed great astonishment at finding themselves so near the Southern lines.

It was now obvious that no time was to be lost in bearing off the General, and Lieutenant Morrison, one of the staff, exclaimed: "Let us take the General up in our arms and carry him off!"

"No; if you can help me up, I can walk!" replied Jackson, faintly.

And, as General Hill, who had drawn his pistol and mounted his horse, hastened back to throw forward his line, Jackson rose to his feet.

He had no sooner done so, than a roar like thunder came from the direction of Chancellorsville, and a hurricane of shell swept the road in which we stood. A fragment struck the horse of Captain Leigh, of Hill's staff, who had just ridden up with a litter, and his rider had only time to leap to the ground when the anima. fell. This brave officer did not think of himself, however; he hastened to Jackson, who leaned his arm upon his shoulder; and, slowly dragging himself along, his arm bleeding profusely, the General approached his own lines again.

Hill was now in motion, steadily advancing to the attack, and the troops evidently suspected, from the number and rank of the wounded man's escort, that he was a superior officer.

" Who is that?" was the incessant question of the men; but the reply came as regularly, " Oh, only a friend of ours."

" When asked, just say it is a Confederate officer!" murmured Jackson.

And he continued to walk on, leaning heavily upon the shoulders of the two officers at his side. The horses were led along between him and the passing troops; but many of the soldiers peered curiously around them, to discover who the wounded officer was.

At last one of them recognized him as he walked, bareheaded, in the moonlight, and exclaimed, in the most piteous tone I ever heard:

" Great God! that is General Jackson!"

" You are mistaken, my friend," was the reply of one of the staff; and, as he heard this denial of Jackson's identity, the man looked utterly bewildered. He said nothing more, however, and moved on, shaking his head. Jackson then continued to drag his feet along—slowly and with obvious pain.

At last his strength was exhausted, and it was plain that he could go no further. The litter, brought by Captain Leigh, was put in requisition, the General laid upon it, and four of the party grasped the handles and bore it on toward the rear.

Such, up to this moment, had been the harrowing scenes of the great soldier's suffering; but the gloomiest and most tragic portion was yet to come.

No sooner had the litter begun to move, than the enemy, who had, doubtless, divined the advance of Hill, opened a frightful fire of artillery from the epaulments near Chancellorsville. The turnpike was swept by a veritable hurricane of shell and canister —men and horses fell before it, mowed down like grass—and, where a moment before had been seen the serried ranks of Hill, the eye could now discern only riderless horses, men writhing in the death agony, and others seeking the shelter of the woods.

That sudden and furious fire did not spare the small party who were bearing off the great soldier. Two of the litter-bearers were shot, and dropped the handles to the ground. Of all present, none remained but myself and another; and we were forced to lower the litter to the earth, and lie beside it, to escape the terrific storm of canister tearing over us. It struck millions of sparks from the flint of the turnpike, and every instant I expected would be our last.

The General attempted, during the hottest portion of the fire, to rise from the litter; but this he was prevented from doing; and the hurricane soon ceased. He then rose erect, and, leaning upon our shoulders, while another officer brought on the litter, made his way into the woods, where the troops were lying down in line of battle.

As we passed on in the moonlight, I recognized General Pender, in front of his brigade, and he also recognized me.

" Who is wounded, Colonel ?" he said.

" Only a Confederate officer, General."

But, all at once, he caught a sight of General Jackson's face.

" Oh! General!" he exclaimed, " I am truly sorry to see you are wounded. The lines here are so much broken that I fear we will be obliged to fall back !"

The words brought a fiery flush to the pale face of Jackson Raising his drooping head, his eyes flashed, and he replied:

" You must hold your ground, General Pender! You must hold your ground, sir !"

Pender bowed, and Jackson continued his slow progress to the rear.

He had given his last order on the field.

Fifty steps further, his head sank upon his bosom, his shoulders bent forward, and he seemed about to fall from exhaustion. In a tone so faint that it sounded like a murmur, he asked to be permitted to lie down and die.

Instead of yielding to this prayer, we placed him again upon the litter—some bearers were procured—and, amid bursting shell, which filled the moonlit sky above with their dazzling corruscations, we slowly bore the wounded General on, through the tangled thicket, toward the rear.

So dense was the undergrowth that we penetrated it with difficulty, and the vines which obstructed the way more than once made the litter-bearers stumble. From this proceeded a most distressing accident. One of the men, at last, caught his foot in a grape-vine, and fell—and, in his fall, he dropped the handle of the litter. It descended heavily, and then, as the General's shattered arm struck the ground, and the blood gushed forth, he uttered, for the first time, a low, piteous groan.

We raised him quickly, and at that moment, a ray of moonlight, glimmering through the deep foliage overhead, fell upon his pale face and his bleeding form. His eyes were closed, his bosom heaved—I thought that he was about to die.

What a death for the man of Manassas and Port Republic! What an end to a career so wonderful! Here, lost in the tangled and lugubrious depths of this weird Wilderness, with the wan moon gliding like a ghost through the clouds—the sad notes of the whippoorwill echoing from the thickets—the shell bursting in the air, like showers of falling stars—here, alone, without other witnesses than a few weeping officers, who held him in their arms, the hero of a hundred battles, the idol of the Southern people, seemed about to utter his last sigh! Never will the recollection of that scene be obliterated. Again my pulses throb, and my heart is oppressed with its bitter load of anguish, as I go back in memory to that night in the Wilderness.

I could only mutter a few words, asking the General if his fall had hurt him—and, at these words, his eyes slowly opened. A faint smile came to the pale face, and in a low murmur he said:

"No, my friend; do not trouble yourself about me!"

And again the eyes closed, his head fell back. With his grand courage and patience, he had suppressed all evidences of suffering; and, once more taking up the litter, we continued to bear him toward the rear.

As we approached Melzi Chancellor's, a staff-officer of General Hill recognized Jackson, and announced that Hill had been wounded by the artillery fire which had swept down the turnpike.

Jackson rose on his bleeding right arm, and exclaimed:

"Where is Stuart!"

As though in answer to that question, we heard the quick clatter of hoofs, and all at once the martial figure of the great cavalier was seen rapidly approaching.

"Where is General Jackson?" exclaimed Stuart, in a voice which I scarcely recognized.

And suddenly he checked his horse right in front of the group. His drawn sabre was in his hand—his horse foaming. In the moonlight I could see that his face was pale, and his eyes full of gloomy emotion.

For an instant no one moved or spoke—and again I return in memory to that scene. Stuart, clad in his "fighting jacket," with the dark plume floating from his looped-up hat, reining in his foaming horse, while the moonlight poured on his martial features; and before him, on the litter, the bleeding form of Jackson, the face pale, the eyes half-closed, the bosom rising and falling as the life of the great soldier ebbed away.

In an instant Stuart had recognized his friend, and had thrown himself from his horse.

"You are dangerously wounded!"

"Yes," came in a murmur from the pale lips of Jackson, as he faintly tried to hold out his hand. Then his cheeks suddenly filled with blood, his eyes flashed, and, half rising from the litter, he exclaimed:

"Oh! for two hours of daylight! I would then cut off the enemy from United States Ford, and they would be entirely surrounded!"

Stuart bent over him, and their eyes met.

"Take command of my corps!" murmured Jackson, falling back; "follow your own judgment—I have implicit confidence in you!"

Stuart's face flushed hot at this supreme recognition of his courage and capacity—and I saw a flash dart from the fiery blue eyes.

"But you will be near, General! You will still send me orders!" he exclaimed.

"You will not need them," murmured Jackson; "to-night or early to-morrow you will be in possession of Chancellorsville! Tell my men that I am watching them—that I am with them in spirit!"

"The watchword in the charge shall be, 'Remember Jackson!'"

And, with these fiery words, Stuart grasped the bleeding hand; uttered a few words of farewell, and leaped upon his horse. For a moment his sword gleamed, and his black plume floated in the moonlight; then he disappeared, at full speed, toward Chancellorsville.

At ten o'clock next morning he had stormed the intrenchments around Chancellorsville; swept the enemy, with the bayonet, back toward the Rappahannock; and as the troops, mad with victory, rushed through the blazing forest, a thousand voices were heard shouting:

"Remember Jackson!"

CXXXII.

IN A DREAM.

HERE I terminate my memoirs for the present, if not forever.

The great form of Jackson has disappeared from the stage. What remains but a cold and gloomy theatre, from which the spectators have vanished, where the lights are extinguished, and darkness has settled down upon the pageant?

Other souls of fire, and valor, and unshrinking nerve were left, and their career was glorious; but the finger of Fate seemed to mark out, with its bloody point, the name of "Chancellorsville," and the iron lips to unclose and mutter: "Thus far, no further!" With the career of this man of destiny had waned the strength of the South—when he fell, the end was in sight. Thenceforward as good fighting as the world ever saw seemed useless, and to attain no result. Even the soldiership of Lee— such soldiership as renders famous forever a race and an epoch —could achieve nothing. From the day of Chancellorsville, the battle-flag, torn in so many glorious encounters, seemed to shine no more in the light of victory. It drooped upon its staff, how- ever defiantly at times it rose—slowly it descended. It fluttered for a moment amid the fiery storm of Gettysburg, in the woods of Spottsylvania, and on the banks of the Appomattox; but never again did its dazzling folds flaunt proudly in the wind, and burn like a beacon light on victorious fields. It was natural that the army should connect the declining fortunes of the great flag which they had fought under with the death of him who had rendered it so illustrious. The form of Jackson had vanished from the scene : that king of battle had dropped his sword, and descended into the tomb: from that moment the star of hope, like the light of victory, seemed to sink beneath ebon clouds. The hero had gone down in the bloody gulf of battle, and the torrent bore us away!

In the scenes of this volume, the great soldier has appeared as I saw him. Those of his last hours I did not witness, but many narratives upon the subject have been printed. Those last moments were as serene as his life had been stormy—and there, as everywhere, he was victorious. On the field it was his ene- mies he conquered : here it was pain and suffering. That faith which overcomes all things was in his heart, and among his last words were : "It is all right !"

In that delirium which immediately precedes death, he gave his orders as on the battle-field, and was distinctly heard direct- ing A. P. Hill to "prepare for action !" But these clouds soon passed—his eye grew calm again—and, murmuring "Let us cross over the river, and rest under the shade of the trees !" he fell back and expired.

Such was the death of this strange man. To me he seems so great that all words fail in speaking of him. Not in this poor page do I attempt a characterization of this king of battle: I speak no further of him—but I loved and shall ever love him.

A body laid in state in the Capitol at Richmond, the coffin wrapped in the pure white folds of the newly-adopted Confederate flag; a great procession, moving to the strains of the Dead March, behind the hearse, and the war-horse of the dead soldier; then the thunder of the guns at Lexington; the coffin borne upon a caisson of his own old battery, to the quiet grave—that was the last of Jackson. Dead, he was immortal!

As I write that page here in my quiet library at Eagle's-Nest, in October, 1865, I lay down my pen, lean back in my chair, and murmur:

"Have I seen all that—or was it only a dream?"

The Rappahannock flows serenely yonder, through the hills, as in other years; the autumn forests burn away, in blue and gold and orange, as they did in the days of my youth; the winds whisper; the sunshine laughs—it is only we who laugh no more!

"Was that a real series of events?" I say; "or only a drama of the imagination? Did I really hear the voice of Jackson, and the laughter of Stuart, in those glorious charges, on those bloody fields? Did Ashby pass before me on his milk-white steed, and greet me by the camp-fire as his friend? Did I fight by his side in those hot encounters, watch the flash of his sabre, and hold his bleeding form upon my breast? Was it a real figure, that stately form of Lee, amid the swamps of the Chickahominy, the fire of Malvern Hill, the appalling din and smoke and blood of Manassas, Fredericksburg, Chancellorsvil e—of Gettysburg, Spottsylvania, and Petersburg? Jackson, that greater than the leader of the Ironsides—Stuart, more fiery than Rupert of the Bloody Sword—Ashby, the pearl of chivalry and honor—Lee, the old Roman, fighting, with a nerve so splendid, to the bitter end—these were surely the heroes of some dream, the forms of an excited imagination! Did Pelham press my hand, and hold the pale face of Jean upon his heart, and fall in that stubborn fight with Averill? Did Farley smile, and fight, and die near the very same spot—and was it really the eyes of Stuart that

21

dropped bitter tears upon the pallid faces of these youths, dead
on the field of honor? Were those spring flowers of Incognita,
which lay but now before me, real clusters from the sunny
slopes of Georgia, or the flowers of a dream? Was that proud,
bronzed face of Mordaunt real? And the blue eyes, peering
from the golden curls of Violet Grafton—were they actual
eyes?"

It is like a dream to me that I looked upon these faces—that I
touched the honest hand of Hood; gave back the courteous
smile of Ambrose Hill; spoke with the hardy Longstreet, the
stubborn Ewell, Hampton the fearless, and the dashing and
chivalric Lees. Souls of fire and flame—with a light how steady
burned these stately names! how they fought, these hearts of
oak! But did they live their lives, these men and their comrades, as I seem to remember? At Manassas, Sharpsburg, and
Chancellorsville, was it two, three, and four to one that they
defeated?—and at Appomattox, in that black April of 1865, was
it really a force of only eight thousand muskets, which Lee long
refused to surrender to one hundred and forty thousand? Did
these events take place in a real world, on an actual arena—or
did all those figures move, all those voices sound, in some realm
of the imagination? It was surely a dream—was it not?—that
the South fought so stubbornly for those four long years, and
bore the blood-red battle-flag aloft in so many glorious encounters, amid foes so swarming and so powerful—that she
would not yield, although so many brave hearts poured their
blood out on the weird plains of Manassas, the fair fields of the
valley, by the sluggish waters of the Chickahominy, or amid the
sombre thickets of the Spottsylvania Wilderness!

But the dream was glorious—not even the *immedicabile vulnus*
of surrender can efface its splendor. Still it moves me, and
possesses me; and I live forever in that past. Fond violet eyes
that shone once at The Oaks, and now shine at Eagle's-Nest!—
be not clouded with displeasure. It is only a few comrades of
the old time I am thinking of—a few things I have seen in the
long-gone centuries when we used to wear gray, and marched
under the red flag of the South! It is of these I dream—as

memory goes back to them I live once more in the days that are dead. All things recall the scenes and personages of those years; and bring back from the tomb the phantom figures. They speak to me, as in the former time, with their kindly voices—the pale, dim faces flush, the eyes flash.

At all times—everywhere—the Past comes into the Present, and possesses it. As I awake at morning, the murmur of the river breeze is the low roll of drums from the forest yonder, where the camps of infantry are aroused by the reveille. In the moonlight nights, when all is still, a sound comes, borne upon the breeze, from some dim land—I seem to hear the bugles. In the thunder of some storm, I hear the roar of artillery.

Even now, as the glory of the sunlight falls on the great land-scape of field and forest and river, a tempest gathers on the shores of the Rappahannock. The sunlight disappears, sucked in by the black and threatening clouds which sweep from the far horizon; a gigantic pall seems slowly to descend upon the land-scape, but a moment since so beautiful and smiling; the lurid lightnings flicker like quick tongues of flame, and, as these fiery serpents play amid the ebon mass, a mighty wind arises, swells, and roars on through the splendid foliage of the forest, where the year is dying on its couch of blood.

That is only a storm, you may say, perhaps—to me it is more. Look! those variegated colors of the autumn leaves are the flaunting banners of an army drawn up there in line of battle, and about to charge. Listen! that murmur of the Rappahannock is the shuffling sound of a great column on its march!—hush! there is the bugle!—and that rushing wind in the trees of the forest is the charge of Stuart and his horsemen! How the hoof-strokes tear along! how the phantom horsemen shout as they charge!—how the ghost of Stuart rides!

See the banners yonder, where the line of battle is drawn up against the autumn woods—how their splendid colors burn, how they flaunt and wave and ripple in the wind—proud and defiant! Is that distant figure on a horse the man of Port Republic and Chancellorsville, with his old yellow cap, his dingy coat, his piercing eyes—and is that humming sound the cheering of the

"Foot Cavalry," as they greet him? Look how the lead banners—red as though dyed in blood—point forward, rippling as they come! See that vivid, dazzling flash!—is it lightning, or the glare of cannon? Hear that burst of thunder, like the opening roar of battle—Jackson is advancing.

A quick throb of the heart—a hand half reaching out to clutch the hilt of the battered old sword on the wall—then I sink back in my chair.

It was only a dream!

Americans in Fiction

*A series of reprints of 19th century American novels important
to the study of American folklore, culture and literary history*

THOMAS BAILEY ALDRICH
The Stillwater Tragedy

JAMES LANE ALLEN
A Kentucky Cardinal

GERTRUDE ATHERTON
Los Cerritos: A Romance of Modern Times
The Californians
Senator North
Aristocrats
The Splendid Idle Forties

ARLO BATES
The Puritans

OLIVER THOMAS BEARD
Bristling With Thorns

ALICE BROWN
Tiverton Tales
The County Road

FRANCIS H. BURNETT
Through One Administration

WILLIAM A. CARUTHERS
Kentuckian in New York, or the Adventures of Three Southerns
The Cavaliers of Virginia

CHARLES WADDELL CHESNUTT
The Conjure Woman
The Wife of His Youth; and Other Stories of the Colour Line
The House Behind the Cedars

KATE CHOPIN
Bayou Folk

JOHN ESTEN COOKE
The Virginia Comedians
Surry of Eagle's Nest
Mohun: or the Last Days of Lee and His Paladins
My Lady Pokahontas

ROSE TERRY COOKE
Rootbound and Other Sketches

MARGARET DELAND
John Ward, Preacher

THOMAS DIXON
The Leopard's Spots
The Clansman

EDWARD EGGLESTON
Roxy
The Faith Doctor

MARY HALLOCK FOOTE
The Led-Horse Claim

PAUL LEICESTER FORD
The Honorable Peter Stirling

HAROLD FREDERIC
Seth's Brother's Wife

MARY E. WILKINS FREEMAN
A New England Nun; and Other Stories
The Portion of Labor

HENRY B. FULLER
The Cliff Dwellers